CELESTE

Also by V. C. Andrews®
in Large Print:

Broken Wings
Midnight Flight
Cat
Cinnamon
The End of the Rainbow
Eye of the Storm
Falling Stars
Honey
Ice
Lightning Strikes
Rain
Rose

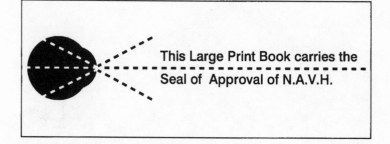

V.C. ANDREWS®

CELESTE

Thorndike Press • Waterville, Maine

Published in 2004 by arrangement with Pocket Books,
a division of Simon & Schuster Inc.

Thorndike Press® Large Print Core.

The tree indicium is a trademark of Thorndike Press.

The text of this Large Print edition is unabridged.
Other aspects of the book may vary from the original edition.

Set in 16 pt. Plantin by Elena Picard.

Printed in the United States on permanent paper.

Library of Congress Cataloging-in-Publication Data

Andrews, V. C. (Virginia C.)
    Celeste / by V.C. Andrews.
        p. cm.
    ISBN 0-7862-6647-3 (lg. print : hc : alk. paper)
    1. Mothers and daughters — Fiction. 2. Brothers —
Death — Fiction. 3. New age movement — Fiction.
4. Teenage girls — Fiction. 5. Sex role — Fiction.
6. Twins — Fiction. 7. Large type books. I. Title.
PS3551.N454C45 2004
    813′.54—dc22   2004047999

CELESTE

INSERT NAVH

Prologue

⸺●○●⸺

The Voices
Mommy Heard

I can't exactly remember the first time we saw our mother stop whatever she was doing, look out at the darkness, smile, nod, and softly say something like, "I understand. Yes. Thank you," to no one we could see, but every time she did it, I felt an eerie excitement, a pleasant chill like the quiver I might feel sliding down a hill on my sled or leaping off the rock to splash in our pond. When I was very little, seeing and hearing Mommy speak to her spirits was simply scary fun, and no matter what I was doing at the time, I would stop and listen and watch her, and then Noble would stop playing and listen, too. Sometimes we would hear Daddy talk to himself and Mommy as well, but this was different, and only Mommy did it.

I would look at Noble to see if he made

any sense of it, and he would look at me with a confused expression, the dimple we both shared in our left cheeks flashing prominently, his eyebrows, like mine, raised and twisted. Neither of us understood, but neither of us asked her about it.

I knew in my heart that in time, she would tell us.

And yes, one day she pulled us aside and hugged us to her, kissing both our foreheads and cheeks, perhaps kissing Noble a little more because she always seemed to think he needed more of her kisses than I did, and then she told us everything with great excitement in her voice, as much excitement as someone learning what she was going to get for Christmas.

"I am going to let you both know a great secret," she said. "It's time for me to tell you. Do you know what a secret is, Noble?" she asked.

She didn't ask me because she knew I knew. I was a far better reader and listener than Noble was, and I had twice the vocabulary. He nodded, but not with any real confidence in his eyes, so she explained.

"It's something you must not tell anyone else, something you must keep locked up here and here," she said, pointing to his head and his heart. "It's a very bad thing to tell a secret after you have promised not to do that. Understand?"

Noble nodded firmly now and Mommy relaxed, took a deep breath, and continued.

She told us she heard voices no one else could hear, not even Daddy, and she could see people — spirits, she called them — that he couldn't see.

"Who are they?" I asked.

She said they were the spirits and the voices of all her dead ancestors, and then she drew up a ghostly mélange of men and women with distinct and interesting personalities, girls who still whined about their lost lovers, men who were stern but wise, women who were beautiful and women who were plain, even disabled, like Auntie Helen Roe, who had polio when she was very young and was in a wheelchair until the day she died. She told us they buried her wheelchair with her and she was still in it, even in the spiritual world. She made it sound as if they were actually in the room with us, sitting there, smiling and watching her tell all about them. I kept looking around, expecting to see someone.

Whether they were all true ancestors or merely inventions of Mommy's imagination didn't matter at the moment. I wanted them to be as real as the occasional visitors who came to our ancestral home, a large three-story Queen Anne house first built by my mother's great-grandfather William De Forest Jordan, who had laid claim to acres and acres of rich riverbed land in an upstate New York valley nestled almost in camera by Mother Nature.

His portrait hung in the living room over the fireplace. He was stocky, with a thick neck and heavy shoulders that looked like they were straining the seams of the suit jacket he wore. When the portrait was painted, he had a neatly trimmed Van Dyke beard and a full head of stark white hair brushed back with a part in the middle. His skin was dark and leathery because he spent most of his time outdoors in the sun.

I didn't like looking up at him often because his dark brown eyes seemed to follow me about the room, and he wasn't smiling in the portrait. In fact, he looked angry, I thought. When I asked Mommy if he was angry or upset about having to sit for a portrait, she told me that people took their pictures and portraits very seriously in those days and believed smiling made them look frivolous. To me, he always looked like someone who was incapable of smiling, even if he had wanted to smile. He was one spirit I wasn't all that anxious to meet.

Family legend had it that he was hiking alone in the famous Rip Van Winkle Catskills and turned a corner to behold this stretch of land comfortably set between two slopes where once the Sandburg River had run when it was free to race along, unchecked by dams upstream. Now it was more like a creek, albeit often a raging one after heavy spring rains or a winter of particularly heavy snowfalls.

"Your great-great-grandpa Jordan's heart pounded the way a man's heart pounds when he sees a beautiful woman," Mommy told us. "He fell in love with every tree, every blade of grass, every rock he saw, and just knew he had to live here and work his farm here and build his home here, and yes, dear children, my sweet dear and precious twins, die here."

On the north side of the house, he was buried along with our great-great-grandmother Elsie and a child of theirs who had died in childbirth, an unnamed creature of misfortune who had the door of life slammed shut before she could sound a cry, take a breath, behold a color or her

11

mother's face. The three granite tomb-stones were in a small square created out of fieldstone about three feet high with an entrance. Their stillborn child's gravestone reads INFANT JORDAN and her date of death. There was, of course, no date of birth. Her stone is smaller, with two baby hands embossed in a clasp above the inscription. Mommy says that sometimes when she touches the hands and closes her eyes, she can feel them moving, feel their softness.

The vivid way she described it made me think that the dead reach up through their tombstones to see and hear and even touch the people who come to visit their graves. Mommy's great-grandmother Elsie died before her great-grandfather. Mommy said her mother told her she often saw him hugging the stone as if he was actually hugging his departed wife, and he would kiss it, too!

All of our other family members lay at rest in church cemeteries, except they didn't lie at rest, according to Mommy. They rose almost immediately from their cold, dark graves and began to walk the earth, eager to speak to our grandmother, our mother, and now eagerly waiting to be able to speak with us. That was the prediction Mommy made to us.

"Soon, children, soon, you too will see and hear them. I promise. They've promised. When they feel you're ready, they have promised they will," she told us that day, and she looked out the window with her beautiful angelic smile softly sitting on her full and perfect lips and nodded as only one who had heard the voices would nod.

How could we not believe it would all come true?

1

Our Family History

We sat on the chintz sofa originally bought by Grandma Jordan. Every stick of furniture in our home was pristine and cared for with love and affection, for every piece seemed to have its own history, whether it be Great-Great-Grandpa Jordan's hickory wood rocking chair or Great-Grandpa Jordan's homemade stepladder. Nothing could be discarded or misused.

"Personal possessions that are cherished hold the spirit of the owner in them," she said. "Sometimes, when I sit in my great-grandfather's rocking chair, I can feel him in me," Mommy told us, and I'd be fascinated by the expression on her face as she rocked herself. Her eyes seem to grow darker and her lips tightened. Folds formed in her forehead suggesting she was filling with heavy thoughts, and for a long moment, she didn't hear us or see us.

14

Then she would blink and smile. "My grandfather spoke to me," she would say.

It was an idea that took seed in my mind. Everything I touched in our house had power, I thought. Perhaps some day I would look into the old mirror in the downstairs powder room and see the face of my grandmother or even my great-great-grandmother Elsie. Maybe I would sit on a kitchen chair and see one of my cousins sitting across from me. Mommy made me believe it could happen that way. Surprises just waited to be unpacked and opened in our home.

On the sofa Mommy put her arm around Noble and made me sit close. Through the open living-room window, we watched twilight begin and night seep in through the maple, oak, hickory, and pine trees and over the long, wide lawn and meadow that surrounded our house and the barn. Sitting here after dinner was something we often did now, especially when Daddy was out late working on one of his big jobs. Mommy thought our time to "cross over," as she put it, was getting near, and I was very excited.

Even when we were very little, playing with our toys at her feet, Mommy would sit quietly and look out the window for hours and hours. I would glance up at her from time to time, especially when I would catch her eyes widening and narrowing like the eyes of someone listening to another. Sometimes, she would smile as if she had heard a funny story; sometimes she would look sad. Noble never seemed to be interested in her looks. He was always too wrapped up in his playing.

Occasionally, she would catch me looking at her and she would tell me not to stare. "A lady doesn't stare. It's not polite," she would say. "Staring in, politeness out," she recited.

When we began to sit with her at twilight on the chintz sofa, it was late spring of our sixth year and the aroma of freshly cut grass flowed in over us. Noble was restless and squirmed a lot more than I did, but Mommy kept him close to her breast, and he took deep breaths and waited, glancing at me occasionally to see if I was behaving or if I was as bored as he was.

I barely looked at him, afraid to take my eyes off the approaching shadows for fear I would miss the sight of one of Mommy's spirits. I so wanted to see one of our ancestors, and I was not at all afraid of ghosts. Mommy had spoken so long about them and how they would always protect and

16

watch over us. Why should I have any fear?

"You must never think of them as ghosts anyway," she once told me. "Ghosts are fantasies, storybook inventions meant only to haunt. They are silly. When the day comes that you see one of our family spirits, you will understand just how silly ghost stories are."

Noble was always impatient when we sat on the sofa. Tonight, before it became too dark to see anything, he wanted to go out and explore the anthill he had discovered. Mommy knew that. She knew he had far less patience than I had, and he wasn't as intrigued about the possibility of seeing one of her spirits, but Mommy had been a grade school teacher before she married Daddy and so she knew how to keep Noble attentive.

"Stop worrying, Noble. We'll take your flashlight if we have to, and I'll go look at your anthill with you," she promised him. "But only if," she added, "you watch night fall with me and perhaps see them come in with the shadows. They ride shadows like surfers ride waves. You must see them. You must understand and feel what I feel," she told him, and me of course, but she always seemed to want Noble to feel it more and to see them before I did. In fact, some-

17

times it seemed to me she was talking about the spirits only to him or to me through him.

It wasn't something she talked about in front of Daddy, however. Not only didn't he believe in her spirits, he was upset that she spoke about them to us or in front of us. At first he told her she would frighten us, and then, when he saw we weren't exactly frightened and rarely, if ever, had any nightmares because of her talking about spirits, he began to complain that she was distorting our view of reality and making it impossible for us to be social.

"How will they get along with other children their age in school if they have such weird ideas, Sarah? It's all right for you to believe in such things, but wait for them to grow older before you tell them these stories. They are just too young," he pleaded.

Mommy didn't respond. She often didn't when she disagreed with something he said, which could make him angrier or just send him mumbling off, wagging his head.

"Your father means well," she told us afterward in soft whispers, "but he doesn't understand. Not yet. Someday he will, and he won't be as unhappy with me. You must not let it bother you, children," she said.

"And you must not let it blind you to the wonderful visions that await you."

Noble didn't understand the disagreements anyway, and again, all this talk about invisible people and voices only Mommy could hear was something boring to him. He was far more interested in his insects. I didn't want to make either Mommy or Daddy sad and favor one over the other, but I didn't know what to do.

"Listen to me, Celeste," Daddy would say when he pulled me aside or when it was just me who was with him. "You and Noble were born the same day, practically the same minute, but you're brighter than he is. You'll always be smarter and wiser than your brother. Look after him and don't let Mommy make him crazy with her strange ideas.

"She can't help herself," he explained, speaking about her as if she were someone with a terminal incurable illness. "It was how she was brought up. Her grandmother was out there somewhere all the time, mumbling chants, finding magical herbs, and her mother wasn't much different, often worse in fact.

"Don't misunderstand me," he said quickly when he saw me curl my eyebrows toward each other. "Your mother is a wonderful, very intelligent and loving woman. I couldn't be happier about being her husband, but when she talks about seeing and talking to her ancestors and spirits, you have to listen to her with half an ear," he said.

He loved that expression: half an ear. I knew that he meant to pretend to pay attention, perhaps to take in what was said, but not to let it stay long.

"Sometimes," he said, "words just rent a space in your head. They don't stay forever, and lots of times there are words you don't want to remain even for a minute. And then," he said with a sigh, "there are those words you want to be permanent residents, especially words of love."

When Mommy and Daddy weren't arguing about her obsession with spirits and the forces of the other world, they were truly a loving couple and the handsomest and prettiest daddy and mommy that could be. I was sure they had just stepped out of a storybook to become our parents.

Mommy was the most beautiful woman I knew or had seen, even in the magazines or newspapers Daddy brought home. She kept her soft, rich hazel brown hair shoulder length and spent hours and hours brushing it. Daddy said she had a figure and a face that belonged on the front

20

covers of magazines, and sometimes he would just stop, look at her, and say, "Your mother moves with the gracefulness of angels. She sheds her years like a snake sheds his skin. She'll never look old."

I thought she wouldn't either.

And Daddy never looked his age. Of course to me, thirty-two sounded very old back then, but he was athletic and strong with raven black hair he kept swept back and eyes the color of rich wet soil. He always had a tan, a light almond complexion, even in the winter because he worked outdoors as a building contractor. He wasn't very tall, maybe just a few inches taller than Mommy, but he had wide shoulders and never slouched. He told us that his mother always made posture important.

"When I was your age, children," he said, "my mother made me walk around the house with a book on my head, and if it fell off, I had to stand in the corner with it on my head for twenty minutes. I hated doing that, so the book never fell off, and you can see how that helped."

"Should we walk around with books on our heads, Daddy?" I asked him.

He smiled and said no, because our posture was fine. We never met our grandmother, his mother. She had died a year before we were born. He made his mother sound like an army general sometimes, describing how she shouted orders and marched him about his home to do chores, but Mommy told us he liked to exaggerate.

"The truth was, your father was a spoiled brat," she said, and she said it in front of him. He would pretend to be angry at her, but they would always laugh about it.

So many things were heard with only a half an ear in our home those days.

But not Mommy's spirits. At least, not to her.

And soon not to me!

I had yet to hear them, but I knew Mommy was right in saying I would. I could feel it in the air. Their voices were almost in my ears. There was a faint whisper here, a faint whisper there, maybe waiting in a closet, a cabinet, or behind a closed door. I'd stop and listen hard, but I didn't hear anything really, or at least nothing that made any sense. I wasn't quite ready yet, I guess.

None of the spirits came from Daddy's family, only Mommy's. Mommy said that was because her family was special. They were people born with mystical talents and spiritual gifts. Some could read fortunes;

some could see the future in signs in Nature. Some had healing powers and could stop disease with just a touch of their hands, and one, it was said, even rose from the dead and returned to his family. Daddy said he must have been a sight to see and a smell to smell.

Mommy didn't get angry at him when he made fun of her stories. Instead she made those light brown eyes of hers small and tightened her lips as she gazed at him. Then she put her hands on our shoulders and leaned down between us.

"He'll see someday," she whispered in both our ears, but kissing Noble's. "Someday, he'll know."

Like Mommy, Daddy had no brothers or sisters. He had cousins and uncles, of course, and a father who was still alive, but was in a home now for very sick elderly people. All we knew was he couldn't remember anything or anyone, not even Daddy, so there was no point in our visiting him. Daddy did visit whenever he could, but Mommy said our grandfather was already gone. He had just left his body behind for a while like some statuary, "a living tombstone," she called him.

"If he was kind, he would take his body with him," she muttered.

Her own mother had passed away when Noble and I were only two. I had no real memory of her or of my maternal grandfather, because he had died ten years before we were born. He had fallen off the ladder when he was repairing a leak in the roof of this house, and he had died almost instantly when the fall broke his neck.

Daddy told me he remembered Mommy's grandmother well. If he talked about her, he usually spoke with a twist in his lips, since as we knew he blamed Mommy's interest in spiritual matters on her and Mommy's mother. Daddy said her grandmother had come from Hungary to marry her grandfather, and besides her two suitcases, she was laden down with a bag of superstitions, many of which Mommy still believed. To this day Mommy wouldn't let Daddy put his hat on a table because that would bring death or tragedy. He couldn't whistle in the house because that was calling the devil, and if a knife fell, she would predict we were getting a visitor.

Sometimes Daddy teased Mommy by calling her his gypsy lover because of all these superstitions and the stories he said Mommy's mother told him about the gypsies, who she said stole children and wandered about the Hungarian countryside, putting on carnivals and magic shows and reading fortunes. Daddy stopped just short of calling Mommy's mother a witch, herself. He told us she had ways with herbs and natural cures that, he had to admit, seemed magical. Mommy knew a great deal about those things, too, and relied on them more than she relied on modern medicine.

In fact, she and Daddy had some serious arguments about our getting our inoculations. He finally convinced her by assuring her he would just sneak us off and do it anyway if she didn't cooperate. She relented, but she wasn't happy about it.

Daddy was a healthy man who was hardly ever sick. Both Noble and I thought he was invulnerable, an extension of the wood and metal, the steel and cement, he used to build houses. He could work in bitter cold weather and in hot, humid weather and never get discouraged. When he came home to us, he was always happy and energetic. He didn't fall asleep on the sofa, or drag himself about the house. He loved to talk, to tell us about his day, mentioning people or places as if we had been there with him. Both of us wished we had, but Mommy would never let us go to a work site even though Daddy wanted to take us.

"You'll get distracted," she told him, "and they'll get hurt. And don't tell me you don't get distracted, Arthur Madison Atwell. You and your political speeches. When you make them, you're oblivious to everything else and don't even know you're standing in the cold rain."

Mommy was right, of course. Whenever Daddy had an opponent he deemed worthy, he would argue politics, but that wasn't often at home because we had so few visitors and Mommy wasn't very interested in politics. Daddy criticized her for that and said she cared more about the politics of the afterlife than of this life.

Most of the time, Noble and I would sit at his feet and smile and laugh at the way he shouted back at the television set when he watched the news. He did it with such vehemence, the veins in his temples popping, that we actually expected he would be heard and whoever it was on the screen would pause, look out, and address him directly. Mommy was always chiding him about it, but her words floated around him like so many butterflies who were too terrified to land, fearing they would flame up instantly if they dared touch his red-hot angry earlobes.

No matter how she yelled at him, or how

sharply either of them spoke to each other, we could see and feel how strong was the love between them. Sometimes, unexpectedly, Daddy would take Mommy's hand and just hold it while they sat and talked or when they were walking about our house and land. Noble and I would follow behind, Noble more interested in a dead worm, but my eyes were always on them.

And then there were times when Mommy would get a chill, even on hot summer days, and Daddy would throw his arms around her and hold her. She would lay her head against his shoulder and he would kiss her temples, her forehead, and her cheeks, raining his kisses down upon her like so many warm, soothing drops. She would hold on to him and then feel better and walk on or do whatever it was she was doing before the evil spirit hiding in a breeze had grazed her forehead or touched her heart.

Noble rarely saw any of this. He was always more distracted than I was. Everything competed for his attention, and Mommy always complained that he wasn't listening properly or thinking hard enough about what she had just said.

"Your thoughts are like nervous birds, Noble, flitting from one branch to another.

Settle down, listen to me," she would plead. "If you don't learn to listen to me, you'll never learn to listen to them," she would say and glance out the window or into the darkness.

Noble would raise his eyebrows and look at her and then steal a look at me. Mommy didn't know it, but I knew he didn't want to listen to them; he didn't want to hear any voices. Lately, in fact, the very idea of it had suddenly begun to terrify him. I could see that he dreaded the day he would hear someone speak and see no one there, whereas I longed for it. I wanted so much to be like Mommy.

"You should be happy they will speak to you, Noble. You'll know things other people don't," I told him.

"What things?" he asked me.

"Things," I said, and made my eyes small like Mommy often did. "Secret things," I whispered. "Things only we can know because of who we are," I recited. I had heard Mommy say it so often.

He grimaced with skepticism and lack of interest, and I couldn't make him listen like Mommy could.

I didn't look as much like Mommy as I wanted. Both Noble and I resembled Daddy more. We had his nose and his strong mouth. Although both Mommy and Daddy had brown eyes, both Noble and I had blue-green eyes, which Mommy said had something to do with our spiritual powers because sometimes our eyes were more blue and sometimes more green. Mommy claimed it had to do with cosmic energy. Daddy shook his head, looked at me, and pointed to his ear.

Half an ear, I thought, and smiled to myself, but never out loud in front of Mommy. I always thought of smiles as whispered or spoken or even shouted because Mommy seemed to be able to hear our feelings as well as look at us and see them.

When I was older, I would wonder how it came to pass that two people with such different ideas about the world and what was in it fell so deeply in love with each other. Mommy would tell us that love was something that had no logic, no formula, and was, in her opinion, the hardest thing to predict, even harder than earthquakes.

"Sometimes, I think love just floats in the air like pollen and settles on you so that whomever you're with or see at that time is your love. Sometimes I think that," she whispered, as if it was sinful to think it, to believe that something as powerful and important as love could be so carefree and incidental.

She whispered this to us after one of those beautiful times when she told Noble and me the story of her and Daddy. She had told it before, but we both loved hearing it again and again, or at least I did. She told it like she would tell a fairy tale with us sitting at her feet and listening, me more attentively of course.

"One day, a little more than five years after my father had died, we had another serious leak in our roof," she began. "Since my father had died trying to fix a leak, my grandmother thought it was an evil omen, and she was adamant we get the new leak repaired immediately."

"What's adamant?" Noble asked her.

We had just turned six when she told us her story this particular time. We were having a geology lesson when something made her think about it, and she closed her book and sat back, smiling. The year before, Mommy had decided she would home tutor us, at least for the first few years. Daddy was not happy about that, but Mommy told him that her experience as a grade school teacher made her more than qualified to provide us with the best possible early education, and the early years are the most formidable ones, she insisted.

"Besides," she said, "postponing all the extraneous and foolish issues surrounding public education today can only be a good thing, Arthur. Parents, boards of education, and educators are all bickering, and the children are getting lost and forgotten in all this."

In the end Daddy reluctantly agreed. "But, Sarah, only for the first year or so," he added. Mommy said nothing, and Daddy looked at me with a worried expression. It was she who was using only a half an ear now, I thought.

"Adamant," Mommy told Noble, "means determined. Nothing can change your mind. Stubborn, like you get too often," she said and then smiled and kissed him. Mommy never said anything bad about Noble without kissing him right afterward. It was as if she wanted to be sure what she said didn't linger, didn't matter, or maybe wasn't heard by any evil spirits in the house, a weakness it could exploit to get to his very soul.

Yet she didn't do that for me, I realized. Why wasn't she worried about an evil spirit touching me?

"Anyway," she continued, "the first nice

day after the rain, Grandma Jordan had me on the telephone searching for a builder to fix our roof. It wasn't easy to get someone fast, and in truth, it wasn't easy to get anyone at all."

"Why?" I asked.

Noble looked up, surprised at my question. He very rarely had any to ask, and I had not asked this question during the previous times she had told us her story.

"The job wasn't very big. It was more a handyman's job than a licensed contractor's, but your great-grandma Jordan wanted what she called 'a real carpenter,' so I had to call and plead with people," Mommy said. "Almost all of them said either they had no time for it or they couldn't get to it for weeks and weeks, maybe.

"Finally, I called your father's number, and as luck, or maybe something more, would have it, he picked up the phone himself. He heard me pleading, and he laughed and said, 'All right, Miss Jordan, I'll be there this afternoon.'

"The way he said 'Miss Jordan' told me he knew of me, knew I was what people called a spinster schoolteacher just because I was in my late twenties and still not married."

She paused and looked thoughtful a moment.

"To tell you the truth," she continued as if something she hadn't thought before had just occurred to her, "it made me a little nervous to hear him speak so casually to me."

"Why?" I asked. Mommy was never nervous about speaking to Daddy now, I thought.

"Why? Well," she said, looking at Noble as if he had been the one to ask, "I never had a boyfriend, not really. Dates occasionally, but no steady beau."

"Beau?" Noble asked looking up quickly. "You mean with arrows and everything?"

"No, silly. Beau — b . . . e . . . a . . . u. It means lover," she said, smiling. "Some day when you're a teenager, you'll accuse me of being old-fashioned, even in my speech."

Noble grimaced with disappointment. It was obvious to me that none of this was very interesting to him. He looked at his hand and moved his fingers as if he had discovered an amazing thing about himself.

"Your father drove over in his truck, and Grandma Jordan went out to inspect him," Mommy continued, her voice straining with some disappointment at Noble's small attention span. "That was the way your grandmother was with people. She didn't meet them. She inspected them. She looked for flaws, for something dark. I thought to myself, Oh no!" she cried, seizing Noble's attention again. "She'll get a bad feeling about him just like she had about a plumber we called, and we'll lose him.

"But she surprised me," she said, running her hand through Noble's hair. "She smiled and nodded her approval of your father. I brought Daddy into the house, and he looked at where the roof had stained the ceiling. He had this flirtatious smile on his lips every time he talked to me. I'm sure I was blushing. I'm blushing now, just thinking about it," she told us, and I saw that she was. It put a small feather in my stomach, and the tickle went right to my heart.

She sighed before she continued.

Noble was beginning to lose interest again. He had a dead caterpillar in his pocket and brought it out to straighten on the carpet.

"Where did you get that?" Mommy snapped at him. It made me jump because turning her sharp voice on Noble was not something she did very often. Most of the time, she turned it on me.

"I found it on the porch step," he said.

"You didn't kill it, did you?" she demanded with a note of fear in her voice. He shook his head.

"Never kill anything as beautiful as that, Noble. Every bad thing you do is kept in an evil bank account, and when there is enough in it, Nature will punish you severely," she warned, her eyes now not full of anger as much as they were full of real worry.

He widened his eyes, but he didn't look afraid. Somehow, nothing Mommy said or did frightened Noble. It was as if he had been inoculated against threats, especially ones that emanated from the world of mystery. If he couldn't see it for himself or hear it, he didn't believe in it. Nature was just too abstract an idea.

I was so different. I looked for Mommy's spirits in every shadow and corner. I listened to every breeze that threaded through the trees or through our open windows. I even sniffed after odors that were different or strange. In my heart of hearts, I felt it was all coming to me faster and stronger now. Soon, soon, I would be as Mommy was, and maybe then she would kiss me when she whispered in my ear or be worried more that an evil spirit would touch me. Maybe then.

After all, hadn't she told me often that the reason she insisted I be named Celeste was that something divine would be passed on to me?

"Anyway," Mommy continued, refusing to be distracted from her wonderful, romantic story, "your father went out and set up his ladder. Just the sight of it against the house drove my mother and my Grandma back inside. The memory of my father falling was still too vivid for my mother. She found him lying there unconscious while I was at school, you see. I'll never forget that phone call when they summoned me to the office, and she was screaming and crying. He wasn't moving. He wasn't breathing."

She wiped away an errant tear and sucked in her breath.

Noble was attentive again. Any reference to death captured his imagination, but I sensed it also frightened him a little. He moved a little closer to me so that we could touch.

" 'Be careful,' I told your father when he went up that ladder. He looked down at me, smiled in that way of his that can put you at such ease, and then he went up to the roof so gracefully and confidently, I had no anxiety about it.

" 'What a beautiful view from here,' he called down to me. 'Your home is in a perfect place in the valley. I can see clear to the lake that feeds the creek and a beautiful pond. You ever go swimming there? I would,' he said, sitting on the edge of the roof as if he was sitting in a rocking chair on someone's porch and had all the time in the world.

" 'Please hurry,' I shouted up at him," Mommy told us, and then paused to give us the same explanation why. "There were nasty spirits twirling about the house, and I did all I could to keep them from climbing the walls to get at him."

"What did you do, Mommy?" I asked in a whisper. This I had asked before, but it was like it was my part in a play. She looked to me for the question, anticipated it.

"I chanted at them, and I recited the Lord's Prayer. Finally, Daddy was finished and started down the ladder. I held my breath and watched him nervously. He jumped down the last five steps or so and smiled at me.

" 'Fixed,' he said.

" 'Thank you,' I told him.

"Then he asked me about my school-teaching job and about the house itself. He was truly intrigued with the construction. We didn't go back inside right away, and Grandma Jordan didn't come out and interrupt us. My mother was always so anxious for me to meet a man and get married, you see. Anyway, I showed him around the property and we talked.

"There were few long pauses between us. I wanted to hear his voice, and he wanted to hear mine. Finally," she said, smiling that soft smile that made her even more beautiful, "he asked me out on a date. I was so surprised I didn't say yes and I didn't say no. I just stared stupidly at him until he said, 'I have to know before I go or before I go on social security.'

"Of course you know I said yes, and the rest is history," she concluded, folding her hands over each other as if she were folding the covers of a book.

"What's history?" Noble asked. His interest in the word surprised both of us.

"All the events, the time that passed, our marriage, your birth, up until today," she explained patiently.

Noble thought a moment.

"Is tomorrow history, too?" he asked.

"It will be," she said, and that seemed to please him. Why did it matter at all to him? Of all the parts of the wonderful love story, why did that matter?

Noble was always a puzzle to me, even though we were as close as identical twins. Daddy said we were so close in our looks and mannerisms, we could have been born Siamese. It was true that we looked so much like each other, but there was something different in his eyes from what was in mine. I guess it all had to do with his being a boy and my being a girl. It was something I would learn about very soon, but never quite understand.

Although Noble wasn't looking for the spirits or listening for their voices as I was, he did a lot more pretending than I did. Mommy often complimented him on his imagination. I used to think that maybe his inventions, space creatures and the like, made him more capable of eventually hearing the spirits, but that wasn't so.

All we had were our books and our imaginations anyway. Mommy wouldn't let us watch much television, and we had never been to a movie. She believed television and movies could muddle up our brains and make it harder for us to be good students. Daddy couldn't oppose her when it came to our education. He would say, "You're the expert when it comes to all that, Sarah, but it didn't do that much damage to me."

"How do you know? How do you know what more you could have been?" she fired back at him, and he shrugged.

"I guess I don't. I just don't want them to be odd, Sarah. It's going to be hard enough for them to attend school when you finally let them attend, as it is."

"They'll be so far ahead of the other students, it will be easier for them," she assured him.

He backed off, but whenever he could, whenever Mommy wasn't home, he would let us watch children's television shows. Only we had to promise we would never tell Mommy.

We promised, but she'll know, I thought.

The spirits will tell her.

That was the way it had always been in our house. We couldn't keep secrets from Mommy. There were too many ears and eyes around us, ears and eyes friendly only to her. I think there came a time when even Daddy began to believe it.

"I didn't see anything again," Noble told Mommy when darkness had stolen the last rosy glow of dusk and was all about our home now. Another time on the chintz sofa had proven to be a failure. "I wanna go out with my flashlight and look at the ants," he whined, squirming under her embrace.

Mommy looked at me, and I shook my head. How I wished I could say otherwise, tell her I had seen or heard something, but I hadn't. She closed and opened her eyes with that patient confidence that told me I would. Don't worry.

"Can I, Mama? Can I?" Noble cried. "You promised if I sat still. You promised."

"All right. We'll all go out and look until your father comes home," she relented, and Noble leaped off the sofa, out of the living room and down the hallway to fetch his flashlight, a present Daddy had given him on his last birthday. It was a long black-handled one, almost as long as his little arm, with a powerful beam that reached the tops of trees bordering the lawn and meadow. He liked to surprise owls.

Mommy and I followed him out, walking slowly behind him. It was a warm, relatively cloudless early spring night. Stars were twinkling so brightly they looked like they were dancing. Noble rushed around to the east side of our house. The half moon was already behind it so that the lunar illumination stretched the shadow of our home into the darkness.

Mommy's great-grandpa Jordan had built a house that drew a lot of interest from passersby. We had a long driveway off one of the main highways.

Sometimes, when I was alone or Noble was off doing something that occupied him completely, I'd look toward the highway to see cars. It was just far enough away so that I couldn't make out the people well, only shapes I imagined to be families, husbands and wives and children who surely wondered who lived so far off the road in that grand old house. These were people I longed to know, children I wished were my friends, but whom I knew I never would know. Even then I knew. Sometimes people would stop and look at our house. Occasionally, I saw some take pictures of it.

It had a steeply hipped roof with two lower cross gables, but it was the tower at the west corner of the front facade that drew the most attention, I thought. The round attic space was used only for storage, but for Noble especially it made our home into a castle and a setting for his pretending.

"Look!" he screamed, shining his flashlight on the anthill.

Lines of them were marching up and

down, in and out, busy and determined, carrying dead insects and pieces of leaves.

"Ugh," I said, imagining them getting into the house as they did from time to time. Daddy had to spray and set traps.

"You shouldn't reject Nature," Mommy chastised. "Noble's curiosity is healthy and leads to learning, Celeste," she told me.

It seemed to me that she proudly pointed out Noble's best qualities whenever she could, but merely acknowledged mine or leaped upon my shortcomings.

She went into her schoolteacher voice, as I liked to call it.

"What you see, children, is cooperation at its peak. Every ant contributes to the success of the hive. They don't think of themselves as separate. They are like cells in our bodies, interacting, building, existing for the success of the whole and not themselves. When we're like that, we do the best work. A family is a team, too.

"In fact," she said, "don't look at the ants as ants. Think of the whole hive as one living thing, and you will understand them better. Can you do that, Noble?"

He nodded, even though I could see in his eyes that he had no real idea about what she had been saying. Nevertheless, Mommy ran her hand through his hair and squeezed him against her. Whenever she embraced him without embracing me, too, I felt as if I was floating in space, lost.

We stood there watching the ants work, Mommy holding Noble's hand and I standing beside them, tears waking under my eyelids for reasons I didn't quite understand. I swallowed against a throat lump and took a deep breath.

Mommy turned and looked at me. A long, thick cloud began to block out the moon, and the light on her face went out as if someone had turned it off in the sky.

Mommy spun and gazed out at the now thickening darkness, her arms locking, her body so still. My heart began to pound. She hears something, sees something, I thought. The invading cloud had almost completely covered the moon.

"Mommy?" I said.

She waved at me to be silent.

Noble knelt to look closer at his ants. He was oblivious to anything else.

"We've got to go back inside," Mommy said suddenly and reached down to seize Noble's arm, forcing him to stand.

"Why?" he whined.

"There's something evil out there, something dark and evil circling us. Quickly," she said.

She started for the house. I followed, afraid to look back. Noble was near tears, his body turned so he could look back at his ants.

"But you said we could look at the ants!" he moaned.

"Just walk," Mommy ordered, practically dragging him along now.

As soon as we were back inside, she slammed the door shut and hurried us to the living room, where she closed the curtains. Then she went to light one of her candles.

Noble stood there looking disgusted and angry.

"I'm going to sneak out and go back to my ants," he vowed.

"Don't!" I said, fearing for him. "You heard Mommy."

"I didn't see anything evil," he said sharply and ran through the house and up to his room.

Mommy returned with a candle and placed it near the front window, which she closed quickly.

She looked at me and then at her watch. What was she so worried about? I wondered.

And then I thought . . . Daddy.

Shouldn't he be home by now?

2

Daddy's Amulet

Daddy was at a meeting with a prospective home builder. When he and Mommy were first married, he had his own construction company, but it was very small and Daddy actually only did work in conjunction with bigger companies. He didn't have the financing to do much more. Mommy remained a schoolteacher until we were born. She went on extended maternity leave and then decided not to return, but instead to spend her time raising us. She said she believed the early years were the most important when it came to bringing up children.

For a while it was a financial struggle, but a little more than a year after we had been born, Grandma Gussie died and Mommy and Daddy inherited the house and the land and money left in an interest-bearing bank account that was from Grandpa Richard Jordan's life insurance policy. Little of it had been touched after he had fallen off the ladder and died. With that money Daddy and his partner formed a bigger construction company and began to build custom homes. Although he wasn't educated as an architect, his imaginative ideas attracted the interest of more discriminating home buyers, and soon he had three outstanding examples to show other prospective buyers.

One of his homes was written up in a statewide magazine and brought him even more attention. Soon he had five men working for him full time in his offices, and then he was given the opportunity to build a custom home development with a very big firm out of New York City.

Mommy was very proud of his accomplishments. I never thought of us as being rich people, but apparently we were doing so well we could afford expensive things like a luxury car, a company jeep, a company truck, better lawn tractors and tools, and nice clothes for Noble and me, although Daddy complained often that no one saw us dressed nicely because Mommy kept us at home so much.

"I'm making all this money," he practically bellowed at her, "but you won't take an expensive vacation. You won't consider putting the children into private school. You hardly spend anything on your own wardrobe. You rarely ever want to go to a fine restaurant."

"We must not let money change us, Arthur," she warned. "It can do that."

"Oh," he said, nodding and pacing about the room when he argued with her. "And where did you get that tidbit of wisdom? One of the dead relatives?"

"If you must know, yes," she said without hesitation. "I had a great-uncle, Uncle Samuel, who made a lot of money in the stock market. He forced his wife to do fancy things, dress fancy and go to balls and charity events, have her picture in the newspaper on the society pages, become friends with other wealthy women."

"So?"

"She met someone who seduced her, and she became pregnant again."

Daddy looked at Noble and me. We were sitting at our little desks, doing our spelling workbooks. Actually, Noble was sketching insects in the margins. He was very good at it. I was listening to Daddy and Mommy, but pretending I wasn't.

"And?" Daddy said.

"And my uncle threw her out. Her lover disowned her as well, and she died when she went to a filthy place to have an abortion."

"How come I never heard this story before?" he asked suspiciously.

"I just heard it myself recently," she replied.

He looked at her and shook his head.

"Okay, Sarah," he said with a deep, tired sigh. "We'll pretend I'm not successful."

"I'm not saying we have to do that, but we have to be sensible about what we do with our money and ourselves."

He smiled.

"Sorry," he said, digging into his pocket and plucking out a small box. "I couldn't help not being sensible this one time."

He handed the box to her, and I stared in wonder. Noble continued to draw.

"What is this?" she asked, not opening it. She held it as if it would turn into something too hot to hold any moment.

"I told you. I couldn't help myself," he said. "I saw it, and I envisioned it on you. Complain to your spirits about me."

She shook her head at him as if he were an errant child, opened the box, and then looked up at him without taking out what was in it.

"Is it real?"

"Of course it's real," he said.

Carefully, timidly, she took out the necklace. There was a pear-shaped diamond in the middle, almost as big as my thumb. It glittered so brightly, I thought it had a tiny bulb inside it.

Daddy rushed forward and took it from her.

"Let me put it on you," he said, undoing the chain and going behind her.

She let him, and then put her hand over the diamond when he stepped in front of her.

"Don't cover it," he said.

"I wanted to feel it, feel its energy," she said.

Daddy raised his eyes to the ceiling and glanced at me to pull on his earlobe. I bit down on my lower lip. Mommy walked to the mirror on the wall and stared at herself for a long silent moment. Both Daddy and I were holding our breaths, I think.

"It's beautiful," she finally said, and then added, "too beautiful."

"Nothing is too beautiful for a beautiful woman, Sarah," he said.

She relented, turned and smiled at him.

"You're incorrigible now, Arthur Madison Atwell."

"I hope so," he said with a twinkle in his eye. "Maybe later you'll continue explaining all this to me in private," he added, and Mommy blushed, glanced at me, and shook her head, turning quickly to hide her smile.

The necklace was the first very expensive gift Daddy ever gave Mommy. Spending money, enjoying their new wealth, really did seem to frighten her. She talked a lot about the evil eye and said it was something her grandmother had described and warned her about when she was a little girl. It always made Daddy angry to hear about it, so she rarely spoke about it in front of him.

"Jealous spirits," she told us, "see your happiness, especially when you flaunt it, and then they do something, throw down a curse, a trap, and make you miserable. Never be too proud, too ostentatious, too showy about the nice things you have and the wonderful things that happen to you or you achieve. Always be modest, children," she warned us.

Noble tucked in his cheek and stared at her blankly because there were so many words he didn't understand, but I knew enough to make my heart thump. How do you know when you're tempting evil spirits? I wondered. I wanted to ask, but I didn't like talking about them either.

Anyway, Daddy's gift gave Mommy an idea. It was an idea that needed to be nurtured between her and her good spirits. She went out alone night after night and listened for advice, and then, one day, she told Daddy she wanted him to take her shopping. She knew exactly where she wanted to go, and she said she would take us to lunch, too, which surprised him, but he was so happy to take us all out for the day, he didn't question anything. He didn't have any idea what it was she wanted to buy either.

She took us to a jeweler whom we would discover she had known for a long time. He had moved his shop to the main street of a village almost thirty miles away from us, which was where Mommy preferred to do most of our supermarket shopping anyway. Daddy complained about that and made her shop locally whenever he could. It was as if she never wanted local people to see us and ask her any questions about us or her. As soon as we arrived in the town, Daddy grumbled.

"I don't know what was so important about driving this far. There's nothing much here for the children," he said.

"Yes, there is," she insisted. "What's here is exactly for the children," she told him.

Still puzzled, he drove along the main street until she told him to stop, and she got out, taking us both by the hand and leading us into the jeweler's shop called Bogart's Estate Jewelry. Daddy followed, scratching his head, amused, but also a little embarrassed. What was this all about? He wondered. I could see it in his face because the same look was in mine. Noble was disappointed it wasn't a toy store.

When the store owner revealed he knew Mommy well, no one was more surprised than Daddy because Mommy never bought herself any jewelry, at least that he or I knew.

"Hello, Sarah," he said. "It's been a long time."

"Mr. Bogart, how are you?" Mommy asked him.

He shrugged.

"I don't ask myself so I don't have to worry about the answer," he said, smiling.

About Mommy's height, Mr. Bogart had a mostly bald head but curly gray hair along the sides. His eyes were like Noble's and mine, blue and then green when he moved from the dimmer light to the bright sunshine streaming in through the small front window. He had soft, very light red lips and a slight cleft in his round chin. He

53

was dressed in a black leather vest over a white shirt and a pair of black slacks, but wore what looked like black leather slippers with no socks. I saw how red his ankles were, as red as a rash.

His shop wasn't very big. It was narrow with dark wood and glass cases on both sides. The cases were filled with all sorts of jewelry, including watches of all kinds. There was something burning on one of the counters. I recognized it to be similar to the incense Mommy burned occasionally.

"These are my children," Mommy said, taking us both by the shoulder and pushing us forward to stand in front of her.

Mr. Bogart looked at us carefully and nodded slowly, smiling.

"Gussie's eyes," he said.

"Yes," Mommy replied, smiling. That was the first time I had heard that Noble and I had our maternal grandmother's eyes. Why hadn't Mommy ever said so before? It was as if she needed Mr. Bogart to confirm it first and had brought us here to his shop just for that.

Daddy cleared his throat.

"Oh, this is my husband, Arthur Atwell, Mr. Bogart."

"Pleased to meet you," Mr. Bogart said,

extending his small, puffy hand.

Daddy shook it quickly, nodded, and then looked at Mommy with an expression that said, "What are we doing here?"

She turned away from him quickly.

"I've come because it's time the children had their amulets, Mr. Bogart."

"Of course," he said. "I was expecting you."

"Huh?" Daddy couldn't help uttering. "Amulets?"

Why was Mr. Bogart expecting us? I wondered, too. A little while ago, he didn't seem to have known who we were or that Mommy had a boy and a girl.

"I know what I need," Mommy said.

"I'm sure you do," Mr. Bogart replied with a twinkle in his eyes and stepped around to walk to the case on the left, closest to the front of the store.

Mommy moved us toward it, too. Daddy, now looking more upset, stood back and folded his arms, which was something I knew he did when he was growing angry.

"Sarah," he said through his clenched teeth, "what are you doing?"

"Please, Arthur, this is important," she muttered and turned back to the jewelry case. She studied everything and then nodded and pointed to a pendant on a gold chain.

"This one is for Noble," Mommy told Mr. Bogart.

"Ah yes, the Krena," he said, opening the back of the case and reaching for a round gold pendant. On it was a design that looked like a worm with arms and legs in the process of running. That was exactly what Noble thought, too.

"A worm?" he said.

"No, no," Mr. Bogart said, smiling. "It isn't a worm, young man. This is a powerful talisman." He looked up at Daddy, who was glaring down at the amulet. "The Krena activates psychic powers," he said.

"What does that mean?" I asked softly, and he looked at me and smiled warmly.

"It helps you focus yourself on your wishes, makes your dreams come true. Everyone has psychic powers, but most of us never use them," he said, lifting his eyes a little toward Daddy, who was embracing himself harder. The veins in his neck were becoming prominent. "The Krena absorbs the energy within your aura and focuses it on the wish of your choice."

"What?" Daddy asked grimacing. "More gobbledygook magic?"

Mr. Bogart looked at us and then at Mommy.

"You haven't told them about this, Sarah?"

"I wanted them to see it and hear it from you, Mr. Bogart," she said, and Mr. Bogart smiled.

He handed the pendant and chain to Mommy, and she turned to Noble, keeping her eyes diverted from Daddy and stepping between him and Noble.

"You need this, Noble. I want you to wear it always. Never, ever take it off, understand?"

He looked up at Mr. Bogart.

"It's a worm," he said firmly.

"No, it's not, but you will understand what it is later. I'm sure of that," Mommy said, and she put it around his neck and fixed the clatch.

He looked down at it and then at me.

"What about Celeste?" he asked, now more intrigued with what I would be getting. So was I. For a long moment, I thought Mommy had decided to buy only Noble something. I was practically in tears already.

Mommy turned to Mr. Bogart, and then she pointed to another.

"Yes, yes," he said, reaching in.

He took out one that had a seven-pointed star with a small diamond at the center.

Mr. Bogart held it in his palm before me. The diamond had a tiny glitter in the light, which made me happy.

"This is the Mystic Star," he said. "The seven points radiate a mysterious and intense energy said to bestow the seven treasures of the kings — wealth, happiness, love, luck, wisdom, respect, and glory." He pointed to each point as he enumerated the treasures.

Mommy took the pendant from him and put it around my neck.

"It is said you often feel the energy the moment you wear it," Mr. Bogart told me.

I did feel something, a warmth, and I looked up quickly at Mommy, who smiled.

"Hocus-pocus," Daddy muttered. "I can't believe you're doing this, Sarah."

He turned away.

"One more," Mommy told Mr. Bogart. She looked into the case again and pointed to a necklace that held an unusual-looking stone.

"What is that, Mommy?" I asked her.

"It's amethyst," she said. "A semiprecious gem."

Mr. Bogart brought it out. The gem was

held in a gold case and on a gold chain.

"I want you to wear this, Arthur," she told Daddy.

"What?"

"It's special. Amethysts can protect you. It can warn you of oncoming danger, accidents. It will change color, and that's how it will warn you."

"Oh, please, Sarah. This is going too far. Really. Change color?"

"It does work," Mr. Bogart said.

"Umm. I don't doubt for you. How much is it?"

"Stop that, Arthur."

"I tell you what, Mr. Atwell," Mr. Bogart said. "Take it at no cost."

Daddy raised his eyebrows and looked at the stone.

"To make me happy, Arthur," Mommy said. "Please, take it."

He shook his head and then took it and put it into his pocket quickly.

"It will do you no good in there," Mr. Bogart told him.

Daddy sighed deeply and then took it out and put it on.

"Can we go now, Sarah?"

She nodded.

"Take the children out to the car, Arthur. I want to talk to Mr. Bogart for a few minutes. I'll be right there," she promised.

Daddy practically seized our hands and pulled us out the door, mumbling to himself as he marched us back to the car.

"Why do I get a worm and she gets a star?" Noble complained.

"You're better off, Noble. At least your thing looks like something funny. Someday you can show it to your buddies, if you ever get a chance to have buddies."

Noble sat back, considering.

"Worms don't have arms and legs," he said. Then he brightened and thought aloud, "Unless I just haven't seen any yet. Do they, Daddy?"

"None I've met," Daddy said. "But your mother hangs around in different circles."

"What's that mean, Daddy?"

"Please. Just let's think about lunch. How about a Whammy burger?"

That excited Noble enough for him to forget his pendant. I fingered mine.

Seven points, the treasures of the kings! Mommy did love me very much after all, I thought, maybe even as much as she loved Noble.

After we had our lunch, Mommy and Daddy had their first really bad argument in front of us. They rode home in silence, but when they arrived, Daddy started to complain about Mr. Bogart and the amulets, and Mommy didn't ignore him like she usually did. She shouted back at him, her eyes full of red rage like we had never before seen. It made Noble and I cringe. We sat close to each other in the living room. They were arguing in the hallway.

"You had no right to be so rude to Mr. Bogart, Arthur."

"Rude? I thought I was quite controlled. This is getting way out of hand, Sarah," Daddy cried. "They don't play with other children their age. You practically keep them locked up here, and when we take them somewhere, where do we take them? To some kooky guy's weird jewelry shop. Who was he, a friend of your grandmother's?"

"Yes, he was, and he was a good friend, too."

"Figures. Do you realize you don't have any normal friends either? And it's getting so neither do I. I'm afraid to invite anyone here for fear you'll see dark, evil spirits hovering around them, see their aura, and do what you did when I brought Dick Calhoun and his wife here. Do you know how embarrassing that was for me? You locking yourself up in the kitchen and leaving me with them for nearly two hours?

I partnered with him on a number of big projects, for crissakes, and now he's part owner of my business."

"I told you why I didn't feel comfortable with them, Arthur."

"You told me? You had a bad feeling about Betty Calhoun. Something dark whirling around her? Really. And now this . . . this voodoo stuff with the children. You're poisoning their heads, Sarah. They won't be at any advantage when they go to school. They'll be thought weird, just like we are. Do you know what Ben Simon told me the other day, the story he heard from the postman?"

"I don't care to hear it," she said.

"Well, you're going to hear it," Daddy insisted. "Simon said the postman claims that he heard Noble and Celeste speaking what sounded like Arabic or some very foreign tongue. Then he said he swore he saw Noble change into a bird and fly into a tree. They all think our kids are weird. They enjoy making up stories about them."

"Stop saying that! Stop saying they're weird!" she shouted at him.

"Then stop doing what you're doing to them. And send them to school, for god's sake," he replied and left the house, slamming the door behind him. The whole house shook.

Mommy said nothing to us, but I could see she was very troubled. She went off for one of her long, quiet walks through the meadow and into the woods.

When she returned, she looked like she had been crying for days.

Daddy didn't really wear his pendant much, and Mommy assured me as we sat waiting for him that night that he wasn't wearing it this day.

"He goes out with it on, but he takes it off as soon as he drives away."

"How do you know?" I asked.

"I know," she said, nodding and staring out at the dark through the slightly parted curtain. The candle flickered as if some spirit was indeed circling the small flame.

I had no doubt Mommy knew Daddy had taken off his amulet. The way she said it put the jitters in my bones.

Noble, calmed down from his tantrum, came into the room complaining about my not playing with him, but I couldn't help it. I was too nervous to pretend anything. I wanted Daddy home. I wanted us all to feel safe again.

"There's no reason for you to sit here

63

with me like this, Celeste," Mommy told me. "Go amuse your brother." She waved me off.

"But —"

She turned sharply.

"You two should feel the same things," she said as if she was just realizing a bigger problem. Her eyes grew small again as she thought. "When one of you is sad, the other should feel sad, too."

I didn't understand why. Noble never felt what I felt, and I rarely if ever did feel what he felt. We were twins, yes, but we were individuals, too, and after all, he was a boy and I was a girl.

"Why is that, Mommy?"

My confusion seemed annoying to her. She twisted her lips and closed her eyes.

"Just go," she said with her eyes still closed. "Play! Occupy yourselves!"

I got up quickly, but before I reached the doorway, Mommy released a cry. She put her hands on her heart, one over the other, and stood there looking up, her face bathed in terror, her eyes wide, her mouth twisted.

Noble seized my hand, and I put my arm around him. She began to waver as if the floor was moving under her feet.

"Mommy?" I cried.

She started to look toward us, and then . . . she fainted.

The sight of her collapsing to the floor was the most frightening thing either Noble or I had ever seen. She folded, her body pouring downward as if all of her bones had turned to liquid.

Noble started to cry, and I couldn't move for a moment. All the breath had gone out of me.

"Mommy!" I screamed.

Her face was turned away from us, and her arm looked so twisted, I thought for sure it was broken.

"What's wrong with Mommy?" Noble shouted through his sobs. He covered his face so he couldn't see her.

I let go of him and edged closer to her, my heart pounding so hard, I could feel the thump in my throat and even into my teeth. I knelt beside her slowly and touched her shoulder. Then I poked it.

"Mommy?"

She didn't move, and I poked her harder. Noble was crying hysterically in the corner now, still hiding his face, squatting. I shook her as hard as I could, and finally, I saw her hand twitch and then her arm move as she moaned and turned slowly toward me.

She looked at me, closed her eyes, and opened them again.

"Mommy, what's wrong with you?"

"Just help me sit up," she said, and I got behind her and started to push on her shoulder.

"Noble, help," I called.

He looked at us but turned away quickly, still too frightened to move.

Mommy managed to sit and catch her breath.

"I'm all right, Noble. I'm all right. Don't be frightened," she said. "Go to the bathroom, Celeste, and run a washcloth under the faucet. Cold water only. Wring it so you don't drip all over the floor and bring it back to me. Go on," she ordered, and I did it quickly.

When I returned, she was on the sofa, her head back. Noble was sitting now, sitting and staring at her. I gave her the washcloth, and she put it over her forehead.

"I'm all right," she said, seeing how terrified I still was. "I'm all right."

"What happened, Mommy?"

She just shook her head, her lips trembling. She wouldn't talk. I sat beside her and held her hand. Noble finally rose and came to us. He buried his head in

66

Mommy's lap and she ran her hand over his hair and his neck.

We sat there like that for a long time. Noble actually fell asleep. Mommy lifted him in her arms and carried him upstairs to the room we shared. He was so tired he barely opened his eyes as she undressed him and put on his pajamas. Then she kissed him and hummed one of the songs her mother and her grandmother had hummed to her to help her sleep. I stood by, feeling forgotten. Finally she realized it.

"You get to bed, too, Celeste. Go wash your face and brush your teeth," she told me and left, seemingly floating down the stairs.

I went to the bathroom to do what she said, but I didn't get into my pajamas right afterward. Instead, I stood by the window and looked out at the road that led to our house. Way off in the distance I could see the headlights of an automobile. It's Daddy, I thought, finally coming home. It's Daddy driving his truck.

Whatever it was that had gripped my heart relaxed and loosened its hold as I watched the headlights get brighter and bigger the closer the vehicle came. I was so full of joy again, I thought I could dance like the stars seemed to be dancing earlier in the evening, but when I looked up, I noticed that even the stars were gone now. The heavy clouds that had earlier begun to cover the moon had continued unfolding across the sky.

It would rain tonight, I thought. Most of the time, I liked the sound of rain at night. The pitter-patter on our windows put me to sleep, but I didn't want rain. I wanted to see the bright, happy sky again, especially when Daddy came home.

However, as the vehicle turned into our driveway, I saw it wasn't a truck after all, and it was an automobile that was a much lighter color than Daddy's car. Who was it? I wondered. I saw someone get out and approach the house.

Curiosity drew me to our bedroom door and then to the top of the stairway when I heard our door buzzer ring. Mommy seemed to take forever to go to the door. The buzzer sounded a second time. I almost went down the stairs myself to see who it was, but finally I saw her walk to the door, her head down. She opened it slowly and stepped back, nodding as if she knew exactly who it was and why he had come.

When the man entered, I recognized Mr. Calhoun. He stood there with his cap in his hands.

"Sarah," he began.

"Where is he?" Mommy asked quickly.

"At the hospital," he said without wondering how Mommy knew something was wrong.

"The hospital," she repeated.

"It all happened so quickly."

"When did he die?" she asked.

Mr. Calhoun lowered his head.

"When did he die!" she screamed.

"About an hour or so ago," he replied. "They wanted to phone you, but I said it wasn't something to tell someone on the phone, so I volunteered to come out here. Did someone call you after all?"

She shook her head.

"No," she said.

"No? But —" He looked down and then up at her again. "I'm so sorry. It makes no sense to anyone. The doctor looked like he had lost his hands or something when he came out to tell us."

"What happened to Arthur? What did the doctor tell you?" she asked, still not crying.

"Some massive hemorrhaging . . . a cerebral aneurism, they called it. How a man that healthy could suddenly . . . they made it sound like getting a flat tire . . . an artery ballooning and bursting. I don't understand. One minute he was talking animatedly to the general contractor on the project, and the next he was . . . collapsed. We tried CPR immediately, of course, and sent for an ambulance. They did the best they could at the hospital. We got him right into the emergency room, and . . ." He looked down at the floor and then shook his head and took a deep breath.

Mommy stood there like a statue, still not crying, and now not speaking.

It seemed to spook Mr. Calhoun. He looked up, shifted his eyes, and backed up a bit.

"Is there anything I can do for you right now? I mean . . . you'll have to contact the hospital . . . there'll be arrangements to be made. If there's anything . . ."

"No," she said.

"I'm really sorry, shocked and sorry. We're all devastated down at the project."

She nodded, but still didn't cry.

Later we would learn that Mommy's reaction would be more interesting to people and a more interesting topic of discussion for them than Daddy's surprising death.

"Did you know he was sick or something?" Mr. Calhoun finally asked to break the heavy silence. "I mean, did you have any idea? Did he?"

"I knew he was in trouble," she said.

"Well, why didn't he go to a doctor, get examined or something?"

"He didn't know he was in trouble," she explained. "Maybe, if he had worn the amulet —"

"Amulet?"

Mr. Calhoun shook his head.

"He didn't know he was in trouble? I don't think I understand, Sarah. How could he not know if he was getting sick, but you knew?"

"I just realized it about an hour or so ago myself," she said. "It was too late."

"I don't understand, Sarah. How is it you knew but he didn't?" he asked with more demand.

"I had a message, a feeling," she told him.

He stared for a moment and then nodded, everything about Mommy coming back to him.

"Oh. Sure. I've heard of things like that," he told her. "When people are so close as you and Arthur were . . . sure." He was backing up more now. He was practically out the door.

Mommy took the door in hand and looked out at him.

"Thank you for coming rather than

calling," she said, and she closed the door before he turned to leave.

She stood there staring at the closed door. I felt as if a part of me was lifting and floating out over the stairs, down to her. I had no doubt that she sensed I was standing there. She turned and looked up at me. And then she held out her arms, and I hurried down and into them.

She held me so tightly, the tightest she had ever held me, and I held on to her, thinking that as soon as I let go, I would fall into a dark hole.

Finally she relaxed and held me at arm's length.

"We won't wake Noble and tell him yet," she said. "Let him sleep."

"Mommy, where's Daddy?" I asked, refusing to understand the words I had overheard.

"He's gone over to the other side, Celeste," she said. "We can do nothing about it. They took him."

"Who took him?"

"His own spiritual family," she said. "He's gone. He died," she uttered.

"How could Daddy die?" I moaned through a constricting throat. "He was never sick!"

"He must have burned himself out.

We're all given a certain number of heart-beats at birth, Celeste, and if we get excited too often or are too vigorous, whatever, we can very well shorten our lives."

"No, not Daddy," I said, shaking my head and backing out of her arms. Why wasn't she crying hard if Daddy was really dead? This was just a dream.

"Go get some sleep, Celeste," she said in a very tired voice. "We're all going to need our sleep and our strength more than ever now."

She was talking as if she was under a spell, hypnotized. Her voice didn't sound like her, and her eyes were cold and gray. I kept shaking my head, my own tears starting to flow and fly off my cheeks.

"I've got to go out," she said suddenly.

"Where are you going?" I cried.

"I have to go out there. I have things to do, things to say to people," she said.

She turned to the door.

"I want to go with you, Mommy," I said. "Please. I'm afraid. I want Daddy."

She opened the door and shook her head.

"You can't go with me," she said. "You're not ready for such things yet. Stop being afraid," she ordered. "Go back to

73

bed. And whatever you do, don't wake Noble. Don't let him know anything, not yet. Do you hear me, Celeste?"

I nodded.

"But I want to be with you, Mommy," I moaned.

She closed the door, and I screamed for her. Then I opened the door and saw her walking quickly into the darkness as if she knew exactly where to go. I started after her until she disappeared from sight, until she was swallowed up by the night. The sky had become totally overcast. There was no moonlight or starlight. How could she walk into that ocean of black and know where she was going? I wondered.

I called for her again, but heard nothing. My voice died in the dark.

For a while I stood there, listening, searching the shadows, wondering who it was she was going to see. Would it be Daddy? I saw nothing. I felt only a bad chill. Then I went back inside, but instead of going upstairs, I curled up at the foot of the stairway, embraced myself, and waited for her to return. I heard our phone ringing, but I didn't answer it. I couldn't keep my eyes from closing. My whole body wanted to close up, and I welcomed it. Moments later I was asleep, and when I awoke with the sunlight on my face, I found myself in my bed.

My first thought was, it had all been a horrible nightmare. I sat up quickly. Noble was just waking up, too. He rubbed his eyes and yawned and then he stretched.

"I'm hungry," he said. When I didn't respond, he grimaced. "Why are you just looking at me, Celeste?"

Without replying, I leaped out of bed and went to the window to look down for Daddy's truck. It wasn't where he always parked it.

"What are you looking for?" Noble asked, sliding off the bed and putting his feet into his slippers.

"Daddy," I said.

"Look downstairs. He's probably having his coffee," he said and stretched again.

I started to nod. Why not? Why not force it all to be a nightmare? Yes, I thought. Daddy's downstairs having his coffee. Everything was just a bad dream.

I started for the door when it opened and Mommy stood there looking in at us.

She was dressed in black, her eyes bloodshot, her lips trembling.

"Mommy?" I said, my own lips trembling just as hard.

"Did you tell him anything?"

"No," I said.

"Tell me what?" Noble asked.

"Daddy's gone," Mommy said.

"Gone? Where did he go?" Noble asked.

"To the bosom of his family," Mommy replied.

The nightmare I had hoped would replace reality was just beginning.

3

Crossing Over

The darkness that fell over our home that night never lifted for months and months. Even in the morning when the sun came out, the darkness lingered. I felt like it stuck to everything around me. It was in every corner, over every window, like a thin film of dark gray. Mostly it was in our eyes, especially Mommy's and mine.

Many people had come to the church for Daddy's funeral service and even to the cemetery. Mommy didn't really know most of them. They were people with whom Daddy had done business: bankers, attorneys, real estate people. Mr. Calhoun was as attentive as he could be, but his wife looked afraid of Mommy and held him back. They didn't come to the cemetery with us, in fact, but one of Daddy's close friends, Taylor Kotes, a man about Daddy's age, was beside us constantly. I knew from the previous times I had seen him with Daddy or heard Mommy and Daddy talk about him that he was now the owner of the biggest lumberyard in the community and he had lost his wife, who had developed some vicious form of muscular dystrophy and died two years ago. On this dark gray day, both he and Mommy seemed to wear the same mask of sorrow, his own cemetery memories returning.

Mommy had decided against having any sort of gathering at the house afterward. I heard her mumbling how many of these mourners had come out of curiosity. They wanted to see her and especially us, the mysterious twins. I could feel dozens of eyes on me in church and especially at the cemetery. Noble was distracted by everything as usual and for a while was more interested in a crow on a nearby tree then the minister's words and the sight of the coffin held on poles above the empty grave. Because Mommy didn't cry, I didn't.

Noble was still having trouble understanding and accepting Daddy's dying. For a long time afterward, he would stop and stare down the long driveway and over the road, expecting to see Daddy's truck approaching. Even after the funeral, he waited with anticipation, sometimes kicking a rock about the driveway for nearly an hour, periodically sitting on the side and scratching pictures in the earth. I watched him from a window. I didn't have to ask him what he was doing.

Mommy didn't permit us to see Daddy in his coffin, so we didn't see him dead. She believed the body had nothing more to do with Daddy. His spirit had left it. Therefore, there was no reason to gaze upon him just to confirm he was gone.

To demonstrate her belief, she filled a paper cup with water and told us the water was the spirit.

"When you die, your spirit leaves your body," she said and poured the water out. "This empty cup is your empty body. It's not you anymore. It is worthless," she said bitterly and crushed the cup in her hand. "I could burn it; I could bury it; I could seal it up in a tomb. It doesn't matter. No one will ever look upon it again."

Noble's eyes grew small and angry. I could see how he thought Mommy was all wrong. She couldn't possibly be right. There was no way Daddy wasn't coming home, not our daddy. He shook his head at her and stamped his foot. "No! Daddy's not a cup! Daddy's not a cup!" he screamed and ran off to hide in his room and sulk, his footsteps pounding the floor and echoing in my heart.

When Mommy had called Noble stubborn, she had no idea how deep that well of stubbornness was. She looked at me and shook her head.

"We've got to make him understand, Celeste. It's important," she said.

Why didn't she even wonder if I had understood? Was it just because I wasn't shouting and crying like Noble? I didn't want to understand and accept Daddy's death any more than he did. Why wasn't she throwing her arms around me and soothing me as much? Why was she sending me after him?

Eventually, I mistook Noble's stubbornness for his being able to reach Daddy's spirit, and I was terribly jealous. He held onto his obstinacy so long I thought, what else could it be? Time wasn't working its magic on him as it was on Mommy and me. There was no concession in him, no willingness to go on without Daddy, even if we performed the smallest and most insignificant of chores about the house.

"Daddy doesn't want us to do this," he would say. Or, "Daddy wants me to help him tonight." He even said, "Daddy was here and he said we should listen to Mommy and never be bad and give her a headache."

"When?" I asked. "Where did you see him? When did you hear him speak? What did he look like? What was he wearing? Did he ask about me?"

Questions about details confused him and sent him running off. Was he hiding something from me? I had to wonder. Did the spirits tell him not to reveal anything? Finally, I asked Mommy.

She looked at me sadly and said, "I wish that were the case, Celeste, but I'm sure everything Noble is telling you comes from his imagination."

"But how do you know, Mommy? Maybe he does speak to Daddy's spirit."

"I would know," she said. She said it with such confidence that I had no doubt she would. "It's not time for that yet. Your brother just won't face our loss. He's a very sensitive child. He has my heart," she said, and I felt as if a bee had stung me.

He had her heart?

What did I have of hers?

"Go find him. I don't like him being so sad all the time, Celeste. Occupy his mind. You must watch over him more," she told me. However, she didn't say it in a way that would make me feel proud and grown-up. She said it with anger. It was a criticism like I wasn't doing my job. She made me feel I was born with him simply to watch over him, to keep him from harm and sadness, a tagalong without a life of her own.

"You came out first," Daddy used to tell me with a smile. "So you're really older, Celeste. You're the older sister."

When I said that in front of Mommy and Noble, Noble started to cry.

"I was first, not you!" he wailed.

"No, you weren't," I insisted. I shook my head, and he wailed harder and louder, and Mommy jumped up and shook my shoulders.

"Stop it!" she told me. "Don't you see you're making him unhappy? You won't have any dessert tonight for this. Meanness in, sweetness out," she recited.

"I didn't say it to be mean, Mommy," I cried.

"Well, it was, and you did," she insisted.

She pulled Noble to her and told him Daddy was just fooling with me. Daddy didn't mean it. He was first, after all. Who knew better than she did? His sobs relented, and Mommy kissed the tears off his cheeks. I stared at her and she looked at me with those eyes that could frighten me, and I shifted my gaze quickly.

It doesn't matter what she tells him, I thought. I know I was first. Daddy wouldn't lie about it.

Now, lo and behold, Mommy was changing her story. I was more mature. I was truly born first, born to grow faster and wiser, but it didn't give me any pleasure to hear her say this now because she made it seem like an added burden. An obligation that I would never shed had been attached to my being born first. I got so I wished Noble really had come before me.

I went to Noble to comfort him as she wanted me to do, however. In the end I always did what Mommy wanted. I played one of his games with him and got his mind on other things, but I couldn't stand the way he talked about seeing and hearing Daddy all the time.

"You've got to stop saying you're talking to Daddy and you're seeing Daddy, Noble. It's making Mommy very upset and it's not right to lie about such a thing," I told him one day.

"I did see him," he insisted.

"Then you must tell me where and when," I demanded and folded my arms about my chest the way Daddy would when he was angry. "Well?"

He covered his face with his hands, and I knelt down beside him and pulled his hands away. He was stronger than I was then, but he was crying now and too sad to be stronger.

"I don't want Daddy to be dead," he moaned.

"Me neither, but that's what he is," I said firmly. "Or at least his body."

"His cup," Noble muttered angrily under his breath.

"His spirit is out there, Noble, really out there, and you know what Mommy has promised us: Someday all the spirits will talk to us and we'll see them and we'll see and talk to Daddy for real again. Don't you want that?"

Noble had always been reluctant to believe in all this, but now with the possibility of it including Daddy, he had no choice. He nodded.

"When?" he asked me.

"Soon," I said. "Mommy says soon."

Not long after our little talk, Noble started to accept the truth about Daddy's death. Ironically, I was actually sorry to see him do that. Sometimes, when he had stood staring out at the driveway or watching the road, or had turned quickly at the sound of a car or truck engine in the distance, my heart would quicken its beat and I would look, too. It wasn't Noble's skepticism as much as it was hope, a dream, a prayer, but the engine sound would dwindle and die and the road would remain empty, lonely. I'd catch myself and shake my head at myself for being so foolish, so childish.

Even at that early age, I disdained looking like or behaving like a child. Mommy's constant prodding for me to be more responsible, for me to be older and more mature, had taken seed in my little body. Often now I would catch myself in the hallway mirror and see how I was standing with a military stiffness, my lips pursed, my face full of little wisdom. The little girl in me was disappearing, shrinking. She would soon be gone after far too short a childhood. The dolls on the shelves in our room stared hopelessly at me and with little expectation. They seemed to know that I'd pick them up no more for many reasons. I had no idea that one in particular was waiting for me like a patient demon.

Instead of playing with my dolls, I was busy helping Mommy with the dinner or cleaning rooms in the house, moving a vacuum cleaner about that was taller than I was. Instead of dressing my dolls and serving them tea, I was helping Noble with our schoolwork, chasing after him for not picking up after himself. By now I had a voice that was a perfect mimic of Mommy's when I wanted it to be, and I could posture like her and glare like she glared at him when she was upset. Noble even told me to turn my Mommy's eyes away from him because they burned like a flashlight in his head.

But I couldn't help it. Even when she wasn't looking at me, I could feel her behind me, watching to be sure I was being a big girl.

On the other hand, Noble seemed to be regressing. He didn't want to grow up, to be responsible, to hear about chores, and he was always angry at me for reminding him. Mommy confused me about this. Most of the time she wanted me to be the big sister, but whenever Noble whined or complained about me, Mommy wanted me to be more of a companion, a playmate.

"He doesn't have anyone else yet, Celeste. You have to get along."

I didn't have the patience for Noble's childish games, but I had to swallow back my reluctance and go along with his pretend. Our house was a castle again. He made me draw a moat around it with a sharp stick. He drew a line, and I drew one about six feet or so apart from his. We went around the whole house, tearing up grass. It took hours and hours, and when I complained about my hands getting sore and I wanted to stop, he had a tantrum. There were actually calluses forming on my palms. I showed him, but he didn't care.

"We have to know where the alligators and the snakes will be swimming, Celeste," he insisted, his eyes wide and full of his fantasy.

I saw Mommy watching us from a window in the house. Her face was strange, caught in a mixture of sadness and fear. It had been so long since I had seen a smile on her lips, even after Noble said something silly. I wondered if she would ever smile again or if smiles had died with Daddy. Had she opened his coffin and thrown all her happiness inside it to be buried with him?

It was not as if we were without all possibilities of being happy again. We didn't have financial problems for her to worry over. Daddy had a big life insurance policy. I overheard Mommy and her attorney, Mr.

Lyman, a short, plump man with cheeks that looked like they were patched with the skin of cherries, talking about it. I stood back in the doorway of the den. I never liked being too close to him. He always smelled like sour apples and his hands were small, with thick cucumber fingers that looked like they didn't have any knuckles. I hated it when he brushed my hair with one of those hands, and Noble would actually bob and weave to avoid any contact.

Mommy said death was a feast for lawyers and accountants. There was so much that had to be done. They descended on our house like mayflies, buzzing around Mommy's ears. Fortunately, all of it left us well off. Daddy's partner bought up his share of the business, the truck, and the jeep, and Mommy had that money, too. There was money put away in trust for Noble and me. We had no mortgage on the house, and anything that was bought on credit was paid up because of all sorts of death benefits Mommy didn't even know we had.

"You're in fine shape, Sarah," Mr. Lyman assured Mommy. I hated him saying that.

How could we be in fine shape with

Daddy dead and gone? Mommy saw me listening and glaring angrily at Mr. Lyman from the doorway. She told me to go see what Noble was up to, and waved me away.

What was he up to? Nothing different. He was out there fighting imaginary battles with imaginary demons. Small trees were enemy soldiers, or tall weeds were monsters. He made a sword out of a slab of wood from a crate in the garage and went charging at the vegetation, slicing everything in sight while he howled his battle cries. If I didn't join him and imitate him, he would cry and complain to Mommy.

One thing she insisted was we remain within the boundaries of our lawn and meadow. We were not yet old enough to wander into the woods, she told us, but Noble was beginning to challenge that prohibition. I would have to remind him continually that he was going out too far, like someone swimming in the ocean and going beyond the reach of the lifeguard.

"Daddy used to take us to the stream and the pond to swim," he complained.

Mommy promised to do it and did one afternoon, but mostly as a lesson in botany. Noble was bored with all that. He swiped at tree branches or shot imaginary arrows at dragons emerging from behind thick oaks.

"Stay close," she told him when he went too far off. Her reprimands wrapped around him like a leash and a collar, snapping him back. How he hated it.

"We don't need Mommy every time we go into the woods," he told me. "It's not dangerous."

He whined and groaned about it so much, Mommy relented and permitted us to go in a short way without her, but Noble was never to go in without me, and if he did, I would be blamed. The burden of my responsibility grew a little heavier every day, it seemed.

I remember I was feeling more and more lonely, too. Noble's games were no longer any challenge or any fun for me and seemed more and more strained and unimaginative. He hated that I didn't contribute to his make-believe, and every time I crossed into our imaginary moat, he would scream and jump, shouting that I had nearly been eaten by an alligator. Of course, I didn't act frightened. It made him so angry and upset that he would cry and complain to Mommy.

"She won't listen! She won't obey the rules!"

"It's silly," I said. "Those are silly rules."

"Oh, just walk over the bridge when you

come into the house, Celeste," she told me. "I don't like him being so upset. Not now," she added.

"What bridge? There's no real bridge," I said, shaking my head.

"Pretend there is a bridge just as you always did," she said, pronouncing each word distinctly, her eyes wide. "It was easy to do then. It will be easy to do now. Just do it!"

I felt tears burning in mine and looked away so she wouldn't see. If I cried, she would only get angrier and make me feel as if I was letting her down, or more important, Daddy, because Daddy was watching. Daddy saw us. She knew.

Yes, Mommy spoke to Daddy often after the first month of his passing. I'll never forget the first time she told us.

All during that first month after Daddy's death, we had visitors from the town and nearby, people we had never seen or Mommy had seen so infrequently, she had forgotten them. Mr. Kotes was the most frequent visitor. She told us that was because Daddy had been a good friend to him after his wife had died. He didn't have any children. His parents were long dead. All he had was an unmarried sister who was a partner in his family business.

Daddy used to say he was a man whose heart had gone to sleep. His face seemed to have forgotten how to smile. Whenever Mommy and Mr. Kotes were together, it seemed to me she was helping him deal with Daddy's death more than he was helping her. It was something she was happy to do and something he wanted her to do.

Just like some other visitors, he always brought something when he came to our house. Most visitors brought cakes and pies, flowers, and even toys for Noble and me. I was given dolls, but Mommy wouldn't let us have any of it. Everything was put away in a special place because they were meant to "make us forget our sadness, and we should not permit anything to do that. Your sadness about the death of someone you loved," Mommy insisted, "will be the avenue over which you will travel to see and hear your ancestral spirits. It's too special and precious an emotion to be treated like coming down with the measles or some other childhood ailment."

Noble was very upset about having to give up trucks and trains, toy soldiers and popguns, but when Mommy put on her angry face, he just turned away to sulk.

She reinforced it all by telling him it would be painful to Daddy to learn that he was forgetting him so quickly, and because of what? A toy? Was that all he meant to him?

He muted his tears and swallowed them back. To compensate, he returned to his make-believe world outside and made do with sticks and rocks, bushes and trees. No one had given us that to help us forget, and besides, if Mommy had told us once, she had told us a hundred times, Daddy's spirit was here. Daddy was in the trees and bushes. Daddy was in the house. We were with Daddy as long as we remained here. If we did that, we would always remain a part of him.

Of course, I was waiting desperately now to see and hear him so when Mommy called us into the living room and sat us down on the sofa to tell us what had just happened, I was filled with anticipation and joy.

She pulled open the curtains and then opened the window slightly as if she was letting Daddy's spirit into the house.

"Children," she said, turning and clasping her hands over her breasts. "I have been with your father today."

"Where?" Noble cried, practically jumping out of his seat. "Where was he all this time? Building a house? Where's his truck?"

For a long moment Mommy simply stared at Noble. She could see that I knew exactly what she meant, and it bothered her to no end that Noble did not, still didn't understand all she had told us and continued to tell us about the spiritual world.

Slowly, just the way she taught him his math sometimes, with painstakingly perfect pronunciation of every vowel and consonant, she said, "What did I tell you about the spirit and the body, Noble? Go on, tell me what I told you."

He glared back at her and then glanced at me. I wasn't going to help him. Let her see how much he knows on his own, I thought. Maybe she wouldn't still say he has her heart.

"I don't remember," he said petulantly. "Why didn't Daddy come into the house?"

"I want you to remember, Noble," Mommy insisted. "What did I tell you?"

He looked down, and then he raised his head slowly and said, "Daddy's body is a cup, and his spirit is all over the place."

"Yes," she said, nodding. "Only, his body isn't exactly a cup. It's like the cup. I just used the cup as a way of explaining it. Do you understand?"

94

Stubborn, he wouldn't respond.

"If you don't tell me you understand, I won't tell you about Daddy," she threatened.

He softened his shoulders and looked at her again.

"I know," he said. "Daddy died, and his body isn't here."

"Okay, Noble. Very soon you'll understand everything," she said. "I'm sure you will."

She looked at me and nodded. I knew she meant, "and you will help him, Celeste."

"Daddy came to me a little while ago. It's not that easy for a spirit to return to talk to the people he or she loves. When you go over to the other side, there are so many changes, so many different things to understand about yourself and about what you were," she said.

Even Noble was paying attention now. Of course, I was barely breathing. I didn't want to miss a word.

"For a while you can't help thinking like a living person. You can't get used to not having to touch the ground, to seeing everything at once as if you were looking down from a cloud, to hearing people's thoughts," she continued, raising her eyebrows. "Yes, the dead can hear your thoughts, children, so be careful about that, be careful you don't think something terrible or evil and then face your father or your ancestors, for they will know and be upset."

Noble began to chew on the inside of his left cheek, and Mommy told him to stop.

"Anyway, it takes a while for someone to understand and get used to being on the other side. He or she loves those left behind just as much, but it's frustrating."

"What's frustrating?" Noble asked immediately. He wanted to understand all this because it involved Daddy.

"Annoying," she said quickly and flicked her right hand as if to chase away a fly.

"The spirit can't take direct action. If you are about to cut yourself or fall into a hole or get hit by a car, anything, he or she can't stop it from happening. What they can try to do is warn you if you'll listen."

"I'll listen," Noble said with his eyes wide.

"Will you? I hope so, Noble," Mommy said with a sigh. She glanced at me. I was staring at her impatiently, and I saw that annoyed her. But I didn't need all this preliminary information about what spirits could do and couldn't do. I wanted to hear about Daddy. She was doing this for Noble only, and she and I knew it.

"To listen, to really hear," she continued, looking only at him. "You have to believe and concentrate, Noble. You cannot flit about when I tell you things."

"Okay," he said in a small voice. "I won't."

"Well, I hope you will remember what you've just promised," she said. "Now then, I was walking in the meadow —"

"Which meadow? Where?" Noble asked quickly.

Mommy raised her eyes toward the ceiling and then, after a moment, looked at him.

"Let me talk without any interruptions, Noble," she said sternly.

He pressed his lips together.

"I was walking in the meadow near the old well. I had my head down and I was thinking very hard about Daddy, picturing him in my mind. It's how you make contact," she explained. "I wouldn't let any other thought enter my head. He never said good-bye to me, you see. He went off to work and never came home."

"Me neither," Noble said, nodding at me. "He never said good-bye to me."

I thought Mommy would be very angry

with him for interrupting again, but all she did was close and open her eyes.

"When I talk and I refer to myself, Noble, I am referring to all of us. Understand?"

He nodded, even though he didn't. Mommy glanced at me again and saw I did.

"Anyway, suddenly, there he was sitting on the edge of the well like he used to when he wanted to tease me about his falling back and down into it. He was smiling, so I knew he was not suffering."

"Did he ask about me?" Noble demanded.

"Of course not. I told you he sees you every moment of the day, Noble. He knows all about you. This is most important, so be still," she commanded and leaned toward us. "He told me you were both very close to being able to see and hear the spirits."

"But Daddy made fun of the spirits. He never believed in them," I said.

Maybe I shouldn't have. Mommy snapped back as if her spine was made of elastic, and for a few seconds she glared at me angrily, much more angrily than she had glared at Noble. Then, suddenly, she smiled, only it wasn't a loud smile. It was a whispered smile, like an offhand remark in someone's ear.

"I know he made fun of me with you sometimes, Celeste," she said.

I started shaking my head.

"And you listened to him. You had that secret little thing about half an ear, didn't you?"

My mouth opened. I never knew that she knew. She held her smile.

"I suppose he thought he had won you to his side, the two of you laughing behind my back."

"No, Mommy," I said. "I never laughed at you. Never."

"No matter," she snapped and smiled again. "He's certainly changed his mind about all that now," she said. "One of the first things he told me was, he wished he had been wearing this," she added and held up the amethyst and dangled it before us. We both stared at it like two candidates for hypnotism as she dangled it.

"So," she emphasized before putting it away, "never forget to wear what I bought you at Mr. Bogart's store."

Noble looked at his amulet, which he still insisted was a worm with arms and legs, and then looked up at her quickly.

"We talked for quite a long time. He

kept apologizing for dying, for not listening to the warnings, for thinking he was invincible."

"What's —"

"Can't be defeated, beaten down, destroyed," Mommy said quickly. I could see she had no more patience for interruptions now, even to explain something.

"He realized he had hurt us more than he had hurt himself, despite the fact that he was the one who died. We were left without him, and you were left without a father. He wanted to find a way to punish himself, but I told him we needed him more now and he had to do whatever was required of him to stay around us and protect us, especially you two.

"But," she continued, "I want to stress that he won't be able to do that for you until you are able to see and hear the spiritual world.

"This is not something you can pretend, Noble," she told him sternly. "You must never ever lie about that, do you understand? Lying, being false, angers the spirits. Don't come to me and tell me you have seen or heard anything if you really haven't. That goes for you, too, Celeste," she said, nodding at me.

"I wouldn't, Mommy," I said.

"I won't," Noble promised.

"Good. But when it does happen, I want to know about it right away. Okay?"

"How will it happen?" I asked. "With you, sitting on the sofa?"

"Maybe. Maybe when you're by yourself or playing or woken in sleep. There is no way to know that. Be alert, be ready, but most of all, I want you two to concentrate for an hour at least every day."

"What's concen—" Noble started to ask.

"I'm going to teach you now how to meditate, how to fix your mind on one thing and stay glued to that one thing so firmly that you will hear or see nothing else around you. You need to learn how to do that, Noble. It will help make it all happen faster," she said, nodding to herself. "It will help you to connect to your psychic energy, along with the Krena."

"Is Daddy here now?" Noble asked.

"Yes," she said, and he looked about the room. "He's right beside you," she said. "Listening to everything we're saying and hearing all your promises."

Noble's mouth dropped open. Slowly, he turned and looked, and then he looked at me to see if I saw anything. He could tell I didn't, but I was quiet. He looked again.

"You can't see him or hear him yet, Noble. I told you."

"I want to," Noble whined.

"Then you'll do what I tell you," Mommy insisted. "It's time for bed. Go up and get ready," she concluded and stood up.

Noble, full of disappointment, rose. I took his hand and we walked to the stairway.

"Did you see him?" he asked in a whisper.

"No," I said. "But we will," I said.

He looked back. Through the doorway, we could see Mommy smiling at what was for us nothing. She was nodding, too. How I envied her.

When she came to our room that night to say good night, she told us Daddy was alongside her. I closed my eyes after she had kissed Noble and then me, and I waited to see if I could feel Daddy's lips again. His kiss was always different from hers. He held his lips on my cheek longer and then tickled the tip of my nose with the tip of his nose. I didn't feel his lips, but I was sure I had vaguely felt the tip of his nose. My eyes snapped open. Mommy was leaving the room, closing the door softly, and in the wake of the hallway light, I was sure I saw Daddy's shadowy figure. I wanted to call out to him, but I didn't. My heart was pounding. The door snapped closed.

"At least Daddy could fix the wheel on my wagon," Noble muttered. "I don't have to see him for him to do that."

I shook my head and turned away.

He'll never understand, I thought, and I wondered how Mommy would live with that.

Mommy's decision to start us on meditation was really her way of trying to get Noble to concentrate and make contact with the spiritual world. I didn't mind it when we began, but Noble hated it more than anything else Mommy made him do.

She surprised us the next morning by having three cushions on the floor in the living room, one for each of us and one for herself across from us. She told us we could not have any breakfast until we practiced our meditation. Noble whined that he was hungry and wanted a mushy egg, which was a soft-boiled egg Mommy crushed with a fork until it sat on the plate like a yellow and white pancake.

"This has to be done on an empty stomach," she insisted and then she demonstrated how she wanted us both to sit on the cushion. Her directions were very specific, and she demonstrated.

"Cross your legs and relax your shoulders," she directed and rose to help Noble get into the position. "Put your arms comfortably on your thighs. That's it. Don't bend over like that, Noble. I want you to keep your back straight, but not stiff. Do it," she ordered, and he groaned and followed her instructions.

She glanced at me and saw I was doing it correctly.

"Okay," she said, sitting across from us.

"What are we doing?" Noble moaned. "I'm hungry."

"We are learning how to concentrate so you can do what you have to do to see and speak to Daddy again. Do you want that?"

"Yes."

"Then just listen and do what I tell you to do," she said. "It's important you be relaxed. You open your mouth just a little, children, and notice your breathing. Just notice it. Don't breathe harder or faster. Notice how your breath goes out. Every time something else comes into your mind, toss it away and go back to noticing your breath."

She closed her eyes and looked like she was doing exactly that.

"I can't stop thinking about my egg," Noble complained.

Mommy raised her eyes to the ceiling and then took a deep breath herself and said, "Okay, here's what else I want you to do. When you breathe in and out, I want you to say, *hamsa*."

"What?" Noble asked.

"I want you to say *h-ah-m* as you breathe in and *s-ah* as you breathe out. Go on. Let me hear it."

I did it, and Mommy nodded.

"Good, Celeste."

Noble made it sound like "hamster." Mommy corrected him, and then she rose and knelt beside him and held her hand on his shoulder and had him do it repeatedly until she said he had it right. She told him to continue.

Soon, we were chanting in a chorus. Noble tried to be louder than I was, and Mommy stopped us.

"It isn't a competition, Noble. You're making the sound to help you not to think about anything else. Now start again."

He groaned, and we did it. We sat like that and chanted along with our breathing for nearly fifteen minutes before Mommy decided our first lesson was over. Noble jumped to his feet and cried for his egg.

"We're going to practice this every day from now on," Mommy said. "Once in the morning and once before dinner until you both can do it without me."

Noble never took it seriously. He did what he had to do to get it over with and be able to eat, but sometimes, during the day when he was outside building a fort or battling dragons, he would call to me and chant *hamsa* and then laugh. Mommy didn't know it, but I practiced on my own. I wanted to do everything I could to bring me closer to the spirits, and especially Daddy.

A few times Noble fell asleep during our meditation practice, especially before dinner because he was tired from a day of running and jumping and climbing rocks and trees. Because I had to follow and watch over him, I was climbing and running as well. Lately, it seemed to take more effort for him to do these things than it did for me. We grew at about the same rate. Maybe he was slightly taller by the time we were seven, but my arms and legs looked as muscular, and he didn't have as easy a time of pushing me and wrestling me to the ground as he used to. In fact, he stopped trying to bully me.

Months had passed since Mommy had

told us Daddy was here with us. Although I had yet to hear Daddy's voice, I thought I did hear voices at night. Often I woke and thought I could hear mumbling or whispering, sometimes right outside my window. It never frightened me. Instead, it filled me with excitement and anticipation. Once in a while when I was outside with Noble or working on our garden with Mommy, I would turn and see what looked like a shadow moving around the house or into the woods. It was a bright, sunny day, too, so I knew it wasn't just clouds crossing through the rays.

Once I glanced at Mommy right after I had one of these visions. She looked at me knowingly, but said nothing. It pleased her though, I thought. Noble never saw anything or heard anything, and if I would stop what we were doing and ask him if he had, he would grimace, shake his head, and then tell me I was a liar. I got so I didn't ask him or tell him about anything I thought I had seen.

I enjoyed our meditation. It made me feel peaceful. Noble got to hate it more and more and continually used it to catnap. Mommy grew terribly frustrated and then decided she would soon try something else. The meditation time was ended. Of course, I did it on my own, which was forever annoying to Noble, who would do everything he could to break my concentration. When he was unable to do it by talking to me or even shouting at me, he took to poking me with a stick or throwing dirt at me.

I complained about it to Mommy.

"Don't do it in front of him or when you're with him," she advised rather than reprimanding him.

"But when I'm meditating, I don't know he's near me. I don't hear him."

"Just try to avoid him, Celeste," she said firmly and left me quickly.

Whenever I did anything that annoyed or bothered him, she would reprimand me. Why wasn't she doing it to him? All she would say if I asked was, "We've got to do what we can to protect Noble. Remember that, Celeste. You have to watch over him. I can't be everywhere at all times."

I didn't cry about it in front of her or in front of Noble, but when I was alone and I wasn't meditating or thinking about the spiritual world, I felt the tears burn under my eyelids. It wasn't fair. Why was she favoring Noble? Why was I the one bearing all the responsibility? None of it was fair, I thought.

And then one night, hours and hours after we had fallen asleep, when the stars seem so bright it dazzles you and even the trees seem to be asleep, I woke with a start. Someone was holding my hand. I looked at it first and then slowly I raised my eyes, and there he was. I was sure of it, even though someone else might say I was dreaming.

Daddy was there.

Smiling at me.

He was no longer a shadow.

I had crossed over.

4

A Trip to School

"She's lying!" Noble screamed.

I had said nothing to him when we both got up, washed, dressed, and went down to breakfast, but as soon as we entered the kitchen to help Mommy set the table, I told her what I had felt and seen.

She nearly dropped a cereal bowl.

"Quiet, Noble," she snapped.

Then she sat and reached out for me. I gave her my hands. She held them tightly, her fingers pressing so hard they actually hurt, but I didn't complain. Noble stood off to the side, glaring at us angrily.

"If you are lying, Celeste, I will know," she warned.

"I'm not lying, Mommy," I said firmly. I could feel her eyes moving over my face and even into my brain. Then she nodded and let go of my hands. There were red spots where her fingers had clamped down on them.

"Tell me about it," she said in a whisper.

I described how my fingers felt while I was sleeping, and how I had opened my eyes and had seen Daddy standing there holding my hand.

"Did he speak to you?"

"No. He just stood there, looking at me and smiling."

"Yes," she said, nodding. "It is truly the way it begins. That's how I know she's not lying, Noble," Mommy told him, and his angry expression wilted into one of disappointment only. "It's like easing yourself into a hot bath. You don't cross over quickly. First, you see them, and then, when they know you are ready, they speak to you and you hear them."

"I didn't see him," Noble whined. "Why wouldn't I see him, too?"

"You will. Now that Celeste has seen him, it's only a matter of time for you," she said.

"Why did she see him first?"

"Because she paid more attention to the meditation and she tried harder," Mommy practically shouted at him.

I held my breath. It wasn't that often that she took my side against him or that she showed her anger at him as clearly and firmly. I was sure it was only because I had

111

seen Daddy's spirit. If I hadn't, nothing would change. Despite his failure to fully understand it all, Noble looked like he understood this. He looked down.

"It's not fair," he muttered.

"Go into the living room and sit quietly," she told him. "Go on."

"But I want my cereal."

"Not yet. I want you to sit and think about what's happened and what you can do to make it happen to you, and I warn you again, Noble, if you should pretend, if you should make up something and not be honest about it, you will drive your father's spirit away from you. He might never show himself to you or speak to you if you are not honest. Do you understand? Do you?"

"Yes," he said.

"Go sit by yourself and think," she ordered, pointing to the doorway.

He threw me an angry, covetous look and went out, his head still bowed.

"Tell me more," Mommy asked me. "How did he look to you?"

"He looked younger than I remembered him, Mommy."

"Yes," she said. "Exactly."

"And he didn't look unhappy. He looked very happy."

"That's right," she said. She was so

112

happy I had to go on, think of more.

"And I felt so warm all over."

"Protected," she said nodding. "Exactly. You've done it, Celeste," she cried, tears coming to her eyes. "You've done it."

She reached out and pulled me to her and gave me the warmest, strongest embrace I could remember before she kissed my forehead and closed eyes. My heart was so full of joy, I thought it might burst in my chest.

"Have your breakfast," she said. "You have no idea how much has been opened to you now. Every day of your life will bring a new surprise. You should feel better about yourself, about everything, already."

She was right. Now that she showered so much love and affection on me, I couldn't remember being happier. Nothing I had done had pleased her as much. It was truly as if Daddy's dying never mattered because he would be with me always and I would have Mommy loving me more than ever.

"Now, we have to concentrate on Noble," she said. "We've got to help him to see, and then, then we will all be closer as a family. We'll all have Daddy again," she told me.

After a few more minutes, she called him

back into the kitchen and again told him how he must try harder and do what I had done.

"You know you haven't tried hard enough, Noble," she told him. "You do know that, don't you?"

He didn't respond, and she hovered over him with her eyes full of desperation and anger. He glanced up and looked down quickly. I felt sorry for him.

"You will try harder," she said, and he nodded again.

Noble was as repentant and as cooperative as he could be for days and days afterward. He looked at me differently, too. I could see it in the way his eyes grew smaller, his gaze more intense. He watched me more closely, interrupted his own activities to loiter around me when I planted or weeded our garden, something he had little interest in doing, or when I helped Mommy clean the house. Whenever we took walks with or without Mommy, he paid keen attention to whatever attracted my attention, and he was always asking me whether I saw Daddy and especially whether or not Daddy had said anything to me.

He hadn't yet, so I wasn't going to say he had, and I couldn't tell him anything more because I hadn't seen Daddy again since that night, and I would never say I had. I took Mommy's warnings very, very seriously: never lie about the spirits.

However, since I had seen Daddy, I was sure that I began to see other spirits. Sometimes they were just walking about the property, talking softly to each other, although I couldn't hear them. I saw their mouths moving, their hands going. Occasionally they would pause and look my way, always smiling and nodding at me.

I told Mommy I had seen them and asked her what I should do, and she said, "Do nothing. Smile and nod back. It takes time. They have to get used to you, to believe in you."

She studied me. My eyebrows were scrunching together. Why would they have to get used to me? I'm not the dead one. They are.

"I see that is odd to you, but yes, Celeste, it's harder for the spirits to believe in a living person being able to see and hear them than it is for a living person to believe in seeing and hearing them. Time has made it more difficult for them to understand what we are and what they were. They can't understand why we place so much value on things that have no lasting quality or why we get upset over trivial matters. It's almost like one of Noble's ants trying to understand Noble," she added, and I nodded. When she explained it that way, I understood everything she was saying. Mommy must have been a very good teacher, I thought. We're lucky to have her all to ourselves.

"You're very bright," she told me, but she didn't sound as happy about it as I thought she would. "To be honest, Celeste, I didn't expect it to happen this way. I expected Noble would cross over first."

"Why?" I asked quickly, maybe too quickly. She didn't turn back to me. She stared out the window.

"I don't know," she finally replied. "It was supposed to be that way. That's all I know."

Her voice drifted off. I hated it when she couldn't give me a reason for something.

We both saw Noble running about, holding his sword above him and screaming some war cry. To me he looked further away from crossing over than ever. I guess he looked the same way to Mommy. She turned back to me, and her expression hardened.

"We've got to help him," she said with desperation. "I'm afraid for him."

"Afraid? Why, Mommy?"

"I just am," she said, "and you should be, too. Remember, you have a special responsibility to watch over him, Celeste. Remember that," she warned.

Why? What have I done to give me this special responsibility? I wanted to ask, but I thought it would sound too selfish and mean. After all, she had so much on her shoulders, so much responsibility. She had to be a daddy and a mommy all wrapped up in one person.

Almost a year had gone by since Daddy's death. Our lives had taken on a comfortable routine. For the most part, Mommy was able to do everything we needed done herself. She had even come to understand our oil burner, our circuit breakers, and diagnosed and corrected our minor problems almost as quickly and efficiently as Daddy had. When she was convinced she couldn't solve a problem, and only when she was convinced, she would call for help. Usually she called Mr. Kotes, who came over so quickly, it was as if he had been on his way before she had called.

When she thanked him, he told her not to and practically begged her to call on him again.

"No matter how small the problem

might seem," he said.

"That's very kind of you, Taylor," Mommy told him.

I liked him. He always had a warm, friendly smile on his face for me, but I could see that Noble did not like him. He resented him.

"Those are Daddy's tools he's using," he would mutter when Mr. Kotes went to fix something.

"He needs them to do the job," I would say, but Noble was still distraught.

"He shouldn't be able to use them. He isn't as smart as Daddy, and he isn't as strong."

Mr. Kotes was a smaller-framed man who, even though he was a few inches taller than Daddy was, probably weighed twenty pounds less than Daddy had weighed and didn't have Daddy's firm build and posture. He had light brown, very close to blond hair he kept trimmed short, and a light complexion with swirls of redness in his cheeks and over his temples.

He tried to get Noble to accept his friendship, giving him tools from his lumberyard occasionally, or trying to, because Noble would respond with, "Mommy says not to take gifts that will make us forget Daddy."

"Oh, I don't want you to forget your father, Noble," Mr. Kotes said. "I'm sure he would want you to have these things," he added. "Take them and keep them for when you think it's okay to use them," he urged.

Battling with his own conscience, Noble did take them and hide them in our toolshed. Sometimes, I would see him use the small hammer or screwdriver set, but always quickly and with lots of guilt. He would try not to let Mommy see.

Other than Mr. Kotes and some other service people and the postman, her attorney, and her accountant, few, if any, people ever came to our home.

Even on Halloween, no one brought their children to trick-or-treat at our door, and that wasn't just since Daddy's death. For years Mommy had put out the candy in anticipation, and every year, no one had come. Mommy said it was probably the ride being too long or the driveway being too long. Noble, and even I now, longed to have the company of other kids our age. I often asked Mommy when she would be sending us to the public school.

"We'll see," was all she would say. Once, she added, "When they tell me."

I didn't have to ask her who *they* were.

I came to believe that we couldn't go to the public school until Noble had crossed over. I tried to help him to meditate, to concentrate, but he just didn't have the patience for it, no matter what I did for him or promised him. Finally, one night, Mommy decided to try something else. It had been nearly two months since I had crossed over, and Noble had yet to see a shadowy figure that he didn't invent himself.

She called us to the kitchen table after we had done the homework she had assigned. There was a single candle burning at the center, a black candle. She had us sit on both sides of her, and then she said she was going to try something new, some other way to help Noble cross.

We were told to give her our hands and then to close our eyes and lower our heads. For a while that was all we did. Noble squirmed in the seat, and Mommy snapped at him to sit still.

"What are we doing?" he finally asked.

"I'm trying to get the spiritual powers to move through me and into you. Since they have already begun to move through Celeste, we have a combined strength that might work," she explained.

None of it made any sense to Noble. If

there was one thing he couldn't do well, it was sit still for a long period, and that was exactly what Mommy was demanding of him.

"I've got to pee," he declared after another five minutes.

Mommy groaned and slapped both our hands at the table.

"Ow," Noble moaned. "That hurt, Mommy."

"Just go to the bathroom," she said impatiently.

He got up, glanced at me from a lowered head, and walked off. Then Mommy turned to me with the most frightening expression on her face I had ever seen. It was truly as if she had seen something terrible.

"There is something moving around us, something very, very evil that is keeping Noble from crossing over, Celeste. I want you to be alert and aware. If you feel it, if you see it, you come to me immediately. You understand? There are things I can do only if I know what it is."

I nodded, holding my breath.

"It might come as an icy feeling on the back of your neck or a dark, dark shadow over your eyes in the brightest of sunlit days, or a shiver in your spine. Something, some way, and when it does happen, I want you to be sure to come to me quickly and tell me. Promise and swear to me you will," she said.

"I promise and I swear, Mommy," I said as firmly as I could.

Still, she didn't look relieved at all.

Noble returned sheepishly. He took his seat, and Mommy held our hands again, but she shook her head after a good ten minutes and released her grip on our fingers.

"It's not working. Not tonight, at least," she said. "We'll try again, soon," she promised, and we were excused.

A few nights later, Mommy had another idea. She had waited for there to be a full moon. It was fall, so the nights were growing cooler and cooler until they were downright cold. We couldn't go out after dinner without putting on heavier clothing. There had already been a few nights of frost.

All of the beautiful amber, brown, and crimson leaves had been blown off the branches of their trees. The forest had a gray and darker look. Noble called the saplings bones and the bigger trees skeletons, and they did look like that to me, too, especially when there was moonlight shining through them.

Mommy had yet to take us to Daddy's grave in the cemetery. Because she didn't believe his spirit resided there, she saw little reason to put flowers in front of his tombstone or visit it just because it was something people expected she would do, but Mommy did on occasion stand before her great-grandpa Jordan's and her great-grandma Elsie's tombstones with Infant Jordan's small stone between them. I wanted to ask her why his and her spirit and the baby's spirit would be at their graves and Daddy's not at his, but I was afraid to ask because it might seem like I didn't believe in what she could see and do.

Most of the time she visited the graves herself, but this one night she decided to take us along.

"Noble," she said, "I want you to place both your hands on your great-great-grandpa Jordan's stone and just stand there," she said.

"Why doesn't Celeste have to do it, too?" he asked quickly.

It was only on a very rare occasion that he was asked to do something I wasn't asked to do. We shared all our chores in the house. We shared our homework. We shared our room. We ate the same foods.

For as long as we both could remember during our seven and a half years, that was how it was, maybe because we were twins.

"She doesn't have to," Mommy replied. "She'll do something else that will help. Now do what I tell you," she ordered, and he stepped forward, gingerly placing his hands on the top of the tombstone. He looked back at me. I saw he was shivering.

"Give me your hand, Celeste," she said, and I did. Then she surprised us both by falling to her knees and lowering her head. We didn't hear her, but she was whispering a prayer.

I turned and looked to my left. I felt sure I saw Daddy standing there watching us. I was excited because I hadn't seen him again since that first night, but he didn't look happy this time. I wanted to tell Mommy, but I was afraid to speak, to interrupt her. By the time she was finished, Daddy was gone.

She looked up expectantly, her eyes on Noble. He had his head down now, and he was visibly shaking.

"It's cold," I heard him say.

She looked at me and shook her head. Then she rose slowly, seized Noble's hand, and pulled him away from the tombstone. We walked back to the house, Mommy's

124

face as dire and as gloomy as it had been when we had walked from the cemetery after Daddy's funeral.

That night after Noble and I had gone to bed and he had fallen asleep, Mommy came to my bedside. She knelt down and stared through the darkness at me. I held my breath and waited for her to speak because she was taking so long.

"I told you before," she finally said. "For reasons I don't yet understand, the spirits will not show themselves to Noble, will not protect him the way they will protect you and me. Not even Daddy," she said with her voice dripping disappointment, even anger. "It is your special responsibility to protect him and watch over him, Celeste, for you have been blessed and he will not see dangers as you do. I am relying on you for this," she said. "Don't fail me," she warned.

I couldn't respond. It frightened me to hear her repeat this admonition so vehemently. It was too much responsibility for me. How could I watch over him day and night? Why wasn't that her job, solely her job?

She saw the questions in my eyes, I guess. She reached out, stroked my hair, and smiled.

"We are truly a team now," she said. That made me feel better.

Then she kissed me on the forehead and left our room. I watched her close the door.

Even though it was nearly pitch-dark, I thought I saw Daddy standing there.

He looked as troubled as he had out at the gravestones.

"Daddy," I whispered. "What's wrong?"

He started to speak, and then he stopped as if he was listening to some other voice, turned, and left through a shadow in the corner.

I stared into the darkness hopefully, but soon my eyelids closed like the doors of two safes, locking my visions away for the night. In the morning I wasn't sure if I really had seen Daddy again or if it had been a dream. My mind was so hazy. I thought about telling Mommy and asking her what I should do, but she was very distracted and barely paid any attention to either Noble or me.

"We're going for a ride," she said. She had opened an envelope and had the letter spread before her on the table. From the way she was glaring down at it, I knew it was something that had made her very angry.

126

"Where?" Noble asked, excited.

Going anywhere, even to the supermarket, was like going to Disneyland for us.

She looked up at us, the anger in her face so strong, it thinned her lips and put small dots of white in the corners.

"I have to bring you to the school," she said, "for a meeting with the superintendent and for you two to take a test. Even though I am a certified New York State teacher, the superintendent again insists on one of his staff administering the test. I won't be objective or honest, I suppose," she added through the side of her mouth.

"Are we going to go to school from now on?" Noble asked, even more excited.

"No," she said firmly, "but we have to follow the regulations of the New York State Commissioner of Education," she said, making it sound like regulations issued by the devil. She picked up the letter and read, " 'to comply with section 100.10.' I just love the way they try to fit everyone into a little box that they design," she added.

She stood up, holding the letter almost at arm's length as if it could somehow contaminate her.

" 'Dear Mrs. Atwell,' " she read, " 'Perhaps it has been an oversight on your part, but the superintendent wishes to inform you that you are required to provide written notice to the superintendent by July First of each school year of your intention to educate your children at home. As of this date, we do not have any such notice on record, nor do we have your required IHIP, your individualized home instruction plan for your two children.'

"I just love the way they make sure to include things really meant to be threats, to intimidate people." She continued, wagging her head after each sentence she read. " 'Be aware that students instructed at home are not awarded a high school diploma. A high school diploma may only be awarded to a student enrolled in a registered secondary school who has completed all the programs required by the Regents, the school, or the district.'

"Little boxes," she spit.

She continued to read as I set out the bowls for our cereal and Noble got the cereal from the pantry, both of us moving as quietly as mice in the shadow of her anger.

" 'Home-instructed students are not eligible to participate in interscholastic sports. Districts are not required to loan textbooks to home-instructed students.'

" 'Primary responsibility for determining compliance with Section 100.10 rests with the superintendent of schools of the school district.' As if he really cares about you two," she added and crumpled the letter in her hands.

Noble's face was full of confusion. I could see he was disappointed, too.

"I want to go to school," he dared say. "I want to play baseball."

"You're not ready," Mommy said, "and you can play baseball here with Celeste."

"She can't play baseball, and you need more people," he insisted.

"Noble!"

Mommy leaned over and slapped her palm on the table, and we both felt our insides jump.

"I have enough to do without your whining today. I want you both to eat your breakfast and then go back upstairs and put on your Sunday clothes."

She called our nice clothes that even though we never went to church. It was what her mother and her mother before her had called their best clothing.

"I'll be up to brush your hair properly, Noble," she added.

Noble hated Sunday clothes because he couldn't get them dirty, and he always complained that his Sunday shirt collars irritated his neck.

"Eat, get dressed, and we'll go," she concluded. "I have some forms to fill out quickly," she added and left us.

"I want to go to school," Noble muttered after he began to eat his cereal.

"We'll go when Mommy tells us to go," I told him.

He glared at me.

"You don't want to go, so you don't care, Celeste."

"That's not true. I do."

"No, you don't," he said with eyes narrowed in accusation. "You're happy with your spirits. I want friends."

I shook my head.

"No, Noble, you're wrong."

He grimaced and continued to eat, still mumbling complaints about putting on his Sunday clothes. Afterward, he was at least happy about going for a ride. Mommy let him sit up front, and he sat with his face against the window, looking at everything.

"Stop gaping at people," Mommy ordered. "It's not polite, and you look like a refugee."

"What's a ref—"

"Never mind what it is. Stop gaping!" she yelled, and he sat back unhappily. Neither of us could remember seeing her so upset about taking us somewhere.

I was quiet in the rear. It wasn't that I was uninterested in everything. I was probably as excited inside as Noble was about going for a ride and seeing other houses, stores, traffic, and people, but I knew how much Mommy wanted us to love our home and our world.

What really surprised me, however, was seeing Mr. Kotes waiting for us at the school parking lot when we pulled up. We didn't actually see him until we were parked. Both Noble and I were fascinated by the sight of dozens of children our age or a little older out in the play area. Their screams and laughter were like music we never heard. Even I was pressing my face to the window now.

Mommy stopped the car and turned off the engine. Mr. Kotes approached us quickly.

"I've already put in a call for you, Sarah. I don't expect you'll have any great difficulty, but I thought I'd come around just in case you needed something."

"Thank you, Taylor," she said, getting out of the car. She opened the rear door for me. Noble had already hopped out and was looking at the children. He looked poised to run to the play area if someone would just beckon. "Noble," Mommy snapped. "Come on."

He looked back longingly at the children and then joined us. Mr. Kotes walked with us into the building.

"It's down left," he said, nodding.

"Yes, I remember," Mommy told him. She held my hand and Noble's and marched us to the superintendent's office. Mr. Kotes remained with us. I looked back at him, and he smiled, but I didn't understand why he was with us.

The superintendent's secretary put the phone down just as we entered the office and turned our way.

"Mrs. Atwell?" she said, smiling.

"Yes," Mommy said. She glanced at Taylor.

"Hello, Mr. Kotes."

He simply nodded and looked stern.

"I'll let Dr. Camfield know you're here," the secretary said and buzzed the superintendent.

Noble's eyes were everywhere. He couldn't drink in machines, plaques, and other personnel fast enough.

"Stop gawking at everything," Mommy muttered, shaking his hand and his arm hard. He quickly lowered his eyes.

"Please go right in, Mrs. Atwell," the secretary said. She smiled at me, but I didn't smile back. I sensed that for Mommy this was not friendly ground, and therefore I was on guard against everything and everyone.

Mr. Kotes did not follow us in. Mommy glanced back at him, and he whispered that he'd be waiting if she needed him. We entered the office. It was darkly paneled with a very big dark wood desk. Mr. Camfield stood up and came around his desk to shake Mommy's hand and greet her.

He was a tall man, as tall as Mr. Kotes, with hair that was as ebony as Daddy's. He wore a light brown suit and was a handsome man with a strong, firm mouth, firm jaw, and two very dark brown eyes. He smiled at Noble and me and stood back as if to admire us from a distance.

"Good-looking children," he said.

"I got your letter, Dr. Camfield. You might have been told that I lost my husband just a little less than a year ago and that I —"

"Yes, yes, please, sit," he said, indicating the sofa to the side. There was a chair across from it with arms made of the same wood as the desk.

Mommy tugged us both to the sofa and sat.

"I must admit I didn't know about your personal problems, Mrs. Atwell. It's difficult enough for me to know about the family matters concerning the students who actually attend the school," he began.

Mommy didn't look like she cared. She reached into her soft briefcase and pulled out a folder.

"These are the IHIP's you demand."

"I don't demand them, Mrs. Atwell. The state demands them," he said softly, holding that smile around his eyes.

"Yes, well, here they are," she said and dropped them on the coffee table.

He glanced at them and nodded.

"Fine. I'll look them over and get right back to you," he said.

"And here is my letter of notification. As I said, I was concerned with many, many other matters this year, and this just slipped past me."

"I understand fully, Mrs. Atwell. Please accept my belated condolences as to that," he added.

That? I thought. Was *that* supposed to be Daddy's death?

"I'd like to get the testing done as quickly as possible," Mommy responded without saying thank-you.

"I have everything set up for the children. Mr. Katzman is waiting for you in Room 32. My secretary, Mrs. Donald, will show you and the children to the room."

"I could have just as easily administered the tests at home," Mommy muttered.

"Oh, I know, but this way we alleviate any possible conflicts of interest and avoid anything unpleasant," he said.

He was being so nice, I had to wonder why Mommy had come with such an angry face. Despite his smile and his soft, understanding voice, she still didn't relax or smile.

"If that's all, then, we'll go right to Room 32," she told him.

"Well, I don't want to seem like a salesman or anything," Dr. Camfield said, not making any attempt to rise, "but while the children are being tested, I could arrange for you to meet some of our teaching personnel so you could see for yourself what sort of instruction they would be getting here, and you might even consider applying for a position yourself. We're always looking for excellent teachers, and —"

"You have all the required information in that folder," Mommy snapped at him. "I don't need any tours of any schools, and I

135

have no interest in returning to public school teaching," she added, making "public" sound dirty.

His smile hardened, but he held onto it like someone who knew it was slipping away quickly. He rose, and Mommy stood up and urged us to stand as well.

"Thank you for coming by, then," Dr. Camfield said.

Mommy marched us out, and Dr. Camfield followed to the doorway.

"Mrs. Donald, if you would please escort Mrs. Atwell and her children to Room 32."

"Yes, of course," she said rising. "Right this way, Mrs. Atwell."

"Good luck, children," Dr. Camfield called to us.

Mommy spun on him.

"Luck? It's a matter of good instruction, dedication to the priorities, not luck," she said. "In public school these days, it's all luck."

He finally lost his smile.

Mr. Kotes quickly came down the hallway when we left the office.

"Well?" he asked Mommy.

"It's fine," she said. "Thank you, Taylor." She reached for his hand, and he smiled.

"I'll wait for you outside and take you

for coffee while they take the test," he offered.

"Thank you," she said, and we continued down the hallway behind Mrs. Donald.

My mind was reeling.

"Why did you thank Mr. Kotes, Mommy?" I asked her.

She leaned down as we walked.

"He's on the board of education for the school. He's Dr. Camfield's boss," she said and stood up, smiling triumphantly.

My heart thumped.

It was the first time Mommy was so happy about another man beside Daddy doing something for us.

More important, it was the first time she needed another man, the first time the spirits weren't enough.

All I could think was Daddy wouldn't be very happy about it, and maybe, maybe he wouldn't come around again.

5

A Magnifying Glass

The tests weren't difficult for us. Even Noble, who hated sitting that long, didn't struggle with anything. He loved being at a real school desk, and every once in a while he looked up and around the room, studying the charts and posters and pictures on the bulletin boards. He smiled at me. His face was full of excitement and happiness. I was just as excited and as happy, but I was afraid to show it.

While we were taking the test, a bell rang and students came pouring into the building from outside and hurrying down the hallway. Even with the door to our room closed, we could hear their charged-up voices, their laughter and footsteps.

There was a small window next to the door so we could see them passing. Another bell rang and it grew quiet once again.

Noble flashed me a look of disappointment, and then he returned to his test paper. I did the same. Mommy appeared at the doorway to the room just a little while after we were finished.

"Right on time," Mr. Katzman said and collected our test booklets. "We should have the results for you tomorrow," he added.

Mommy said nothing. She didn't even thank him. She gathered us up and led us out of the room. She marched us through the school very quickly, practically dragging Noble along because he slowed down to look at everything. It wasn't until we were outside that she asked about the exams. Although she asked us both, she looked to me for the answer.

"It was easy. I knew everything on it," I said.

"Me, too," Noble said. "Does that mean we can go to this school soon?"

"Soon," Mommy said, but not with any real assurance. Even Noble heard the hollowness in her voice and looked away with disappointment.

As we drove out, he stared at the school grounds like someone who wanted to remember it until the day he died. When it was gone from sight, sadness draped over his face like a shadow. For the first time in a long time, I actually felt sorrier for him than I did for myself. He needed to be here more than I did, I thought, although a secret part of me wished Mommy had given in and had decided to let us attend the school. I even wished she had gone back to being a teacher.

"We're having a guest for dinner tonight," she said when we were almost home.

"Who?" Noble asked quickly.

"Mr. Kotes," she replied.

"Why?"

"He did me a favor today," she said and looked into the rearview mirror quickly to see my expression. I couldn't help showing surprise. We hadn't had a guest for dinner for well over a year, one of Daddy's business associates whom Noble and I found boring. But this was going to be different, I recognized. This was going to be a lot different.

As always when Mr. Kotes came to our house, he brought gifts. He brought Mommy flowers, a bouquet of blazing red roses that put a blush into her cheeks that I hadn't seen there since Daddy had died.

"I understand you're quite the little reader, Celeste," he told me and handed me a book. "I thought you might like that."

I turned it around in my hands and read the title, *Alice in Wonderland*. Immediately I looked up at Mommy to see if she approved or disapproved.

"That's fine," she said. "Celeste should know what fantasy is and what it isn't. Perhaps we'll read it to Noble as well," she added pointedly.

"I hope you don't mind me bringing the children more things," Mr. Kotes continued, and gave Noble something wrapped in brown paper. He took it very gingerly, his eyes more on Mommy. She gave a slight nod, and then he practically seized it, tearing off the paper to reveal a box that contained a large magnifying glass. Noble's eyes brightened.

"I know you like looking at insects," Mr. Kotes said. "That will help you see them better."

It wasn't hard to tell that Noble was just itching to get outside and try it out.

"We have a little time before dinner," Mommy said. "You can go see how it works," she told him. "You go, too, Celeste."

"But don't you need help with the dinner, Mommy?" I asked. I always felt closer to her when I worked beside her in the kitchen.

"No. I'm fine. Go on," she ordered.

We started for the door.

"You two should say thank you to Mr. Kotes, don't you think?" she called to us.

"Thank you, Mr. Kotes," we recited simultaneously.

He laughed.

"They're sure a pair of twins," he remarked. "A perfect pair."

Mommy nodded.

"Yes, they are," she said. "Go on. I'll call you," she said when I lingered in the doorway. Although Noble was intrigued with his gift and the possibilities it presented, I couldn't help but wonder what made these presents different from all the others people had given us, even the ones Mr. Kotes had given us. What made it all right to accept them now? Was it just the passing of time?

Noble rushed out, heading for his precious anthill. I hovered about the front windows. Was Daddy in there, too? I wondered. Would Mommy tell Mr. Kotes if he were? How much did he know about the spirits? Did he believe in them? Could he see any or hear any?

"Come here, Celeste," Noble called. "Look at this. It's terrific. You can see their eyes better. Come on."

I plodded up to him and looked through his magnifying glass.

"We probably look like monsters to them through this glass," I remarked.

"Really?" The idea intrigued him. He turned it on me and pretended to be frightened. Then he turned and looked out at the meadow through the magnifying glass.

"What are you doing?" I asked him. "You can't see anything better that way."

"I wondered if I could see spirits with it," he said.

"Don't you listen to what Mommy and I have told you? You can't see them until they want you to see them or until you do what you have to do to focus on them. A magnifying glass won't help. Don't be stupid."

"You're stupid," he countered. Then he looked at the magnifying glass and looked at the house.

"He better not sit in Daddy's chair," he said angrily.

I looked at the house, too. Funny how such a possibility occurred to Noble, but not to me, I thought. Both of us stood there, side by side, and I thought Mommy was right. I do feel the way Noble feels when he feels something very strongly. I have the same rage burning in me. I wasn't sure why, but it was there, at least for the moment.

He threw down the magnifying glass. Then he ran toward his favorite tree.

"You better not get dirty," I called to him. "Mommy's calling us to go in for dinner any minute."

He pulled himself up on a branch and sat in his tree, glaring at the house. I returned to the porch and hovered about the window. I could hear their muffled voices within, and then I heard a sound I hadn't heard for a very long time.

It was the sound of Mommy's laughter. It was so strange to my ears, I thought it might be someone else for a moment. Mr. Kotes laughed, too. Mommy put on some music, and they laughed again. When I looked through the opening in the curtain, I could see that he had his arm around her waist, and he was showing her some dance step. Mommy threw her hands up in despair after a few tries, but he seized her arm and brought her back to him to try again.

I sat sulking in a chair gazing out at the forest, searching the shadows for signs of any spirits, but there was nothing but the darkness and the trees.

They're upset, I thought. They're all upset, maybe Daddy the most.

Finally Mommy called us to dinner, and I had to call to Noble. He climbed down and we entered the house.

"Where's your magnifying glass?" Mommy asked Noble immediately.

"Outside," he said.

"Well, you shouldn't leave things outside, Noble. You should take better care of things you are given," she chastised. "Go out and get it," she told him.

He turned and ran out.

"I'm sorry, Taylor," Mommy said.

"He's just being a boy," Mr. Kotes said. "I was probably worse at his age."

"I bet," Mommy said, and they laughed.

What made them so friendly all of a sudden? I wondered. Teaching her dancing? Bringing her flowers?

Mommy called me into the kitchen to help bring out the sliced bread and butter, a jug of cold water, and some cranberry sauce. She had roasted a chicken and made her famous small potatoes in the gravy, something Daddy just loved. I saw she had prepared an apple pie, too. She had made this a very special dinner. Everything looked and smelled as wonderful as ever. My stomach churned in anticipation.

145

We had just sat, Mr. Kotes indeed in Daddy's chair, when Noble returned. He was empty handed.

"Where's the magnifying glass?" Mommy asked immediately.

"It's not there," Noble said.

"What?"

"It's not where I left it."

"That's ridiculous, Noble."

"Someone took it," he said and glanced quickly at me.

Mommy was speechless for a moment. Mr. Kotes sat with a silly smile on his face.

"Someone took it? Someone came to our home and took it?" Mommy finally asked.

Noble shrugged.

"It's not there," he declared, his arms out. He looked at Mr. Kotes to see his reaction. Mr. Kotes continued to smile, but said nothing. I imagined Noble wanted to see him upset, especially now that he saw Mr. Kotes was sitting in Daddy's chair.

Mommy turned to me, her lips taut, her eyes burning.

"Celeste, take your brother by the hand. Take him outside and find that magnifying glass immediately," she ordered. "Now!" she emphasized, raising her eyebrows. I got up quickly.

"Oh, let it go, Sarah," Mr. Kotes said.

146

"I'm sure he'll find it later."

"No, he'll find it now," Mommy said sternly. "Or he won't have any dinner, and neither will Celeste," she added, glaring at me.

I took Noble's hand and quickly turned him to the doorway.

"Sarah, really —"

"Don't interfere," Mommy snapped at Mr. Kotes. "He needs some discipline, and he needs to know the value of things and what responsibility means. They both do," she added.

"You're probably right," Mr. Kotes agreed quickly.

"That was stupid, Noble," I said as we walked out of the house. "You just made Mommy mad at us for nothing."

He was silent. I marched him back to the anthill, but the magnifying glass was not there.

"See?" he said.

"Where is it, Noble?"

"I don't know," he said.

"This is dumb, Noble. Where is it?" I demanded, my hands on my hips.

"I don't know."

"I'm going to go back inside and tell Mommy you won't tell me," I warned.

"Tell her to come out and look for herself," he said defiantly, standing back with his arms folded. "You can see it's not here."

"Well . . . where is it then?" I asked.

He looked around. The darkness had thickened. The overcast night sky seemed to be closing in on us. The wind picked up in intensity. I walked all around the anthill and searched and searched, but I couldn't find it.

"Did you throw it away, Noble?"

"No," he said.

"Did you hide it somewhere?"

"No," he insisted. "I didn't do anything. When I came down from the tree, it wasn't here."

"I'm hungry, Noble," I whined. "I want to eat. Everything is hot and ready, and Mommy has your favorite pie."

He shrugged and looked away.

"Mommy's going to be madder at you than me," I warned. He didn't respond, so I ran up to him and shook him. He pulled out of my grip.

"Leave me alone or I'll kick you, Celeste."

"Where's the magnifying glass, Noble? Where is it?" I shouted at him.

"I don't know."

"If you didn't throw it away and you

didn't hide it, then where would it be?" I demanded, stepping closer to him. He didn't turn away.

"Daddy probably took it," he offered after a long moment, his eyes fixed on mine.

I felt my throat close and a wave of heat rise up my spine. When it reached my neck, it turned into a chill.

"What?"

"He's mad, very angry," Noble continued. "Mr. Kotes is sitting in his chair."

I started to speak and then stopped and looked back at the house. I shook my head.

"Ask him," Noble challenged. "You can see him, ask him. You'll see I'm right."

"I don't see Daddy," I whispered and kept shaking my head. I didn't know why I was whispering. What he had said made me lower my voice. "I can't demand him to appear. I told you so many times."

Suddenly the front door was pulled open and Mommy stepped out on the porch.

"Celeste, Noble, where are you two?"

"Go on," Noble urged. "Tell her what I said. She'll believe you."

"No," I said. "You don't lie about that. You don't lie about spiritual things." I backed away from him, and then I ran to the house.

Mommy stood there with her hands on her hips, glaring down at me.

"Well?" she asked.

"It's not there where he left it," I told her.

"What are you saying, Celeste?"

"He threw it down by the anthill. I saw him do that, but it's not there, Mommy."

"Then where is it?"

"I don't know, Mommy," I said and started to cry.

"Well, until you do or until he does, you can go without any dinner," she said. "Just go up to your room and think about it," she added as Noble drew closer. "Go on," she ordered, pointing toward the stairway.

Noble walked in quickly and rushed toward the stairs. I followed with my head down.

"I'm disappointed in you, Celeste," she said.

I spun around.

"Why *me*? *He* did something with it, not *me*."

"You *know* why," she said, glaring at me. "Go on upstairs," she commanded and then marched down the hallway to have dinner with Mr. Kotes.

Noble threw himself on his bed facedown. I sat on my bed, staring at him.

Through the floor we could hear Mommy's and Mr. Kotes's muffled conversation. My stomach groaned with disappointment as I thought about what they were eating now. The house was still full of the wonderful aromas.

"Aren't you hungry, Noble?" I asked him softly.

His body shuddered.

"I am. I'm so hungry, I could eat my pillow," I said, and he turned and looked at me. I saw he had been crying.

"I can't find it, Celeste. I looked, and it was gone. I'm not lying," he insisted, holding his arms out. He did look like he was telling the truth, but that made no sense.

"Spirits don't take things," I told him.

"How do you know? You don't know everything about them. You should have told Mommy. You should have," he asserted. "She would have let us eat. She would have believed you."

"I told you. I can't tell her something that isn't true, especially about that. I might not ever see Daddy again if I do."

"I don't care. I don't see him," he said and turned over to lie facedown again.

The muffled conversation below grew softer, and then there was laughter. They played music again, too. How could Mommy do this? How could she be happy with us up here starving?

I lay back. Maybe if I meditated, I thought, I could stop being so hungry. Eventually I fell asleep and so did Noble. Much later, I woke with a start and heard some footsteps descending the stairs. I rose slowly and opened our door. There was no one there, but I heard Mommy talking to Mr. Kotes below. I heard the front door open and heard her say good night.

"Thank you," he said. "A wonderful dinner, especially the dessert," he added. "And I don't mean just the apple pie."

I heard Mommy laugh.

"I'll call you tomorrow, Sarah," he added, and the door was closed.

I listened. Mommy moved about downstairs, shutting off lights, and then she started up the stairway. I waited in the doorway and when she saw me, she stopped.

"I tried to get him to tell, Mommy. Really, I did try, but he wouldn't. He fell asleep."

"Maybe he will tomorrow," she said, "when he sees there is no breakfast for either of you until that magnifying glass is brought back inside the house."

She marched past me to her room. I saw the lights were on already, and the bed was unmade. Why was the bed unmade? Mommy never left her room sloppy. She paused, turned, and looked at me.

"I'd advise you to get some sleep, Celeste," she said and closed the door.

I turned and went to one of our windows to look out at the night.

Daddy, I thought, if you're here, please tell me what to do. Please, I begged, and then I turned off the lights and went to bed.

Noble was up ahead of me in the morning. He had fallen asleep in his clothes and didn't bother changing into different ones. He just rose and went downstairs, expecting to have breakfast. I heard him come charging up the stairway, his feet pounding.

"Get up, Celeste!" he cried, charging through the door. He shook me.

"What is it?" I groaned.

"Mommy won't give us anything to eat until we find the magnifying glass."

"I told you," I said.

"We've got to find where Daddy hid it," he said.

"Noble, you know where it is. Just get it, please," I said and closed my eyes.

153

He shook me again.

"Stop it!" I screamed at him. "Shaking me won't help. Bring in the magnifying glass."

"I don't know where it is," he said. "We've got to look everywhere. You have to help me. Get up," he commanded. "Mommy says you should."

I groaned, ground the sleep out of my eyes, and then slipped my feet into my shoes.

"C'mon," Noble cried, pulling my hand.

"I want to at least wash my face with cold water and wake up, Noble," I complained.

He stood by impatiently, waiting. I had to pee, too. He opened the bathroom door while I was still on the toilet.

"Get out!" I shouted at him.

Although we shared a room, I didn't like him in the bathroom when I was there, and I no longer took baths with him or let him see me in the tub.

"Hurry up," he cried. "I'm hungry."

I joined him in the hallway, and he shot down the stairs.

"This is really stupid, Noble," I muttered. I could hear Mommy in the kitchen. She sounded like she was unloading dishes from the dishwasher, something she ordinarily wanted me to do. She was so angry at me that she wouldn't even permit me to do my chores.

I followed Noble outside and stood on the porch.

"Okay, so now what?" I asked him.

"We'll search everywhere," he declared. "I'll use my magic wand," he added and went for a broomstick that he had painted yellow and red. Somehow, despite his own hunger, this had all turned into one of his silly, childish games, I thought.

I traipsed behind him from the house to the garage to our barn. He would lift his broomstick and then say some gibberish he had invented, which was probably what the postman had overheard and thought was a real foreign language. Noble's magic stick supposedly leaned toward one direction or another, and we followed it as if it were a bloodhound. How long, I wondered, would he keep this up?

He opened closets in the garage. He looked under the vehicles and in the vehicles. He went through shelves, and then he went to the old barn, where I thought he would produce the magnifying glass for sure. He looked through tools, looked in a wheelbarrow, looked in carts, and even looked under the lawn mower. I stood by watching him and waiting.

"The magic wand isn't working. It lost its power," he decided and threw it down outside the barn. Then his eyes brightened. "No, it didn't!" he cried.

"What now, Noble? I'm tired and hungry and Mommy is so mad at us, she'll never be nice to us again."

He lifted his arm and pointed to the broomstick.

"Look at where the wand is pointing," he said.

"How can you tell where it's pointing?"

"The end, silly. It's pointing there," he said and pointed his right forefinger toward the old gravestones.

"Noble —"

He broke into a run, and I followed. When we reached the tombstones, he stopped, and then he turned to me and smiled.

"Told you Daddy did it," he said and went to Infant Jordan's stone. There atop it was the magnifying glass.

I felt my breath stop.

"You did that, Noble," I said in a hoarse whisper.

"No, I didn't! If you tell Mommy I did, I'll throw it away again," he warned.

"Okay, okay, I won't," I said. "Let's just

bring it into the house and make her happy."

I started toward the house and paused to look back once. For an instant, I thought I did see Daddy, but then I decided it was just a shadow caused by a cloud drifting in the wind. I shook my head to shake out my heavy thoughts that felt like cobwebs, and I continued toward the house. Noble followed with a soft smile on his face, the smile of someone who thought he had been validated. He might even believe what he's saying, I thought. He certainly looked and acted like he did. Was that his dream, or was it the truth?

When we entered, Mommy came into the hallway. She was wiping a dish.

"Well?"

"I found it," Noble said. "My magic wand helped."

"I see," she said when he held up the magnifying glass.

"You know where it was, where we found it?" he asked her.

"I can't imagine," she said.

"On the Infant Jordan tombstone," he said. He looked at me and then at Mommy, who stopped wiping the dish.

"Tombstone? Why was it there?"

"Daddy didn't want me to have it," he

told her, "because Mr. Kotes was in his chair."

She recoiled as though she had been slapped.

"Put it away, wash up, change your clothes, and sit down to breakfast," Mommy ordered. She looked at me fiercely. "Now!"

We both hurried up the stairs to do what she had said. Did she think I told him that? My heart was pounding.

"I told you not to say such a thing, Noble. I told you," I chastised.

"It's the truth," he asserted.

When we went downstairs again, our food was on the table. Mommy stood aside and watched us for a while. Then she stepped up to the table and looked down at Noble.

"Where did you get such an idea about your father?" she asked him.

"I don't know. I just thought because Mr. Kotes was in Daddy's chair, that Daddy was mad."

She looked at me.

"I didn't tell him to say that, Mommy. I swear I didn't."

She turned back to Noble.

"I don't want to ever hear you say such a thing to Mr. Kotes or anyone else, Noble. Do you understand?"

He nodded, but he looked so satisfied with himself. Even Mommy sensed it and turned quickly to look at me. I bit down on my lower lip and shifted my eyes quickly back to my cereal.

"There is nothing worse than lying about them," she said in a hoarse whisper. "Nothing."

I couldn't swallow. The food lumped up in my throat, and tears came to my eyes, tears that burned.

Afterward, when Noble was outside, I went to her and again told her that I had nothing to do with what he had said.

"He made it all up himself, Mommy. I swear."

She shook her head.

"He couldn't do that, Celeste."

"Why not?"

"He just couldn't," she insisted.

"I'm not lying," I moaned and started to cry.

"Maybe you said something under your breath or to yourself, and he overheard it."

"No, Mommy."

"I don't want to talk about it anymore," she snapped. "Go see what he's doing and watch over him. Go on," she ordered.

I couldn't help being angry at Noble for getting me into so much trouble. None of it seemed to bother him. It was truly as if he mixed his imaginary world, his pretend and his games, with our spiritual community. He didn't understand, but more important, he didn't care.

Maybe Mommy was right. Maybe he was in some grave danger, only, what could I do about that?

We didn't talk about it anymore that day, and Mommy didn't either. I think it was because she was so happy about our test results. Mr. Katzman commented that we had done better than most students who attended school. Mommy made a point of reading that aloud to us.

As to the magnifying glass, Noble refused to use it again, believing Daddy didn't want him to use it. I knew it, but Mommy didn't. I warned him not to tell her, and he at least listened to that. When Mr. Kotes asked about it, he simply told him we had found it, but he wouldn't talk about it or talk to Mr. Kotes much at all, if he could help it. I could see that annoyed Mommy, but she seemed reluctant to complain or reprimand him for being sullen.

Mr. Kotes began to appear at our house more and more often, either for dinner or just to visit. Getting Noble to accept him was obviously important to him. He lavished more gifts, bought him an air rifle, and then spent time showing him how to use it correctly and safely. The agreement, which Noble hated, was that he wouldn't use it unless Mr. Kotes was there with him.

He bought Noble and me new fishing poles, too, but I knew it was mostly for Noble. With Mommy tagging along, he took us to the creek to fish and talked about how his grandfather used to take him fishing when he was about our age. Actually, I thought Mr. Kotes was a gentleman, a nice man who always seemed concerned about us. I couldn't harden myself against him as easily as Noble could. Mommy had to pull thank-yous and pleases out of Noble constantly.

Most of all I saw how comfortable and content Mommy was in Mr. Kotes's company. There were very few people whom she tolerated, much less liked. I told Noble that if she liked Mr. Kotes, we should, but that well of stubbornness inside him was still too deep to permit compromise. The only thing that did worry me was the fact that I had not seen Daddy's spirit again. However, I did remind myself that if Mr. Kotes's presence in our home and his keeping us company was the reason Daddy's spirit stayed away, Mommy would surely be the first to know.

I didn't have the courage to put it exactly like that, but I did come to her one night and ask her why I hadn't seen Daddy's spirit for so long. She put down the book she was reading and looked at me quietly, calmly, her eyes blinking slowly. I could almost hear and feel the thoughts rising up in her.

"He's waiting for Noble," she said, "waiting for Noble to be able to cross over."

"But that's not fair to me, Mommy," I said.

Her eyes seemed to snap, and she turned sharply to me.

"How can you say such a thing? How could you think only of yourself? I have told you what danger there is for your brother."

"Well, what should I do?" I whined.

"Be patient," she replied. "Just be patient."

She returned to her book, and I left feeling more confused and full of trepidation than ever.

All during the time she was with Mr. Kotes and he was with us, I was keen to hear how Mommy would tell him about the spirits, about our family, about our powers. I listened in on one conversation when they discussed spiritual energy and the power of psychics. I was surprised at how much Mr. Kotes believed or said he believed. I could tell Mommy was very happy about that. What she was doing was gradually easing him into our world, revealing a little more each time, as if she knew what he could accept and what he couldn't.

I knew they laughed about how the people in the community talked about Mommy. I overheard that conversation, too. I wasn't exactly spying on them all the time. Well, maybe I was.

"I can tell you many people are surprised I'm seeing you as much as I am, Sarah," Mr. Kotes told her.

"I know your sister is one of them," she said. "I hear how she feels whenever she calls here for you."

"Well, she's just overly worried about me all the time, that's all."

"Maybe you shouldn't come around so often, Taylor," she said sharply to him.

"The day I let the busybodies in this community determine what I do and don't do will be one sad day for me," he replied.

"And that includes my sister."

She liked that.

She liked him more and more, and with every passing day of growing affection between them, I sensed Daddy's distance from us growing as well. Sometimes it felt like a light dwindling or a shadow retreating into the woods, shrinking until it was barely visible anymore.

Daddy's dying a second time, I thought. It was an idea that came bursting upon me, making me shudder. I dreamed of his coffin, the lid closing down firmly. His voice was muffled within, his cries diminishing. I saw myself desperately trying to pry it open until my fingers bled.

It woke me with a start. I might even have screamed. I didn't know for sure. Noble moaned in his sleep. Was he having the same nightmare? Was Mommy right about our sharing of thoughts and feelings, even when we slept?

I sat up in a sweat and caught my breath. Then I lowered myself back to the pillow, but I kept my eyes open for the longest time, falling asleep again only after I thought I had heard Daddy's voice softly say, "Don't worry. Soon it will all be all right."

I had no idea what "soon" meant. As for

Mr. Kotes, he continued to come to see us often, and finally Mommy agreed to his taking us all out to dinner, as long as it wasn't a restaurant in the nearby community.

"I don't want to see the busybodies gaping at us, Taylor," she told him, and he said he understood.

Traveling to another community to go out to eat was at least something that pleased Noble. He wasn't as sullen, and he was, of course, very interested in everything he could see along the way and when we arrived. He even asked questions and listened when Mr. Kotes gave him answers. Mommy seemed to be pleased about all that.

Since she would never permit us to have a babysitter from the community, Mr. Kotes always had to take us along whenever he wanted to take Mommy somewhere. It was either doing that or eating at our house. There was talk between them about taking us on a trip to New York City to see the Bronx Zoo, which filled Noble's eyes with excitement.

"We could go there and back in one day easily, if you want, Sarah," he told her.

Noble was pleading with his eyes, urging Mommy to agree.

"We'll see," she said with some real interest in her eye, which at least gave him some hope.

Despite his reluctance and efforts to remain aloof and disinterested in Mr. Kotes, Noble was succumbing. I saw it happening more and more. He no longer complained about him sitting in Daddy's chair, and he began to use the magnifying glass again. Soon after that, he was openly using all the tools Mr. Kotes had given him earlier.

He even began to look forward to Mr. Kotes coming to see us, anticipating that he would be bringing something new each time. It was on the tip of my tongue to ask Noble why he didn't think about Daddy as much anymore. Wasn't he afraid he would never, ever see Daddy's spirit or speak with him again? I was afraid to ask these questions, afraid he would just go running to Mommy to tell her.

Actually, I was more surprised at Mommy. Didn't she think that the more Noble grew to like Mr. Kotes, the less chance he would have to cross over and see Daddy's spirit? Why would this occur to me and not to her?

I was building up my courage to ask her that.

It was a question teasing at the tip of my

mind, threatening to burst out on its own if I didn't agree to phrase it myself soon.

I was truly about to do that finally.

But I didn't get the chance, and I didn't have to ask after all.

The answer was already written in the darkness, scribbled on the wind, circling the house and preparing to enter our hearts.

We had only to listen.

6

"Someone Pushed Me"

It happened the night of our ninth birthday, which to me made it even more significant. Mommy made a special dinner and a wonderful chocolate fudge cake with our names spelled out in vanilla icing. When Daddy was with us, our birthday parties were usually big events. He would bring us more gifts than we received on Christmas. Mommy always complained about how he was spoiling us, but he was undeterred.

"Birthdays are days that by definition are meant to spoil children," he said. "It makes them feel special, makes them feel significant and loved."

"Our children feel that every day of their lives," Mommy countered.

"I'm sure they do, but birthdays are still different, Sarah. I'm surprised you don't remember your own when you were their age and how important all that was to you."

"I don't have anything foolish to remember. My parents weren't foolish people," she remarked.

Even when I was very little, I remember wondering what that meant. Didn't Mommy have birthday parties, too?

"They were if they didn't treat you extra special on your birthday," Daddy asserted.

She couldn't slow him down when it came to lavishing love upon Noble and me, no matter what warnings she had received from her spiritual world or fears of evil eyes she pronounced. His voice was the loudest singing "Happy Birthday" to us, and he looked as excited and anxious to see our presents as we did. Whether they were his or ours, birthdays turned him into a little boy again.

Maybe Mommy was remembering all that, or maybe Daddy had come to her and told her to do it, but this time she decided to make us a real party and not just a cake. We had no friends to invite, but Mommy had us decorate the dining room with crepe paper and balloons Mr. Kotes brought. One of his presents, which Mommy permitted to our surprise, was a clown-magician who arrived just at the start of our dinner party. Mr. Kotes had located and paid for him, as well.

Noble was fascinated with the tricks, the way he found money in his ear, pulled strings of thin balloons out of his throat, made cards disappear, poured water down his sleeve and didn't get wet, and then popped a baby rabbit out of a bouquet of fake flowers. Mr. Kotes said the rabbit was ours to keep, too. One of our presents was a cage for it, but one day Noble let it out and we never saw it again.

After the clown-magician left, we had our dinner, and then Mommy lit the candles. Ever since we were old enough to blow out candles, we did it together, Noble on one side and me on the other. As soon as we did it, Mommy and Mr. Kotes began to sing "Happy Birthday to You," and I looked off to the corner and saw Daddy standing there, smiling. I was absolutely positive I did. I turned quickly to Mommy, who smiled and nodded at me, and then I looked at Noble in hopeful anticipation. His attention was on our gifts, and even though he was looking in Daddy's direction, he didn't appear to see him.

After the singing, Daddy was gone. I felt like crying even though we had so much happiness around us. Noble began to rip open gifts, lunging for another one as soon as he saw what the one in his hands was, especially if it was clothes. I was given clothes mostly, and more books to read. The gift that made Noble the happiest was a set of electric trains from Mr. Kotes. He was so excited about it, he gobbled down his cake and anxiously waited for the rest of us to finish. Mr. Kotes had volunteered to help him get it all set up in the living room, where Mommy had said they could be, on the floor beneath the grandfather's clock that never bonged or ticked. So many things in our house were there just because they were always there.

Noble and Mr. Kotes went in and began to connect the tracks. While they did that, I went into the kitchen to help Mommy with the dishes, but really to tell her I had seen Daddy again, finally.

"I though you had," she said. "I could see it in your face, Celeste," she said.

"Didn't you, too?" I asked, a little confused.

"Sometimes, on very special occasions, the spirits can select whom they want to see them, and even if you have the gift, you might not see them. I think your daddy wanted to give you something special. It was his gift.

"But —" She paused as if just realizing something. She shook her head. "I

171

couldn't see any awareness in Noble's face, and it is his birthday, too. Why wasn't he given a special gift? What is it?" she asked, pounding her hand so hard on the sink, I was sure she hurt herself. "What am I doing wrong?"

"It's not your fault, Mommy. Noble's just not ready," I said and held my breath. Whenever I talked about Noble's failure, it was like walking on thin ice.

She turned to me after a moment and told me to join Noble and Mr. Kotes. I had the feeling she hadn't heard what I had just said.

"It's your birthday, too," she told me. "You don't have to work in the kitchen tonight."

"I don't mind helping you, Mommy."

"Just go. I need to be alone for a few moments," she said sharply.

I left feeling like I had been slapped. I certainly wasn't feeling like the birthday girl. Mommy didn't want me around her, and when I went into the living room, Mr. Kotes and Noble paid little attention to me. Suddenly Mr. Kotes had turned into a boy again, it seemed, and Noble looked more comfortable and happy about him than ever. When they actually got the train going, they were both ecstatic.

As I watched them, I wondered, was Mr. Kotes going to become our daddy? Was it terrible even to think such a thing? He was doing everything our daddy had done: helped make our party, bought us presents, helped Mommy around the house, took us for rides, everything. What happens to people who die and get replaced? Do their spirits get shut out? Do they disappear entirely and forever?

Noble's happy laughter shattered my thoughts. I could feel the questions floating down around me like deflated balloons.

The little engine sent up tiny puffs of smoke and had lights. There was a way to switch the track and make the whole train go in a different direction.

"I'll have to get you an engineer's cap," Mr. Kotes told Noble. "You're good at it."

Noble looked up at me, his face beaming.

"You wanna work the controls?" he asked me.

I joined him, and he started to give me orders.

"Make it go faster. Now slower. Stop and put it in reverse. I wish we could go around a bigger circle," he added, already wanting more.

"You add to the set as you go along," Mr. Kotes explained, standing and looking down at the train chugging around the tracks. "Although I bet your mother isn't going to want to give up any more of her living room," he added, seeing Mommy standing in the doorway with a strangely distant look in her eyes. Then she realized we were all looking at her and waiting for her to speak.

"We'll move it when we have to," she said. "Maybe into the garage."

"Is everything all right, Sarah?" Mr. Kotes asked.

Lately, I had noticed how sensitive he was to Mommy's moods and how important it was to him that he make her happy all the time.

"Yes, of course," she said. "Everything is just fine. Better than fine," she added and smiled.

"I'm glad," he said, looking relieved.

They held each other's gaze for a moment, and then Mommy put on music they both liked. She and Mr. Kotes sat and watched the two of us working the train set.

"I think this is the best birthday we ever had," Noble whispered, which surprised me.

Even with a clown, decorations, and all these presents, how could it be the best birthday without Daddy?

I wasn't sure if Mommy had heard him or not, but she looked as if she had, and I thought she had turned sad.

Eventually I grew bored with the trains and started to read one of my new books. Noble was upset that I wasn't paying attention to his train, and then Mommy decided it was time we went to bed. He whined and groaned and begged to stay up later, but she was firm about it, so we straightened up the living room and then went upstairs.

"I don't know why we have to sleep so much," Noble complained. "Why can't we just take naps once in a while?"

"It wouldn't be enough. We'd be too tired all the time," I said.

As if he thought he could rush the night into morning, he hurriedly brushed his teeth and changed into his pajamas in the bathroom. Then I did. By the time I came out, Noble looked asleep. I guessed he hadn't realized how tired he actually was. Happy times make you tired too, I thought.

I crawled into bed and pulled the covers up to my chin. What was it like to have a birthday that was only yours? I wondered, and then I wondered if it was selfish of me to think about such a thing. All my short life, I had known only sharing with Noble. I suppose nothing would seem right for me if it weren't that way always.

It was a good day, I decided. I could hear Mommy and Mr. Kotes below, their voices muffled, but occasionally their laughter louder. I struggled to keep my eyes open because I kept hoping Daddy would appear again. Why did he have to stand in a corner, and why did he go so quickly? I wondered. Again, it made me question whether or not I had really seen him. Mommy's explanation about his giving me something special made sense, and yet it surprised me that she couldn't see him, too. Maybe I had wanted to so much, I just imagined it, I thought sadly.

My eyes closed and opened, closed and opened. Vaguely, I thought I heard the sound of footsteps on the stairway. I heard whispering, and then I heard Mommy's bedroom door open and close. I tried to stay awake to listen more, but sleep was like a heavy black sheet being drawn over me. Try as much as I wanted, I couldn't push it away.

At least not until I heard the sound of

Mommy screaming at someone. It came from downstairs.

"What are you saying?" she was shouting. "What are you saying?"

My eyes snapped open, and I looked around, surprised that it was still very dark. The clock said two thirty-five. Why was Mommy talking to someone on the phone this late? I gazed over at Noble, but he was still, his back to me.

I rose slowly and went to the doorway. Mommy's voice was shrill now, and she sounded like she was crying and saying, "No, no, that can't be."

Slowly, I emerged from the room and started down the stairway. I heard her hang up the phone and then go into the living room. I reached the bottom of the stairway just as she started shouting again, shouting, I first thought, at Mr. Kotes.

"Why did you do this? How can you be this cruel? These children need a father, especially Noble. What you couldn't provide, he could have provided. You could have warned me. You could have, Arthur!"

Arthur? She's talking to Daddy, I thought, and hurried down the hallway.

I found her sitting on the chintz sofa, looking out the window. She had her legs drawn up and under her. Dressed only in her robe and slippers, she was dabbing her eyes with her handkerchief. I quickly looked about the room, but I didn't see Daddy's spirit anywhere. Mommy turned slowly and looked at me. She wasn't upset that I had gotten out of bed and come down. She just stared at me and then shook her head and looked out the window again. It was pitch-dark outside. What was she looking at? I wondered and drew closer.

"Why were you shouting, Mommy?" I asked.

She sighed deeply and nodded her head. Then she took a deep breath and turned to me.

"There has been a terrible, terrible accident," she said. "On his way home from here tonight, Mr. Kotes was hit head-on by a pickup truck driven by drunken teenage boys. Nothing much happened to them. They were too drunk to even realize what they did," she added.

"Mr. Kotes?" I said.

"Yes. He's dead. That was his sister who called. She was hysterical. She blamed it on me because he was here, because he was with me. She called me all sorts of terrible names."

"He's dead?"

"He's dead!" she screamed. "Are you deaf? Dead!" She paused and then took a deep breath. "Maybe it really *is* my fault. I don't know . . ."

"Why, Mommy?"

"I shouldn't have encouraged him," she said softly. "I should have known they wouldn't like it. It's why they stayed away." She stared at the floor and then she looked at me. "Go on back to bed, Celeste."

"Did you see Daddy? Was that who you were yelling at?" I asked.

"Go back to bed!" she said. "Just go back to bed."

She turned away from me and scrunched up on the chintz sofa. She suddenly looked so small, as if she was a little girl herself. I wanted to go to her and put my arms around her, but I was afraid. The house was so dark and silent, but her screams still echoed in my ears.

Mr. Kotes was dead?

But he was just here. We were all singing and playing together!

I walked up the stairs slowly. Tired and groggy, I returned to bed, and after looking over at Noble, who was still in a deep sleep, I closed my eyes. The last thing I thought about was Mr. Kotes's face when he was singing "Happy Birthday" to us.

I woke in the morning when Noble did. He was moving quickly and making lots of noise because he was anxious to get up and dressed and back to his electric train.

"When Mr. Kotes comes back, he might bring more cars and bridges and little people and houses. He thinks we could build a whole city," he told me excitedly.

I rubbed my eyes and sat up. He already had his hair brushed and was buttoning his shirt on the way out.

"Mr. Kotes isn't coming back, Noble," I told him. "He's never coming back."

"Why not?" he asked from the doorway.

"He was in a terrible accident last night, and he was killed," I reported. Mommy hadn't told me not to tell him.

"What? You're lying," he spit at me. "You're a big, fat, stupid liar!"

"No, I'm not, Noble."

He stood there a moment, and then he went out and slammed the door. I heard him charging down the stairway. Mommy's voice was muffled, but the tone was not hard to feel. I rose, washed, and dressed. When I descended the stairs, I found Noble at the table, sulking over his bowl of oatmeal. Mommy was standing by the window, looking out, her back to us. She was in the same black dress she had worn for Daddy's funeral.

Noble raised his eyes slowly and looked at me, but he didn't say anything. He looked very angry.

"It's not my fault," I muttered.

Mommy turned slowly and looked at me a moment and then back out the window. I poured myself some juice, put a piece of bread in the toaster, and stirred some oatmeal into a bowl for myself. When I returned to the table, Noble was sitting back, his arms so tightly embracing himself that he looked like he was pushing all his blood into his face.

"Mommy won't let me play with my trains," he complained. "She wants me to take it all apart and put it back into the box."

"You help him, Celeste," Mommy added, still looking out the window.

I didn't say anything, but I, too, wondered why we had to do that. Noble just glared ahead.

"I'm not," he said finally.

Mommy turned slowly.

"If you don't, I will scoop it all up and throw it all into the garbage," she threatened.

"Why do I have to?" he whined.

"Because I told you to," she said. "That

should be enough reason. This is a house in mourning. We don't simply go on as though nothing terrible has happened."

"Something terrible is *always* happening," Noble muttered. He rose from his seat and ran out of the room. We heard the front door opening and closing.

"Noble!" Mommy screamed after him.

I froze, afraid to eat another bite.

"Go after him," she ordered. "See that he doesn't do anything stupid. I don't want him too far from the house today. And don't you *dare* go into the woods, Celeste."

She looked out the window again.

"They're hovering out there like mosquitoes against the windowpane."

"Who, Mommy?"

She shook her head slowly.

"The spirits," she whispered. "Evil spirits."

When I stood up, I felt my whole body trembling. How close were the spirits? Would I be able to see them?

"Go on," she said. "Quickly."

I walked to the door, hesitated, and then went outside. I couldn't see Noble anywhere, and that frightened me for a moment. What if he had already run into the woods? What if the evil spirits had already gotten him?

"Noble," I shouted. "Where are you?"

I went around the house, looked up at the old graves, and then walked to the barn. All during the time I was searching for him, he was sitting up in his favorite tree, the old maple off to the right, just watching me grow more and more frantic. When I finally saw him, I screamed at him.

"Why didn't you answer me! Mommy wants you to stay close to the house. She won't want you up there. Come down this minute, Noble!"

"No," he said defiantly. "I'm not coming down until she lets me play with my trains."

"Noble, come down."

To demonstrate his firmness, he climbed a little higher and sat on a thinner branch. All I could think was, an evil spirit would swoop down and push him off. My heart thumped.

"Please come down," I begged, tears filling my eyes. "I'll play anything else you want to play. I'll obey the moat. We'll fight dragons, anything?"

"No. I want to play with my trains," he insisted. "I'll never come down until she lets me."

"Noble! Please."

He turned away from me.

"I'm telling Mommy," I said and ran back to the house.

Mommy was in the kitchen, cleaning up the breakfast dishes and pouring out the rest of the oatmeal. I had forgotten my piece of toast. It was burned. She looked at me and threw it into the garbage.

"Where's your brother? Didn't I tell you to stay with him?"

"He climbed up in his tree, and he says he's not coming down until you let him play with his trains," I rattled off quickly. "He's even climbed higher than ever."

Mommy's eyes widened. She dropped what was in her hands and rushed past me to the front door. I followed her out of the house.

"Noble Atwell, you come right down here," Mommy screamed up at him. "This instant."

"Will you let me play with my trains?"

"You will not play with those trains today. You will not play with them ever again if you don't come down this instant," she added.

Even I was surprised at how defiant Noble could be. Instead of obeying, he turned and reached for a higher branch.

"Noble Atwell!" Mommy shouted.

He grabbed the branch and started to

pull himself up, but the branch snapped. For an instant it was as if the whole world had gone into stop-action, been put on pause. The realization that he was without any support and had lost his balance flashed on Noble's face in bright astonishment.

Mommy screamed.

He flailed about as if he thought he might be able to fly his way out of danger, and then he fell from the tree in a swift, graceful drop like someone who had concluded there was nothing else to do but relax and face the music. He was high enough up so that when his left foot hit first, it twisted sharply. He hit next on his buttocks and then rolled head over heels to stop on his stomach.

When he hit the ground, I was sure I felt the thump in my own body as well. Almost immediately, he let out a wail of pain that sent birds loitering on nearby trees shooting into the air. Mommy caught her breath and then ran to him. He was crying hard. His forehead was bleeding where he had scraped it rolling over, but his leg was twisted in a strange angle. Mommy fell quickly to her knees beside him and gently turned him onto his back.

I couldn't move. My heart seemed to

have fallen into my stomach. It took me a few moments to realize I was sobbing profusely. The thick tears were already dripping off my chin. Noble was screaming in pain with such effort, his face was bright red and his screams rose to a shrillness that made them inaudible. It was as if I was watching it all in a silent movie.

Mommy carefully rolled up his pants, and I saw the way his lower leg bone was pressing against his skin, threatening to tear it open any moment. Without hesitation, remaining remarkably cool, Mommy pressed on the leg bone and put it back into place. Noble was in such pain at that moment, his eyes went back in his head and he passed out.

I thought he had died.

My own heart stopped.

"Is he dead, Mommy?" I somehow managed when she rose to her feet.

She looked at me, and I saw there wasn't even a tear in her eyes.

"No," she said. "He's better off for the moment. Don't let him move until I get back," she ordered. "Come here!" she screamed at me when I hadn't walked a step toward Noble. "Sit next to him and don't let him move this leg if he wakes up before I return, Celeste."

I hurried to his side.

"Keep him calm," she ordered. I had no idea how, but I took his hand into mine and sat while she went off toward the barn. Noble was just starting to groan and move his head from side to side when she returned with two pieces of wood slabs. I saw she also had some tape.

"Mommy," Noble muttered.

"Just stay still, Noble, completely still. You've broken your leg," she said.

He looked up at her, dazed.

"Someone pushed me," he said, and she stopped working. "I could feel it," he muttered and closed his eyes. "Someone pushed me."

Mommy looked at me for a moment, the expression on her face confusing. She looked like she wanted me to explain. I bit down softly on my lower lips and shook my head. I didn't know what he was talking about. I hadn't seen anything.

"Go into the house and get the antiseptic I use on your cuts and bruises, Celeste. I want a wet cloth with soap, too. Go on," she ordered, and I jumped up quickly and ran into the house.

By the time I returned, she had the splint on Noble's leg firmly put together. She took the cloth and soap and washed off his forehead scrape, and then she applied the antiseptic. Noble continued to cry, his whole body shaking with sobs. Mommy slipped her arms under him and then, with great effort, lifted him as she stood. He let his head roll against her breast and closed his eyes as she carried him toward the house.

"Will he be all right?" I asked, following.

"Get the door for me," she said in return. I hurried ahead and opened it.

I stood back and watched her carry him up the stairs to our room. She told me to pull his blanket back, and she set him softly onto his bed. After she began to undress him, she sent me for a pair of scissors and used them to cut his pants leg so that she could slip his pants off. After that she put pillows under his broken leg.

"I'm going to get an ice pack and something for him to take so he can sleep for a while," she said. "Stay with him and just keep him calm and still," she told me.

Noble groaned. His face was streaked with charcoal channels his tears had drawn over his cheeks and down his chin. I took the washcloth and very lightly wiped them away. He kept his eyes on me. I thought he looked half asleep already. Before I spoke, I looked back at the doorway to be sure

Mommy hadn't returned.

"You didn't really feel someone push you up in the tree, did you, Noble?"

"Yes," he said.

Mommy returned with the ice pack, a glass of water, and one of her herbal drinks. She gave it him and made him swallow it.

"I want you to sleep for a while, Noble."

"It hurts," he complained.

"I know it hurts, and it will hurt for quite a while. Celeste will stay with you and keep this ice pack on your leg. She will get you what you need," she added.

She put my hand around the ice pack.

"Keep it on as long as you can. When he complains it's getting too cold, take it off for a while and then put it back on, understand?"

I nodded.

"Doesn't he have to go to the hospital, Mommy?" I asked her when she stood up and started for the door.

She turned to me slowly.

"No," she said. "They won't do anything more than what I have done and will do."

"Will he be all right?"

"I don't know. Will he?" she shot back at me. I couldn't understand why.

I scrunched my eyebrows. Why did she

think I knew the answer?

She stared at me a moment, and then she walked out of our room. Noble groaned.

"It hurts, Celeste. It hurts so much," he said. "More than splinters or cuts, more than anything."

I looked at the empty doorway, and then I returned to him and held the ice pack on his leg. I stroked his arm softly.

"I know it hurts. I'm sorry it hurts, Noble."

"Why doesn't Mommy stop it from hurting?" he asked me.

"She did. She gave you something. This ice pack will help, too. It will all help you soon," I said.

He closed his eyes and whimpered. I looked at his leg. It was black and blue around where the bone had protruded. I thought it looked horrible. He should be in a hospital, I concluded. Maybe Mommy will realize it soon and take him.

"I . . . want . . . to play with . . . my trains," Noble whispered, and then he fell asleep.

The ice pack melted, and I grew stiff sitting there and hardly moving. I kept wondering where Mommy had gone. Why wasn't she coming back quickly to see how

Noble was? Suddenly, I heard a loud engine sound and rose slowly to look out the window. I didn't see anything, but the sound became louder. I thought for a moment. A memory returned of Daddy in the woods getting us firewood.

Curious now, I headed downstairs and went to the front door. The moment I stepped out, I stopped. It was such a shocking thing to see. Mommy had Daddy's chain saw, and she was cutting at the tree from which Noble had fallen. It was a good-size maple tree and a beautiful tree. I didn't understand why she was doing it, but even more difficult to understand was how she was able to hold that saw and work like a man.

She didn't see me standing nearby, and she couldn't hear me calling to her above the chain saw engine. Finally, she caught sight of me when she stopped to rest a moment.

"Why are you out here?"

"I heard the noise and wanted to see what you were doing, Mommy. Noble's fast asleep and the ice pack is all melted."

"I don't want you leaving him, Celeste. Empty the water out of the ice pack and fill it with ice cubes again. Keep it on the bruise. You and I are going to have to take care of him until he mends," she said.

"But . . . why are you cutting the tree?" I asked.

She looked up at it and then turned back to me.

"It's touched by evil now," she said. "We have to get rid of it." She started the saw again, but I heard her add, "We have to get rid of anything that welcomes the evil. Get back upstairs and stay with your brother!" she shouted at me.

I backed away, watched her for a few more moments, and then ran into the house. For a long moment I just stood in the entryway, catching my breath. Then I went upstairs, fetched the ice pack, and did what she had told me to do. Noble didn't wake up for hours, and when he did, he was very uncomfortable and very unhappy.

"Where's Mommy?" he asked. "I want Mommy."

"She's outside cutting down the tree just because you fell out of it," I said, "and because you said you felt someone push you."

"Cutting down the tree?"

"Listen. You can hear the chain saw."

"I don't want her to cut my tree."

"You can thank yourself for that, Noble."

Finally, the sound of the chain saw stopped. Noble started to squirm, and I stopped him.

"Mommy said you shouldn't move, and especially not your broken leg."

"But I have to pee," he said.

It didn't occur to me until that moment that his going to the bathroom was going to be a big problem. What would we do?

"I have to pee!" he said again.

"I'll go tell Mommy. Please don't move, or she'll blame me, Noble. Please," I pleaded and hurried out and down the stairs.

Mommy was standing beside the fallen tree, the chain saw still in her hand. Her hair was wild, and she had chips and sawdust stuck to her face.

"Noble has to pee," I said. "What should we do?"

"Go get an empty bottle in the pantry and let him pee into it," she told me.

"What?"

"Do it. It's easy for a boy. You'll see," she said. She tugged at the chain saw cord. She was so determined. She had killed the tree, and she would cut it up and get it away from us.

I stood there, stunned, for a moment, and then I went back inside and looked for a bottle with a neck wide enough. I found an empty cranberry juice bottle. Still shocked by her orders, I went back up-stairs. Noble was moaning.

"Mommy wants you to pee into this," I said and showed him.

He stopped moaning and looked at me with his eyebrows scrunching just the way mine often did. There really was so much about our faces that was similar.

"I can't," he said.

"She says you can. She says it's easy for boys to do."

He shook his head.

"That's what she says," I added and handed him the bottle.

He looked at it, and then he brought it down between his legs. I turned my back, but I could hear the pee going into the bottle.

"I'm finished," he said and held it up.

Ugh, was all I could think. I took it from him and hurried into the bathroom to dump it into the toilet.

"What happens when I have to do number two?" he asked, and I turned red and nauseous at the thought of it. I just shook my head.

"I don't know," I said.

He closed his eyes and periodically

moaned about the pain and how he wanted to turn over or get out of bed. His whining seemed never-ending. Finally Mommy came in and up to the room, and he directed all of his complaints at her in shotgun fashion.

"It hurts. I want to turn. I want to get out of bed. I don't like peeing in a jar. How am I going to do number two? Can I play with my trains?"

"Stubborn in, happiness out," Mommy said. "No one told you to climb that tree. You should have listened to me."

She checked his splint and looked at his toes.

"I'm going to make you a cast," she said, "and you're going to have to be like this for a long time, Noble. If you don't listen and obey, you'll make it worse, and you might never walk or run again properly and certainly never run again, do you understand?"

"It hurts," he said.

"It will hurt, and that is good because it will remind you how important it is to listen to what I tell you to do and not to do. I'm going down to make you something to eat. Celeste will read to you to help you take your mind off it," she said, looking at me.

"I don't want her reading to me. I want —"

"What you want doesn't matter now," Mommy said calmly. "Just do what I tell you, and we'll make you better," she added and kissed him on the cheek. "Read to him," she ordered.

At the doorway she paused to voice her own thoughts.

"First they take Taylor," she said, "and then they try to take you." She looked at me. "See why you must be vigilant, Celeste. This is partly your fault. You should have paid more attention to him. You have to *help* me."

"I did, Mommy. I told him to come down from the tree and not to climb higher."

"I don't mean that, Celeste. I mean the darkness, the shadows, the evil. You must watch for it always," she said. "You have been blessed. You have been given the eyes. *Use* them!" she commanded and left us.

I sat thinking for a few moments. How was it my fault? Was there something I had seen and forgotten to tell her? A shadow, a shape, even a strange sound?

"Mommy said read to me," Noble said suddenly, folding his arms across his chest.

"I thought you didn't like it when I read to you. I thought it was boring."

"Mommy said," he repeated. "She said you could help stop it from hurting," he added.

Could I? I wondered.

Maybe I could.

Maybe I did have the eyes.

I began with chapter one of *Alice in Wonderland*, and before I had read five pages, Noble was asleep again.

And he wasn't in pain.

7

Into the Woods

While Noble slept, Mommy left to get what she needed to make his cast. Of course, I couldn't go along. She told me that it would be this way for a long time now. Whenever she went to shop for things we needed, she would have to leave me and Noble behind, and it would be my responsibility to watch over him even more. She said it would be like that until he was able to use a crutch and get around easily.

I was in the kitchen cleaning up when I heard the front door open and then slam shut so hard, the house shook. I stepped out and saw her marching down the hallway, her hair wild, her face red.

"What is it, Mommy?" I asked, practically cringing as she flew by.

"That sister of Taylor's," she ranted, "is going around and telling people I'm somehow responsible for what happened to him. Like I'm a witch or something. I dazzled and beguiled him to the point where he didn't know what he was doing. Forget that two drunken teenagers did this. That doesn't matter. Just what she says about me matters, and people are so ready to believe anything bad about someone else, you know, especially these people in this . . . this narrow-minded small town. I hate these people. We're not going to have anything to do with this community," she vowed. "I'll do all my shopping far away always, and we'll not call on anyone around here for any help. We're alone more than ever, but that's fine with me," she continued.

I didn't say anything, but I told myself that our chances of getting to go to the public school in our community just dropped into a sewer.

She was livid with rage and rambled on about the ignorance of some people while I watched her prepare the cast. She looked as if she had done it many times before, although I had never heard about anyone else in the family breaking his or her leg. Mommy knew how to do so many things, I thought, and I wondered if I would ever be as independent and as strong as she was.

For a while Noble was at least intrigued

with a cast on his leg. Mommy kept him as quiet and still as she could. She gave him sponge baths, helped him go to the bathroom, and had me bring him all his meals and anything else he wanted. After a while I think he just enjoyed ordering me about the house to get him this or that. If I dared voice any reluctance to do something he wanted, he would whine to Mommy and she would lecture me about how important it was to keep him happy, how that would hasten his recovery, and how it was my responsibility — clearly, my *fault* — that he had suffered the broken leg.

I didn't argue. I did what he wanted, and I read to him as much as I could and as much as he would tolerate, but he wasn't one to stand still before he broke his leg. It was quite impossible for him to continue this way now. Mommy finally realized that, and together, we eventually brought him and all of his things downstairs. I was as happy as he was because it made things easier for me, and I had our room all to myself.

Mommy prepared a place for him in the living room and reluctantly gave in and permitted him to play with his electric trains. For some reason she had wanted anything that reminded us of Mr. Kotes to be put away and forgotten, but Noble never stopped asking for his trains. I had to sit and watch him play with them for hours, fixing cars and tracks, creating tunnels out of cardboard, and pretend to be as interested in it all as he was. Mommy watched us, but she didn't look happy. It gave me the willies. I felt like I was touching something contaminated, but we had to keep Noble occupied so he would recuperate.

She even began to permit him to watch more television. Our school lessons continued, but his attention span was so reduced, she reduced our class hours and then had me help him with homework. He hated working in the booklets and, although he could draw well, was very sloppy with his writing, not taking care to keep his script on the lines. Mommy usually made him write things over when he did that, but she was far more lenient with him now and he got away with lots more.

Without Mr. Kotes coming around, and with Noble confined and cranky most of the time, our house felt like a big cage locking us away from the world. Aside from the postman, some utility people, and the occasional car that paused on the highway so the travelers could gape at our house and property, we saw no one. Of course no casual callers came to our door. At the start of our driveway, there was a big sign that read KEEP OFF. PRIVATE PROPERTY. NO TRESPASSING. The phone rarely rang. The one time I remember it ringing and Mommy talking was the time the administration at the home where Daddy's father was living called to let her know that he had died. With Daddy gone, we never spoke about his father, and I had forgotten all about him.

"He died long ago," I heard her tell whomever it was that called.

She left to make arrangements, but we never attended any funeral. Mommy took care of the burial, and that was that. I had hardly known my grandfather, so it was hard to feel any sadness. I told myself at least now he was with Daddy.

To keep Noble occupied even more, Mommy went and bought a wheelchair. He enjoyed having me push him about the house and then outside through the back door because there were only two steps to navigate. Once outside, he demanded to be pushed everywhere, and that was not easy. If I complained or protested, he whined and screamed until I made an superhuman effort and rolled him up a hill or through the gravel.

I was more grateful and happier than he was when Mommy finally let Noble get around on a crutch. In the beginning he thought that was fun. He even turned the crutch into an imaginary friend upon whose shoulder he would lean. Billy Crutch, he called it and would tease me, telling me Billy Crutch didn't like me to touch him or Billy Crutch wanted me to do this or do that. Mommy let him paint the crutch the same colors he had painted the broomstick he had called his magic wand.

Consequently, he no longer complained much about any pain, although he was always moaning and groaning about itching. He didn't eat as much as he normally ate, and he grew thinner. We were still about the same height, although my added chores made me tougher, stronger. Noble used to be the one who brought in firewood, for example, and now I was doing it.

I wondered how much Mommy missed Mr. Kotes. She never played any music, and she let her hair grow uneven, not trimming her bangs. She no longer put on any lipstick and went days wearing the same housedress. I felt sorry for her, but her lack of companionship seemed to bother her less and less as time went on. She kept busy looking after the house, making our meals, washing our clothing. Sometimes she wanted me to help, and sometimes she resented me working beside her and lessening her load. It seemed she wanted to be busy and occupied. If I was around her too long, she chided me about not paying enough attention to Noble. I knew she believed that as long as I was right by his side, nothing more terrible would happen to him.

I was as vigilant as I could be, but I was bored most of the time, and Noble was very unhappy about being confined either to the house or just outside. If he dared start toward the woods, Mommy would scream and then rage at me for permitting him to even contemplate doing such a thing. What could I do but pull his crutch out from under him, his Billy Crutch?

"I don't know why she's so upset," Noble complained. "I'm not going to climb any trees, at least not for a while."

"She doesn't trust the shadows," I told him, and he grimaced and shook his head. None of it made any sense to him. He was like a wild bird, caged and told it was for its own good.

However, one night soon after, Mommy came charging up the stairs and burst into our room. Noble had gotten so he could move about much more easily and navigate the stairway, too, so he was back upstairs. We were just getting ready for bed when she threw open our doorway and stood there, breathing hard, her eyes wide, her face flushed. Her hair looked like she had been running her fingers through it for hours. Neither Noble nor I spoke. We froze and gaped at her. After a moment, she caught her breath and looked at me.

"Did you see anything, hear anything?"

"No, Mommy," I said.

She looked so hard at Noble that he stepped back and closer to me.

"Your father," she said in a whisper that seemed to come from somewhere deep down in her throat, "he told me we should be especially alert and careful. Especially you, Celeste," she added, nodding at me.

I felt a sheet of ice slide down my back. I couldn't swallow. I couldn't move. She looked up at the ceiling and let her eyes sweep the room while she embraced herself.

"Me?"

"You have the eyes," she emphasized, widening her own for emphasis.

She looked around our room again and then embraced herself and nodded.

"He's right. There's something," she muttered. "Something not right. Be *vigilant*," she warned me and stepped back, closing the door.

Even after she left, neither Noble nor I moved for a long moment. Finally he turned to me, biting the inside of his cheek as he often did when he was annoyed or confused.

"I hate this cast," he said, as if that was the whole reason for what had just happened. Why wasn't he just as frightened for us as I was? He went past me into the bathroom and closed the door.

I took a deep breath finally and sat on my bed. It had been so long since I had felt anything spiritual around me, so long since I even thought I had seen Daddy or any of our spiritual family. Maybe there was just too much darkness, too many gray skies. Winter had come earlier this year, crowding fall out of our lives. The winds swept the yellow and golden brown leaves off the trees and turned our surrounding forest into gloomy watchmen waiting for the crisp light of morning to drive back the shadows that thickened and lengthened their reach toward our home and us every night.

Inside our cage the three of us hovered

in the living room, the fire in the fireplace crackling. Mommy knitted or worked on some needlepoint, listening to Noble and me recite our lessons or, occasionally, me reading aloud. From time to time she would turn toward a window, her eyes small with suspicion at the sound of the wind. It always made my breath catch and hold, my heart thump.

With Mr. Kotes now long gone from our lives and the breaking of his leg changing his life so, Noble eventually lost interest in his trains and finally agreed to help me and Mommy pack them away to store in the garage. They were to be resurrected and put together on some future date. It was a date left vague, as vague as our future seemed to be in every way, whether it be when we were going to the public school, when we would have friends, when we would go to movies or see ball games or concerts, when, in essence, we would eventually emerge from this thickly woven protective web that Mommy had spun around us.

And adding to all that, I thought, she had cast this very frightening, very general warning over us like a net consisting of icicles. If I felt like I was walking on eggshells before, I certainly did now. Just as it was for her, every sound, every tinkle, caused me to spin around and search for something. I had no idea what it was I should be looking to see, but I did look. I was even afraid to fall asleep too quickly, and many nights I woke up listening hard for any unusual sounds.

Occasionally I could hear Mommy chanting something in the living room below or even behind her closed bedroom door. She lit candles all over the house and burned her special incense. Every day, especially every night, I would catch her shifting her eyes quickly toward a window or toward the door, her head slightly tilted back as she listened hard.

"Did you hear anything, Celeste?" she would ask me quickly.

I would shake my head, but she would remain still for so long, I thought she might have gone catatonic.

All of this made me more and more nervous. Often I would get up to check on Noble and be sure he was comfortably asleep. If he ever groaned, I felt my body tighten in fear. I would turn on my lamplight on my nightstand quickly. A few times it woke him, and he was angry about it.

"I'm doing it for you, Noble," I would tell him.

He would grunt and turn away.

"You're the one who told us you were pushed off the tree," I reminded him every time he yelled at me for crowding him or spying on him.

Finally, one day he told me he had said it because he was afraid of Mommy, afraid she would be even more angry at him for climbing the tree. He knew she would believe him and blame someone or something else for what he had done. I was surprised because I realized he was smart enough to know not to use any excuse like that for anything else he did wrong.

Still, I wanted to be sure.

"You really didn't feel anything?"

"I really didn't," he said, "so stop telling me what to do and warning me about this or that. You never leave me alone anymore," he moaned.

One of the reasons he hated being confined was just that, I could see him do anything he did. He couldn't get away fast enough or climb up to the loft in the barn. He turned his frustration and rage into hatred for his cast. Sometimes, when Mommy wasn't looking, he would jab a pen into it and tear just a little of it. He never stopped complaining about itching.

So it was no surprise to me that on the day Mommy decided Noble's cast would be removed, we were to have a party. The celebration hung out there with as much excitement about it as Christmas or birthdays. A special dinner was to be made, and of course, Noble's favorite cake.

"Let's make a fire and burn my cast," Noble suggested eagerly.

To my amazement, Mommy actually thought it was a good idea.

"Fire is a purifier," she said. "That's why fires rage in hell, why evil things flee from it."

"We'll roast marshmallows, too," Noble continued.

Mommy didn't like that idea and told him you don't mix up such a thing.

"Either we keep the fire sacred or we don't do it at all," she said.

He was disappointed, but at least he could get his fire and vent his anger and his vengeance on his cursed cast.

His leg looked so white and skinny when Mommy cut and peeled the cast off. She rubbed in creams and lotions she had concocted with her herbs, and then she had Noble stand and walk very slowly and carefully. He was stiff and moved with a little limp. I don't think he realized it himself, but Mommy's eyes grew small and full of concern.

"Just take it easy for a few days," she told him. "Definitely no jumping, Noble."

He promised to be good, and then we all went outside and gathered the wood for our fire. Noble said he wanted it to be so big it singed the stars. Mommy got it started by throwing some gasoline on the wood. It flamed up almost immediately and threw off so much heat, we had to step back.

"Okay, Noble," Mommy said without a smile, "toss in your cast."

He looked at me. Now that he was about to do it, he was a little timid, especially of getting too close to the fire. He seized the cast and then he threw it at the fire. It dropped in and immediately flamed up. Mommy stepped closer to Noble and put her arm around his shoulders.

"This is good," she said, watching the smoke twirl into the night and disappear. "We burn away the evil that has touched us. This is good."

We watched the fire until Noble became bored. Mommy sent us into the house and turned on the hose to be sure the fire was out and no danger.

"We should have had marshmallows,"

was Noble's comment about it all.

After that our lives returned to the schedule we had always followed. Noble's leg grew stronger until his limp was hardly discernible. He put on weight, and because he was permitted to run about outside again, regained his healthy, slightly crimson complexion. Too often, however, the weather kept us indoors. Winter was particularly severe this particular year. We had some major snowstorms, and it was left to Noble and me to plow the driveway out, using our rider mower, which had a plow attachment. Noble wanted to be the one who drove it most of the time. I had to wait until he grew bored, and then I would take over.

When he was alive and visiting regularly, Mr. Kotes had suggested that Mommy hire one of the local men who went around plowing out people's driveways, especially because ours was so long and wide, but Mommy wanted as few strangers on our property as possible.

"We've taken care of it ourselves up until now," she told him. "We'll continue as long as we can."

I didn't mind the winter and the cold weather so much, and even enjoyed building the snow forts and snowmen with

Noble on sunny days. We had a nice Christmas. Mommy kept to her vow never to shop in our community, so all of our presents and decorations came from the stores miles and miles away. Neither Noble nor I minded it, because it gave us an opportunity to take long rides.

The spring thaw was late in coming, but when it did, the earth was so soggy we had to wait an extra few weeks to begin our garden. Between doing that, our schoolwork, and performing some minor repairs about the house, we three seemed constantly busy. Noble took advantage of Mommy's leniency during his recuperation and wormed his way into more and more television time, too.

When the warmer spring days started and the trees began flowering again, Mommy seemed more at ease. Her periods of tension and suspicion dwindled, and her moods became lighter, happier. She even talked about taking us to a movie or perhaps to a fun park this year.

I helped her plant more flowers, weed the small cemetery, and spring-clean the house. Noble volunteered to whitewash the old barn, and for a while we were the happiest we had ever been since Daddy's death. In fact, I began to have high hopes that Mommy would indeed permit us to go to the public school the following year. Her "We'll see" when Noble asked her periodically sounded less hollow. I knew Noble was the happiest he had been for months and months, especially after Mommy gave him permission to go farther into the woods to build his fort. As long as I tagged along, of course. I didn't mind. Noble was very creative and skilled when it came to constructing the fort, and when Mommy saw it, she even considered permitting us to sleep out one night during the summer. All of the darkness seemed to be lifting from our lives. The beautiful idyllic world our great-great-grandfather had seen the day he set foot on this property was once again within our reach.

And then, one twilight when Noble and I were walking back to the house from the barn after we had cut some lawn and raked up the grass, I saw them. They began as shadows, shifted into confusing twisted shapes with distinct legs and feet, and then returned to shadows, one of which passed right through Noble before they both disappeared around the corner of the house. I was sure of it, and for the moment, the sight staked my feet to the earthen floor. My heart thumped and echoed down my spine. Noble, who saw and felt nothing, kept walking until he realized I had stopped.

"What are you doing?" he asked.

I looked about, hoping for sight of Daddy to reassure me, but there was nothing but darkness crawling in everywhere behind us like globs of ink.

I was choked up and battled to swallow a throat lump.

"I'm going into the house," he said, frustrated when I still hadn't responded, and he kept walking.

After a moment I followed quickly. Noble had already run up the stairs when I entered. Mommy was in the kitchen. I walked down the hallway and stopped in the kitchen doorway. She looked like she was talking to herself, but I knew it was one of her chants. Suddenly, she stopped what she was doing. I didn't have to call to her. She spun around and looked at me, her eyes small and dark.

"What is it, Celeste?" she asked.

"I saw something, I think," I said.

She wiped her hands quickly on a dishcloth and walked toward me, nodding slightly.

"Go on, tell me," she said after taking a deep breath.

I hated to say anything. I knew it was going to bring doom and gloom back into our lives, but I described it all.

"Maybe it was just a shadow from the sun falling below the tree line," I suggested hopefully.

"Moving that fast? I doubt it," she said and looked up as if she could see through the ceiling into Noble's and my room. "No," she said shaking her head, "I have had some bad vibrations, too, lately."

She returned to preparing dinner. Afterward, when we were all sitting at the dinner table, Mommy paused and looked at Noble.

"Celeste has seen an evil thing tonight, Noble. I don't want you going into the woods anymore."

"What? But I'm not finished building the fort in the woods, and I want to go fishing this weekend. It's time to go fishing again."

"Don't disobey me, or I'll keep you confined to the house for the entire summer," she warned him.

He looked down, and then he looked at me angrily.

"She's just making it up," he said, "because she doesn't like going into the woods and she hates fishing."

"That's not true!" I cried. "I love the fort and I like fishing."

Mommy turned her head very slowly toward me and fixed her eyes on my face.

"Celeste knows better than to lie about such things, Noble," she said without taking her eyes off me.

"I didn't lie," I protested.

Mommy nodded.

"No, you didn't lie."

Noble went into a sulk and refused to eat.

"What you don't eat tonight, you'll eat tomorrow," Mommy told him. "We don't waste food, Noble Atwell."

He sat with his arms wrapped around himself and kept his head stiff, his lips sealed.

"I have apple pie and ice cream tonight," Mommy reminded him. "But meanness in, sweetness out," she recited. "If you don't eat your meal, you have no pie."

Stubborn as always, Noble did not retreat from his sulk. Finally, Mommy told him to go upstairs and stay in our room. He jumped up.

"I'll go into the woods, and I'll fish whenever I want to," he threatened and ran up the stairs, pounding his footsteps so hard, they vibrated in the walls.

"He needs more of our protection than I ever imagined," Mommy said in a loud whisper. She rose slowly and started after him. I heard doors slamming. It was very quiet, and then suddenly I heard Noble pounding on our bedroom door and stamping his feet.

I couldn't swallow the food I had in my mouth and gagged until I got it out. I rose slowly and went to the dining room doorway. Noble's shouting was muffled, but I could make out that he was screaming he wanted Mommy to let him out.

Let him out? Out of where?

I went to the stairway just as she was coming down.

"You're sleeping in the living room tonight," she told me as she descended. Her arms were full of my things. "Take this," she ordered, and I hurried forward to accept it. "Put it all in the living room."

"Why am I sleeping there, Mommy?"

"Noble is to remain in his room by himself until he swears that he will not disobey me," she said. "It's for his own good."

She returned to the dining room. I heard Noble's stamping on the floor get louder, and then he grew quiet.

After I put my things in the living room,

I returned to the dining room, too.

"How long does he have to stay in there, Mommy?"

"I told you. Until he promises," she said.

I felt very bad for him and terribly guilty for telling Mommy about the shadows. Maybe that was really all it was, and look at what was happening to Noble. I shouldn't have spoken. I shouldn't have brought all this unhappiness into the house. All the commotion had made me lose my appetite, and I had to force down my own supper. Afterward, while Mommy was distracted, I took a chance and snuck a piece of apple pie upstairs to Noble, but to my surprise, the door was locked from the outside. I never knew our door could be locked that way.

"Is that you?" he asked through the cracks when I fumbled with the knob.

"I'm sorry, Noble," I said.

"You and your big, stupid mouth," he said and kicked at the door so hard, I jumped away.

Mommy heard it and came to the foot of the stairway.

"What are you doing up there, Celeste?" she called up. "Let him think about what I told him. Come downstairs and finish cleaning up," she ordered.

I looked about frantically for a place to hide the piece of pie and then hurriedly went to the bathroom in Mommy's room and dumped it down the toilet.

"What were you doing up there?" she asked.

"I wanted him to behave and come out," I said.

She kept her eyes on me so long, I had to shift mine away.

"Just do what I told you," she said and returned to the kitchen. I helped her clean up, and then I went into the living room and helped her set up the chintz sofa for me. I kept waiting to hear Noble call for Mommy and make the promise, but he didn't give in. Mommy was surprised, too. Nothing bothered him as much as being confined.

"Something's gotten hold of him already," Mommy muttered with conviction.

She didn't open his door to speak to him about it again. Later she went to bed, and I lay there listening and hoping Noble had decided to make the promise Mommy wanted, but he must have fallen asleep under a blanket of anger, and I was too tired to wait any longer.

In the morning Mommy woke me to wash up and come to breakfast. I expected to find Noble at the table, but he was still locked in our room. Mommy went about her business. Finally, when it was nearly lunchtime, we heard Noble calling, and she went up to let him out. I remained at the foot of the stairway, listening.

"Do you promise and swear, Noble Atwell?"

He mumbled a yes.

"If you disobey me, you'll be kept in this house for the whole summer," she threatened. "I mean it."

He came downstairs looking tired and defeated. No matter what I did or said, he wouldn't talk to me. He wouldn't even look at me. Mommy tried to make things up to him by promising to take us for a ride and maybe, just maybe, if he was good, take us to the fun park that was nearly forty miles away. It would be a full day away. That did put the light back into his eyes.

"But will I ever be able to back into the woods and go fishing?" he asked her.

"Yes, Noble. When I say," she said.

He seemed satisfied, but on the weekend, when we were supposed to go to the fun park, Mommy woke with a very bad cold. It was the first time we had seen her so sick. She had a fever and a cough that made her so tired she had to stay in bed. I made breakfast and lunch, and Noble and I waited on her.

"I'll be better in no time," she promised and fell asleep, sleeping most of the day.

Noble was far more disappointed than I was. He sat on the lowest front step and scratched shapes in the dirt with a stick. Every once in a while he would look out at the woods in the direction of his fort.

"I don't know why I can't go in there," he muttered. "And this is a great day to go fishing. I could catch something for supper. I bet that would change her mind."

"Don't you even think of it," I told him. "Noble?"

"Leave me alone," he said.

I went back inside to see Mommy. She was still sleeping, so I thought about what we would have for dinner. Maybe I could get Noble to help me, I hoped. Maybe that would distract him and keep him from thinking of his fort and his fishing. I went out to tell him, but he was not on the stoop.

"Noble?" I called. I went about the house looking for him, and then I went to the barn. He wasn't there, but my heart stopped and then started.

Where our new fishing poles and tackle

box were kept, his were gone.

My first thought was to go tell Mommy, but I knew she was sleeping, and she would be so upset to hear about Noble doing this, she would get up and maybe get even sicker. I decided instead to go after him and make him come back. He couldn't be too far ahead of me, I imagined, and I knew exactly where we had always gone to fish.

I ran through the forest, paying little regard to the branches and bushes that slapped at my legs and scratched me. I had to find Noble and bring him home before Mommy woke up and asked for him. When I got to the stream, I stopped and looked around. At first, I didn't see him.

"Noble!" I screamed. "Where are you?"

He didn't respond. I walked along the shore. The water was flowing faster and wider than I could ever remember it. It was no longer a bubbling brook. It actually roared as if it was remembering itself when it had been a river. I went upstream a bit and then, after not finding him, ran back downstream until I turned a corner with the creek and saw Noble squatting on a large boulder out in the water. He had obviously followed a trail of smaller rocks out to it. He reached back with his pole and flicked it forward, just the way Mr. Kotes had shown him.

"Noble!" I called.

If he heard me, he ignored me.

"Noble, come back home this instant!" I screamed. He didn't turn around.

I had to go into the water, stepping on rocks toward the boulder. They were like ice because of the glistening water rushing over them.

"Noble!"

Finally he turned around and smirked at me.

"What do you want?"

"You can't stay here. You have to come home now. Mommy doesn't want you here, Noble."

"Go away," he said. "I'm going to catch a big fish and make her happy."

"I'm not going away. You're coming home."

"I'm not," he said defiantly. "Get away."

"I'll drag you home. I swear I will, Noble Atwell. Now come home."

He turned his back on me again. I worked my way closer to him, and this time, when he reached back with his pole to flick his fishing line, I managed to grab hold of the end of the pole. He jerked forward and fell back with surprise.

"Let go!" he shouted.

"No. You come home right now. I'm not getting into trouble because of you." I pulled on the pole, and he pulled back. For a few moments we were in a tug-of-war, which he seemed to relish.

"Stop it, Noble!" I screamed, nearly losing my balance on the smaller rocks.

"No, you let go," he shouted.

He stood up to get more leverage and pulled very hard. The pole began to burn my palms, so I had to release it. When I did so, however, he kept his momentum and fell backward off the rock. I didn't see him for a moment, and then I saw his leg and the rest of him turning in the water. Streaming around his head was a line of crimson. His body hit another boulder and then dipped under the water and came up. For a moment I couldn't move a muscle, and then I screamed and charged through the water toward him.

The ground beneath me seemed to sink, and I was in as deep as my waist. The stream of red looked like it was flowing out of Noble's ear. For a moment he was caught against another boulder, so I thought I would get to him, but then the water just lifted him away and he floated faster and faster downstream, his body bouncing against rocks like a rubber tube.

I kept screaming his name, but he didn't lift his head, nor did he try to stop himself from being carried away. As I went forward, I sank deeper and deeper until the water was up to my neck. It was icy cold, but I didn't really notice. My body was already numb from what I had seen. Unable to go farther, I stopped and watched Noble disappear around another turn. The brook raged on around me, sounding more like it was growling now.

I made my way back to the shore as quickly as I could, and then I stopped, looked down the creek to where I had last seen Noble, before I spun about and charged through the forest, screaming and crying all the way home.

8

Death and Rebirth

Mommy looked like she didn't understand what I was saying. Maybe that was because I screamed it all so fast. She kept her head on the pillow and stared at me in the doorway, her eyes blinking rapidly as if she was trying to decide whether I was real or a dream. I probably looked like a nightmare. I was soaked through and through, dripping on the floor. Finally, she braced herself on her elbows and sat up.

"What did you say, Celeste? Speak slowly. I don't understand you."

I struggled to catch my breath. The words just felt bunched up in the base of my throat, and I couldn't stop crying. All I could do was stand there and shiver. My whole body trembled so hard, I thought I could hear my bones rattling.

"Noble . . . went . . . fishing," I managed.

"What? What did you say? He did what?"

She emerged from under her blanket and found her slippers.

"I want him back here immediately. Why are you soaked?" she asked as she stood up. "Talk!" she screamed and then had a coughing fit.

She spit into a tissue, turned, and charged at me. Her eyes were bloodshot and runny, her face pale. She seized my shoulders and shook and shook while I bawled uncontrollably. Finally, she slapped me hard. My head nearly spun around and my skin stung. I gasped. She rarely, if ever, struck me or Noble like that.

"Talk!"

"He fell off the boulder," I said. Her eyes were so wide now, they looked like two dark tunnels into her brain.

"Fell? What boulder? What do you mean he fell? Where is he? How is he? Tell me quickly," she said shaking me again.

"The big boulder in the creek. He floated away," I said. "He must have hit something when he fell. He was bleeding from the head."

Her mouth held open, and then she threw me aside as if I were a large rag doll. Without thinking about what she was wearing, which was only a nightgown and slippers, she charged out of the bedroom and down the hallway to the stairs. I hurried after her, my body so numb I couldn't feel my feet touching the floor. She nearly fell going down the stairs and caught herself on the bannister. Then she waved her arms about as if she was driving away bats, screamed something I couldn't understand, and lunged for the front door. It wasn't until she was outside and down the porch steps that she paused and looked back for me.

"Take me to him!" she shouted. "Take me to that boulder. Hurry!"

I walked quickly ahead of her.

"Faster!" she ordered, her voice like a whip, and I broke into a run until we were in the woods. For a moment I couldn't remember the direction. It put a panic in me, and I spun around and around. My skirt got caught in some bramble bushes and tore. I fell, but got up instantly.

"Where is he!" Mommy screamed at me.

Desperate, I turned toward an opening and walked faster. A sense of direction returned, and I moved more determinedly toward the roaring sound of the creek. Mommy was right behind me now. When I glanced back at her, I saw her nightgown had been caught on branches and bushes, too, and had a deep rip from her waist across the front of her thighs. She had lost her slippers somewhere behind us and was barefoot. There was already some bleeding about her toes. She was coughing and choking, but she didn't seem to notice or care.

When we reached the creek, I stopped. I immediately realized we were too far up. I plodded along the shoreline, hurrying down toward the big boulder upon which Noble had been sitting.

"He was on that," I said pointing. "Fishing."

"Where is he?" she cried looking about frantically.

"He fell back, and then he floated away," I said. "I tried to get him to come home, but he was stubborn."

I didn't tell her about our tug-of-war with the fishing pole.

"I tried to go after him, but it's too deep in there," I added.

She moved past me and hobbled along the sides of the creek. I followed, imagining how painful it must be for her to step barefoot around the rocks and broken roots. She paused, looked, and listened.

"Which way?"

I just pointed downstream, where I had last seen his body rebounding off rocks that glimmered in the water, their jagged edges now looking more like jagged teeth.

"Noble!" she screamed. "Noble, it's Mommy. Noble, where are you?"

I joined her and screamed his name as well. The biggest crow I had ever seen swooped down from a tree and soared over the creek before threading its way between two tall pine trees and disappearing. Mommy stopped and watched it and then turned to me, her face crumbling in tearful agony.

"No," she said and shook her head. "No." She swung her arms madly again, just as she had done on the stairway. I thought she looked like someone being attacked by bees.

I stood there and searched over the water, combing the shore of the creek until she stopped swinging her arms, turned, and continued. We plodded along, and then suddenly Mommy paused and brought her hands to her mouth, jabbing her fingers so hard between her teeth, her jaw looked like it would crack.

I studied the creek in the direction she was looking and saw him. His body was caught between two large rocks about five or six feet out in the stream. The water was rushing past his legs and making it seem as if he was kicking. His head was turned away from us. I saw his right arm was below the water. Somehow, his fishing pole had followed along and trapped itself in a nearby set of smaller rocks.

"Noble," Mommy muttered and then shouted, "Noble!"

She stepped into the raging creek and slowly made her way to him. I waited on the shore. With the water rushing about her waist, she gently lowered her hand to Noble's face and then she lifted his head out of the water so she could kiss his cheek. I watched her embrace him under the arms and bring him to her, holding him against her. The creek rippled and spun around them as if it impishly had them trapped.

Mommy lifted her head away from Noble and tilted it back to scream his name. Her voice echoed and died in my heart. Coughing harder, but undeterred, she started toward the shore, dragging him along through the water and taking care to keep his head high.

"Mommy?" was all I could manage.

Struggling, she pulled him until he was on the ground. When I went to help, she reached out and slapped at my hands.

"Get away!" she screamed. "Get away!"

I stood aside and sobbed, my legs growing weaker and weaker until I could no longer stand and sat hard on the ground. Mommy hacked and coughed over Noble's body. Finally, I managed to look at his face.

His eyes were open with an expression of surprise. There was a trickle of blood leaking from a gash in his right temple. His mouth was open just enough to show his tongue, which looked blue, but other than that, he looked like he could get up and start complaining about me pulling on his fishing pole and ruining his fishing.

"It's her fault. All of this is her fault!" he would shout and point at me with a finger of accusation.

I truly expected it and waited with my throat tight, my breath trapped below what felt like a rock in my gullet. Mommy would hate me. She would hate me forever and ever.

I stood up when she tried to lift him to his feet, but he was too heavy for her now. She was exhausted, her coughing relentless. Finally, she sat back again.

"Will he be all right, Mommy?" I asked.

She just stared up at me, then she held

him against her breasts again and rocked back and forth, coughing.

I felt as if I had run out of tears. I wiped my face and waited.

"Go back and get the wheelbarrow," she said in a voice without any emotion, a dry, dark voice that didn't at all sound like hers.

I got up quickly and ran through the woods again, taking care to remember exactly where I had left Mommy and Noble. By the time I got to the meadow, I was exhausted, but I found the strength to run to the barn. The wheelbarrow was just inside and to the right. Leaning against it was Noble's magic wand. It stunned me to see it there for a moment because it looked like it was pointing directly at me like that finger of accusation I feared at the creek. I took it away and gently laid it down before pulling the wheelbarrow out of the barn.

It wasn't easy manipulating it through the forest. I got stuck a few times and had to break through brush and saplings, but finally, after what seemed like hours and hours to me, but was probably only ten or fifteen minutes, I broke out on the shore of the creek.

I saw that Mommy had dragged Noble up farther.

"Here!" she screamed, and I rolled the wheelbarrow to her.

She scooped Noble under his arms and lifted. I went to lift his legs.

"Don't touch him!" she shouted at me.

I practically fell over backward jerking myself away. She coughed and struggled, but managed to get him into the wheelbarrow. Then she turned toward the forest and grabbed the handles. I stood there, waiting for her instructions.

"Go in front," she said. "Find the clearest way. Quickly!" she screamed.

I rushed into the woods and waited. It was very, very hard for her to roll that wheelbarrow over the rough ground, the stumps, and the tree roots. She never stopped coughing. Once she let me help her push the wheelbarrow over a ridge, but then she ripped me away from it.

"Just lead," she ordered, and I continued, searching for every opening.

Finally we managed to battle our way through until we had reached the edge of the meadow.

"Go get the wheelchair," she told me in a coarse whisper. "It will be more comfortable for him. Hurry."

I ran to the rear of the house, where she had stored it in the pantry. It had to be unfolded, and then I wheeled it as fast as I could to where she waited in the meadow. Noble's legs dangled over the end of the wheelbarrow. Mommy tipped it slowly toward her and again scooped him under his arms. She held him up enough to turn and lower him into the wheelchair. Then she carefully arranged for his legs and feet to fit. His head fell to the side, his eyes still open and now, it seemed, fixed on me. He looked like he was smiling madly, happy that I would bear the blame for all of this. I had to turn away.

"Put the wheelbarrow back," Mommy told me and started for the house.

I grabbed the wheelbarrow handles and followed her across the meadow.

I could hear her talking now between her coughs.

"Why did you go fishing when I told you not to? I'm going to have to lock you in your room again. You disobeyed me. I told you I would keep you locked up all summer. I might just do that now. How can I trust you ever again?

"Fishing," she continued and coughed. "Why is fishing so important? Boys are so foolish. Your father is going to be very upset with you and very, very upset with Celeste. He may never appear for her again," she added, which brought me to a complete stop.

Why did she say that? Did she know about our struggle with the fishing pole? Had he managed to tell her?

"We have lots to do," she said as she moved farther away, "lots to do."

I watched her go to the side of the house and then around to the rear before I continued toward the barn. When I got there, I put Noble's magic wand back where he had placed it. Of all the things I had heard Mommy say, the one that disturbed me the most was that Daddy would be upset with me and never come to me again. Hadn't I tried to bring Noble home? Wasn't that what I was supposed to do? I didn't mean for him to fall. I didn't know my letting go would ruin his balance on the boulder. Why would Daddy be upset with me? It wasn't fair. None of this was fair.

I walked very slowly to the house. I was actually afraid of going inside and hesitated on the porch steps. Luckily, it had become a warm spring day. I just barely noticed being soaked to the skin, and I was no longer shivering through and through. I was exhausted, perhaps too tired to shiver. The scrapes and scratches on my legs burned, but for some reason, I didn't mind it. I almost welcomed pain. It was bringing me back to life.

Some teenager beeped his horn loudly and continuously as he and his friends rode by on the highway. I could hear their shouts and laughter, too. It was something teenagers had been doing for quite a while now. They thought it was funny, I suppose. All sorts of stories continued to be spread about us in the village. I watched the car disappear around a turn, and then I walked up to the front door and entered.

For a moment I just stood there listening. At first I heard nothing, and then I heard Mommy upstairs. I waited until she appeared on the stairway. She had her arms filled with Noble's wet clothing.

"Look at you," she said. "Go into my bedroom and take off those clothes. Then take a hot shower immediately. Do not disturb your brother."

My heart leaped for joy. Disturb him? That sounded so good to my ears. I would never again disturb him. I vowed I would never complain about him teasing me either. He could order me all over the farm, if he liked. I wouldn't care. I'd pretend anything he wanted me to pretend, and I'd play any game he wanted to play, no matter how silly or childish.

"He's going to be all right then?" I asked quickly.

"We'll see," she said, continuing down the stairs. She coughed when she reached the bottom and leaned against the banister for a moment.

"Do you want me to help you, Mommy?" I asked.

"No," she said quickly. "Just do what I say," she told me and walked to the laundry room.

I looked up the stairway. He must have regained consciousness as soon as she brought him into the house, I thought. How wonderful. Most important, Daddy wouldn't be angry at me and never, ever show his spirit again. We'll be all right after all.

I went up, pausing at Noble's and my bedroom door to listen. I heard nothing. Of course he's sleeping, I thought. Mommy might have given him one of her herbal drinks, too. Hurrying along, I went into her bedroom, took off my wet clothing, and went into a hot shower as she had ordered. When I came out, I saw she had put my clothing on her bed. I dried off quickly and got dressed. When I descended the stairs, I found her in the kitchen, working on dinner. Her hair hung down limply, and she looked so worn, so exhausted.

I saw she had the ingredients out to prepare a meat loaf, and I knew just how to do it now. The last few times we made it, she had let me do most of the work.

"You're sick, Mommy, and more tired than I am, I'm sure. Let me do that," I said.

She shook her head.

"I have to be the one to make him dinner," she insisted. "Just set the table for the two of us. Go on. Do it," she commanded, and I went ahead and did what she asked.

A little while later, I saw her prepare a tray and start for the stairway. Everything on the tray was covered, I imagined to keep it warm.

"Should I bring that up for you, Mommy?" I asked.

She didn't seem to hear me, or if she had, she didn't want to answer. Like someone in a trance, she walked down the hallway, her eyes so still. I watched her go upstairs and waited, listening to her go into Noble's and my room. She didn't come out for quite a while. I finally went to the dining room, where I sat and waited for her. Finally, she came downstairs. Once again, she looked to me like she was walking in her sleep. I got up and followed her into the kitchen, where she went through all the motions to set out our dinner, but she really did nothing.

She opened the stove, took out the meat loaf pot, took off the cover, and put nothing on a large plate because there was nothing in the pot. Then she uncovered another pot and scooped out nothing into another dish before turning to me.

"Put the meat loaf and the string beans on the table while I mash the potatoes," she told me.

I stood there staring.

"Do it now before everything gets cold!"

"But —"

She turned away and started to mash potatoes in a bowl, only there was nothing in the bowl. As she worked, she coughed, sniffed, and wiped her eyes. She took deep breaths and kept herself hovering over the counter with her back to me. I didn't know what to do, so I took the empty dishes into the dining room and put them on the table. Then I sat and waited. Except for the sound of her tapping fork on the inside of an empty bowl in the kitchen, I heard nothing. Our house was so quiet. The pipes didn't groan, the walls didn't creak.

It was as if the house was holding its breath, too.

After a minute or so more, she came hurriedly into the dining room, carrying the bowl. She dipped a serving spoon in it and slapped air on my empty plate.

"Start eating without me," she said. "Don't let everything get cold. I'm not hungry."

She returned to the kitchen. I sat there, not sure what I should do. I wanted to cry, but I was afraid to utter a sound. I snuffed down my sobs and sat waiting to see what she would do next or what she wanted me to do next.

Suddenly, she burst back into the dining room, this time with her hands over her ears.

"I can't stand the humming. Do you hear it?" she asked.

"No, Mommy," I said, my lips trembling. I couldn't help myself. I started to cry again.

"I've got to go upstairs. I've got to get some rest. I want you to clean up when you're finished, and put everything away. Fix the sofa in the living room for yourself tonight. And keep quiet, keep as quiet as you can," she whispered, her eyes wide. "Do you understand? Do you?"

I nodded quickly. She didn't even notice I was crying.

"Good," she said, straightening up. "Good."

Then she walked through the dining room and out to the hallway. I heard her going up the stairway. For a while I just sat at the table. I was still too frightened to move a muscle. Finally, I rose slowly and took the empty plates back into the kitchen.

Except for putting the meat loaf ingredients back into the pantry, there was nothing else for me to do. I really wasn't very hungry myself, just thirsty, so I poured myself some orange juice, washed the glass, put it away, and went into the living room to fix the sofa. Afterward, I sat and listened for Mommy, but I never heard her moving around. I thought she might have fallen asleep.

My curiosity about Noble was too strong to contain. I went to the stairway, listened, and then when I thought it was safe enough, walked quietly up to the door of our bedroom. I tried the knob, but found it was locked.

"What are you doing?" I heard. It didn't sound at all like Mommy, but when I turned she was standing there in her bedroom doorway, and she was totally naked. "Well?"

"I just . . . I wanted to . . ."

"Go to sleep!" she ordered. "Didn't I tell you to stay quiet? It's important. Do it!"

She stepped forward threateningly, so I turned and hurriedly descended the stairs. I went into the living room and stood listening, my heart pounding. The lights went out above. I went to my pullout sofa bed and sat until I was tired enough to close my eyes and lie back. I didn't fall asleep quickly. I listened to every sound in the house because now it was creaking again and the wind threaded its way through every small opening in the roof and shutters. Finally, mercifully, sleep took me prisoner, and I, like an exhausted combatant, surrendered without delay.

Spirits swirled around me like the water in the creek. My dreams tossed and turned me. I felt hands on me and muttered for Mommy, but I didn't wake up fully.

I fell back into the raging water of my twisted nightmares, where I was carried off into a darker and darker place.

The morning light woke me, and for a long moment, I really didn't remember why I was sleeping in the living room. My body ached in places it had never ached. My empty stomach rumbled. I took a breath and sat up, grinding the traces of sleep out of my eyes. When I pulled my hands away, I gasped and felt as if I had just swallowed a spoonful of pure ice.

Mommy was standing in the doorway, her face nearly as white as milk. She was dressed in black, the same dress she had worn for Daddy's funeral and the day after Mr. Kotes had been killed. Her lips were caught in a crooked smile. The way she was looking at me frightened me.

"Mommy?" I said and nearly burst into tears.

"Your sister is gone," she said. "She has been taken from us to live with our ancestors and her father. We can do nothing but accept it."

"What?" I asked, puzzled over her remark.

"You must come outside with me now," she said. "We're going to say good-bye to her body. You remember," she added, now smiling nicely, "the cup and the water?"

"Outside?"

"Yes, follow me now," she said. "Come along."

She turned and went to the front door. I slipped my shoes back on quickly and stood up. I had fallen asleep in my clothing.

She waited at the open door. I saw she had our old family Bible in her hands. What was all this? Why did she say "your sister"?

As soon as she saw me, she walked out. I followed behind, moving slowly, as slowly as she was moving. As she turned toward the old cemetery, she began to chant something I didn't recognize at all. Then she stopped, lit a candle she was carrying, and carefully, so as to keep the flame from going out, cupped it and continued toward the cemetery. At the gate, she lifted the candle, let the wind snuff out the small flame, but then waved the smoke around her.

I watched everything she did with my eyes so wide my forehead folded in pain. The moment she stepped through the gate, I started and stopped.

So did my heart.

There was an open grave right beside Infant Jordan's. When had she dug that? She had to have done it during the night when I was asleep.

"Quickly," she said, turning toward me. "Under the smoke," she indicated, nodding at where she had twirled the candle.

My feet were in mutiny. They didn't want to obey, but I forced myself to walk into the cemetery and stand beside her. Every part of me was trembling.

"We've come to say our final good-bye, Noble," she told me, and she nodded toward the open grave.

Why was she calling me Noble?

I stepped up to the grave.

I will never forget that moment. The scream that began inside me nearly blew out my eardrums, because I did not utter it. I was too shocked, too frightened. Nothing that had happened to me before and nothing that has happened to me since will ever clap thunder as loud, singe the sky with fire as hot and bright, burn through my heart or capture and hold my breath as long as this.

There in the grave lay my brother, Noble . . . dressed in my clothes, wearing my shoes and my amulet.

She had somehow taken it off me during the night, and it wasn't until that very moment that I noticed I was wearing his talisman instead of my own. In my clothes, with a bonnet on his head that I hadn't worn for years, he truly did look like me. I did feel like I was gazing down at myself.

"Good-bye, Celeste," Mommy whispered. "Now you must join our ancestors and walk with them. You must have become so worthy in their eyes. I can be only happy for you for that, and of course, now you will keep Daddy company. How lonely he must have been to let this happen to you."

She turned to me and smiled softly.

"Your brother wants to say good-bye, too," she said, looking at me. "Go on, Noble," she urged. "Don't be afraid. She can hear you for a little while longer. Go on."

I gazed down at him and then at her. She was still smiling and waiting. What was I supposed to say?

"Mommy —"

"Just say good-bye to your sister, Noble. Sleep well. Go on. Say it," she instructed.

I looked at my brother, and then I muttered a good-bye.

Mommy opened her Bible and began to read.

"The Lord is my shepherd . . ."

I listened, unable to move, practically unable to breathe. Every time I looked down at him, I grew dizzy. The clouds above seemed to spin and spin, dropping lower and lower, coming at me. Her voice droned on. I could hear the wind in the trees. The clouds continued to drop.

Suddenly, all was black.

I awoke in my bed, or what I thought was my bed. When I gazed around, I realized I was in Noble's bed. My head felt different, too. I brought my hands to it and quickly realized that my hair had been cut. Then I looked down at myself and saw I was wearing Noble's shirt and pants. I sat up quickly, and just as I did, Mommy appeared in the doorway, a tray in her hands. This time it had a cup of herbal tea on it and two pieces of toast with her homemade blueberry jam.

"Now, there you are," she said setting the tray down on the nightstand and then pulling a chair up to the bed. "Sit up, Noble," she said and fixed the pillow behind me.

"Mommy, why am I wearing Noble's clothing, and why did you cut my hair?" I asked.

"She was very close to them, Noble," she replied instead of answering me. "I knew in my heart she would be taken. That's why they appeared to her so soon. We should be grateful for the time we had with her. No one else will understand. I know that. You know how these people around us can be. It has to be our secret, my darling. Our secret."

"But . . . I'm Celeste," I said.

"No, no. You must be your brother forever and ever now. It's what they want, what they expect. Every day you will understand more and more. You will hear the spirits telling you what I am telling you. You will hear them just as I do. You will know I am right.

"If you betray them, if you disobey, the evil spirits will take you as well, but you will not be with your father, for you failed to protect your brother's spirit, so you must *take* his spirit into you. You must *be* his spirit. Noble must not be gone," she added. "It wasn't his time. It was Celeste's time. That's what we now know."

She reached for the tray.

"Eat and drink some tea," she said, smiling lovingly. "I need you to be strong again. We have much to do together, Noble."

I stared at her, but she continued to smile.

"I will never again call you anything but Noble, and you must never again answer to any other name. To abandon this destiny is to condemn yourself to the darkness and the fire, to be forever in a place where there is no love, no hope. Ugly in, beauty out, forever and ever," she said. "Go on, eat, sip your tea, get well, and then we will begin."

Begin what? I wondered.

It was as if she could read my thoughts.

"Begin your rebirth," she said and rose slowly. "We'll have to contend with the outsiders for a while. They would never be able to understand us, so we must tell them things they will be able to understand. After that they'll be gone from our lives, and we will be able to continue, just as always," she said, smiling, and continued walking toward the doorway.

She turned back to me, her smile deeper, brighter.

"Guess what I've done," she said. "To cheer you up."

I couldn't speak. All I did was shake my head.

"I've brought out the trains again," she said. "When you're ready, you can go downstairs and play with them, okay?"

Her smile faded.

"We'll miss her, Noble. We'll miss Celeste very badly, but we'll have to content ourselves with the knowledge that she is with spirits who want and love her dearly. She is in a happy place. She'll forever walk beside her daddy.

"As you will someday, and as I will, too. Don't you see?" she said anxiously. "I've found a way to keep us together."

She turned and walked out. I heard her descending the stairs slowly, and finally, I released the breath that had been locked in my lungs.

I looked over at what was my bed. I almost expected to see myself there. How strange it felt to be looking at it this way, I thought.

I got out of the bed and immediately stopped to look at the mirror on the wall. My hair was Noble's length, and in his clothing, I did not see myself. I saw him.

It was as if he had been standing beside me and suddenly slipped into me, and I was gone, to be replaced by him. I would be Noble. Mommy had said it was my destiny, and I knew destiny was something you couldn't prevent, you couldn't change.

But why was it so?

As if I knew exactly what he would say, I glanced at my bed and then back at the mirror.

"It was her fault," I said to the image of Celeste sinking in the mirror. "If she hadn't pulled on the fishing rod, I wouldn't have fallen. This is right. Mommy is right.

"It's what has to be.

"Forever."

And like someone closing a book, I turned my back on what had been my side of the room and drank the tea and ate the toast Mommy had brought up for Noble.

For me.

And then I went downstairs to play with the trains.

9

Celeste Is Gone

Mommy asked me to help her plant grass over the newly dug grave. For as long as I could remember, she had taken tender loving care of the old cemetery, not only weeding, but scraping the mold off the stones and the walls. She told me many times that it was our sacred responsibility to do so, for the heart of her family, our family, lie buried there. She said the spirits that hovered about our home often gathered together there and sang hymns. If I listened carefully to the wind as it circled our house at night, I could hear their sweet, melodic voices. She revealed that often now, especially since Daddy's death, she went out there in the evening and joined them. She promised me she would wake me next time and take me out with her to sing at the graves of our precious ancestors.

I raked the earth, planted the seeds, and

watered them. There was to be no marker with CELESTE written upon it, however, which made me happy.

"We cannot ever reveal anyone else is buried here, Noble," Mommy told me as we worked. "They wouldn't understand, and that's why we must make this earth look unturned. It will always be our secret to be guarded with our very lives. Put your hand upon the earth above our precious dearly departed and swear with me to keep this secret locked in your heart forever and ever. Swear," she said and fell to her knees.

I did, too, and we put our palms on the cool, fresh ground. Mommy recited the pledge.

"We shall never tell anyone ever that Celeste is here," she recited with her eyes closed. "I swear."

"I swear," I followed, and she smiled at me and leaned over to kiss me and run her fingers through my hair.

"My precious Noble, my beautiful Noble," she said.

I had never seen her look at me with such love and admiration. Despite everything, I couldn't help but feel my heart fill with joy, even with the strange new lessons that followed nightly for days and days.

"This is truly your rebirth," she began

after sitting me down in the living room. "It will take time, maybe as long as a baby takes, nine months, maybe even a little longer, but now that Noble's spirit is in you, eventually you will become as Noble was meant to be. You will be so successful that even your daddy will recognize your spirit as Noble's spirit. He will be so proud of you," she promised. "When you see him again, he will have a father's pride written all over his face."

How wonderful. My father would love me, and my mother would love me as she had never loved me, I thought. I thought about it every night, and especially in the way her voice filled with bells and music whenever she spoke to me now, or called to me. She had never embraced me or kissed me as much. The happiness in her eyes fed my own. She even seemed to grow younger and more beautiful as I grew taller and stronger.

"Let us begin," she said the very night after Celeste's burial, for I had come to think of it that way. It was what Mommy wanted, what the spirits wanted. "From now on, you must never, ever let anyone see you naked," Mommy warned. "Keeping you here in home schooling will make that so much easier. You see that now, don't you? You won't ask me constantly when you are going to public school anymore, right?"

"No, Mommy," I said.

"Good."

"Boys have a rougher edge," she continued. "I really don't mind your love of insects, your collection of dead things."

I swallowed hard. I minded it.

"In time, of course, I would expect you to focus yourself on more important things, Noble. A boy must become a man. You must assume more responsibility. Your day will be filled with more serious work and less playtime. We have a lot to do here together. There is just the two of us now, and I will depend upon you to help with the harder chores. It will take much more strength than you have shown in the past, but you will grow if you listen to me. Will you?"

There was nothing in her face that revealed she did not really see Noble in me when she looked at me now. Sometimes, when she spoke, I listened for hesitation, but there was never any. She looked at me just the way she had always looked at Noble. I had envied him for that, and now it was mine, forever and ever, my mother's eyes were mine.

"Yes, Mommy," I said. "I will listen. I promise."

"Good."

She reached out and took my hands into hers, turning them palms up.

"Your hands will get tougher, rougher, too, Noble. Don't be afraid of calluses. Calluses protect your hands from the pain of hard work. Remember how rough Daddy's hands were and how strong?"

I nodded.

"Yours will be like that. Don't be worried about skin lotions, and don't try to be like me," she warned. "Boys don't think of such things for some time, and you're rapidly approaching that age when things begin to be different, so different between boys and girls.

"Anyway," she said, "I want you to know that for now it's all right for you to go back into the forest and finish your fort. Your childhood days are limited, and you should be able to get the most out of them. I know how precious those memories will be to you when you're older and mature and unable to do things like that anymore.

"Try to recall all the stories your daddy told you about himself when he was a little boy. Remember how much he enjoyed reminiscing and describing the things he had done?"

"Yes," I said, smiling at that memory.

"Well, it will be the same for you. Oh, there is so much for you to learn, Noble, so much to know and be aware of so you don't make mistakes, especially with people who could never understand us, appreciate us. We don't need them barking at our heels, peeping through fences, whispering about us," she said with anger tightening her lips and filling her eyes with bright new rage. "Fortunately, as you know, I was a schoolteacher for a long time. I know about boys and girls better than most mothers know about them, and I will always be here to help you. So you need not worry. Okay, my darling?"

She ran her fingers through my hair, mussing it. I started to fix it, and she stopped me.

"Don't worry so much about your looks yet, Noble. Boys get dirtier, more messy, and don't think about it until they are older and think about the way they look to girls. You're not going to be a Little Lord Fauntleroy. Arthur Atwell's son will never be called a sissy, never," she pledged.

"When I was studying to be a teacher, I studied what is called the gender differences. Gender is another word for sexual differences. Boys hate to be compared to girls, to be thought too much like a girl, but girls aren't as frightened of it, and do you know why?"

I shook my head.

"Boys in general are more aggressive, more competitive. It's why men still make more money than women in this country and why women have a harder time being successful. Women aren't supposed to be tough, relentless, ruthless, which are often things people must be to claw their way to the top. See? I even said 'claw.' Most women don't want to claw. Most women don't want to break their fingernails."

She looked at my hands.

"I've got to cut yours back, I see. Okay, enough of this lecture for now. Go on out and work on your fort. I'll be by later to see how you're doing."

I really wasn't sure what to do exactly, but I went out to the barn and located the tools I had seen Noble use. The walls of the fort were not quite complete. There was a pile of wood slats beside what had been done, so I began to fit them on the shell Noble had built. I worked for hours, and when I stepped back, I noticed that my slats were put on more neatly and evenly. I was thinking about it so hard and remembering my brother so much, I didn't realize Mommy had been standing behind me for a while.

"Stop worrying so much about how pretty it is," she suddenly said, and I spun around. "It's just a little boy's imaginary fortress in the woods, Noble. Get it done," she said, and I saw that it had become more important to her than it had ever been to my brother.

I went back to work, and a little while later, I caught a splinter in my palm. It hurt, so I threw down the hammer and went to the house. Mommy was sitting in the living room in her great-grandpa Jordan's rocking chair, staring out the window and moving back and forth very gently. She heard me come in, but kept looking out the window.

"What is it, Noble?" she asked.

"I got a splinter," I said.

"So? You've gotten splinters before, and you kept working because you were afraid I'd tell you to stop building your fort, remember? Remember how I saw them only when you got into your bath and I lectured you about infections? Remember?"

I started to shake my head, but she turned to me sharply, and I stopped.

"Yes."

"Go back to your fort. I'll call you when it's time to have dinner," she said.

It was on the tip of my tongue to ask if she wanted me to help, to set the table at least, but she anticipated it.

"Without Celeste now, I will do everything in the kitchen, and I will set the table. You were never good at it, Noble. You broke one of my pieces of china, an heirloom, remember? You were always a bit clumsy, Noble, but boys are more clumsy. Don't worry about it. It's expected," she added and turned back to the window.

"There's a lull out there," she said. It seemed like she was talking to herself more than she was talking to me now. "So much has happened. Everyone has retreated for a while. But don't worry. They will return. Everything will be fine again soon when they see we're doing exactly what we were told to do. Don't worry," she whispered.

I thought about it. Was that why I didn't feel or see any spirits?

I looked at my splinter, and then I went back to the fort and continued, not really doing all that much before she called me to dinner. Only then did she help me get the splinter out of my hand. I didn't cry about it, but she talked to me as if I were crying.

"Boys are such babies. Actually, they never stop being babies. Even when they're men, grown, they need to be treated with tender loving care much more than women do. You hate to hear it, I know, but women are actually stronger than men, especially when it comes to endurance, Noble. Women endure. They are the ones who give birth, you know. Men stand by and grimace, giving thanks they are not having the labor pains. This splinter is nothing. Most women would gladly endure a splinter rather than give birth, believe me. There," she said. "See? It's all over. Wipe away your tears and wash your hands. It's time for dinner," she told me, even though I had no tears. I pretended I did and went to wash my hands.

Dinner was the most lonely time of all for me. I never stopped expecting my brother to appear and take his seat. I missed the way he squirmed or complained about having too many vegetables.

"You're eating too fast as usual," Mommy told me. I had barely started, but it was something she always said to Noble. "Take your time and chew every mouthful. Your poor stomach will complain if you don't," she warned.

How many times had I heard her say that to him? I actually looked at his chair, and then Mommy, not realizing it until that very moment, practically leaped out of hers.

"Noble!" she cried.

I held my breath.

"What?"

"You're sitting in your sister's chair. It's not right to do that. Get back into your own seat immediately. Go on," she ordered.

I looked at my plate and Noble's chair and rose slowly. It was very hard to do it, to sit in his seat. I hesitated. Mommy leaned toward me, her hands on the table.

"You have to do this," she said in a whisper. "You have to do it all."

I sat, and she put my plate of food in front of me.

"Gobble your food," she said. "Go on."

I started to eat fast, and then she stopped me.

"Please, eat slowly. I told you. Someday you'll have to eat with more people, and you want to be polite, don't you, Noble? You don't want people to think you were brought up in a pigsty." She smiled. "Remember when Daddy used to tell you how his mother chastised him at the dinner table? If he didn't eat slowly, he would have to eat a second dinner. That's what he said. Of course, I didn't believe that. Not for a moment. Half an ear, remember? That was what he told you children. Half an ear," she muttered.

She sat again and sighed.

"Once there was so much joy around this table. I wonder if there will ever be as much again."

She ate in small bites, pecking at her food like a sick bird. When we were finished, I started to reach for a plate, and she cried out.

"Don't touch anything. Go play with your trains or look for night crawlers," she told me. "You want to go fishing again, don't you?"

The very thought of it put an electric fear into my bones. I started to shake my head.

"Of course you do. You must. It's part of what I need you to do. You'll understand later," she promised. "Go on. You're excused from the table, Noble," she concluded, waving her hand at me.

I rose and walked out. Noble would take his flashlight and search around the house for worms. He'd pluck them and drop them in his empty coffee can. He would tease me and call them pieces of spaghetti, which made it hard for me to eat real spaghetti when Mommy served it. I stood there for the longest time, and then I put my hands in my pants pockets and brought my right hand out quickly. What was that?

Gingerly, I put my hand back in and brought it out. It was the dried remains of a dead snail. My stomach churned, but I caught hold of myself when I turned and saw Mommy peering out of the living room front window curtain, watching me. I quickly went to find the coffee can and, swallowing back my reluctance, began to pluck night crawlers with as much glee as I could manage.

Mommy was smiling.

For her, every day that passed with me doing the things that Noble had done was another day confirming that Noble was indeed coming back. Mommy felt it when she saw the dirt on my face, the sores on my hands, the tears in my jeans, and the mud on my shoes. My completion of the fort in the woods was a crowning achievement. She talked about it as if I had built one of Daddy's wonderful houses.

"You do take after your father," she said. "You've inherited his penchant for construction. The next house you build will be even better. I always knew you'd be good with your hands. You're mechanically inclined. You draw well. You have that vision," she continued.

How would I ever draw as well as my brother had, or at least good enough to please her? I wondered. When I tried to draw some of the things he had, they came out terrible, but Mommy didn't see it that way. She raved about my sketches just the way she always did when my brother made them. Was she blind to my awkward lines, or did she really see something good in them?

She was right about the calluses coming, just the way they had come to Noble's hands. The roughness was distasteful to me at first, and then I did get used to it. I swung my hammer better, drove nails in faster, and worked with a saw without the fear I used to have of cutting myself. Mommy had me chopping wood and showed me how to split logs to prepare them for the coming winter, when we would use them in our fireplace. It was very hard work. Most nights, I ached terribly and wanted nothing more than to soak in a hot tub, but she told me to just shower quickly and get to bed.

"You don't soften yourself. You toughen yourself," she said. "There will be harder things for you to do in the coming days and weeks, months, and years, and you'll thank me for helping you get stronger and stronger."

Sometimes I would lie in bed and think about my beautifully scented soaps, especially the gift packages of them Daddy had bought me. I would go into Mommy's room and stare at everything on her vanity table like some beggar staring through a bakery window at the fresh loaves. I longed to lift a brush and run it through my hair the way I used to, but Mommy kept my hair very short. There was actually nothing to brush anyway.

One night she caught me in there, smelling the scent of her cologne, and she screamed from the doorway.

"What are you doing? Don't touch my things!" she snapped and marched in to rip the bottle from my hands.

"I'm sorry, Mommy. I just wanted —"

"Tomorrow, I'll go into town and buy you some of the men's cologne your father used to use. You like that smell, don't you?"

"Yes."

"Good." She squeezed my upper arm. "Good," she said. "You're firmer. Good."

She made me leave the room and go work on my school problems. Ironically, if I did them as quickly as I used to do them, she was upset. She tried hard to find things wrong and picked on the smallest mistakes, demanding me to write things over or redo math problems, even if I got them all right.

"You didn't do them correctly. It was just luck," she said.

"Do it again."

I began to realize that I was better off working slower, making deliberate mistakes, and not writing as neatly as I could. It pleased her.

"You'll get it eventually," she would say as she had always said to Noble. "Just keep at it."

If I completed a reading assignment, I couldn't reveal it. When she looked in on me, I had to flip the pages back and pretend I was only up to the middle. She would smile and encourage me to concentrate.

"It's usually more difficult for boys than it is for girls until after puberty," she explained. "For some reason, boys do better then, and more often than not, girls don't do as well."

She paused and nodded at me, her eyes getting that far-off look she often had when she was sitting in the rocker or on the chintz sofa and looking out the window.

"It's good," she said. "You're doing well. I'm sure they will be pleased with both of us. I'm sure they will return to us, and we'll be safe again, safer than any of those skeptics and busybodies out there."

Except for the postman, who had seen me chopping wood and watched me for a few moments, and the fuel oil delivery man, no one from what Mommy now called the outside world saw me. In time they would have to, I thought. I would have to go take the test for my progress at home school, at least, not to mention accompanying Mommy when she went shopping, even when she went far away. It made me nervous to think about it. Would they see Noble or Celeste when they looked at me, and how would that affect Mommy? More important, how would it affect our spiritual family?

It wasn't until the grass had thickened over the newly dug grave to the extent that a stranger could not look at it and tell any difference that Mommy finally decided to call me into the living room one night to tell me her plan for dealing with the "nosy, ignorant community."

"I want you to go fishing tomorrow, Noble," she began. "I want you to go with Celeste."

I looked at her, my face heavy with confusion. She smiled.

"The two of you scrunch your eyebrows the same way. I told Celeste many times she would develop two deep wrinkles and regret it someday."

She sighed.

"Someday. What a word that is," she rambled. "It's full of so much hope, so much promise. It trails off ahead of us, floats around us, brightens our darkest moments. We can always turn to it to pull ourselves out of our quicksand of doldrums. Someday this, someday that. Well, it works almost always. We can't really do that now, can we? It's far, far too late for that," she said, thought a moment, and then cleared her throat and sat firmer.

What did she mean by "go with Celeste"?

"You will go with your sister. You will get separated. And you will come running home to me when you can't find her late in the day. Take her pole. Where is yours?" she asked, and my eyes widened. "Well?"

"It was in the creek, Mommy," I said. I almost said, "Remember?"

She thought a moment and then nodded to herself.

"That's fine, I suppose. They'll find it."

"Who?"

"The search party," she said. "The police will be here, and they will question you and me in great detail, so we'll talk about it now. I've been thinking about it for a long time, as you can imagine, and I know exactly what you will say.

"Oh, don't you see, my darling boy, how important this all is? Stop grimacing like that. I've told you many, many times about these people around us, how they talk about us, think about us. They would never understand us, never believe anything but their own stupid, nasty thoughts.

"We have to do this now. Soon there would be questions, otherwise. I have reports to turn in, and there is always the possibility of a visit from the school, you know. That interfering know-it-all, Dr. Camfield, would just love to pounce on me, especially now that Taylor is gone and no longer any threat to him.

"But all of that is not important. We have a life to live here, and we don't want people snooping about forever, now do we, my precious?" she asked, running her hand over my hair and down my cheek. I closed my eyes to keep the pleasant loving touch forever and ever locked in my heart. I had longed so for that so many, many times and watched with envy as she caressed

Noble and not me.

"Do we?" she repeated.

"No."

"Good. Right. Okay. You and Celeste will go off in the morning to fish. You will decide to separate. You go upstream. She'll go downstream, below that horrible boulder. Midday, you will come running home to tell me you can't find her. She didn't meet you where she was supposed to meet you. We'll go look for her. We'll find the fishing rod, and then I'll call the police," she continued.

It sounded like a story I would read in one of the books in our library.

"Why did you split up with your sister?" she asked, pretending to be a policeman.

"What?"

"Why didn't you fish together?"

"She talks too much," I said, and she smiled.

"Yes, that's right. That's true. Very good."

I loved when Mommy appreciated me. I went on.

"And she doesn't like to fish all that much. I thought she was just going to go off and find a place and read one of her books, like she has done many times before, and I didn't care. I wanted to fish."

"Excellent. And when she didn't show up, what did you do?"

"I ran about, shouting for her, until I thought she might have gone home without me."

"That's very clever, Noble. Very clever," she said, smiling, with appreciation lighting her eyes. I felt good basking in that glow.

"But when I got home . . ."

"She wasn't here. Exactly. So we both went looking, and —" she encouraged, gesturing for something more.

"We found the rod but not her. Where is she?"

"Where is she?" she mimicked. "Celeste . . . my Celeste . . . I hate to think of the horrible possibilities. . . . Someone . . . did you see someone?"

"No, but I thought I heard someone once. I even thought I heard a scream, but I couldn't tell. The stream is so noisy these days."

"Yes, it is."

She smiled again and leaned over to kiss my cheek.

"And," she said, "we found her shoe, didn't we?"

"Her shoe?"

"Exactly. One shoe, just one shoe." She sat back, a look of contentment on her face, and nodded. "They will never bother us after this," she said. "Never."

That night when I went to sleep, I dreamed the story just as Mommy and I had told it. I saw myself walking into the woods with . . . with Celeste. It was so strange at first to turn and see her traipsing behind me, her head down, hearing her mumble complaints about the bushes, the effort to get through the forest, the dirty job of putting a worm on a hook.

"You're going to do it for me, Noble," she said. "Or I won't go along. And don't tell me it doesn't hurt them. They bleed, don't they?"

"You're so stupid, Celeste," I told her.

"I am not!" she whined, and I smiled. It was fun to tease her. It had always been fun.

"Why don't you just ask your spirits to put the worm on the hook for you?" I threw back at her. He had said that. I remembered it well.

"I told you. They don't do things like that, and Mommy's told you, too. Someday when you see them, you'll understand."

Someday . . . someday . . . someday . . . Promises drifting like white ribbons through the darkness of my sleep, leading me into the light of morning.

Mommy was jubilant in the morning. She was singing one of her happier old songs. She had prepared Noble's favorite breakfast: blueberry pancakes with maple syrup and little sausages. The aroma was tantalizing, which surprised me. I was never that fond of the sausages. Sometimes they upset my stomach, but this morning, I had a big appetite.

"Now, I'm holding you to your prediction today, Noble," she told me as she put out the breakfast and poured my orange juice. "You're bringing home our dinner. And I don't want to hear about any arguments between you and your sister. You two behave. I have fixed you peanut butter and jelly sandwiches, and there's chocolate milk in the thermos. Share it evenly. I don't want to hear, He drank it all and didn't give me any. I'm warning you," she said, wagging her finger at me.

I ate as much as I could, surprised at how much I did eat, and then I rose, took the lunch pail, and walked to the front door. The fishing rod, which was really Celeste's, was in the foyer with the can of fresh worms. Mommy kissed me in the doorway and told us to be careful.

"I love you both!" she cried as I walked toward the woods.

My heart was thumping hard and fast. I hadn't been back to the creek since that day, of course. I feared the sight of it, the sound of it. As I stepped through the bushes and pushed aside any branches that grew over the pathway we always followed, I heard Mommy telling the story again, how she had prepared a wonderful breakfast for us, how we had gone out together, excited, full of energy, Celeste looking particularly bright and beautiful, her hair gleaming in the sunlight.

"I'll never forget the way it danced around her face, that sunlight, my precious little girl," Mommy said with tearful eyes. I cried myself.

As I listened to her speak in my mind, I could hear a second set of footsteps just behind me. I paused.

"Catch up," I cried. "I don't want to take all day to get to the creek."

He had said that, so many times before, he had said that.

I walked on and found the spot from which Daddy and Mr. Kotes had shown us how to fish. I set down the lunch box and reached into the can of worms. A small pool of revulsion started at the base of my stomach and then quickly disappeared. I had a thick nightcrawler between my fingers. It squirmed slightly, nearly dead already.

Carefully, with more expertise than I imagined I had, I threaded the hook through it until it was perfectly secure, and then I tossed the fish line into the creek and sat on a rock. Celeste was bored quickly, of course, and drove me mad until I chased her downstream. She was happy to go.

"I'll call you when I'm hungry," I shouted.

Across the way a crow stared at me and moved very slightly on a thick oak tree branch. I could see its beak open and close as if it was talking to itself.

"Yaaa," I shouted at it the way Noble used to, and it lifted and flew downstream, screaming a complaint. I laughed, sat back, and grew mesmerized by the sound of the water rushing by, the breeze fanning the leaves and small branches, and the distant roar of a jet plane.

Maybe I dozed off. I don't know, but I realized that I was hungry. Nothing had taken my hook and worm yet. The string remained limp. I reeled it back and then looked at the hook. Something had nibbled on the worm. It was gone nearly to the edge of the hook.

Smart fish, I thought, and then I did something that surprised me.

I shouted for Celeste just the way Mommy told me I did. I shouted and shouted. Disgusted with no response, I threw down my pole and walked downstream, shouting. Something caught my attention across the way. Was it the movement of branches, the sound of someone running, and then, was that a scream?

I walked a little farther and then I stopped, true waves of shock and fear rushing at and over me.

There before me near the edge of the water was a shoe, a girl's pink and white shoe.

Mommy, I thought. Mommy!

I turned and ran through the woods, pushing bushes and branches out of my way until I broke out to the meadow, where I shouted louder and harder. Mommy was squatting by her tomato plants. She rose and looked out at me.

"What is it, Noble?" she cried.

I ran toward her, and I told her. As if she had planned it, the postman came and saw me screaming and running. He got out of his vehicle and walked toward us.

"What's wrong, Mrs. Atwell?" he asked.

"My little girl," she shouted back. "She's missing!"

He walked faster, and then he stood and listened to me.

"That doesn't sound so good," he muttered. He looked at his watch. "Is that creek far?"

"Not too far," Mommy said and started toward the woods.

"I'll be with you in a moment," he said. "I'm calling in to let them know back at the post office."

"Celeste!" Mommy screamed, and we ran toward the woods.

The postman came after us, but we stayed ahead of him until we reached the creek. There, I led Mommy to where I had seen the shoe. The postman followed and stood by, looking at the shoe.

"That's hers?"

"Yes," Mommy said. "Where is she?" She screamed and screamed for Celeste. The postman ran downstream and then ran back.

"We better get some help," he said. "I don't like what he's telling us," he added, nodding at me.

"Where's my daughter?" Mommy shouted at him, as if it was his fault.

He shook his head.

"Take it easy, Mrs. Atwell. Let's get help. Don't panic. Maybe it's nothing."

He ran back through the woods.

Mommy plucked the pink and white shoe off the sand and then put her arm around my shoulder.

"I fear she's gone, Noble," she said, "but you must not blame yourself. You must never blame yourself."

It didn't take the local policeman long to get to our home, but a little more than a half hour later, he was followed by the fire truck and a half dozen volunteer firemen. After that came two state policemen.

Just as Mommy had predicted, they questioned me repeatedly about the events. I led them back to where I had been and then where I had found Celeste's shoe. The firemen fanned out and searched both sides of the creek until one of them shouted and we all converged on the discovery of the fishing pole. It was stuck on shore, caught in some tree roots.

Word spread back to the village, and more volunteers arrived to help search for some sign of Celeste. Someone found a piece of cloth on a thorny bush, and Mommy confirmed it came from Celeste's skirt. Later, the county sheriff brought in some bloodhounds, and they went barking and chasing in small circles.

Mommy and I returned to the house, where we waited in the living room, Mommy lying on the sofa, a cold, wet cloth over her forehead. Outside, groups of men and some women conferred. The postman was questioned repeatedly and quickly became the most popular person. I watched and listened to him. He seemed to enjoy retelling the events.

"Some sick person must have been watching those kids, just waiting for an opportunity like this," I heard a sheriff's deputy tell another.

Night fell, and with the darkness came retreat and a promise to continue the search in the morning. Mommy was asked to produce as recent a picture of Celeste as she could and had to admit that she had nothing more recent than two years previous. She gave a full description.

The sheriff brought a detective to question me, and I told him how I thought I had heard noise across the creek and then a scream. I told him why we had separated, and I cried. He thanked me and told me to do what I could to help my mother.

"She'll need you to be strong," he advised and left.

When I went to sleep that night, I felt

terrible for so many reasons, most of which I couldn't understand. I had never seen so many people on our farm. The lights, the police cars, the dogs, were overwhelming.

Mommy came up the stairs slowly, her footsteps slow and heavy. She appeared in my doorway, silhouetted by the hall light.

"Are you all right, Noble?" she asked.

"Yes," I said in a small voice, more Celeste's voice, which was something that was happening less and less. Mommy had been teaching me how to think before I spoke and bring my voice up from a deeper place. She said it would soon come natural to me.

She walked into the bedroom and sat on my bed. Then she reached out and stroked my hair and my cheek.

"You did very well today," she said. "I know they will be proud of you. We can expect them to return."

"Who?" I thought she might mean the firemen and the police.

"You know who, and Daddy, too. I am sure. Just a little longer, and those people from town will leave us alone forever, my darling."

She leaned forward and kissed me on the cheek.

"Get some sleep. We will have to be

283

strong to deal with them tomorrow."

She stood up.

"But soon, soon, it will be over, and then there'll just be the two of us and our loving spirits. Sleep tight," she said and walked out, closing the door softly.

I listened to the wind outside my window for a while, and then I sighed and turned toward Celeste's empty bed.

"I'm sorry," I whispered before I fell asleep. I had no idea why.

Mommy was right about the police and the volunteers. They came in bigger numbers the next day. The local newspaper sent a reporter as well, and Mommy gave him a detailed description of Celeste. He was the first one to look at me and comment, "So they are twins?"

"Yes, yes," Mommy said and gave him the two-year-old picture. At least there would be something. The following day the story ran and more people came to our farm, many just to gape, some supposedly to help search the woods. Dozens of people traipsed through the property and crossed over to our nearest neighbor, an elderly man named Gerson Baer who lived alone. He had nothing to offer, but because he was a loner and a neighbor, he fell under some suspicion for a while. He was wise enough to permit a full search of his house and property, and eventually the police left him alone, but Mommy predicted nasty, stupid people would always suspect him. She sounded like she really did feel sorry for him, but she also mentioned that it helped us.

A week went by, and the story stopped being published in the paper. Occasionally one of the sheriff's patrolmen appeared. The detective returned and went back over the story. Mommy looked terrible. She didn't eat. She didn't do anything to make herself attractive. Some people, old friends of Daddy, and his former partner, Mr. Calhoun, sent over flowers and candy with good wishes. The detective offered to contact any family to assist us, but Mommy thanked him and told him we would be all right. He promised to keep us up to date on any new developments.

"Something will turn up," he promised. "We really searched that forest. Nothing bad happened to her there. I feel certain of that," he said to be encouraging. He told Mommy to call him any time she wanted.

From time to time she did. When I heard her speaking on the phone, I actually felt sorry for her. She sounded so desperate about it.

And then, one day, we felt it. People weren't coming by any longer. Cars still slowed down at the property line, and people gaped out at our home and at us if we were outside, but for the most part the phone stopped ringing. The days drifted on. Occasionally the newspaper did an update, but even the size of the stories grew smaller and smaller and they occurred less and less. Statistics on children who went missing and were never found were impressive. When Mommy read it aloud to me, it was like someone pounding a door shut forever.

She folded the newspaper and went outside. For a few moments she just stood there, looking over our property. It was a warm day. Summer was just over the horizon.

"Well," she said when I stepped up to her. "That's it. We have done all they have told us to do."

She turned and went back to her garden, back to our life.

When I went up to my room that night, I found it to be quite different. Celeste's bed had been stripped down to its mattress, and the pillow was gone. The closet door was open, and I could see the empty hangers where her clothing had once been.

All her shoes were gone as well. The shelves above and to the side of my bed were empty. Every doll on the shelves in the room had been taken away. There was no longer a trace of her, not a ribbon, not a hairbrush, nothing. Where was it all?

Excited, Mommy came upstairs quickly after me to tell me she had just seen her grandfather walking quietly through the meadow with her grandmother. They were arm in arm, she said, and they looked very happy.

"The curtain has been lifted," she told me. "And it's largely thanks to you."

She insisted on tucking me in and singing one of her grandmother's old folk songs. Her voice was melodic and full of so much nostalgia, I saw her eyes tear. When she was finished, she kissed me good night and left my room.

It took me longer than usual to fall asleep. I lay awake for a very long time, occasionally turning to look at the naked mattress on the bed beside mine.

Celeste was truly gone.

I didn't realize I was crying until I felt the dampness on my pillow.

10

A Fine Young Lad

There was nothing that frightened me more than failing Mommy and therefore failing Daddy. I *must* be who they want me to be, I thought. Even though Noble couldn't read as well as I could read or do as well on tests, or see Daddy's spirit when I believed I had seen him, Mommy always seemed to have some reason to like Noble more, and what I feared the most was whatever that reason was, I wouldn't ever know it and everything would go wrong.

Still, I had to try and do the best I could. I quickly realized that Mommy's happiness depended on it, but more important, perhaps, her ability to see and communicate with her spiritual family was directly related to it. The more like Noble I became, it seemed, the clearer were her visions and the more frequent.

And then I thought, the same surely will

be true for me. When I do well, Daddy will return to me. So whenever I would think of Noble being gone, I would stop myself and recite, "Noble is not gone. Celeste is gone. My sister, Celeste, is gone and buried."

With everything feminine being removed from my room and with Mommy giving me harder and heavier chores to do daily, I was able to reinforce the assumption of Noble's identity. I worked as hard as I could at every task she gave me. I didn't care about my hands or my hair. I never looked for a doll or a teacup, and I tried to avoid housework with the same dislike for it that Noble always had.

I could feel Mommy watching me, studying me, ready to point out the smallest mistakes. If I didn't do something Noble used to do, like track in mud occasionally, Mommy behaved as though I had done it anyway, chastising me for not wiping my shoes or taking them off, for staining my clothing or touching her clean walls with my muddy hands. Sometimes there really were stains on my clothing and mud on the walls, and I wondered, had I done that?

She raged about another pair of pants I had torn, a pair I had supposedly left lying on the floor by my bed. Then she pulled me aside the way she always pulled Noble and softly lectured me about being more careful outside.

"You're too involved with your play and your imagination, Noble," she said. "You have to think about consequences."

One evening when I was doing my schoolwork, she appeared in the doorway with a jar of dead spiders and told me I had left it in the pantry next to jars of jam. I remembered when Noble had done that, but I hadn't done anything like that recently or otherwise. However, I dared not deny anything.

And then, one day, when I was peeing and I had left the bathroom door open, Mommy came by and looked in at me. I heard her scream, and I quickly finished.

"Boys don't sit on the toilet to pee, Noble. You want people to laugh at you? Boys stand," she said.

I was shocked enough at the criticism to simply stare at her with my mouth slightly opened. I didn't know what to say or do. It wasn't something I had ever considered.

"Just remember to lift the toilet seat," she warned. "Sometimes your father would forget. Men and boys," she said as if she was spitting out something bitter, and shook her head.

I didn't know what to do, but next time, I straddled the toilet with the seat lifted. It was uncomfortable, but I was able to do it. When she saw me a few days later, she was very pleased, and that day, she claimed she had a nice talk with her great-aunt Sophie, who had lost her little girl because she had a heart defect. According to Mommy, it had happened before the improvements in heart surgery.

"She gave me comfort," Mommy said. "I feel much better about my own loss after having spoken with her. I'm so lucky to be able to do it."

Despite all that I was doing and the satisfaction I saw in Mommy's face, the world of spirituality that Mommy visited was still not opened to me as I thought it was going to be, especially with the intensity and frequency Mommy experienced. I was afraid to question why not, afraid to say anything, afraid she would blame it on something I was doing or had forgotten to do. Or worse yet, something I had done.

Just be patient, I told myself, and do what Mommy says. It won't be too much longer now. Daddy will return to me, and Mommy's wonderful spiritual ancestry will become mine as well. We'll truly be a happy family again.

One afternoon, however, while Mommy was walking someplace on the farm and talking with her spirits, I grew bored and wandered up to the little tower room, where I discovered all of my things had been stored. I was overcome with the strangest, yet warmest feeling of nostalgia. For a while, at the start at least, it was as if Noble had truly visited his sister's old things and realized how much he missed her.

I stood there with my hands on my hips, the way he often stood, and surveyed the room. This is a good opportunity to be Noble, I told myself. Think as Noble would think. See everything as Noble would see it.

It came easier than I had imagined it would.

How I wish I could tease her now, I thought. I'd even been nicer to her. My happiest days were surely the days when we played together, pretended together, created the magical world outside. And she did help me so often with my schoolwork. I need her. I need Celeste.

I was doing fine just wading in Noble's pool of thoughts and gazing at everything until I squatted beside a carton and opened it to see all the dolls crushed together. A rush of overwhelming warmth and excitement passed over me.

Daddy had bought me two antique rag dolls when I was sick with the chicken pox. He said they were authentic Raggedy Ann and Raggedy Andy dolls, and when he brought them to me, he told me they were created in 1915 by an artist and storyteller named Johnny Gruelle whose stories helped his little girl when she was very sick. Daddy was very excited about the dolls. He had been redoing an old house, and they were discovered in the basement. The owner wasn't interested in them, and when he heard that Daddy had a little girl, he said Daddy could have them.

"I didn't hesitate to take them," he told me. "The man had no idea what he was giving away. These dolls are very valuable, Celeste. They are real antiques. Take good care of them," he advised.

No matter how valuable they were, Noble thought they were uninteresting because the eyes didn't move and they didn't have any strings to pull to make them say anything. I tried to feel that way about them now, but I just couldn't. The memories of playing with them, Daddy's smile, sleeping with them beside me, all came rushing back as if the floodgates I had locked were broken. I couldn't help but hug them to me. They were so precious.

I guess I had made noise pulling things apart and looking at everything. Mommy had come into the house, heard me, and hurried upstairs to discover me sitting on the floor, clutching the dolls in my arms and rocking gently with my eyes closed. Her scream shattered my recollections. They crumbled in my mind like thin china, and I gasped at the sight of her standing in the doorway, her eyes wide with fear and rage.

"What are you doing up here? What are you doing with those dolls?"

I wasn't sure what to say, so I replied, "I can't help it, Mommy. I miss Celeste."

It calmed her for a moment, but not enough. A light seemed to come into her face. She nodded at her own thoughts and charged into the room to rip Raggedy Ann and Raggedy Andy from my arms.

"Come with me," she said and hurried down the stairs, in each hand a doll clutched at the neck like one of our chickens after she had cut off its head.

I followed, my heart racing, the thumps feeling like a steel marble rolling around in my chest. Mommy practically leaped at the front door. She hurried off the porch to the toolshed, where she seized a shovel and thrust it at me.

"This way," she said.

We walked around the house to the far east corner, where she told me to dig a hole. She stood by and watched. She wanted the hole deep. I had a hard time with some rocks, but she didn't move, didn't offer to help. She seemed to be pleased by my struggle. Finally, it was deep enough to satisfy her, and she dropped Raggedy Ann and Raggedy Andy into the hole.

"Celeste is gone! She's gone! And so should her dolls be, gone as far as you're concerned. Cover them up and forget them forever," she said. "I hope it's not too late," she added, looking about and shaking her head.

I had no idea what she meant by "too late," but it frightened me, and I worked as quickly as I could. She stamped down on the earth when I was finished, and then she told me to put the shovel back into the shed. She returned to the house.

Later I found her sitting in the old rocker, staring out the window in the living room. When I entered, she turned on me, her face almost as red with rage as it had been up in the tower room.

"Because of what you did," she said, "they have retreated into the shadows. Even your father has cowered back into the darkness. Who knows when they'll return?" she angrily added.

"I'm sorry, Mommy," I said.

"Don't whine like a little girl, Noble. It's time you tried to be more like your father, full of inner strength. You want to be a man like he was, don't you?"

I nodded quickly.

"Go out and split some firewood until I call you," she ordered.

These days, we had the logs delivered, but we still had to split them to let them dry properly.

"It's going to be a bad winter this year," she said. "They've told me. We'll need twice the wood we had last year. Go on."

She turned away, and I left with my head down. I worked extra hard and fast, and at one point, I realized my left palm was bleeding because I had worn the skin right off one spot. It burned, but I didn't stop. Every once in a while I would pause and look around the meadow and into the woods, studying every shadow, but I saw nothing but pockets of unshaped darkness.

"I'm sorry," I muttered. "I'm sorry, Daddy."

I quickly flicked off any tears. One thing I didn't want was for Mommy to catch me crying.

"Big boys don't cry," she had told me time in and time out since the tragedy. "When you're in pain, you squeeze it like you are closing your fist on a fly, and you squeeze and squeeze. It makes you hard on the inside where you have to be hard, and then it seeps through until you're harder on the outside. Someday you'll have a shell as tough as a turtle's," she promised.

I lifted the ax and struck the log. With concentration and new strength, I could often split them in one stroke now. Whenever I did and Mommy saw me, she would smile.

"When I see you out there working like this, you're the spitting image of your father," she would tell me.

I wanted her to smile at me like that again. I struck the logs, and every time my ax made contact, I recited, "Celeste is gone. She's gone! And so are Raggedy Ann and Raggedy Andy, forever."

In the days and months that passed, I didn't go back to the spot where they were buried. I avoided it as much as I could, and soon grass and weeds grew so quickly and thickly, it was hard to look out and see where the dolls' grave was anyway. Mommy was happy about that. She was settling into her comfortable world once again.

I went about my work, my studies, took my tests, and grew taller and stronger. Finally, Mommy told me that the spirits, as if they had been frightened by something they had seen or heard, slowly had begun to return out of the shadows. Not a day passed afterward when Mommy hadn't spoken to some spirit, and then one day she suddenly began to talk about Celeste. She told me she had finally seen her.

I had just come in from feeding our chickens, and she popped out at me from behind the den door, her eyes wide and bright with excitement.

"I was putting clothes into the dryer," she said, "when I felt a presence and turned slowly to see her standing there, looking up at me and smiling."

My heart began to pound. Celeste's spirit was in the house? But how could that be? Had Noble and I truly exchanged our souls? Had Mommy made that happen?

"How wonderful it was!" she exclaimed and hugged me to her.

"I'm glad, Mommy," I said, unable to stop myself from trembling. Mommy didn't notice. She was too absorbed in her vision.

"I know, I know. I worried and worried about it, Noble. I was afraid she was being punished for something, or I was. No one could tell me anything. You see, my sweet child, there are even more mysteries in the spiritual world than there are here. And for good reason, if you think about it," she said, quickly regaining her composure and assuming her teacher's voice. "Here we have science to help explain things to us. All those questions you ask me day in and day out about insects and animals, plants and birds, I can answer for you. Soon enough, you will be able to find most of the answers yourself in your reading.

"But it's not that way in the other world. They tell me it's like walking in a cloud most of the time. It's pleasant and without any fear or anxiety, but it's so vast. You no longer touch anything. Poor Celeste couldn't help with the clothing the way she used to help me. She looked a little flustered about it, but I reminded her she would never be flustered in the world she now lived in, and she must give up this world," she said, smiling. "Nothing there is frustrating. Nothing there is unpleasant. She looked a little put-off, but I'm sure she'll adjust. At least, I hope she will, for her sake as well as ours," she added thoughtfully. "Otherwise . . ."

"Otherwise what, Mommy?" I asked, holding my breath the way I used to when she was coming to the end of a wonderful story that could have either a sad or a happy resolution.

"Never mind," she said sharply. "She'll be fine. She'll be fine where she is."

Mommy always sounded as if she liked what she knew and learned about the other world. I was often afraid because of that, afraid that she would like it so much, she would leave me. She saw that in my face, I think, for she promised me she would always be with me.

"I'll be right by your side until you no longer need me, Noble, at least until then."

I couldn't imagine when that would be.

Mommy and I will be together forever and ever, I thought, and when she dies, I'll die with her. What would I do without her? I'm sure she felt the same way about me. What would she do without me?

Of course, I was constantly afraid that some morning she would wake up and look at me and no longer see Noble. No matter how well I did, how strong I grew, she would be unable to see him, and she would hate me even more, for she would blame me for his being gone from her life forever. I had nightmares about it.

"Where is he?" she asked me in these dark dreams. "How could he fall off that rock? Tell me again how it happened. Tell me every little detail."

"He just leaned back too far," I would say, but in my nightmare her eyes grew larger, brighter, and turned into little flashlights sweeping away every hidden word.

If I hadn't grabbed his pole, if I hadn't played tug-of-war with him, would he have fallen? Did I push or pull? Did I want him to fall?

In my dream the questions seemed to come from Mommy and not me, and when that happened, I woke up shuddering.

Just as every old and precious piece of furniture in this house held the spirits of those that had come before us and lived here, Noble's bed held his spirit, and that spirit entered me in the same fashion Mommy's great-grandpa entered her when she sat in his chair. I looked at Celeste's bed, stripped and bare as it was. I imagined what it would be like if I saw Celeste's spirit lying there. I was sure she would be smiling at me, looking so self-satisfied.

"You pushed me," I would accuse. "You

didn't pull the rod. You pushed it and you pushed me backward."

The smile would pop off her face just as it did in my imagination now, as she disappeared quickly.

"You deserve to disappear. You deserve to be gone with all your dolls!" I shouted at the emptiness.

It's what the spirits thought, too, and what Mommy thought, and what would be. Celeste was gone. She was gone. She couldn't face me with guilt staining her face. As surprising as it seemed, I felt good about that. Mommy would never see anyone else but Noble when she looked upon me, I thought confidently. She'll never be disappointed.

All will be well.

And it was well for the longest time, even when we left the farm to go shopping or did other chores. I know Mommy was more anxious than usual when she brought me to the public school for my tests the first time after our tragedy. She was anticipating all sorts of complications, but Dr. Camfield was nicer to us than she had expected he would be. He tried to be very accommodating, too, and I remember after the test results were in, this time the same day because of his intervention, he complimented Mommy on how well I had done despite our difficult times.

"Usually, siblings have setbacks when something like this happens," he told her. "It's remarkable that your boy has actually shown improvement. I sure wish you would reconsider and come back to public education, Mrs. Atwell. You're obviously a talented teacher."

"We'll see," Mommy said, pleased with the compliments and with me, but I knew the empty promise resonating in that "We'll see" of hers. She would never go back to public school teaching, never.

I couldn't help wishing she would, however. When we left the school that first time after Celeste's disappearance from our lives, I looked back at everything as Noble would look back on it all, the longing to be on that ball field clearly in his eyes, the reluctance to leave, the covetous way he gazed at the classrooms, the smile he had on his face when he heard the shouts of the students.

I pressed my face to the window and looked out at the world I had only glimpsed. Anyone looking at the car would think I was like some pauper with her face pressed to the front window of a restaurant, watching all the lucky people eat more than their fill while my bones showed clearly through my thin skin.

"Don't gape," Mommy snapped. "They're not as lucky as you are, Noble. You'll see," she said. "Someday, you'll see what you have is wonderful."

I wanted to believe her, but what would be so wonderful that it could replace having friends my age, going to parties and dances or to the movies together? Couldn't I do all that and still know the spiritual world? Couldn't I just keep all that secret?

Maybe it was because of my growing loneliness, or maybe it was because I was doing well at what Mommy and the spirits around us wanted me to do, but I was sure I did begin to see shadows take shape again, and soon, they were faces smiling my way. I told Mommy because I knew she would want to know, and she was very pleased, even though I couldn't tell her any more because I still couldn't say I had spoken to anyone or anyone had spoken to me.

"We're all going to be fine again, Noble," she said. "Just fine. Just be patient. Just do what you have to do and believe. When you fill your heart with faith, it will all happen for you just the way it happened for me," she said and described the first time she had seen one of the family spirits. Her mother and her grandmother had told her it would happen.

"And it did. Just the way they said it would. One day a shadow molded itself into a spirit just as they do for you. That first spirit was my great-grandmother Elsie. She was happier to see that I could see her than I was. Nothing makes them feel more complete again than when one of us, the living, crosses over, my darling."

How pleasing and wondrous she made it all sound, and how anxious I was to have the experiences again and forever, especially with them finally speaking to me. I studied every wisp of smoke. I peered into the fog. I watched the twilight creep in from the forest, and I listened and waited. It wasn't easy being patient, especially because I feared I wouldn't be worthy and I would spend my whole life deaf and blind to what they had to offer.

Perhaps that was why for me time moved as slowly as maple syrup. One day was the same as the next, despite the heavy load of chores Mommy laid on me. Whenever she saw me stop and start reading, she pounced and ordered me out to gather blueberries or wild strawberries, or pick some eggs. Harvesting our maple syrup was very important, too.

Some time ago, so long ago now, it seemed to me, Daddy had shown us how to tap the maple trees. It was our job to go around to the trees and empty the syrup into a big pot, and then the pot was boiled until it became the maple syrup we used on our pancakes or Mommy used for baking. It was a hard enough job for the two of us, but now it was all mine, even the boiling part.

I know the work hardened me. I was the one cutting the lawn, raking the leaves, turning the earth for replanting. I was the one gathering kindling wood, splitting more and more of the logs for firewood, painting, repairing, cleaning the chicken coop. From time to time, the postman or a serviceman would see me out in the field and remark to Mommy how big I had grown.

"You've got a fine young lad there," the UPS man told Mommy when he delivered our order of seeds and I carried the boxes to the barn.

"Yes," she said proudly. "He is going to be quite a young man soon.

"He's my salvation," she would add, and whoever it was would nod and understand. Mommy needed salvation. Like some fire that had been smothered by tragedy, she needed rekindling.

For well over a year or so after the tragedy, she moped about in a faded housedress and old shoes. Her hair was straggly and unclean and her face pale. She did her best to avoid leaving the farm, but when we went to the supermarket or did some shopping, she made little or no attempt to fix her appearance. People seemed to expect it anyway. She was wearing the cloud of gloom around her like some dark robe. In their eyes and whispers was the reminder that she had suffered a terrible loss. Her little girl had been snatched up and taken away, and who knew what had eventually been done to her or who had taken her, although the suspicions circling our unfortunate neighbor, Gerson Baer, lingered.

However, the stronger I became, the more work I accomplished, the healthier and happier Mommy looked. The compliments I received chipped away at her darkness. Eventually she began to wear pretty clothes again, take care of her hair, even wear some makeup when we went shopping. I saw the way men looked at her, and I knew that there were even some who called and tried to get her to go out on dates, but she brushed them all off like so many annoying flies.

She was content taking care of our home, reading, knitting or doing her needlework, baking, and cooking our dinners, and working beside me in the vegetable garden and having me help her in her herbal garden. I would work and listen to her stories about her younger days, her grandmother's endless stories about Hungary and gypsies, and her mother's wonderful remedies for every problem. Once again she told me about Daddy's coming to the house to fix the roof. I had to remember not to ask the questions Celeste always asked. Then she talked about her and Daddy's courting and his proposing marriage.

She said I shouldn't mind if she repeated things because he liked it when she told me stories about him.

"The dead want to be remembered. They wait for the sound of their names," she assured me. "It's like the ringing of a bell to us. Wherever they are, they perk up and come to us, come to hear us talk about them."

She leaned toward me and whispered with a wink, "I do it deliberately for that purpose sometimes, to get him to appear.

He knows, but he doesn't mind."

This reminiscing was something she did more and more as the years went by with only the two of us managing the property, comforting each other. Our days were always full and busy. We were like two bees doing the work of an entire hive. If something broke, we made every effort first to fix it ourselves. Nothing seemed more important to Mommy than keeping strangers off our land and out of our lives. She said they filled the air with static and kept our spiritual world away. So I learned how to fix a leaking pipe, snake out our septic system, clear the gutters on the roof of leaves, and even splice broken wires. What we didn't know from Mommy's experience, we read about in books she acquired either at the county library or at bookstores.

With every turn of a wrench, rap of a hammer, I felt my arms tighten and my shoulders thicken. Despite my slight frame, my diminutive facial features, my small hands, I eventually presented a tight fist of a figure, wiry perhaps more than muscular, but certainly tougher and thicker than most young people my age, and quite different from any girls my age. That was certain.

Sometimes Mommy would stand aside and look at me for the longest time. I would catch her lips moving and her head turning to someone beside her. I was being admired, and that admiration was strengthening her ties to all she loved and cherished.

At night after I had gone to bed, exhausted half the time, I could hear her muffled conversation below. Most of the time, she was talking to Daddy. I was tempted to get up to see if I would see him as well, but she had once warned me about spying on her and how that would displease the spirits, so I just lay there, listening and looking forward to the day or the night when I would finally see Daddy beside me again and finally hear him talk to me the way he talked to her.

From time to time, I was sure I saw him standing to the side, watching me work, a smile on his face, but when I started to talk to him, he would disappear. I told Mommy, and she said it was normal.

"One day he'll just start talking to you," she predicted. "You'll see."

It was all going so well that I had no doubt she was right. Even birthdays went smoothly, birthdays when there was once doubles of everything and now there was only one. For the first few birthdays after the tragedy, she said Daddy and Celeste were there, and he was holding her hand. I didn't see either of them. I believed I had seen Daddy at my birthday party once, but that was when Celeste was alive in our world. I'm Noble, I reminded myself. There were still miles to go. I complained about it, and again, she promised me I would very soon.

"Patience and faith," she would tell me. "Patience and faith. Just do as you are doing, my darling boy," she told me. "It will all come true."

And then, like a lightning bolt from the reality that hovered around us and over us, I was struck with a realization one morning that burned fear through my body, singeing my very soul. It came with a small, almost unrealized ache. I yawned and ran the palm of my hand down my chest. The bump surprised me, and I sat up quickly. I felt for it again, on both sides. Then I stood up and went to the mirror. It could not be denied.

My breasts had begun to blossom.

I was eleven by now, actually only months away from being twelve. When we were five, Mommy had insisted on teaching us about human anatomy. Daddy thought we were too young to learn about such things, but Mommy insisted the public schools were wrong to treat the human body as if it were an X-rated movie.

Up until the end of that year, Noble and I did many things together that we wouldn't do again. We took baths together. We went to the bathroom in front of each other and put our underthings on in front of each other. I think we were like Adam and Eve before they tasted knowledge.

After the lessons, we began to avoid each other's eyes whenever we did any of these things. If one of us looked at the other, we would scream. Both of us denied peeping, but Mommy told us that it was a natural and good thing to be modest by then.

"Shame in, sin out," she would say, but we didn't quite understand the meaning of it. We only knew we felt uncomfortable doing things we had never thought much about before she had given us the lessons in anatomy and pointed out how different we were and would be.

When Noble learned about the female producing eggs, he thought it was so funny. He teased me often by checking my bed in the morning to see if, like the hens, I had laid one. I would moan and cry. I know

Mommy was considering separating us soon before the tragedy. She was going to convert the sewing room into a bedroom for one of us. But that never happened.

Now that I discovered the bumps growing on my chest, I suppose what surprised and even frightened me the most was the fact that I had forgotten what was coming. It had been so long since I had done what we knew as girl things. I don't think I gave a second thought to myself being pretty or good-looking. Not long after Noble recuperated from his broken leg, Mommy had disconnected the television set and moved it into the back of the pantry, where it was covered by a small tarp. We had no magazines. The only time I ever thought about girl things was when we went shopping and I could catch glimpses of magazines or see girls in the stores or streets or once a year at the school.

I looked at girls the way someone would look at something very foreign, almost extraterrestrial. I was afraid Mommy might see some longing in my eyes, so I tried not to stare or let her catch me looking at any of them. The truth was, I was so different now, caught somewhere in between, floating, waiting to land and become someone.

Sometimes girls in the stores looked at me with something more than just simple curiosity. I could see it in their faces. What did they see when they looked at me? I wondered. Was there something about themselves that they recognized in me, something I couldn't change or cover? It was terrifying. I imagined some girl or even some boy looking my way, pointing and laughing.

"Exactly what is that?" they would scream. "She's not a boy and she's not a girl," they would chant, and I would flee.

Mommy would be devastated.

The best way to avoid it was to look away, and never, never think about it. For a long time, it worked, and then . . . this. I couldn't but help feel my body was betraying me, betraying all of us. How could Celeste insist on returning to this body? Hadn't I not only seen her buried in the old cemetery, but buried her as deep down within myself as possible? I wouldn't even permit Celeste's dreams into my mind anymore.

For a moment I thought about cutting the buds off my chest, smothering Celeste before she could even think of opening her eyes inside me. I even took a knife to myself, but I couldn't do it. Instead, I did

314

what Mommy hated. I sat down and I cried. She heard me as she was passing my room, and a moment later, she opened the door and looked at me.

I was on my bed, wearing only my underpants.

"What is it?" she asked. "What could be so terrible as to make a soon-to-be-strapping young man weep like some infant? Well?" she demanded when I didn't respond immediately.

I turned instead and thrust my chest into her view.

She stared, her eyes widening.

What would this mean? Would she hate me? Would the spirits never speak to me?

She didn't yell. She nodded her head slowly instead.

"Grandma Jordan once told me about a relative of ours, a boy who was developing into a girl. I'll have to go back and study the remedies," Mommy said. "Until I find something, never take your shirt off outside."

It wasn't something I did anyway.

"And stop this baby bawling. We have a problem. We solve the problem. That's what we do and what we will always do, Noble. Now get dressed, and let's start the day," she concluded and left me soon to understand that my sexuality had become my illness, my handicap, a burden to lift and toss aside.

She tried different remedies on me, concoctions of herbal drinks and even some salves. I thought the hair on my arms was growing darker and thicker, but other than that, nothing changed. In fact, my breasts continued to grow. Every morning I woke and stared at myself. One time, I didn't hear Mommy come to the door, and she watched me gently touch my nipples.

"Stop!" she screamed. "You must deny it. You must force it back or . . . or . . ." She couldn't get herself to voice what would be the result if I didn't, but I knew in my heart what she thought. The words, like mold on a bread, formed on my brain: "Or Noble would die again."

A little while later, she reappeared with a roll of gauze, and she wrapped it around my emerging breasts. She went around and around to be sure I couldn't see through it, and then she taped it and stood back.

"For a while I will be the one who changes that and unwraps it," she said. "I want you to put it out of your mind, forget it's there, understand?"

"Yes," I said.

It wasn't easy. Some days, especially on

very hot and muggy ones, I would sweat, and it would itch terribly. I tried not to complain, but there were occasions when it was so uncomfortable for me, I couldn't help myself. She saw me scratching and pulled me inside, marching me back up to my room. There she unraveled the gauze, as she did from time to time. Lately, when she stepped back, she looked more unhappy. I knew it was because I was getting bigger, rounder.

She rubbed one of her salves roughly on and around my breasts and then wrapped me again, so tightly, I complained that I couldn't breathe.

"Just get used to it," she said. "You'll be all right."

Eventually, I was able to ignore the feeling. The itching became less and less severe, and in time, Mommy was right. I was able to forget being strapped down. She continued to give me some of her herbal concoctions. Once in a while they made me sick to my stomach, and one time I threw up for a whole day and was unable to do any work at all.

She paced the house, mumbling to herself.

"Something evil has taken hold," she muttered to me, her eyes full of suspicions.

She made me feel guilty, and I had to look away. That seemed to confirm something for her. She went out to talk to her spirits.

Then, one night, long after I had fallen asleep, the lights went on in my room, and I saw her standing there, her eyes wide.

"It's Celeste," she declared. "It was one thing to come around here and smile at me, and even come with your father and look sweet and lovable on your birthdays, but the truth is that no matter what I've told her and what she has been told by others, she is refusing to rest in peace. I must keep her away from us until she does."

"How can we do that, Mommy?" I asked, more intrigued than ever.

"She is not to return to the house. You must not think of her. You're giving her opportunities, providing a doorway from the other side, a portal through which she is crossing back into our world, not as a good spirit, but as an interfering one. It's happened before," she added. "My cousin Audrey so resisted entering the other world, she caused great stress and turmoil for my aunt Bella. Her son was driven to commit suicide," she added. "It was the only thing that satisfied Audrey. Only then did she rest in peace."

Suicide? Birds of panic fluttered in my chest. Would that happen to me?

She came farther into my room, reading my fear as if it was in big black-and-white letters on my forehead.

"Yes, suicide. Don't you see? Don't you get it, Noble?" she asked with a cold smile. "Celeste wants you with her, Noble. You must drive her away, drive every thought of her away. Don't let her get close to you. Do you understand?"

I nodded, so terrified, I could barely breathe.

"I'm going through the house tomorrow and removing every item, no matter how small or insignificant it might seem, that relates to her, belonged to her. It was obviously not enough to get rid of those rag dolls. I want you to start digging another grave in the cemetery. Dig it behind Infant Jordan's. Right after breakfast, go out there and start."

"Okay, Mommy," I said.

"Good, good." She looked about the room with her eyes small and intense, and then she stopped and charged forward, ripping a picture of Daddy and us off the wall. "Every picture of her, every image," she whispered and left with it snugly under her arm.

I lay back, my heart thumping.

Then I heard Celeste's voice calling to me. I put my hands over my ears.

"No!" I screamed.

Mommy returned.

"What is it?"

"Her voice," I said.

She smiled.

"Good," she said. "That's good. Shut her out," she said, turned off the lights and closed the door.

Silence was soothing. I closed my eyes and tried to think only Noble's thoughts, dream only his dreams. A trail of red ants marched across my eyes, and I counted them into sleep.

Mommy was already at work when I awoke. I could hear her carrying things down from the turret. I hurriedly washed and dressed.

"There's no time for breakfast," she told me when I descended the stairs. "Go out and start digging."

I went to the barn to get the shovel, and then I went quickly to the cemetery. The sky was clouding over quickly, and some of the clouds rolling in from the east looked black and blue. The air was still but heavy. It made it more difficult to work. The ground in the old cemetery was like cement, too. Every few inches, I seemed to run into a rock that I had to dig out and pry away from the soil.

It began to rain, slowly at first, just a slight drizzle, and then a more intense shower. Mommy came out and inspected my work.

"You're going too slowly," she said. "Work faster, work harder."

The rain began to pound around us, and the wind picked up and drove it over the farm in sheets that soaked me through my clothing, but Mommy didn't care. My hole in the ground softened and the sides turned to mud, caving in with every spoonful I brought out. I felt like someone going in a circle.

"We should wait for the rain to stop," I told her.

"No," she said. "Work."

The rain didn't let up for a moment now. I was so tired and so soaked, I began to lose my footing and slip with every thrust of my shovel. The wet earth was far heavier than before, so I couldn't dig as much or as fast. The ground continued to give way around the grave. There was even a small pool of water at the bottom.

The futility of it all put a look of utter terror into Mommy. She spun about, searching for a new idea, and then finally, seeing me work without results, told me to stop. I was aching all over, so I didn't think much of the pains in my abdomen. We both headed back to the house, and on the porch, she had me take off my muddied and soaked clothing. I was shivering badly now. She told me to go in and upstairs before she undid the gauze around my breasts.

In the hallway was the pile of items she had found that even in the slightest way related to Celeste. Of course, all of the clothing, every toy, but even birthday cards, drawings Daddy had loved and were once pinned to the refrigerator, every school lesson and test, pens, pencils she used, her toothbrush, hairbrush, and things that could have been anyone's, like soap, washcloths, even the rug that once was at the foot of her bed. Mommy was ridding the house of anything Celeste had touched!

I stared, amazed, and then I heard her come in behind me and I started up the stairs. She followed me to my bathroom, and she began to undo the gauze, mumbling about the rain. Mud had literally seeped through my clothes and stained my skin. I was still dripping from my hair, short as it was.

"You'll take a hot bath," she decided. "I don't need you getting sick on me right now. Now we need to —"

She paused and stared at me, and then her face seemed to twist so hard to the right that it looked like it might slip off her skull. She brought her hands to her heart and pressed them against her chest. Her mouth moved, but nothing came out for a moment.

I couldn't speak.

I turned instead and looked into the full-length mirror against the inside of the bathroom door.

A thin trickle of blood was crawling down the inside of my right thigh. The cramps in my stomach grew more intense as I looked at myself.

I turned back to Mommy, white fear freezing my heart.

She stepped forward, took my shoulders in her hands, and shook me hard as she brought her eyes to bear down into mine.

"Celeste," she said in a hoarse whisper, "you will go back. You will. None of this will make a difference," she concluded and then went to the medicine cabinet. She fashioned another gauze bandage, this one into a pad.

"Think of this only as what it is, an injury, an injury Celeste has caused, and like any injury, we will mend it," she said.

She made me take a shower instead of a bath, and then she fastened the new bandage between my legs and told me to rest. My stomach cramps grew worse. I moaned and cried. She brought me some tea made from pennyroyal, one of her herbs. It helped. My stomach stopped aching. She then put a twig of rosemary under my pillow, which she said would drive away evil spirits and illness, and soon I fell asleep. I was so tired from the digging that I slept most of the day.

When I opened my eyes, I was surprised to find my bed surrounded by lit candles. Mommy sat beside me, waiting for my eyes to open.

"Do not be afraid," she said. She took my hand and closed her eyes. "Repeat after me," she told me and began. "Celeste, be gone," she chanted. "Go on, repeat it."

We chanted.

The candle flames flickered.

The gray skies outside the window grew darker before they tore apart to let some light graze our house.

"Celeste, be gone," Mommy said and I said until I felt her spirit leave me and Noble's return.

It would be all right, I thought. It would. Mommy would not let go of my hand after all. She would not stop loving me.

Later, after we had something to eat, we returned to the old cemetery, where she helped dig this time, and we were able to make the grave as wide and deep as she wanted. Then together we carried everything she had gathered out of the house and dropped it in the dark, muddied hole.

We worked until dusk, and when it was over, we could see the stars begin to twinkle.

Mommy put her arm around my shoulders.

"Listen," she said. "Listen hard, Noble. Don't you hear them? Don't you?"

"Yes," I said quickly, maybe too quickly. She turned and looked at me.

"What are they saying?" she asked, her eyes full of hesitation, but also full of hope.

I closed my own eyes to listen hard. Speak to me, I prayed. Speak to me. It wasn't just the wind. I heard words. Surely, I heard words.

"Celeste, be gone," I replied. That was what I thought I heard. Was I right?

When I opened my eyes, I saw she was smiling.

"You do hear them," she said. "How

wonderful. How long I have waited."

She hugged me to her and held me tightly for a moment before kissing my forehead and caressing my cheek.

"Now, my darling, I am sure it will all begin for you."

With her arm still around my shoulders, we walked back to the house, where Daddy's spirit surely waited in his favorite chair.

I might even see him, I thought, and envisioned him smiling up at me. How I wished I could run into his arms again. I would do anything for that.

I would even bury Celeste a thousand times.

11

A Boy Next Door

As I grew older and my breasts matured even more, I took to unstrapping myself at night so I could be more comfortable. Mommy knew it, but said nothing as long as I was sure to strap myself down well enough every morning to flatten my breasts sufficiently, but it was getting more and more difficult to do that enough to please her. One morning she came into my room before I had woken and risen. She had an old corset she had trimmed. It was something that had belonged to one of our ancestors.

"Sit up," she ordered, and then she fit it around me, keeping it so that the strings that tightened it were in front.

"You can do this yourself every morning," she said. "Tighten it as you need to."

I was having some trouble breathing, so she loosened it a bit, but only a bit.

Not a morning went by when she didn't

inspect me the moment I descended the stairs. With her hovering over me, ready to pounce on any mistakes, I continued to treat my oncoming sexuality as others treated their illnesses. Mommy was suspicious about every look I had, every change in my temperament. If my face looked flushed, she would make me drink a herbal medication. She seemed to remember when I might be having some abdominal cramps. There was always one of her remedies waiting for me at the breakfast table.

And then one day I think she decided that to compensate for the way my body was taking shape, curving and tightening, I should eat more. Weight could disguise it all.

"There's nothing wrong with a boy being a little overweight," she would mutter as she slapped down another helping of buttery mashed potatoes or cut me another piece of her rich chocolate cake. My thighs did become bigger and my waist wider. I couldn't help not liking the way I was starting to look.

Noble wouldn't be fat at my age, especially not with all the activity and work. I shouldn't be fat, I told myself, but if I didn't finish the food Mommy put on my plate, she would make me sit there until I had. Once, she made me eat so much I threw up, and immediately afterward, she made me eat everything again and wait at the table until she was sure I wouldn't throw it up a second time.

One of the worst things I could do was stop and look at myself in a mirror. To prevent that, she removed every mirror she could, even the full-length one in my bathroom. She told me spirits avoided mirrors, that not seeing their reflection made them unhappy, and everything in our world was to be designed to make our spiritual company comfortable. But in my heart I knew what bothered her was simply my unhappiness with my own appearance.

"Stop worrying about looking too fat. Work harder, and you're muscles will get bigger, stronger," she told me. "Your father wasn't a vain man."

I could almost see her thinking up ways to make me feel more like Noble would feel as I grew older. When I was fourteen, she decided I should have a dog.

"All boys on farms have dogs," she told me, and we went to Luzon, a bigger village about twenty miles south, to shop at a pet store. I had no idea what sort of dog I should have, but Mommy seemed to think a golden retriever made sense since we had so much land. The four-month-old puppy she chose was a male she decided we should name Cleo, because she said he had a face that reminded her of a lion. It seemed to me she wanted the dog far more than I did, but after we brought Cleo home, he became my sole responsibility and I was the one blamed for anything he did wrong, like digging holes in Mommy's herbal garden, terrifying the chickens, or leaving droppings too close to the house. She would threaten me with, "If you don't take better care of that animal, Noble, I'll give him away." She made it seem like I was the one who had wanted the dog more.

I can't say I didn't grow attached to Cleo quickly. He took to following me every-where, and by the time he was a year old, he had grown big enough to challenge any animal he saw, even a bobcat that had wan-dered down the old stone wall toward the pond. He got badly scratched, but Mommy didn't take him to a veterinarian. She treated his cuts herself, and they did heal quickly. She didn't blame me. We couldn't hold him down anyway. He loved charging through the woods, sniffing after every creature that burrowed or hid in the bush. Just watching him chase after wild rabbits was delightful. He never caught one, but he never stopped trying.

As far as water went, Cleo behaved more like a fish. He couldn't look at the stream or the pond without charging into it seconds later. He would splash about, his tongue moving excitedly out of his mouth and his head wagging from side to side. He was a dog any boy would love, I thought, and I took to running with him at my heels or training him to fetch sticks and balls. I saw that Mommy derived great pleasure from watching us play, too.

She pounced on me, however, whenever Cleo tracked in mud, and one day, when she discovered he had chewed on one of the old piano legs, she went into a rage and threatened to make both of us sleep in the barn. She worked on that piano leg like an experienced craftsman until she got it so it didn't look much different from what it had before Cleo had gotten his teeth around it.

Maybe he just hates music, I thought to say, but Mommy wasn't in the mood for any sort of humor about her sacred furniture. Anyway, nothing could be further from the truth. Cleo loved music. He would lie at my feet and listen to the classical music Mommy played for us, his ears sometimes perking up at a high note and his head tilting slightly as if he had heard something very, very curious or strange.

One day, when I heard him barking out front and walked out to see what it was, I looked out over the meadow in the direction he was looking at, but I saw nothing. He continued to bark and growl. I knelt beside him and kept my hand on his neck, feeling his growl rumble down to his stomach. His eyes were fixed in this one direction. I studied it and studied it and then came to the conclusion that perhaps he saw something spiritual and perhaps what he saw wasn't nice. Was that possible? I presented the idea to Mommy.

She put down her needlepoint and thought long and hard. As always, she had a story from her ancestral past.

"My great-uncle Herbert had a golden retriever exactly like Cleo. You know," she said, pausing, "some animals can sense animal spirits and human spirits, too. They have a gift."

She looked at Cleo.

"I had a suspicion he might have that gift. When I looked into his eyes that day in the pet shop, I sensed it. Anyway, Uncle Herbert's dog grew so attached to the spirit of his younger brother, Russell, that he would often go off for days at a time and be with him. Uncle Herbert said that when his dog, I think he called it Kasey, returned from one of his spiritual visits, he would stay even closer to his side. He told me it was as if his brother's spirit had impressed Kasey with how important loyalty is, and how important it was to watch over Herbert.

"When I see you and Cleo out there, I think he might have visited with your daddy's spirit, and perhaps that is why he was growling. He's here to protect you, and he saw something Daddy had warned him about," she added, and I looked at Cleo in a new light. He was staring up at me as if he had understood every word Mommy had spoken.

"There is truly a link, a relationship among all beautiful and loving creatures in this world," Mommy said. "Never forget that. And that was why I was always chastising you for killing pretty butterflies or caterpillars, Noble," she added, wagging her finger at me.

Then she leaned over to kiss me just the way she always did when she reprimanded Noble.

Like Noble always did, I denied it. Mommy gave me that look, half critical, half loving and went back to her needle-point.

Three days later, Cleo was barking at something at the edge of the woods again.

Only this time, it was definitely not any sort of spirit, good or evil.

It was a slim, tall boy in a pair of jeans, an oversize dark blue T-shirt, and a pair of dark brown hiking boots with the laces undone. At first he looked like he had a patch of strawberries growing on his head, his hair was so red. It streamed down the sides of his head, over his ears, until it nearly touched his shoulders. He stood so still beside an old oak tree that he seemed to be part of the forest, something unusual that had just grown there.

It made my heart pitter-patter. I knitted my eyebrows and stared back at him.

Cleo barked harder and started to run toward him. The boy didn't cower. He clapped his hands and called to Cleo as I followed. Cleo's tail began to wave when he reached him, and the boy knelt to pet him. He looked up as I drew closer.

"Hey, how you doing?" he asked.

"Who are you, and what are you doing here?" I demanded.

Mommy's distrust of strangers on our land had become my attitude as well. I rarely answered the postman when he said good morning or waved back at any delivery man if he waved to me.

"That's a nice way to greet your new neighbor," he said, continuing to pet Cleo, who sat contentedly, his tongue out, his eyes on me. Later I would tell Mommy that Cleo trusted him, and that was the reason I didn't just ask him to leave our property and stop talking to him.

"New neighbor? What do you mean?"

"My dad bought Mr. Baer's property," he said. "We moved in yesterday. You people didn't know?"

"We people don't butt into other people's business," I said sharply. "Or walk around on other people's land, either."

He continued to pet Cleo and look up at me, ignoring my tone.

"Nice dog," he said. "I had to give mine up before we moved."

"Why?"

"Something wrong with her hip. She was a beautiful Labrador."

"So where did you leave her?"

"With the vet." He stood up and looked away. "He put her down." He turned back to me. "Put her to sleep for good. I didn't want to hang around and watch it, so I left her. How long have you lived here?"

"All my life. This is our family property, and it has 'No Trespassing' signs everywhere," I said with heavy emphasis on the "no."

He nodded.

"Yeah, I saw. What, do you get a lot of hunters marching through or something?"

"No. Most people don't disobey the signs."

"How old are you?" he asked, still ignoring my attitude toward him. Was he stupid or just stubborn? I wondered.

"Why?"

"Just asking to see if we'll be in the same class this September," he said with a shrug. "You go to the public school, don't you?"

"No. As a matter of fact, if you have to know, I don't attend public school."

"Oh, a parochial school?"

"No."

"What then, some ritzy private school?" he asked, grimacing.

"You're looking at it," I said, nodding back at the house.

"Huh?" He looked over my shoulder as if he thought he did miss something. "That's your house, right?"

"Yes. My mother is a teacher. I'm in home school."

"Home school?" He twisted his nose.

I had always avoided looking too long or directly at anyone because I didn't want to invite them to do the same to me, but I couldn't help but study his face closer. He had turquoise eyes, striking, under very light eyebrows. Down his cheeks were sprinkled very tiny freckles. His mouth was firm, strong with very bright full lips, and there was a slight cleft in his chin, more like a dimple, as if his Maker had just tapped the tip of His finger there while he was being molded.

"Yes, home school. I do better than I would at public school where they spend less and less time on real education," I said, reciting one of Mommy's mantras about the state of education in America. "I'm tested yearly, and I always score in the top three percentile."

"No kidding? I'm lucky to pass, especially English. I'm not too bad at math and usually do all right in science. I hate social studies. Boring," he sang.

"Not for me," I said.

"Maybe I oughta join your mother's home school," he said.

"You can't join it. It's just for me."

"Oh." He nodded. "Sure." Then he smiled in confusion. "Just for you? I don't get it."

"My mother is a professional teacher, and she tutors me in every subject. What's so hard to understand?"

He shrugged.

"You're just the first person I met doing that at so old an age, that's all."

"Well, now you know someone," I said.

He shrugged and looked around. I wasn't chasing him off. That was for sure.

"You stay here all day?"

"Yes, I do. So?"

"How do you make friends?"

"I don't," I said. "For now," I added.

He kept petting Cleo and nodding as if everything I said made absolute sense.

Then he practically leaped at me, his hand out.

"I'm Elliot Fletcher."

I looked at his hand.

"I don't bite," he said.

I shook it quickly.

"My name is Noble Atwell."

"Wow. What do you do, rub sandpaper on your palms?" he asked, turning my hand around in his. "Those calluses feel like rocks."

I pulled my hand away from his quickly.

"I do all the outdoor stuff," I said proudly.

"Like what?"

"Like chop wood, cut grass, plant, take care of our chickens, look after things."

"Yeah, my father was talking about me taking on house chores now, to earn gas for my car when he gives in and buys me one this year after I get my license. We lived in a town house in Jersey. No lawns to cut, and especially no firewood. Man, this is like a real farm, huh?" he said looking at our property. "That's cornstalks?"

"Yes," I said. "It's delicious. We pick it off the stalk and cook it the same day."

"I bet you hunt, too, huh?" he asked me.

"No."

"Fish?"

I looked away, deciding whether I should just chase him off, walk away myself, or what. I thought I saw Mommy come around the rear of the house, and for a moment that made me freeze, but it was just the shadow of a cloud.

"Sometimes," I said.

"I was wondering what was in that creek. It looks pretty deep in spots."

"When we have heavy rains in the spring, there are sections that would be over both our heads."

"It looked like it. I took an exploratory walk around soon after we moved into the house yesterday. Dad was mad, of course.

He wanted me to help with the move-in, but I got bored with unpacking and told him and my sister I was taking a walk whether they liked it or not. I left before either could complain," he added with a smile.

His smile was nice because it started around his eyes and seemed to trickle down to the corner of his mouth, sort of rumble through his cheeks.

"How old is your sister?"

"She's nearly eighteen and a pain, especially for my father."

"Why?"

"She just is, and she's always trying to get out of doing her share of things. That's why I was happy to leave her unpacking the kitchen stuff. I worked this morning and then snuck out again to look around. I saw your fort," he added, nodding in its direction.

"I built that a long time ago," I said. "I don't play in forts anymore."

"So how old are you?"

"I'm fifteen, if you just have to know," I said belligerently.

"I'd be a year ahead of you at school. As I said, I'm getting my driver's license this year and the car. Dad used that as a bribe to get me to agree to move to the boondocks."

"Boondocks?"

"Woods, country, whatever you call it out here. We moved from Paramus, New Jersey. My dad had his own pharmacy there, but the business went to pot when one of the chains moved right on top of him. Can't beat 'em, join 'em, Dad says. He's working at Rite Aid in Monticello now. Says it's better to be an employee than an owner anyway."

"How come you talk only about your father? What about your mother?"

"She died a long time ago," he said quickly.

"Oh."

"What's your father do?"

"He died a long time ago, too," I said.

He nodded. He had a peculiar look on his face.

"What?"

"Actually, I knew that," he said. "I knew your name, too. We heard all about you and your mother and the terrible thing that happened to your sister. It's why we got the house so cheap. No one wanted to buy it from that old guy and live next to you people. At least that's what Dad says," he added.

"Good for you. Now get off our land," I snapped and turned to walk away.

"Hey, take it easy. I didn't say I had

funny ideas about you. That's why I came over to meet you."

"Cleo," I called because he remained sitting in front of Elliot.

"Come on. Don't be so sensitive," he added. "You're acting like a pussy."

I spun around.

"I'm not sensitive, and I'm no pussy. Don't call me that."

"Just trying to get you to calm down," he said, shrugging.

He did look harmless and friendly, but his mentioning our tragedy put trembles into me.

"I know what the stupid people around here think of me and my mother. I don't need to be reminded," I said.

"Sure. I won't say another word about it," he said, raising both his hands.

"I don't care if you do or not," I said and kept walking back toward the house. Cleo followed, but looked back periodically. "Forget about him, Cleo," I muttered. He looked up at me and walked alongside.

"Maybe they're right about you!" I heard Elliot scream.

I didn't turn around.

My heart was still pounding after I went into the house. I could hear Mommy moving around in the kitchen. Should I just go in and tell her about him? I wondered. I'd better, I thought. She would find out and she would want to know why I didn't tell her. We shouldn't keep secrets from each other, ever, I reminded myself.

"What is it?" Mommy said when I appeared in the kitchen doorway.

"We have new neighbors. I just met the son."

"What?" She wiped her hands on the cloth and turned from her chicken stuffing. "What son?"

I described him to her and all he had told me. I practically did it without taking a breath.

"I saw the sign out front of the Baer house, but I never imagined anyone would buy it so fast," she said. "He must have sold it very cheap."

I told her how Cleo had taken to Elliot.

"Don't get too friendly," she advised. "Sometimes people try to get you to be friends and talk to them just so they can make up stories about you. Be careful," she added. "I didn't think that house would sell so fast," she repeated, as if she had been assured of it.

I nodded, and Cleo and I left her looking like she was in deep thought. I was, too. I sat in my room with Cleo at the foot of my bed. I felt torn. I didn't want to drive Elliot away, but I couldn't help myself. Cleo looked disappointed that I had done that. Every time I moved, he lifted his head in anticipation, probably thinking we were going to go back out there and talk to that boy again.

"You heard Mommy," I said. "He's just trying to dig up stories to tell about us."

Still, I couldn't help being intrigued. We finally had real neighbors. I was never interested in knowing or seeing Mr. Baer. He looked like a grouchy old man whenever I did set eyes on him. It didn't surprise me that people would have suspected him of doing something terrible to one of us.

But Elliot, his sister, and his father were different. They were another family. At the moment I was actually more interested in knowing about his sister. What was she like? How did she dress? What music did she listen to? What books and magazines did she read? Learning anything about her was intriguing.

Worst of all, my meeting Elliot and hearing about his family suddenly heightened my loneliness. My room looked like a prison cell, the walls bare now except for the toy cars on the shelves and some of the bug cages. The flow of thick, gray clouds streaming in from the east quickly shut down the little sunshine in the room. *Dreary* was a good word for how I felt, I thought.

Unable to stop myself, I rose and headed downstairs, Cleo close at my heels. Mommy was still in the kitchen, but she heard me and called to ask what I was doing.

"I need some worms. I think I'm going to go fishing tomorrow in the afternoon," I told her.

She didn't reply, and I hurried out. It was a lie, and lies lay in the air like bad odors in our home. I half hoped to see Elliot still in the woods nearby, but he was gone. Gathering up one of my worm cans, I traipsed slowly over the meadow toward the cool dark earth in the forest, where I knew worms were plentiful. Cleo wandered about nearby. I could hear him crashing through brush. Every once in a while, he returned to see if I was still there. I mixed some wet earth with my worms and collected quite a few mushy ones, as Noble used to call them.

The sky was completely overcast now, but it didn't look like it was going to rain. Unable to keep my curiosity under lid, I decided to cross through the forest, following paths well known to me, and reached a point from where I could easily look upon the old Baer property without being seen myself.

I saw Elliot working on setting up some lawn furniture with a man who was obviously his father. He had a similar build, and although his hair was not as red, it was a reddish brown. He was a few inches taller. I watched them together for a while, and then, because of the overcast, I saw a light go on in an upstairs window.

The old Baer property was nowhere as attractive as ours, I thought, but it had a large, two-story Queen Anne house with a wide front porch and a small back porch. The grounds obviously had been neglected to the point that the lawn was overgrown and full of weeds. The vegetation from the forest nearby seemed to be encroaching rapidly, as if it had fully intended to overrun the house itself eventually. There was a broken wagon tipped to the left and a rusted wheelbarrow beside it. The wood cladding looked like it desperately needed a few coats of paint, and some of the shutters were broken and hanging by a single hinge.

Cleo came up beside me and sat, panting. His coat was full of small branches and leaves, and he had mud halfway up his legs. I would have to work him over considerably before taking him into the house. What I feared the most, however, was that he would just start to bark at Elliot and his father, and they would see me spying on them.

"Quiet," I warned him and put my hand on his neck, holding him tightly so he would know I didn't want him charging out of the brush.

Suddenly the lighted window was thrown open and a buxom girl with hair more like her father's leaned out. She was wearing only her bra and a pair of panties.

"Dad!" she screamed. "Dad!"

Elliot's father put down his screwdriver and walked around to the side of the house so he could look up at her.

"What?"

"The water is coming out brown. How am I supposed to take a shower and wash my hair in brown water?"

"Brown?"

"Dirty water," she cried.

"I'm sure it's nothing," he said. "Just hasn't been run in that room for a while. Let it run, and you will see that it clears up."

"I have other things to do than wait for

water to clear up, Dad," she whined.

"Betsy, just give it a chance, please," he pleaded.

"Why did we have to move?" she screamed and backed into the room.

Her father looked up, shook his head, and walked back to join Elliot at the lawn furniture. I could see Betsy pacing, and as she paced, she ran a silver brush through her hair. Although she didn't look that pretty to me, she had beautiful hair, I thought, and I felt a longing in the pit of my stomach. I watched the window for another glimpse of her, and then I grew tired of it and started for home.

It took me a good half an hour to get Cleo cleaned up enough to take him into the house. Mommy already had the dinner table set. Lately, she had agreed to let me help with it, but she made sure to add, "It's something a good son would do anyway."

I could see she still looked troubled about the new neighbors. She didn't want to stop talking about them.

"I was more comfortable with Mr. Baer living there," she said. "As dirty and crotchety as he was, he kept out of our business. All I need is a neighboring woman coming over here to sit and have coffee and gossip. Waste of my time," she spit.

"He said his mother was dead," I told her. For some reason, I had left that out. She raised her eyebrows.

"Oh? Why? What happened to her?"

"I don't know," I said. "He didn't say, and I didn't ask."

"And you were right not to ask. Still," she said looking out the window and speaking in a softer tone, "I wonder if her spirit's followed them here."

The idea raised my eyebrows.

"Would you be able to see her?" I asked.

"Yes," she said. "I would, and so would you," she added firmly.

As if she expected the spirits who hovered about us to be buzzing about the neighbors tonight, she couldn't wait to go out and walk into the shadows. I considered following her, but I knew she didn't like that. She always told me she needed her solitude when she was crossing over.

It was difficult falling asleep that night. I couldn't help thinking about some of the things Elliot had said. Wouldn't it be nice to really make friends with people my own age already? Would he ever come back, or had I made him hate me immediately? I couldn't get his sister out of my mind. The image of her brushing her hair lingered on the insides of my eyelids. I tossed and turned and moaned, but sleep was a door that seemed to have shut on me. I couldn't remember being as restless in a long while.

Mommy heard me and opened my door on her way to her own bedroom, but she wasn't stopping by to see what was bothering me. She had something important to tell me.

"No spirit has accompanied those people here," she said.

"How do you know?"

"I know," she said. "Something's not right. Stay away from those people," she warned and closed the door.

For a long moment, I couldn't move. Something's not right? What did that mean? If I was having trouble falling asleep before, I was surely going to have trouble now, I thought, and I actually didn't fall asleep for another two hours or so.

Every once in a while during the following day, I looked toward the forest, expecting to see Elliot spying on me or perhaps see him walking through the forest. I watched Cleo closely, too, but he didn't bark at anything in particular and mostly just lay nearby me and watched me do my chores. Mommy said nothing more about the new neighbors, but I could see she was still upset about them. When I asked her if she was all right or if there was something else wrong, she ignored me as if I hadn't spoken. What she did remember, however, was that I said I was going fishing.

"I'm glad you're getting back to doing that, Noble, but please be careful," she told me when I went for my pole and the tackle box and can of worms. "Don't stay there too long. I'm going to the supermarket and to do some other shopping. I have to visit Mr. Bogart," she added, which surprised me. We hadn't been back to his jewelry store since she had bought us our amulets years ago. "We'll have dinner a little later tonight."

"Okay," I said.

I went through the woods to the stream, but far down from where the tragedy had occurred. At first I just sat there staring out at the fishing line and waiting to see my sinker bob. I had some nibbles, but nothing significant, and I had to fix a new worm on the hook three times. Suddenly I heard music, rock music. I could tell it was coming from the Baer house, of course, and I couldn't contain my curiosity.

I reeled in my line and put the pole

aside. Then, with Cleo at my heels as usual, I walked carefully through the woods until I reached the Baer property line. The music was coming from the opened upstairs window I knew now to be Betsy's room. I heard a loud peal of laughter, too. Then, there was some shouting, her father's voice. Moments later, the music was turned down and finally turned off.

I could hear the movements they made in their house, and when I went a little farther down on my left, I was able to see into what was their dining room. I saw Elliot standing at the table with his arms folded, and then he sat and only the top of his head was visible.

My curiosity was unstoppable. It grew stronger and stronger until one of my feet followed another and I ran with my head down, almost squatting to keep out of view. Cleo ran beside me, but fortunately kept quiet. It was almost as if he knew he had to be.

When I reached the house, I pressed myself against the wall for a few moments and caught my breath. Then I moved ever so slowly until I was looking through a corner of the window into the dining room. Elliot's father came from the kitchen holding a roasted turkey on a silver platter. He wore an apron. Now that I looked more closely at his face, I saw he and Elliot had the same forehead and nose, but Elliot had a stronger, firmer mouth.

Betsy followed with a bowl of mashed potatoes and set it down. She was wearing a black and red pin-striped short-sleeved shirt with a black tie tied loosely around an open collar and a pair of matching black pin-striped pants. I thought she would have looked more like a boy than I did, except for the fact that her cleavage was prominent in the opened blouse and her hair was beautifully brushed down about her shoulders. I couldn't believe the amount of makeup she had on for a family dinner, too.

Looking at her closely now, too, I could see some resemblances to Elliot, but she had a rounder face with small, brown eyes and a very weak mouth that drooped in the corners, giving her a habitual look of disgust. She practically slammed the bowl on the table and flopped into her seat.

"I'd like to go to the movies," she moaned. "I'd like to meet some of the kids my age before school starts here, and Billy Lester wants to take me."

"We don't know anything about him

yet," her father said.

"What is there to know? He's the son of the real estate agent who sold us the house, Dad. He can't be a serial killer."

"I thought we would just enjoy our first big dinner at our new home."

"So how long is that going to take?" she pursued.

"It would be nice to spend the first few nights together here, don't you think? There's so much to do, Betsy."

She pouted.

"It's your fault, Dad, for letting her buy all these new clothes. She thinks she has to go parade around and show off," Elliot said.

"I do not. Just because you don't care what you look like, that doesn't mean I have to be undistinguished."

"Wow. Excuse me. Undistinguished. Miss America," Elliot teased.

"Come on," their father said. "It's a new beginning for us. Let's all get off to a good start."

"Some beginning," Betsy insisted.

Her father looked frustrated.

"It just takes time to settle in," he emphasized.

"I'll never settle in," she muttered. "It's going to be boring living here, just as I thought," she wailed and sat back with her arms folded under her bosom. When she pouted like that, she looked like a fish we called a sucker.

"Betsy, please," her father pleaded.

"Well, it is going to be if I have to sit home every night and stare at these old walls and run water until it stops being brown and —"

"All right, all right," her father said, surrendering. "After we eat, help with the dishes and then go to the movies, but I want you home early, Betsy. I don't know this area yet. I don't want you going off and getting into any trouble."

"I won't," she said, satisfied.

"Sure she won't. And the sun won't come out tomorrow either," Elliot said.

"You're such a dork," Betsy told him.

"I didn't get into trouble last year," he snapped back at her.

"No, you didn't. You only got suspended twice for getting into fights," she said, wagging her head. "And nearly failed two subjects."

"That's nowhere near what you did, and you know it," he countered, playing Ping-Pong with accusations.

"Can we at least eat in peace?" their father said in a desperate, tired voice.

They glared at each other.

Was this what it would have been like with Noble and me? I wondered. Yet even though they were bickering, there was something attractive about it. It made me smile. Soon they were talking about other things — the house, the plans their father had for fixing it up. He made it sound like a wonderful project for them. Betsy said little, ate fast, but listened and promised to do what had to be done.

"I want to get another dog," Elliot told his father. "The crazy people have a golden retriever."

"We'll see," his father said. "One thing at a time here, Elliot."

Crazy people? Is that what they all thought about Mommy and me?

Suddenly, I thought I saw Elliot looking at the window. I pulled myself back quickly, my heart pounding. Then I turned and, with my body folded again, ran for the woods. Cleo loped behind me, taking much too long.

I looked back when I reached the trees.

Elliot was standing in the window. He had pulled up the blinds and was looking in my direction.

I was sure I clearly saw a smile on his face.

His smile chased me through the woods.

I hadn't realized how late it had gotten. I scooped up the pole, the fishing tackle box, and the can of worms. Then I charged through the woods and back to our house. Mommy was just pulling up the driveway.

"What's wrong?" she asked, getting out of the car quickly. She had her arms full of bags.

"Nothing," I said.

"Why are you running out of the woods so hard? Did you see something? Hear something? What?" she demanded as I stood there panting.

"No," I said.

She stared at me. She looked like she could see right through my head.

"They won't be here long," she suddenly predicted. "I've been told. There are dark days ahead for them. You listen carefully, Noble. You'll hear the same thing, unless you already have. Have you?"

"No," I said, fear draping over me like a gust of cold rain and wind.

"You will," she insisted and started for the house. "I have much to do," she added and mumbled, "much to do. Clean up for dinner," she told me when she turned back at the door. "And get that dog clean before you bring him in."

"Okay."

She went inside, and I looked back at the woods.

What was going to happen to them? I wondered. When would I hear about it?

Where were the spirits, and why wasn't I seeing them more and hearing them?

How much longer would it be before I was as welcome as Mommy was?

Talk to me! I wanted to shout at the shadows.

Maybe I did.

But all I heard was Cleo's panting and the sound of my own heart thumping.

12

Conjugation

It wasn't solely Mommy's cryptic warnings that put the shivers in me at night and made every sound I heard, every creak, resonate like a firecracker. It was the things she did around our house and property that she had never done as intensely or as abundantly that really frightened me.

For one thing, she had candles burning in every window, and not just the window in the living room. Apparently, Mr. Bogart had given her some other things to do as well. She had brought home a decorative long knife. She said nothing about it, but after dinner, she suddenly produced it and without telling me why, she went out with it. I followed and stood on the porch where I watched her use the knife to draw a long line in the earth between the meadow and the woods facing the old Baer place. Then she returned to the house and brought out something else from her package. It was a five-pointed star in a circle made of brass. She pinned it securely to our front door. Above it she pinned two leafy twigs of fennel.

"What does all this mean, Mommy?" I asked, my eyes searching every pocket of darkness around us. It felt more like Halloween.

"It's how we protect ourselves, keep evil away," she told me. She said nothing more.

Afterward, she returned to the living room, where she sat without any other light burning but the candle. Its glow flickered off her face, turning her skin amber. I could see her eyes fixed firmly on the darkness, unmoving. Her intense staring frightened me. She wouldn't talk; she wouldn't even glance my way. How long can she sit like this? I wondered. What was she expecting to see? The silence, the candle flickering, tweaked my nerves. I couldn't remain there watching her. Even Cleo retreated and was anxious to follow me upstairs, where I tried to distract myself with my lessons and reading.

I kept dozing off, so finally I went to sleep, but sometime during the night I awoke and listened hard because I was sure I heard someone singing. I rose and went to my window. It was Mommy outside, singing a hymn. Cleo was awake, too, but I didn't encourage him to get up. When I left my room, I closed the door so he couldn't follow. Then I went downstairs and quietly opened the front door. Slowly I approached the edge of the porch and looked off toward the old cemetery, where I saw her standing with a lantern before the tombstones. When she stopped singing and blew out the light, I turned and quickly retreated, hurrying back upstairs. Cleo was up and waiting for me.

"Go to sleep," I told him and got into bed again. He curled up, groaned, and lowered his head to his paws. I listened for Mommy's footsteps and heard her pause at my door. After another moment, she went to her own bedroom, and all was quiet.

Despite the warm, humid night, I shivered and wrapped the blanket about myself tightly. I was scrunched up in a fetal position, embracing myself. What was the danger Mommy feared? What would happen to us? What was so powerful that even our wondrous spirits couldn't protect us enough on their own? Had I done anything to cause this all to happen?

Every creak in the house snapped my

eyelids open and made me hold my breath to listen harder. I saw Cleo was asleep, and that reassured me. Finally, exhausted, I drifted into sleep myself, as restless as it was. I woke once when I saw myself at the bottom of that grave, and my eyes suddenly snapped open. My arms lifted toward me, and I literally jumped out of sleep. It took me a while to slow my heartbeat and then tentatively, still frightened, lower my head back to the pillow and risk closing my eyes.

However, the morning was so bright it swept away my dark dreams and thoughts as if they had all been cobwebs. Cleo was already panting at the door, anxious to be let out. When I rose, washed, and dressed myself, I found Mommy up and about, looking fresh and relaxed. She beamed a happy, soft smile at me. It was truly as if all I had seen her do the night before was just a dream.

"Looks like you need a haircut," she said. "I'll give it to you right after we have breakfast. Then I have to go to see Mr. Lyman, our attorney. We have some business matters to discuss. He called the other day and pointed out I needed to make some changes in my will, with Celeste gone and all. He's called me many times about it, and I've finally decided to do it," she added.

"Can I go, too?" I asked quickly. My talking with Elliot, spying on his family, hearing the music and the chatter, filled me with more of a longing to be in public, to see things, especially more people my age.

"It will be quite boring for you. All you'll do is sit in a lobby and wait for me. I really have no intention on doing anything else. Just enjoy the day, Noble. Go fishing again. Maybe you'll have better luck. You used to bring home dinner for us, remember? I can still hear you yelling for me to come out to see the fish you were bringing home so proudly," she said, smiling at the recollection. "Celeste usually trailed behind with her head down. She was never very good at catching fish."

I was disappointed at her refusing to take me along, but her relaxed confidence did make me feel better. All of her preparations must be working, I thought. Whatever threatened us was driven back. We were safe again, but when she gave me my haircut, she warned me once more about staying away from the new neighbors.

"My mother always told me that evil was like an infectious disease. If you get too close to someone who is infected, he or she can infect you. No matter how well you're protected," she added. "But you already know all this, my precious one. You know it because you have my heart," she said and kissed me on the forehead.

Afterward, Cleo and I stood on the porch and watched her drive off to our lawyer's office. I really wasn't in the mood to go fishing, but the warm, partly cloudy day was too inviting to ignore by shutting myself up inside and reading. Cleo looked anxious to get some exercise, too, so finally, I fetched my fishing pole and the tackle, found my can of worms, and walked across the meadow toward the woods.

Sparrows and robins flitted from branch to branch excitedly, greeting me like an old friend returning. The scent of pine and fresh earth filled my nostrils, and I was invigorated. I should get out more, I thought. Our home, as comfortable as it was, was too dark and closed these days, too stifling. I felt like a newly born bird eager to test its wings in flight. Everything beyond our farm can't be evil and everything on it can't be good, I thought, and wondered if that was a blasphemous thought.

When I reached my spot on the stream, I fixed my pole and cast my line. Cleo wandered about as usual, exploring on his own. I sat staring at the water, at the way it foamed around rocks and carried branches and leaves downstream. The creek was busy today, I thought. I remembered how Noble used to think it sounded like someone gurgling. That constant sound, the buzz of some bees nearby, birds gossiping around me, and the warm afternoon put me into a daze, I guess. I snapped out of it when I heard a splash.

At first I wondered if it was a fish. I sat up quickly and studied the water, and then I saw another splash to the right of my line. That was followed by a third to the left, and I realized quickly that someone was throwing rocks. I stood up and spun around.

Elliot came walking out of the woods to my right, a wide, impish smile on his lips. He wore a short-sleeved blue shirt and a pair of faded jeans. My first thought was to follow Mommy's orders and pick up my things and run, but I stood my ground. Cleo was wagging his tail, too, and hurried to approach him.

"Don't start talking about 'No Trespassing' signs," he warned as he drew closer. "I saw you spying on us. You were the one trespassing."

"I was not spying on you," I said. He smirked.

"I guess you're not too good of a liar. Can't you even think of some excuse?"

"I don't have to think of anything. Just leave me alone," I said.

"How can you like being alone so much?" he asked with real curiosity. He looked around at the woods and the stream and smirked with disgust. "I hated the idea of moving out here because I knew how isolated we were going to be. Back home I used to just catch a bus or a ride and go to the mall when I was bored. It was easy. Until I get my license and my car, I've either got to walk or ride a bike or something, and what's there to go see and do anyway?

"I know, I know. You can't tell me," he said before I could respond. "Nature boy," he tacked on disdainfully and threw another rock into the water.

"You're scaring off the fish," I said.

"Like you really care," he countered. Then he gave me that impish smile of his again. "What's this, the big excitement of the day?"

"I like it," I said firmly.

"You like it? This is what you do with your free time? Jeez. Don't you even think about girls, or do you have something better?"

"What I do is none of your business," I said.

He laughed.

"I bet. I bet you don't want it to be anyone else's business but yours."

"What's that supposed to mean?"

"Hey," he said holding up his hands. "I don't really care if you found something else to take the place of girls. Maybe a big, pretty fish, huh?"

"You're disgusting," I said.

"I'm disgusting? That's disgusting? What did I do, offend your tender soul? What are you, a mama's boy or something? Is that the story? Mommy doesn't want Junior to get himself dirty by hanging around with dirty teenagers or something? Is that why she keeps you chained to this place?"

"I'm not chained to anything."

"You're not?"

"Think what you like," I said.

He smiled and reached into his top pocket to get a pack of cigarettes. He pounded one out and put it in his mouth. I watched him, unable to not be intrigued with his every move. He smiled.

"Want one?"

"No," I said quickly.

"So you don't smoke either, huh?"

"No, I don't," I said.

"Pure in mind and body. Nature boy." He laughed and puffed on his cigarette, blowing the smoke directly at me.

"Stop calling me that. Look, just leave me alone," I said. "This is our side of the creek, and you don't belong here."

"Not so fast with all the orders, nature boy. I was going to ignore you until I caught you peeping into our window. What were you hoping to do, catch my sister undressed or something?"

I felt the heat rise up my neck and into my face.

"No!" I practically screamed. He laughed and flicked the ashes off his cigarette, again in my direction.

"It's all right if that's what you were hoping to see. She's sexy. That's one of the real reasons my father wanted us to move out here. She was getting into all sorts of trouble with boys, actually college men, know what I mean?"

He puffed his cigarette and studied me, which made me very uncomfortable. I turned away.

"Maybe you don't have any idea what I mean. You've never been with a girl or been on a date or anything, have you, home-school boy?"

"I can see you're not going to leave me be," I said and started to reel in my line.

"Man, what a pussy," he said.

I tried to ignore him and continue to gather my things, but he stepped up behind me and pushed me so that I had to step forward, my right foot going into the water. He laughed when I spun around.

"Got to be more careful," he said. "Here, let me try that fishing pole," he added and stepped forward to take it from me, the cigarette burning away in his mouth.

"Get your hands off it," I said, pulling back.

He grabbed hold anyway, and we struggled for a moment. Then I let go and pushed him at the center of his chest as hard as I could. He was holding on to the rod, but he fell backward and sat right in the stream. He jumped up as if the water burned him. He was red with rage.

"Bastard," he said, charging at me. He wrapped his arm around my head and tried to turn me and throw me down, but I pushed up on his arm and slipped out easily. Then I grabbed his left arm and pulled him as hard as I could. It threw him off balance, and he tripped over some rocks and went down again, this time his arm completely submerging in the water nearly up to his shoulder.

Cleo was barking now, but not angrily. He was excited and circled and yapped as if he was finally part of something that was fun. Elliot crawled to his feet, the cigarette soaked and dangling from his lips. He thought a moment, and then he smiled, scooped up some water, and heaved it in my direction. I backed away to avoid it.

"You're not getting away with this," he said, laughing, and he started for me again. One thing I didn't want was for him to throw me into the water.

I turned and ran into the woods, Cleo charging behind and barking and Elliot following and yelling, "C'mon, nature boy. It's your turn to have a bath."

I ran as fast as I could, and I should have been able to pull away from him easily because these were my woods and I knew every path and clearing, but my panic made me sloppy and careless. I was charging through brush that slowed me down. By the time I reached the next clearing, Elliot was right behind me. He leaped at me, tackling me around my knees, and we both slammed into the weeds and wild grass. We rolled about for a moment, he trying to get my arms pinned. I squirmed and pushed at him, but he was over me and was able to hold me down. We were both breathing so hard, we couldn't talk for a moment.

He moved his legs so that he could put his knees on my upper arms and hold me firmly to the ground, while he sat back on my stomach.

"Okay now, you going to stop this crap or what?"

"Let me up," I cried.

"Not yet. I want to know some stuff first."

"Let me up," I said, struggling. He weighed too much for me to move him.

Cleo sat by, panting and watching with excitement. Why wasn't he angry? I wondered. Where was my spiritual protection?

"What do you really do for fun? You don't just fish and study and work a garden, do you?"

"Yes," I said.

"Bull. You have to have some other kind of excitement. Is your mother really a witch?"

"If she is, you better worry, because I'll have her put a spell on you," I said as threateningly as I could. He started to laugh and then stopped. I could feel him relaxing his grip.

"I don't believe in that stuff," he said, and he moved his legs off my arms. He looked a bit concerned. "Come on, tell the truth."

"My mother isn't a witch," I said, rubbing my arms and turning away from him. He sat back. Cleo, the traitor, snuggled up next to him.

"So why do people make up all those stories about her casting spells and having secret ceremonies?"

"They're just jealous and mean because we're independent people," I said.

"What's that weird thing on your front door?" he asked, wiping his sleeve over his muddied face.

"It's nothing. My mother believes in some things, but she's not a witch. Anyway, if you saw that, you must be the one peeping, not me."

"I just happened to see it this morning. I was looking for you. Did you get an earful last night spying on us? And don't deny it again. I saw you at the window. You heard what we were saying. Well?"

"No, I didn't get any earful of anything. I just went there to see if you were telling the truth, that you really did buy the property and move in."

He sat back, petted Cleo, and looked at his pack of soaked cigarettes.

"Thanks a lot," he said. "It's not easy sneaking cigarettes into my house."

"You shouldn't be smoking anyway," I told him.

He shook his head at me.

"I suppose you don't do anything that's supposedly bad for you."

"No, I don't."

"No drinking, no smoking, no pot or anything?"

"I care about myself," I said and stood up and brushed myself off. He sat there watching me.

"Yeah, well, nobody worries about that stuff, at least nobody our age where I come from. You think it's going to be different for me here?" he asked. Then he shook his head. "I forgot. You wouldn't know. Does anyone else about our age live nearby, any normal person I could become friends with?"

"I don't know," I said. "The next house is about a half mile down toward Sandburg, but I think the children living there are all about four or five. And I'm more normal than you are."

"Yeah, right. Home school, weird things

on your front door, fish and garden all day. Very normal."

"You don't know anything," I said.

"You're really not bored? You're happy just hanging out with a dog?" he asked, still amazed.

"I'm very busy. There's a lot to do on our farm. I don't have time to be bored," I told him.

"Man, you are weird."

"So stay away from me," I snapped at him and started back to the stream. He got up and followed alongside.

"I'm sure my father wishes I was bored like you," he said in a more casual tone. I didn't walk as fast because he was talking about himself now. "My sister wasn't the only one getting into hot water. I cheated on a final exam and failed social studies last year. Had to go to summer school to make it up, which meant I couldn't get a summer job. Dad wasn't going to let me get my license this year, so I had to be sure I at least passed everything. Actually, I'm glad he wanted to move, because he had to offer something to get me to go along. That's how I got him to agree to the car. Betsy was giving him a really hard time about it. I knew I had him over a barrel after a while."

I stopped and looked at him.

"What?" he asked.

"You don't sound like a family. You sound like combatants," I said.

"Combatants?" He grimaced.

"It means adversaries. Belligerents? Enemies? You know what that means, at least?"

"Oh. You are smart," he said.

We walked back toward the stream, Cleo following right behind us now and not rushing off to investigate some hole in the ground as usual.

"Maybe your mother did some magic thing to make you that way," he added with a wry smile. "Maybe she could do it for me, too, huh?"

"There's only one magic thing to do to get smarter, Elliot, study, read, pay attention to instructions, and work."

"Right," he said smugly. "You know, my last girlfriend was pretty smart, always on the honor roll. And she was a junior varsity cheerleader, too, for the basketball team."

I saw him smile, but I said nothing. I didn't want him to stop talking. What was it like to be a cheerleader and to go to school games?

"She was very competitive. The only thing I could beat her at easily was ring toss. Of course," he added, "we played strip ring toss. I invented it," he added with a twist in his lips.

"What's that?" I asked unable to stop myself.

"Simple. Whoever lost a round had to take off something. I usually got her naked in less than ten rounds."

I felt my breathing quicken.

"She was nicely built, too. She wasn't the first girl I did it with, though. I did it when I was only twelve," he boasted. "We had these neighbors, the Brakfists, who had a daughter named Sandra. Everyone teased her and called her Sandra Breakfast. She was a brain, too," he added glancing at me. "The truth," he said in a whisper, "was she knew more about the old birds and the bees than I did. Once in a while, I did homework with her because I was such a lousy student."

We broke out of the forest and approached the stream again. My pole was lying over some rocks, the line carried out by the rushing water. During our roughhousing, the can of worms had been knocked over, and most of it had spilled. I knelt down, scooping as much as I could back.

"Don't you want to hear what happened — or are you gay or something?" he asked, annoyed I could get distracted. I wasn't. I just didn't want to show how interested I really was.

"Well?"

"Okay, what happened?"

"You think I'm making it up?"

I shrugged.

"How would I know if you were or you weren't?" I asked, and he folded his brow.

"Because I'm telling you," he said gruffly.

"So tell me," I countered.

"Ahh —" He waved at me and looked away.

"I'm sorry. Tell me," I asked with more enthusiasm. It was easy to see he wanted to tell me.

He sat on a big boulder.

"It was funny, actually," he said. "We were studying science and something called conju . . . conje—"

"Conjugation?"

"Yeah, that's it, but it was about worms," he said nodding at my can.

"So?"

"So, she started to expand the discussion. How's that for vocabulary, smart boy? She began to talk about how important it was to know about human reproduction, and we got into it that way. She was, what's that word that my dad uses about my sister? Pro . . . something."

"Promiscuous?"

"Yeah, that's it," he said, excited. "She was promiscuous. I was certainly not the first boy she fooled around with. To tell you the truth, she scared me, but I went along so as not to be pussy, and one thing led to another."

"What do you mean, led to another?"

"You know. *Another.* Touchy-feely first and then undressing and then conjugating. With her it was like following directions to put something together. First you do this and then you do that. I was excited, but I felt like I was back in school. I didn't do it with her again. She tried to get me to come over to supposedly study, and when I didn't want to, she found someone else. The joke around school became, who had Sarah for breakfast lately? Get it?"

He waited for my response, but I said nothing. I completed reeling in the line instead.

"You don't believe me, huh?"

"It's not important whether I do or not," I said.

"You are weird."

"You want to stop saying that," I said,

spinning around on him.

He shrugged.

"I guess you have reason to be weird."

"And what exactly is that supposed to mean?"

"With what happened to your sister and all. They never found her body, huh?"

I stared at him.

"I'm just asking."

"I don't like talking about it," I said.

"Did your mother think it was that old guy who owned our house?"

"I said —"

"All right." He was silent.

"It's painful," I told him.

"Yeah. Well, sometimes missing kids show up. I read about that girl who turned up ten years or so later. It was in one of those newspapers you get at the supermarket. She had a flashback or something and knew how to get home like a dog or something. Maybe that will happen to your sister.

"You see that movie on television about a month ago about that teenage girl who discovers she was kidnapped by the people she thinks are her parents?"

"I don't watch television," I said.

"What?"

I put the pole over my shoulder, picked

up the tackle box, and then hugged the worm can against me.

"We don't watch television."

"You don't ever watch television?"

"That's right."

"Well, what do you do at night?"

"Read, listen to music, work on projects."

"I'd go crazy without television. Dad promised to get us hooked up as soon as possible. We don't get anything on that old antennae. Do you get to a movie once in a while at least?"

"No," I said starting away.

"Well, don't you want to?" he asked, charging after me. I walked on. "Huh?"

"Sometimes," I confessed.

"But your mother won't let you."

"She says there's not much of any value to see."

"How would she know if you don't go?" he asked. "Oh, I get it. She can see beyond," he said dramatically, and swept his arm out toward the horizon.

"Anyway, let me tell you about this movie last week," he continued, walking alongside me. I felt myself smile inside. It seemed he needed company more than I did. "So they come to get the girl. The cops come to the house and tell her she's been kidnapped by her so-called parents, and they confess. She gets returned to her real family, but the grandmother doesn't want her to be brought back."

"Why not?" I asked.

"Turns out the grandfather is her real father."

I stopped and shook my head.

"I don't understand."

"What's so hard? The grandfather had sex with his daughter-in-law, and she was born, and the grandmother had her stolen off when she was a baby. I bet you wish now you saw the movie, huh?"

I said nothing.

"They replay them sometimes. If I see it's coming on, I'll let you know, and you can watch it at my house."

I started to shake my head.

"You don't have to tell your mother where you're going. You'll just pretend to go fishing or something."

"I don't lie to my mother," I said sharply.

"Yeah, right."

"I don't."

"Well, it doesn't have to be a lie as such. You just don't tell her everything. What they don't know doesn't hurt them," he recited.

"You can't have a loving relationship without honesty," I preached.

He swung his eyes.

"Oh, brother. You've been living alone too long, Noble. When you do break out of here, you're going to be like a kid in a candy store, and that's when you do get into lots of trouble," he said, trying to be the wise one now. I had to smile. "What's so funny?"

"That's the best excuse for doing bad things I've heard or read."

"Yeah, well, it's true. Look at these college kids who are on their own for the first time in their lives."

"What do you mean?"

"They go wild. They drink too much, stay out too late, get pregnant, do drugs, everything. If their parents didn't keep them so chained up all the time, they wouldn't turn out that way," he said, nodding.

"Did your parents keep you and your sister chained up?"

"No, not really."

"So?"

"So what?"

"You just finished telling me about all the trouble your sister's been in with older guys and how you've messed up so much yourself, right?"

"Oh, you're such a puss—"

"Look, go find a dictionary and learn another word, will you?" I said and moved faster.

He stopped.

"Maybe your mother will let me go to your home school and get smart like you," he called after me.

I didn't turn around.

"I tell you what," he shouted, "come around and I'll teach you about conjugation and you can improve my vocabulary. Just in case you're ever with something called a girl!" he screamed.

Cleo paused to look back at him.

"Come on, Cleo," I said. "Leave him be."

I hurried home to clean up before Mommy saw me and wondered why I was so muddied and disheveled. Afterward, I tried to do some reading and move forward on the lessons Mommy had outlined in science and math, but I kept finding myself distracted, pausing for long moments and thinking about the things Elliot had told me. Being with him and listening to him did leave me feeling as if I was stranded on an island. Was this the evil that Mommy was afraid would infect me? Were these images of sex and the stories he told like germs or something? I fought hard to keep them out of my mind. It frightened me that I was having so hard a time doing it. In the end I decided to go out and up to the old cemetery. It was where Mommy went for spiritual guidance, I thought. Why shouldn't I?

As was often the case during these late summer days, the sky changed rapidly. Warm, increasingly humid air warned of an impending shower. Despite our altitude being up in the mountains, we could get a downpour that I'm sure seemed more like a tropical storm. The clouds above circled the patches of blue, closing them off with what looked like real determination. Where was Mommy? I wondered. Why was it taking her so long? She said she was going nowhere else.

I stood before the old tombstones and tried hard to feel some spiritual presence.

"Please come back to me, Daddy," I prayed. "I need you. Please. I don't want to be bad. I don't want to do anything to hurt myself or Mommy."

I touched the Infant Jordan tomb the way Mommy always did, and I closed my eyes and tried to feel those embossed hands move, but all I felt was the cool stone. Nothing happened, even after I sang some of the old hymn Mommy sang. Cleo watched me from outside the gate and then sprawled out and waited, lowering his head to his paws and closing his eyes.

Suddenly he lifted his head and looked toward the driveway. I turned and saw two cars approaching. One was Mommy's, but one I did not recognize. As they drew closer, I saw that someone else was driving Mommy's car, a man in a blue shirt. Mommy looked very upset. The second car was driven by a man wearing a similar shirt. I hurried out of the cemetery and down to the front of the house as they pulled up.

The man driving Mommy got out quickly and went around to open her door. I saw he was wearing some sort of uniform with matching blue pants. The second car stopped, and that man, dressed similarly, stepped out and walked slowly toward them. Mommy's driver helped her out. She looked wobbly.

"Mommy?" I cried.

"She's all right," the man helping her said.

Mommy opened her eyes and looked at me, strangely at first, and then calmly, nodding at the door. I hurried ahead to open it, and they all walked up.

"I'll be fine now," Mommy said, turning to the man helping her. "Thank you. Thank you both."

"You really should have let the doctor look you over and do those tests, Mrs. Atwell," he said. He turned to me. "Keep an eye on her," he said.

They turned and went to the second car.

"What happened, Mommy?"

"Let's just go in," she said quickly, and we entered the house. She closed the door, took a breath, and walked to the living room.

I followed and watched her move as quickly as she could to Great-Grandad Jordan's chair. Once she was in it, she looked relieved.

"What happened?"

"I fainted in the lawyer's office. They took me to the hospital before I could protest, and then those two attendants insisted they take me home and not let me drive myself. I'm fine," she insisted.

"Why did you faint?"

She shook her head, looked away, and then turned back.

"Maybe it was just too hard to be forced to remember everything, losing . . . losing a precious child like that and being made to acknowledge it. It was just like going to a funeral, watching the coffin lowered, the dirt cast over it, facing the reality. My heart skipped beats and I lost my breath. I'll be fine," she insisted. "I just need some rest. Get me a glass of cold water," she told me, and I hurried to do it.

She drank it slowly, and then she leaned back and smiled at me.

"We'll be all right," she said. "This is nothing." She closed her eyes a moment and then opened them quickly. "Did I see you were at the cemetery when we drove up to the house?"

"Yes," I said.

"Why?" she asked.

"I . . . I was hoping . . . I wanted to . . ."

Her eyes grew small.

"You didn't do anything you shouldn't have done, did you, Noble?"

"No," I said quickly, maybe too quickly.

"If we weaken our fortress, they will come marching in," she assured me.

I bit down on my lower lip as she studied my face.

"Go make yourself something for dinner," she said.

"What about you, Mommy?"

"I'm just going to sit here and rest. Go on," she said. "I'll be all right now."

I hesitated, and then I started out. At the

door I turned back to look at her. She had her eyes closed and her head back, and she looked like she had aged years.

It couldn't be just the thought of losing a child, could it, I wondered? How many times did she relive it? Why did our attorney have to force her to face it again? Why couldn't people just leave us alone?

Maybe it had to do with something else. Maybe it was because of how I had strayed and how I had let my mind wander and dream and fantasize. Mommy always warned me they could read my thoughts.

This is my fault, I concluded.

Somehow, some way, this is my fault.

I had to try harder to be good.

Why was it that voices inside me were warning me it would be more and more difficult to do?

I trembled inside just the way Mommy often did when she sensed something dark and dreadful was nearby.

Only it wasn't just nearby for me, I thought.

For me, it was inside, resting comfortably under my heart.

13

Through a Peephole

Mommy seemed better later in the evening, although for days afterward, she did move slower and take more naps, often falling asleep in the living room. Sometimes, when I saw her napping, I noticed that her eyes twitched and her lips trembled. One particular time, she woke with a start and looked about as if she didn't know where she was or how she had gotten there.

"What is it?" she asked me when she caught me standing there and staring at her. "What's wrong?"

"Nothing," I replied quickly.

She looked suspicious and wrapped her shawl around herself.

"Get back to your work," she ordered, and afterward, I was the one catching her staring at me. I don't know what she expected to find me doing or what she thought she might see. It made me very nervous. I wondered if anything dark and foreboding was following me around the farm, something I was unable to see myself.

Summer was fading quickly this year. Nights were colder than usual, and the leaves actually began showing signs of turning by late August. We had an early frost, too, and that hurt some of our late corn and other vegetables. Mommy even complained about her herbal garden and the effect the early cold was having on those plants. It appeared her spiritual advisers were right when they told her this was going to be a longer, harder winter than usual.

I avoided the woods and didn't go fishing. Every once in a while, I was sure I spotted Elliot watching our house and me from the forest's edge, but I did not acknowledge him, and he remained in the shadows or behind some trees. Because of the stories he had heard about us, he was sufficiently afraid of Mommy, I suppose, to keep from approaching our home or me. After a while, I didn't see him anymore, and then, of course, I knew that public school had begun and he would be occupied and have made new friends by now anyway.

Mommy was annoyed about having to do another independent study plan and submit it, but she had to by law. This time she went to the school without me to deliver it, and when she came home, she mumbled and grumbled about the arrogance of Dr. Camfield and all those educators who were full of themselves.

About mid-October, it began to rain a great deal. Some of the downpours were long and hard, so that before the month had ended most of the beautiful yellow, brown, and orange leaves were pounded off their trees and matted down on the forest floor, the cold raindrops like nails. Skeletons appeared again. Dull, dark, naked branches, awkward and twisted, emerged in the twilight. Their grayness was like a single, leaden note resounding around our house. The birds that hadn't already fled south looked depressed, hardly flitting about and rarely singing. They resembled stuffed birds more than live ones at times.

Mommy took to sitting for long hours alone, staring out the living room window into the darkness, which was often undisturbed thick coats of night because of the predominantly overcast skies. She didn't speak much about any spiritual presence.

She never mentioned Daddy anymore. The truth was, she was acting lonelier than me, and because of that, I was more and more worried about her.

We did continue to do all our chores and keep busy. I studied whatever lessons she set out for me to study, and she played her piano, albeit not as much as usual, and the music she chose was rarely light or happy. She seemed to want to bathe herself in a pool of melancholy. She complained about the cold weather's effect on her hands and moaned about the poor quality of some of her remedies these days. Even so, she continued her needlework and kept the house as clean as ever, if not more so.

I did constant battle with my own driving curiosity, which wanted to take me by the hand and lead me back to spy on Elliot and his father and sister. Another world, a family with all of its laughter and tears, anger and joy, loomed just through the island of trees between us. I toyed with approaching their home from the road instead of going through the woods. I lingered at times at the edge of our property and dared myself to go forward, but I hesitated long enough to overcome the urge and return to my own world.

And then, one day in early November,

when I was gathering some kindling wood at the edge of the forest, I heard Elliot call to me. I turned and saw him leaning smugly against a maple tree, that impish smile of his twisting his bright lips. He wore a red jacket and a baseball cap with NEW YORK YANKEES written on it. I heard keys jangling and saw him hold up a set and shake them.

"Guess what these are," he said.

I looked toward the house first to see if Mommy was outside, and then I stepped forward, the kindling wood in my arms.

"I have no idea," I said, trying to imply I had no interest either, even though I did.

"To my car, stupid. I passed the test easily enough, and my father had no choice but to do what he had promised. It's a four-year-old car, but it's pretty sharp. It's black, a metallic black, you know, with chrome wheels."

"I'm happy for you," I said and turned to carry the wood to the house.

"Hey, hold up. Don't you want to know what I've been doing all this time?"

I paused.

"No," I said.

"Liar. I looked for you at the stream from time to time, but never saw you there. How come? Afraid you'll fall in the water again?" he asked, widening his smile.

"No, I'm not afraid of anything. I've been busy, that's all. There is a great deal to do around here," I said, "and little time to waste talking to you."

"Right, like feed the chickens. I'm in school, you know. I made some friends. It's not as terrible as I thought it was going to be. There are these girls who are actually pretty cool."

"Great. I'm happy for you."

"All right, all right," he said, turning serious. "I'm sorry I pushed you around."

"That didn't bother me," I snapped back at him.

"Good. You want to take a ride with me?"

"No."

"Why not? Jeez. We'll cruise the area, check it out. I'll introduce you to some other guys our age and maybe some girls, too. I won't even ask you to chip in for gas."

"I don't want to cruise the area. There's nothing and no one that interests me," I said. "Enjoy your car," I told him and hurried away.

"Even my sister? Even she doesn't interest you?" he screamed after me.

I heard him laugh, but I didn't pause. I

continued toward the house without turning and entered. For a moment I remained at the door. Then I peered out the front window and looked toward the forest where he had been standing. He was gone.

But I didn't feel relieved.

I felt disappointed.

A few days later, we had an early snow. It was actually a welcome sight because the white blanket covered the gray, dreary trees and pale grass and bushes. Even the birds that spent their winter with us looked pleased and more energetic. The day after it was warm again, however, and the cloudless sky gave the sun an opportunity to melt the snow quickly. The world glistened, especially in the moonlit evening when the cold air hovered around freezing. The trunks of the trees and the branches shimmered like someone had painted them all with a glossy clear polish.

I was free in the afternoon. Mommy had fallen asleep again after spending the morning cleaning the house, this time with a vengeance. She seemed to see dirt where there wasn't any, spots where there were none. Toward the latter part of the morning, she went up to the tower room to dust and scrub. I could hear how intensely she was working, and I wasn't surprised when later, after lunch, she practically collapsed on the settee and dozed off.

A terrible new sense of loneliness came over me. It had been so long since I had a companion. Despite the facade I had put up in front of Elliot, work, as hard and as long as it could be, didn't compensate. I was actually running out of ways to occupy my mind, and the school lessons Mommy set out were easier than expected. In the back of my mind I thought the school lessons for Celeste would have been more of a challenge, but I dared not say anything like that.

The truth was, I couldn't ignore the stirring going on within me. Even without mirrors, I found ways to see my reflection, sometimes in a windowpane, sometimes in some shiny silver. The face that looked back at me intrigued me. It wasn't the face I felt I wore. It truly looked more like a mask. Where am I, the real me? I wondered. Where have I gone?

Eventually, a Greek myth I had read recently drew me back to the water, where the stream was caught and circled into something of a pond. Years and years ago, when Daddy was alive, he would take us to the pond to swim. The myth that tickled my brain was the myth of Narcissus.

Looking into the water, Narcissus fell in love with his own image, and when he realized it was only an image, he died. Mommy wanted me to read it so I would learn to be unselfish and avoid caring too much about things that didn't matter. I understood all that, but I still longed to see something beautiful in me. Was that evil?

Cleo was practically ecstatic that I was returning to the woods. His eyes were bright, and he was running about everywhere, his unbounded energy amusing. I tried calming him down, but it was like trying to hold back the wind. Crashing through bushes, digging, barking, chasing every bird, he circled and charged ahead of me. When we reached the pond, he lunged for the water and went in completely, dog-paddling his way across and then back, his head bobbing as if his neck was one big spring. I couldn't help but laugh at him.

Then I sat on a rock and looked at the water to stare at myself. Mommy had my hair very closely cut, even shorter than Noble wore his own. My added weight made my face rounder than I wished it to be, but my lips didn't thicken, and despite all the hard work I had done, I still had slight features. I'm almost pretty, I thought.

"Well, if it isn't the hermit," I heard and

nearly jumped out of my body.

There he was, Elliot, coming out of the woods toward me.

"What do you do, wait around all day to see if I'm in the woods?" I asked, annoyed at being so surprised.

"Hardly. But I did hear the dog barking, and I knew you're the only one with a dog around here. It didn't exactly take brain surgery. Where's your fishing pole?"

"I didn't come here to fish," I said.

"Oh?" He looked around. "Well, you're obviously not here to swim, right? That water is probably cold enough to freeze your ding-dong."

"Ding-dong?"

"I know you know what that is," he said, smiling. I felt my back stiffen.

"No, I'm not here to swim. Sometimes I just like walking in the woods. I need to give Cleo some exercise, too."

"Right, exercise," he said and skimmed a flat rock across the water.

"How come you're not cruising in your car?" I asked. He smirked. "What?" I followed.

"I'm grounded for a month. I got a speeding ticket. Who would ever think they would have a speed trap in one of these one-horse towns? Naturally, my father went nuts. I just get my license and then a speeding ticket, which he says raises the car insurance premium."

He kicked a stone and then sat on a rock near me.

"Fortunately," he continued, smiling again, "my new girlfriend drives."

"New girlfriend?"

"Yeah, her name's Harmony Ross. Her parents are divorced, and she lives with her mother and her younger sister, Tiffany. Her mother is a paralegal and works for an important attorney. She's a knockout. Harmony and her look more like sisters than mother and daughter. Anyway, Harmony's mother's got a boyfriend, a bank executive, so Harmony has the house often. She told me everything about herself and her family. Her mother and father were divorced when she was only five, and he has nothing to do with them anymore, but they have some money, and she has the house. It's a really nice house."

He smiled.

"This was the first time I made love to a girl in her own bed."

I stared at him.

"You don't believe me again?"

"Why shouldn't I believe you?" I said, looking away.

"We did it on the second date, too," he bragged.

I stood up and clapped my hands for Cleo.

"I told her about you," he continued, and I spun around.

"What do you mean, told her about me?"

"Take it easy. She was really curious, and the next day, when she told her girlfriend Roberta, Roberta got very, very interested. They think you're fascinating," he added with a wry smile. "Of course, I built it up a little."

"I bet you did," I said.

"Doesn't hurt anyone. Actually, it made me a big shot," he said.

"Why?"

"Why? No one knows much about you. You're hardly ever seen anywhere. I could have told them you had horns growing out of your head, and they would have believed me."

"Who cares what they believe?" I snapped and started away.

"Relax. I didn't say anything terrible," he quickly told me and caught up. "Actually, I made you look really good. I told them you were really a very nice guy, full of interesting information about the woods, the animals, a true nature boy who could talk to birds. Roberta was practically champing at the bit. She can't wait to meet you. You'll thank me when you meet her, too. I've practically laid out your path to glory."

I stopped and squinted.

"What's that supposed to mean?"

"She'll put out for you without much effort on your part. Just so she can say she's been with you, stupid."

"How do you know I want to be with her?" I asked, partly out of curiosity. How would he know?

He raised his eyebrows and smiled.

"Talk about my sister being built. Wait until you see Roberta Beckman, and from what I hear, she's easy, a little booze or a joint."

"Joint?"

"Marijuana, stupid. You've heard of it?"

"Yes, I've heard of it."

"So. That, a couple of kisses on the neck, and it's open sesame."

"Who says I want to see her?"

"Get off it. You want to. I decided to help you," he added, sounding magnanimous. "What good is all my experience if I don't put it to use to help a buddy, huh?"

I tilted my head skeptically.

"I'm now your buddy."

"Hey, guys have to stick together in this world."

"Why is it I have these doubts buzzing around me like bees?" I asked.

He started to laugh and stopped.

"I gotta get home," I said.

"Wait a minute," he said, reaching out and grabbing my arm. "This is really a good opportunity for both of us. I can get them over to my house this weekend. We can party."

"No," I said trying not to sound panicky. "I'm not interested."

"Why not? You said you weren't gay," he countered angrily. "I didn't say anything bad about you. I made you look good," he whined. "I've set it all up for us."

"I didn't ask you to do that."

"Well, I did it."

"So?"

He stared and then looked away and turned back to me.

"Okay, okay, I'm not telling the whole truth," he suddenly confessed.

"What?"

"Harmony is not really my girlfriend, and I didn't sleep with her in her room. At least not yet, but I'm determined. She's the prettiest girl in the school, believe me, and Roberta is really good-looking, too. The truth is, they're inseparable. They practically only go out on double dates. I got them interested in me by talking about you."

"That's not my problem. It's yours," I said and started to turn away again. Again, he grabbed my arm. "Cut it out!" I told him.

"Wait a minute. Maybe we can make some sort of deal."

"Deal?"

"Just agree to meet with them at my house, that's all. You can talk about fishing or something or carve twigs for all I care, as long as you're there and you occupy Roberta while I occupy Harmony."

I started to shake my head.

"You need some encouragement, that's all. I know you're shy and you haven't seen or done much."

"No thanks."

"Tell you what," he said, sounding more desperate, his voice full of pleading. "I'll show you something you want to see if you'll agree to meet the girls with me. You don't have to do anything if you don't want to. Just be there, is all."

"What would you show me?" I felt my curiosity lift my eyebrows. "What do you think I want to see?"

"You want to see my sister naked, don't you?"

For a moment I couldn't respond. Then I started to shake my head, and he smiled.

"Don't try to deny it. You came around that night to peep."

"That's not true."

"So, big deal."

"You would do that to your sister?"

"I don't care. She shows it off anyway. Guess what? We have side-by-side rooms upstairs, and there was something once attached to the wall in my room. It's gone, but there is now an opening that goes clear through. You can be in my room and see her and she won't even know it."

"I wouldn't do that," I said in a hoarse whisper and backed away.

"Yes, you would. She parades around naked in there, and sometimes . . . sometimes she does stuff."

It felt like my heart had stopped pounding. My chest was hollow. I shook my head and started walking, but he followed alongside.

"You know what I mean when I say she does stuff?"

"No," I said.

"She gets herself excited. It's something to see. I used to think it was something only guys like us did, but it's not. I got to confess. It got me pretty excited the first time I saw her do it. If she knew I had seen her, she'd die."

I tried to swallow but couldn't. My body felt so hot all over, I wondered if he could feel the heat radiating. He walked with me, Cleo moving from his side to mine as we cut through the forest.

"I'm sure without television, never going to the movies, and with what your mother lets you have and do and what she doesn't, you haven't seen anything, Noble. Once you do, you'll thank me, and to thank me, you just have to agree to meet the girls. They want to meet you so much," he said. "You gotta be interested. If you're not, then something is weird, something strange is going on at your house. Maybe your mother is doing something to keep you from being interested in girls. People should know it," he added, a slight note of threat threading through his words.

I stopped and looked at him. He held his ground.

"What's that supposed to mean?"

He shrugged.

"I could tell people anything I wanted to tell them and they'd believe me," he said. "I don't even have to make stuff up. Look at all the things your mother does around the place, and I've been by there when she's been singing in that graveyard. Who's buried in there anyway?" he asked.

"None of your business."

"Yeah, you're right," he said. "I don't really care about dead people anyway." Then he soften. "C'mon, we'll have some fun. You won't regret it. What do you say?"

"I . . ."

"Come over tonight about eight. She takes a bath about eight, and then she's in her room. My father's working tonight, too. It'll be just the two of us. We won't even let Betsy know you're in the house. Whaddya say? Huh?"

Was it the power of evil? Was it some dark force coming over me? I felt myself nod.

"Great." He smiled, and then he stopped smiling. "You'd better come, Noble. If you don't, I swear, I'll come get you."

I started away.

"You'd better come!" he shouted after me.

I walked quickly, my heart returning and thumping with a vengeance. What had I agreed to do? When I reached our meadow, I ran all the way to the house and then stopped at the door, panting as hard as Cleo sometimes did. I worked desperately at getting myself calm again. If Mommy saw me like this . . .

Finally, I entered the house. I could hear her in the kitchen. The first thing she did when she saw me was scream about Cleo's feet being dirty. I practically carried him out and wiped him down. When I returned, her eyes were still wide, her hair disheveled. She looked like she had seen something terrible.

"We've got to keep the house immaculate," she told me. "We must think of our home as a sacred place. They won't come to us otherwise. From now on, leave your shoes outside the door. There will be a washcloth in a pail of soap and water there, too. Wipe your hands clean before you enter. Do you understand? Do you?"

"Yes," I said quickly.

"Good. Good. It's important. Everything is important," she muttered and returned to preparing our dinner.

She was unusually quiet during the meal. Once in a while, she would stop eating and look at me hard, her eyebrows knitting together under the weight of some deep, dark thought she was having, I was sure. Occasionally she would just stare ahead, not chewing, not moving. Finally, something I did, some sound, would cause her eyes to snap back to awareness and she would return to eating.

Afterward, she cleaned the kitchen and had me take out the garbage. When I returned, she was at the door, waiting.

"Take off your shoes," she said and handed me the washcloth. "Remember now. Always clean yourself before you come into our temple, because that is what our home is, a temple, a sanctuary for them."

I did what she asked, and then she returned to the kitchen. A short while later, she went upstairs. I waited for her to come down, but she didn't, and when I went up to check on her, I found she had fallen asleep with her clothes on. I fixed her blanket over her, but she didn't move.

She's just very exhausted, I thought. All the responsibilities, the worries, have taken their toll on her. She just needs a good night's sleep.

I intended to go to sleep early myself, but Elliot's invitation loomed in my thoughts. Try as I would, I couldn't drive the images, the words, out of my mind. Rationalizing that if I didn't go to his house he would carry out his threats and make more trouble for Mommy and me, I slipped out of the house, put on my shoes, and, with Cleo right alongside, ran all the way through the wooded path to the edge of Elliot's family's property.

Once there, I hesitated, looking at the lighted windows. It was nearly eight o'clock. Suddenly I heard the back door of the house open and then saw him standing on the rear porch, looking toward the woods.

I stepped out and walked slowly across the field, Cleo trotting alongside.

"Do you have to bring that dog everywhere you go?" he asked.

"If I didn't, he'd bark and bark, and my mother would wonder where I had gone," I told him.

"Well, he can't come in. My sister will hear him."

"He's going to bark," I warned.

"Okay," he relented. "Jeez, I feel like a ten-year-old when I'm with you."

"So don't be with me. I'll go home," I said.

"Forget I said anything. Man, you are the most sensitive guy I know." He smiled. "C'mon," he said. "I always live up to my side of any bargain I make."

"This is probably a bad idea," I said.

He tilted his head and smiled.

"Trust me, you won't be disappointed."

"I didn't mean that," I said, but he already turned and opened the door.

"Just be quiet," he said in a whisper and beckoned for me to follow.

We entered through the kitchen. Cleo followed behind, sniffing everywhere. When we reached the foot of the stairway, Elliot paused.

"Get the dog," he ordered.

Cleo had gone on to explore other rooms. I snapped my fingers, got his attention, and made him follow us up the stairs, where we turned sharply and hurried to Elliot's room. Unlike mine, it was filled with so many things, including posters of his favorite singers and bands and movies. Books and magazines were scattered about. The bed was unmade, and shirts and pants were draped over chairs and even on the floor. Cleo quickly found a pair of socks and seized them in his mouth.

"I don't know why, but he goes for socks all the time," I said. I tried to get the socks, but Cleo twisted and turned to keep out of my reach.

"Forget the dog. Who cares about the socks? Jeez."

Elliot smiled lustily, and then he went to one of his rock band posters and carefully removed it from the wall. Beneath it was a hole in the wall, just as he had described. He put his eye to it and looked, and then he turned to me.

"Not there yet," he said.

"You really don't feel bad doing this?" I asked. "She is your sister."

"What's the big deal? What she doesn't know won't hurt her, and the way she dresses and parades about, she's practically nude most of the time. She gives my father little heart attacks every day. No one ever speaks about it, but he provides her with birth control pills. He just leaves them in her room like someone would leave a mousetrap."

I stood there listening, intrigued with the intimate details of someone else's family life.

"I guess you can figure out what happened," he added with a smirk. I said nothing, and he turned and looked through the hole again. Then he stood back slowly, smiled, and nodded at me.

"All yours," he said, gesturing at the wall.

I didn't move.

"Well, come on. You want to get in and out and not be noticed," he said. "My father comes home in about forty minutes."

Slowly, my heart tripping, I approached the wall. I couldn't help feeling like I was accepting an invitation from the devil himself, but the power of my curiosity was so overwhelming, I couldn't hold myself back. I brought my eye to the hole and gazed through it.

This was the first time in my entire life I had seen a teenage girl's bedroom. Since Daddy's death, Mommy had done little to change what had been their bedroom. His things were still in his closet. However, it was never a completely feminine room. My own room, once shared, was now as Noble would have it, and all that had belonged to Celeste was gone, buried.

Betsy's room had pink walls and a canopy bed with a sheer pink netting over it. Her bed was still neatly made, and there were two dolls side by side against the pillows. I didn't know what they were, but they both had long hair and very curvy figures.

Their were posters on her walls, too, one of a rock singer with his shirt off and what looked like a bike chain around his neck. He held a guitar below his waist. If his pants were any tighter, they would have to be considered another layer of skin, I thought. I saw a movement and shifted my gaze to the right where Betsy sat before a mirror at a vanity table. She was completely naked.

I watched with fascination as she began to experiment with different makeup, coloring her eyebrows and then putting something on her eyelashes to make them look longer. She rubbed some cream into her cheeks and under her mouth. Then she wiped it off and tested three different lipstick colors, studying the effect each had on her appearance.

"What's she doing now?" Elliot asked from behind.

"Makeup," I said. "Boring," he said rising. I looked through the hole again. It was far from boring to me. I hadn't seen this since Mommy used to do it, but she hadn't for so long.

Finally, Betsy rose and then turned and looked at herself in the mirror. She cupped her own large breasts and stared at her image in the mirror. Then she went to her closet and retrieved some blouses, trying on each and studying how she looked.

"She playing with herself?" Elliot asked.

"She's trying on clothes," I said.

He groaned.

"She'll do that for hours. Forget it," he said.

I hesitated to pull back. I wanted to see every fashion, every article of clothing.

"Hey," Elliot said. "C'mon. You got more than an eyeful anyway, and my father will be coming home soon."

Reluctantly, I pulled back.

"It get you excited enough?" Elliot asked.

I didn't respond. Instead, I started out of his room, urging Cleo to follow.

"Now you'll appreciate Roberta Beckman," he told me as we descended the stairs. "I'm going to arrange it all for Saturday night, okay?"

"I don't know," I said.

"Whaddya mean? We had a deal. You don't welsh on a deal," he said sharply.

"My mother might not let me come here."

"Do what you did tonight. Just sneak over. I know you can do it, Noble, so don't give me any grief," he said, his eyes small and threatening.

"I'll see," I said and opened the door. He followed Cleo and me out.

"You better be here, Noble," he called. "Don't make me look stupid and ruin my chances with Harmony. I won't forget it if you do," he shouted as I crossed toward the woods.

When I reached the woods, I broke into a trot and then ran all the way home. I took off my shoes, cleaned Cleo, and then washed my hands. It was very quiet inside the house, so I imagined Mommy was still in a very deep sleep, but as I walked down the hallway, I saw she had risen and come downstairs, where she had fallen asleep again in her great-grandad Jordan's chair. I stood in the doorway and looked at her, waiting to see if she would wake. She didn't, so I went upstairs, but instead of going directly to my room, I continued down the upstairs hallway to hers.

Practically tiptoeing, I entered her room and went to her vanity table. So much of her makeup, lipsticks, and creams had been untouched for so long, but seeing Betsy at her vanity table filled me with new interest. I sat and gazed at myself in the mirror. My eyebrows were too thick. How I wished they were as trim as Betsy's were.

Only once before, when I was very little, had I put on lipstick. Noble and I were playing house, and I was to be the mother. I messed it up terribly, but Mommy wasn't angry at me. She laughed and called Daddy, who looked at me and went into hysterics.

Slowly, I opened one of her lipstick

tubes. It looked all right, so I brought it to my lips and carefully traced along, pressing my lips together and then patting them the way I had seen Betsy do it in her room. The sight of bright red lips on my face made me smile. Encouraged, I opened one of the jars of cream and began to rub it into my cheeks and under my lower lip, around my chin. My fingers were rough against my face, so I had to rub very gently.

After that, I opened one of the cakes of makeup and began to experiment with color the way I saw Betsy do it. Once I finished that, I found an eyelash brush and started to darken mine. I was nearly finished doing that when I heard Mommy's shrill scream. I had been so involved in it all, I hadn't heard her coming up the stairway.

"What are you doing?" she shouted, rushing to me and ripping the eyelash brush out of my hands. She gazed down at me, her eyes wide. "What are you doing?"

She reached for a towel and, with her left hand holding the back of my head, roughly began to wipe off the lipstick and the makeup, practically tearing my skin off my skull with the fierce effort.

"I was just . . . just —"

"You're contaminated," she said. "You're possessed. Get to your room this instant," she ordered, and I rose quickly and went to my bedroom. "Get undressed and go to bed," she said. She nodded at me. "This will take time," she added, and then she stepped out and closed the door.

What did that mean? I wondered.

Before I finished undressing, I heard her return to my door, and then I heard her insert a key in the lock and turn it. The lock snapped shut.

"Mommy?" I cried and went to the door. It wouldn't budge.

"This will take time," I heard her say, and then I heard her footsteps as she went to the stairway and descended.

There was nothing for me to do but go to sleep. I dreamed about being in Betsy's room, only it was my room. I was at that vanity table, and I was making myself look very pretty, only when I turned and looked at the wall, I saw Mommy's eye in the hole, and it woke me with a start. I smelled something so I sat up, and there, near the door, I saw a candle burning. Its flame flickered slightly. I listened hard. I heard a rustling and then I saw Mommy sitting there near the window, her body silhouetted in the light of the stars and half-moon that poured into my room.

"Mommy?"

"Go back to sleep, Noble," she said. "You'll need your strength. We have a lot to do."

She rose to fix my blanket as I lay back. Then she touched my forehead before turning to go out. I heard the key in the lock, and the lock turned.

Sleep was like a leaf in the wind, just inches from my fingertips and always out of reach until the first light of morning. I was surprised at how late I had slept and surprised Cleo was not in the room. Groggy, I rose and washed and dressed, but when I went to go out, I found the door was still locked.

"Mommy!" I called. "I'm awake and ready to come down to breakfast. Mommy!"

I heard nothing. I pulled on the handle and then I knocked on the door, and I waited.

Still nothing but silence was what I received in return. Where was Cleo? Why wasn't he barking for me? I wondered. I continued to call to Mommy, to knock, to rattle the doorknob. I never heard her footsteps. I opened my window and looked out in every direction for sight of her, but she wasn't in view. I shouted for her and waited and then returned to the door and knocked and shouted again.

Exhausted, I sat on my bed.

The clock ticked on. The morning passed into afternoon. I heard our vacuum cleaner go on below, and I waited for it to end. It was on for so long, I thought it would never be turned off, but finally it was, and then I started shouting for her again. She didn't respond. My throat was dry, so I went into the bathroom and drank water from the sink faucet.

Still, she did not return to my room. My calls went unheeded. Afternoon passed into the early evening. I was so hungry, my stomach was rumbling. I tried to sleep so I wouldn't think of it. Darkness grew thicker. I listened and heard very little, and then I heard her singing and rushed to the window. She was off to the right in the cemetery. I waited until she stopped and then I screamed for her, but she didn't call back.

I waited by the door to listen for her footsteps on the stairway, and finally I heard them. I banged harder and called to her. I could hear her approaching.

"Thank goodness," I muttered.

She did nothing, however. I waited, a new panic building inside me.

"Mommy?"

"Just rest, Noble," I heard her whisper through the door. "You need to fast. You need to cleanse yourself."

"I'm hungry, Mommy, very hungry."

"You need to cleanse yourself," she repeated. "Just drink water. This is what they told me."

I heard her start away.

"Mommy!" I screamed and listened.

Her bedroom door closed and it was silent.

"Where's Cleo?" I screamed.

I went to the window to listen. If she had left him outside, he would be barking by now, I thought. But I didn't hear him, and I couldn't stand the silence. I put my hands over my ears, in fact, to listen to the roar in my head instead.

Truly exhausted now, I returned to my bed. I slept on and off most of the night. I woke hopefully at first light and listened for Mommy. Surely, whatever it was she thought she had to do had ended, I hoped.

But it hadn't. I spent the whole day just as I had spent the day before, and the same was true for the night. On the third day, I was so tired and weak, I didn't bother to get up. I just lay there, waiting, listening, drifting in and out of sleep. I thought I heard the sound of our car starting, but I wasn't sure.

The day passed into night.

And then, in the morning, I heard the door open. My eyelids felt glued together, but I lifted them and looked up at Mommy, who was standing there with a tray in her hands, her face in a smile. There was a mug of one of her teas on the tray, and a bowl of oatmeal and some toast and jam.

I started to sit up. She put the tray on the nightstand and helped me into a sitting position, fixing my pillows behind me. Then she set the tray on my lap and stepped back.

"It's over," she said. "We'll be all right again."

14

A Wild Ride

Although I always enjoyed pretty good health and rarely had colds and coughs, never got measles or chicken pox or anything Mommy told us children our ages suffered, I did on occasion have stomachaches and sniffles with some fever. That was how I felt, even after I had finally eaten something. It took most of the day and another good night's sleep before I felt strong enough to rise, and even then, I moved slowly.

The first thing I did when I finally left my room was ask for Cleo. He wasn't barking for me, and he wasn't anywhere just outside. I checked all his favorite spots. Usually, he would be right at the front door, waiting for me to come out.

"Cleo is gone," Mommy told me.

"Gone? What do you mean by gone, Mommy?"

"Gone is gone, Noble." She stopped what she was doing and turned to me. "He was being used," she said.

"Used?"

"By forces of evil."

"How could Cleo be used by forces of evil?" I asked.

"Remember that story I read to you about the Trojan Horse?" she replied.

I was shaking my head in disbelief, but I stopped.

"You mean, how the soldiers were kept in the big horse and that was the way they got into the city of Troy?"

What did this have to do with Cleo? I wondered.

"Yes, exactly," she said excitedly.

"I still don't understand, Mommy," I said.

She stopped smiling.

"The forces of evil invaded him and when he came into our home, they came in with him, inside him. I couldn't figure out what I was doing wrong until it was pointed out to me, and guess by whom?"

I just stared at her. What was she saying? What did this mean?

"Uncle Herbert. Remember I told you about his dog? That was why he knew about such things. He knew animals could

423

be used for good or for bad. Thankfully, he got to me in time."

"But where's Cleo?" I asked again.

"I told you, Noble. Cleo is no longer with us. He's gone," she said.

I shook my head to shake the words out of my ears. Gone? No longer with us?

"But I want Cleo," I moaned.

"I'll get you another pet. Maybe a bird this time," she said. "Yes, I think a bird that we keep inside and in a cage. It will be safer."

"Mommy, Cleo is probably very unhappy. Where is he?" I pursued.

She put down her dish of chicken cutlets so hard it amazed me the dish didn't shatter.

"Are you deliberately being thickheaded, Noble Atwell? Well? Are you? That was a characteristic your father possessed and a characteristic that came to the fore too often."

"No, Mommy, I'm not deliberately being anything. I miss Cleo. I need Cleo," I said. "He's always been with me."

"Exactly. That was the reason he was chosen. Other than myself, there was no other living thing that was as close to you, as capable of getting to you, Noble. Don't you see? It makes perfect sense."

"Did you give him to someone else?" I questioned.

She stared at me a moment, and then she looked away.

"Yes, I gave him to someone else. I gave him to the pound," she said.

"You mean where they keep the animals in cages, and when no one comes for them, they destroy them?" I asked, my voice no longer diminishing the panic and the rage.

"Someone will take him. He's too attractive an animal, and he's young enough to learn to be with someone else. I don't want to talk about Cleo anymore. You're giving me a splitting headache," she added sharply and returned to her dinner preparations.

I stood there just looking at her.

"Go to the pantry and get me some basil," she commanded. When I didn't move, she turned. "Well?"

I walked away slowly, my heart feeling so heavy in my chest, I thought it might have hardened into stone. When I brought her the basil, she smiled, and then she immediately changed expression.

"One more thing," she said. "Someone had the audacity to call here and ask for you."

"Who?"

"Some impetuous boy. I told him you were sick and couldn't come to the phone, and he said he'd call again to remind you of a bargain. Who is this? What bargain? How would anyone know to call you? You haven't been talking to strangers, have you? Not after all my warnings."

I shook my head. I didn't feel like being honest and cooperative. I was still blistering inside about Cleo.

"Just a prank, I'm sure," I said. "Like we had happen many times before," I added. That was true. For years, kids who lived in our area thought it was funny to call us and say silly things. I went into the living room, where I sat in Daddy's favorite chair and thought about Cleo, how he would be at my feet by now, lifting his head every time I moved practically. The memory brought a smile to my lips and then overwhelmed me with a wave of sadness. I could also imagine him, despondent, lying in some cage, lifting his ears at every footstep, every voice, expecting me to rescue him. How I wish I could.

It made me very angry. Cleo couldn't have brought evil to us. Cleo barked at evil. Mommy had told me that herself. She told me he would protect me. She told me Daddy must have given him that assignment. Surely, she merely forgot. I'll tell her, I thought and then we'll go get Cleo before it's too late. I hurried back to the kitchen.

She listened quietly, and then she turned and smiled.

"You know I'm very impressed with you, Noble. You thought all that out very logically and sensibly."

My heart leaped for joy.

"However," she said, "what you don't know is that evil is insidious. It creeps through shadows and through smiles equally. This is why we have to be on such guard, be so alert always. I told you, it even got past me, but not past Uncle Herbert's spirit. But don't worry anymore. It will be all right now. Everything will be fine again," she said and kissed my forehead, petting my hair. "How noble you are, Noble. How noble you will be," she whispered and returned to her work, leaving me frustrated.

I left the house to be by myself. The rage building inside me was too strong. It would only get me in trouble, I thought. It was fortunate for me that I walked out at that moment, too, for coming down our driveway was a metallic black automobile, and I could see Elliot driving. Panicking, I gazed back at the house and then ran down the driveway so he would stop before he got too close. Once Mommy saw them, she would know I had been lying about the phone call.

There was a pretty brunette in the front seat with Elliot, and as I drew closer to the car, I saw another girl with darker hair in the rear. It wasn't until he stopped the car and I saw the three of them that I realized what day it was. Being locked up in my room, I had lost track of time. Elliot rolled down his window and smiled at me.

"Hey," he said, "we're here just as I promised."

The girl in the front leaned over his shoulder to look at me. She was smiling, but her face was full of curiosity, her hungry eyes looking me over like a fox might look over a chicken.

"Hi," she said.

"This is Harmony," Elliot told me, nudging his head in her direction. Then he winked.

Instinctively, I folded my arms over my chest and stepped back. The girl in the rear rolled down the window, too.

"Hi," she said. "I'm Roberta."

"I thought we might take a little ride first," Elliot told me. "Hop in."

"How did you get your car? You told me you were grounded," I responded.

"I was, but I made a new deal with my father. I'm going to improve my grades." He looked at Harmony and laughed. Then he turned back to me. "Maybe I can get some pointers from your mother. C'mon, get in."

"I can't. I have to take care of some important chores."

"Hey," he said, losing his smile quickly and leaning farther out of the window, "a deal's a deal. I lived up to my end, and as you can see, we're here. We're going to have a good time, remember?"

"C'mon, don't be shy," Roberta called to me and opened the rear door.

I stared at her.

"Maybe I should just go and ask your mother if she'll excuse you from your important chores. I called and spoke to her, and she doesn't sound so bad," Elliot said. He started to open his door to get out.

"No, she's not feeling well," I said quickly. "She's taking a nap."

"Oh." He shrugged. "Perfect. She won't notice you're not here, then."

"Come on, Noble. I won't bite. I promise," Roberta said, beckoning.

"He wants you to bite," Elliot told her,

and she laughed. "Don't you, Noble?"

"No," I said.

"Are you coming or what? Chores. Don't give me any lame excuses about this place," he said and then he looked around the farm. "Hey, where's your faithful dog? He brings his dog everywhere he goes," he explained to Harmony and Roberta.

"That's very nice," Harmony said. "What kind of a dog do you have?"

"Golden retriever," Elliot answered for me. "He's a beaut, too. So where is he?"

"Inside," I said quickly.

The reference to Cleo stirred my pot of rage again. I looked down, thought a moment, and then I moved forward impulsively and got into the rear of the car, closing the door.

"Way to go," Elliot said and instantly put the car into reverse. He backed up awkwardly, causing the girls to scream. Then he turned and churned gravel beneath the rear wheels.

"Slow down!" Harmony shouted at him. "You'll get another speeding ticket."

"Right," he said, and he did slow down.

"What's it like going to school in your own house?" Roberta asked me.

Harmony leaned over the front seat to look at me and listen. She was very pretty,

430

I thought, with perfect, dainty features and interesting blue eyes. They were shaped like two almonds. I envied her smooth complexion and the color of her lipstick. It made her lips look moist and sexy, just like the lipstick Elliot's sister Betsy had.

"It's okay," I said quickly.

"Okay? Going to school in your own house is okay?" Roberta asked.

"Yes," I said with a face as firm as Mommy's could be when she was determined. "I'm fine with it."

Roberta was not half as pretty as Harmony. Her face was rounder, her eyes smaller and dull brown. She was big boned with a very large bosom that seemed to pour out of her chest. She had the top two buttons of her light pink blouse undone, revealing a deep, dark cleavage that had two pink spots at the top on both sides. The remaining buttons of her blouse looked like they were straining to remain buttoned. Both girls were in jeans.

"Do you have a blackboard and a desk and all that, too?" Harmony asked.

"No, not a blackboard. I have a desk, of course," I said.

"Does your mother ring a bell between subjects?" Elliot teased.

"Very funny," I said.

He laughed and drove out of the driveway and away from our property. I looked back at the house. My heart skipped beats because I realized this was the first time in my life I had ever left home in a car without Mommy or Daddy. I couldn't help feeling like someone in outer space who had become detached from his rocket ship and was left weightless and helpless. The farther away we went, the more the butterflies in my stomach fluttered.

"Elliot says you don't have any friends our age. No one comes to see you, and you don't visit anyone. Is that true?" Harmony asked.

"Yes," I said.

"Don't you have any relatives nearby, cousins, anyone?"

"No," I said. How could I tell them about my spiritual family?

"Doesn't it get boring and lonely for you?" Roberta questioned.

I shrugged.

"Sometimes it does," I admitted.

"I'd hate it," Harmony said. "You never get invited to parties or go to the movies with friends or anything?" she followed, her voice rising into a high-pitched tone of skepticism.

"No," I said.

"He doesn't even watch television," Elliot added.

Both girls looked at me with amazement in their eyes. It was as if they had discovered an extraterrestrial creature or something.

"Is that right?" Roberta asked.

"Yes. We don't have a working television set anymore."

"But what do you do at night?"

"I read a lot," I said.

"And he fishes and chops wood and feeds chickens," Elliot added, laughing.

"Do you at least listen to music?" Harmony asked me.

"Sometimes. My mother plays piano, and we have some records."

"Records?" she asked, and they both laughed.

"What's so funny?" I asked.

"You don't have tapes at least?" Roberta asked.

"No," I said. "Just records."

"Like what?" Harmony followed.

I shrugged. "Mozart, Beethoven, Debussy. We have some full operas, too. The Victrola needs a new needle, and my mother hasn't gotten one yet."

"Huh?" Roberta said. "Victrola?"

"Told you he was something," Elliot

cried. "You could at least get with it and call it a phonograph," he threw back at me, and they all laughed again.

I shook my head and looked out the window. I shouldn't have gotten into the car, I thought. This was very wrong.

"Don't you listen to the radio?" Harmony asked.

"Don't you get magazines or newspapers?" Roberta followed.

"Don't you go shopping, go to the mall, and at least see tapes?" Harmony continued, neither pausing to give me time to respond.

"You listen to rock, don't you? Who's your favorite group or singer?"

I looked from one to the other, feeling like I was under interrogation.

"No," I said to answer all their questions. "I have no favorites of anything, and I don't listen to the radio."

"Even in your car?" Harmony asked.

"My mother doesn't turn it on in the car."

Roberta stared at me, a curious smile on her lips.

"You know what this is like?" she said, still staring at me, her face brightening with excitement. "It's like finding someone who was buried alive for fifty years."

I felt myself blanch.

"Yeah," Harmony said. "That's right. You do have electricity, right?"

"Yes, we have electricity," I snapped at her.

They all laughed.

"Where are we going?" I demanded.

"We're just killing some time until my sister leaves the house," Elliot said. He smiled at Harmony. "Unless you would like her to be there when we arrive," he added.

The heat in my neck rose so quickly, I thought my face was lit up like a full moon. What had he told her?

"Stop picking on him, Elliot," Harmony said and smiled at me. Roberta moved closer.

"Why doesn't your mother want you to go to a regular school?" she asked.

"My mother is a teacher, and she thinks I'll have a better education at home. She says there are too many distractions at school, and there is too much politics going on at the expense of the students."

"Expense of the students? What's that mean?"

"He does do better. He scores in the top percentiles every year, don't you, Noble?" Elliot asked.

"Yes," I said.

"There's more to school than school,"

Roberta said. "You could probably be on the soccer team or the baseball team, and you'd meet people and have fun."

I was silent.

"Don't you care?"

I looked out the window. Don't I care? I thought. Yes, deep down I care. I care almost as much as Noble cared.

"Is it because your mother believes in voodoo or something?" she continued.

"Roberta!" Harmony cried. "Stop teasing him."

"I'm not teasing him. I was just interested. Elliot says you talk to birds and other animals and there are all sorts of weird things on your doors and around your home, and he says there's a graveyard. Is that true?"

"Elliot is a stranger to truth. He wouldn't see it if it was on the tip of his nose," I replied, which was something I had heard Mommy say about people. The girls laughed, but a little more nervously.

"Yeah, yeah. I'm not lying. He spends a lot of time in the woods. Don't deny it, Noble."

"I don't deny it. I like nature," I said. "I've always been interested in plants and animals and especially insects, but I don't talk to birds."

"Insects, ugh!" Roberta said, twisting her lips. They looked thick and rubbery.

"Stop it, Roberta. There's nothing wrong with that," Harmony said. "Do you fish for your dinner?"

"Sometimes we eat what I catch, yes, but I don't fish that often anymore."

"I wonder why," Elliot said, laughing again.

"What's that supposed to mean?" Roberta asked him.

"That's between Noble and me, right, Noble?"

"Whatever you say, Elliot. You're doing all the talking, obviously," I replied, and he laughed.

"Does your mother practice witchcraft and put spells on people she doesn't like?" Roberta finally came out and asked.

"No," I said. "But we do believe in spiritual things."

"What does that mean, exactly?" Harmony asked. They were all quiet, waiting in great anticipation.

"It means that there is a spiritual energy in the world and it's possible to feel it, to experience it," I said. "That's all."

"I've heard of that," Roberta said, nodding.

"It's not so strange. I know other people

who believe that," Harmony said.

"Let's see if my stupid sister left with her boyfriend yet," Elliot decided, bored with the conversation. He turned the car sharply and headed for his house.

"I bet you miss your sister, don't you?" Harmony asked me. "It was a terrible thing that happened. One of the most famous terrible things in this small town."

"Yes, it was," I said. "But I don't like talking about it," I added quickly.

"Of course you don't," she agreed in a soft, sympathetic voice.

"Don't be too nice to him. He'll get used to it, and then I'll have to be nice to him all the time," Elliot teased.

"If you're not nice to everyone, I might not be nice to you," she threatened, and Elliot laughed and howled.

"You hear that, Noble, my buddy? I'll be so nice to you people will think I'm your slave."

Everyone laughed. I smiled and looked out the window as we turned into Elliot's driveway. He cheered.

"My sister is gone," he cried. "We've got the place to ourselves."

I wasn't sure why yet, but that sounded ominous to me and set my heart pounding again. I wondered if Mommy had discovered I was gone by now. I kept looking toward the woods, thinking about poor Cleo, remembering how he bounded through the brush and so enjoyed exploring.

"Don't look so worried," Elliot said, looking back at me through the rearview mirror and mistaking my expression of sadness for fear. "No one will give you a test on what we do."

The girls giggled.

"I might," Roberta teased, and Elliot laughed harder.

I sat back and contemplated getting out and running as soon as we stopped.

But I didn't. I got out with them and walked into Elliot's house.

"You've got a lot of catching up to do, Noble," Roberta told me. She put her arm through mine. "I wouldn't mind being your home teacher when it comes to that."

"Comes to what?"

"We'll see," she said.

"Let's go up to my room," Elliot said. "I have that surprise I promised."

Roberta stayed very close to me, her breast pressed against my upper arm. She was only an inch or so shorter than I was, but she was so much broader in the hips that she made me look taller than I was.

"You have such a firm arm," she told me.

Elliot overheard her and turned back.

"Show her your sandpaper hands, Noble."

Instinctively, I closed my fingers into fists.

We followed Elliot and Harmony up the stairs. Outside of his room, I hesitated.

"Are you all right?" Roberta asked me. "You look a little pale. Doesn't he, Harmony?"

She nodded.

"I was sick," I told them. "I just got over something."

"Did you have to go to the school nurse?" Elliot joked. "That would be his mother, and the school principal and the janitor, too."

As soon as we entered his room, he went to the stereo set he had in the corner and turned on a tape. He flopped on his bed and spread his arms. The music blasted, but no one seemed to mind.

"Make yourselves at home, girls," he said and winked at me. Then he reached under his bed and came up with a cigar box. Harmony sat beside him and looked excitedly up at Roberta and me.

"Just as I promised," he said and opened the box to reveal what I thought were poorly made cigarettes. "The last of my New Jersey stash," he declared. "Better than what you guys get up here, I bet."

"I'll let you know," Harmony said, plucking one out of the box.

I stared, confused.

"Noble, this is something called a joint, pot. You've never seen it, I'm sure."

"Yes, I have," I said. "I've read about it."

"Does your mother teach you about such things?" Roberta asked me. "Does she tell you to just say no?"

"No. She never talked about it. I just read about it, I said."

I really hadn't read much about it at all, and the first time I had heard the word was when Elliot mentioned it that day in the woods.

"But you never tried it, have you?" Harmony asked me.

I shook my head.

"How could he? He never leaves the nest," Elliot said and then smiled. "Until now. This is your lucky day," he declared, glanced at Roberta, and added, "in a few ways."

He handed one to Roberta and then held one out to me. I didn't move. He gestured emphatically, pumping his hand at me. I started to shake my head.

"Just take it," he said sharply and shifted his eyes toward Roberta and then back to me. I took it and stepped back.

"Aren't you worried your father will smell it?" Roberta asked. "I always worry about that."

"Not a problem," Elliot said and threw open the windows. "Besides, I'll blame it on my sister. Dad believes everything anyone says about her," he said.

He lit his joint and then lit Harmony's. Roberta lit her own and offered me the match.

"I don't smoke," I said, and the three of them laughed.

"This isn't smoking. This is different," Harmony said.

"It looks like smoking to me."

"Try it once," Elliot said. "Just for the fun of it."

I shook my head.

"Don't act like a nerd in front of the girls, Noble," he warned. "I know for a fact that you're not a nerd," he added. Then, to intimidate me, he nudged the poster behind which was hidden the hole to his sister's room.

He lit a match and held it out. I brought the joint to it, and as soon as I sucked in, I started to cough. They all laughed. Roberta decided to instruct me on the proper way to smoke the joint. I didn't like it, but I played along, and then I felt like I was getting dizzy.

The music got louder and everyone's laughter seemed to merge into one great laugh. Somehow it was then decided that Roberta and I would go downstairs and leave Elliot and Harmony alone upstairs.

She led me out of the room and practically pulled me to the stairway.

"I want you to tell me everything about yourself," she said. "You're the most interesting boy I know."

"You don't know me," I said, and she laughed.

"I mean, I'd like to know. You're so . . . so . . ."

"Literal?"

She grimaced.

"Yeah, I think so. I guess you are smart. C'mon," she urged and pulled me into the living room.

I stumbled, but followed her to the sofa. She flopped down, laughing at everything she did or that happened now. Then she reached up for me.

"Come here. Don't be so shy," she said.

I looked back at the doorway, thinking perhaps I would just bolt, but she lunged forward, seized my hand, and pulled me down to her. I lost my balance and fell awkwardly over her, which made her laugh more. I squirmed to get loose, and she turned, pressed her breasts into my face, and then, before I could get back up and away, brought her lips to mine with such force, she pushed my head back. I felt her tongue jet in between my lips, and I gagged. I shoved her with all my strength. She clung to me, still laughing.

"Don't you like it?" she asked.

"No," I said. "And you shouldn't do that. I just told you I was sick. You'll catch it," I warned, hoping that would make her retreat, but her eyes were so glassy and small, and she continued to wear this silly smile on her lips.

"I'm not worried," she said and started to bring those thick, rubbery lips to mine again.

This time I ducked under her arm and managed to get off the sofa. She spun around, disappointed, and looked up at me.

"You are shy? This won't hurt. I promise," she said.

"I know what hurts and what doesn't," I told her.

"Do you?" She widened her smile. "Then come on back. You won't be sorry," she said.

I watched as she fumbled with her blouse buttons and pulled the blouse apart. Then she sat forward and undid her bra. I should have just turned and run then and there, but the sight of her and what she was willing to do was mesmerizing. She slipped her bra off and then leaned back so her head was on the arm of the sofa. Her breasts poured forward. She smiled at me and put her hands under them, lifting them as an offering.

"Come back!" she urged.

I shook my head.

"I can't," I said. "I have to go. I have . . . things I have to do. I can't," I stuttered and then turned and ran out of the living room, out the front door, and down the steps.

Her shout died behind me when the door closed. I didn't hesitate or look back. I charged across the lawn to the woods and then ran harder and faster as if I was being pursued. It had all put me in a panic. I didn't pay attention to the bushes and the saplings. Crashing through them, I felt my right cheek get scratched, but I didn't stop.

When I broke out of the forest and I was on our land, I slowed down, but I continued walking at a rapid pace, gazing back to be sure they hadn't followed me. I could feel myself crying now, feel my body shaking with sobs, but it was as if I was outside my body, watching myself. The scratch on my cheek burned when the tears ran over and into it. Before I reached the house, Mommy stepped out and stood on the porch, her arms folded, her head high, her lips taut, the corners pulled in with white rage.

"Where were you?" she demanded.

I brushed some pieces of twig off my hair and wiped the tears from my cheeks. I was afraid to reply. She didn't wait. She stepped off the porch and stood before me, glaring at me. Then her eyelids fluttered and she looked confused for a moment. I tried to swallow, but it was as if I had a lump of hard candy in my throat. Slowly, she brought her face toward mine, and then I heard her sniffing.

She recoiled like someone who had smelled death.

"What were you smoking? Where were you? Answer me!" she shouted and seized my shoulders. She shook me hard, and I started to cry again. "Tell me!" she demanded. "Tell me everything and tell it to me right now!"

I blubbered between sobs, confessing everything, every detail, every moment. I dreaded what would happen next. Surely, she would lock me in my room again and again put me on a punishing fast, but when I was finished, she surprised me by smiling and then lovingly stroking my hair, my cheek, before she hugged me to her and rocked with me.

"My Noble, my wonderful Noble."

I looked up at her. I was still quite frightened, but I was confused as well.

"Don't you see, my child, you were honest. You were willing to expunge all the evil from you. You practically spit it out of yourself. You cleansed yourself. Your confessing is your purging. You have nothing more to do except to give thanks. Why do you think you ran home, you left that den of inequity? I am so proud of you," she said.

My sobbing and shaking stopped. She still held me by my shoulders firmly, but her attention lifted from my face and went toward the forest. Her lips twisted with anger, and then she closed her eyes and nodded.

"You don't have to worry," she said. "I'll take care of things now. Go on into the house and clean yourself. I'll be up to put something on that nasty scratch on your cheek. Go on," she told me.

"What are you going to do, Mommy?" I asked.

In my mind's eye, I saw her at the cemetery, praying to an army of spirits, asking them to take vengeance. I was frightened for Elliot and the girls. Something terrible was going to happen to them. I had no doubt that my mother could do it.

"Don't you worry yourself about any of that," she repeated. "Go on. Do what I say."

She released me and stepped back.

I glanced at the forest and then I walked into the house. I stripped off my clothes and threw them in the hamper and then, after removing the corset, went into a hot shower. When I was drying off, Mommy appeared with one of her salves and put some on my scratch. Then she gave me one of her herbal pills to help me relax.

"I want you to lie down for a while, Noble. I want you to take a good rest, a good long nap. I'll be gone for a while. Don't answer the phone. Don't go to the door. Understand?"

"Where are you going?"

"I have an errand. Just do what I say, and all will be well," she said.

She kissed my forehead and then she left me. I was tired. Every part of my body ached. I had jerked and twisted myself in a frenzy when I ran from that house through the woods. Now I was a little ashamed of my show of panic. Could I have made a more graceful exit?

I crawled under my blanket and hugged my pillow. In moments I was asleep, and when I opened my eyes again, it was dark.

It confused me, and for a few moments I couldn't remember what had happened. The pill Mommy had given me had been quite strong, I thought when I began to recall all the events. I sat up and listened. There was music. Mommy was playing the piano. Full of curiosity now, I rose and put on my bathrobe and my slippers. Then I started down.

She wasn't playing anything melancholy. The tune was robust, and when I looked in at her, I saw she was pounding with great energy, the strands of her hair flying about her face as she turned and twisted at the keyboard. Usually she sensed my presence when she played, but if she did this time, she didn't acknowledge it until she had completed what she wanted to complete. Then she sat back, exhausted but satisfied. Finally, she turned to me and smiled.

"How are you, darling?" she asked.

"I slept so long."

"That was what you were supposed to do," she said. "Are you hungry?"

"A little," I said.

"Good. I have some cold chicken and some wonderful potato salad with string beans waiting for you," she told me as she rose. She approached me and then turned my head to look at the scratch. "It will be gone in a few days," she muttered, more to herself than to me, I thought.

She started toward the kitchen.

"Where did you go, Mommy? What did you do?" I asked her.

She turned at the doorway and smiled.

"I told you not to be concerned."

"But I am. I can't help it."

"Yes," she said nodding, "I guess you can't. It's only natural." She paused and then said, "I went to see that man."

"What man?"

"The man who bought the property, who has that miserable son," she said. "I went to where he works, and I pulled him aside and told him everything you told me. He nearly passed out. I never saw a grown man turn so pale. I had to comfort him. Can you imagine? I was the one giving the comfort when I should have been the one receiving it. He went on and on about how difficult it has been for him to raise two teenagers alone.

"Of course, he couldn't thank me enough. He babbled like a fool, apologizing for not coming over to introduce himself, for listening to stupid gossip about us. It became embarrassing, if you want to know. How I miss a man like your father, a man of strength. These people have children and then they shatter like brittle glass. What was a family crumbles into shards of selfish stupidity," she said. "I thought he was going to break out into tears.

"He blamed everything on his wife." She looked away and then she turned to me with fire in her eyes. "She didn't die, you know. That was a blatant lie you were told. The woman left them. She left her own children. She was so self-centered, she couldn't stand the idea of being tied down with children and ran off with someone, leaving this soft noodle of a man with the responsibility of raising two young children.

"Well, he's obviously made a mess of it. He told me more than I wished to know. Apparently, his daughter is an even bigger problem than that boy who tempted you.

"But," she said, punctuating the air with her closed fist, "that's all behind us, all behind our wonderful wall of protection. That imaginary moat and castle you once built with Celeste is all there again, Noble. You need not be afraid. Tomorrow," she said, "is just another day, another wonderful day for us.

"Let me get your dinner now," she concluded and left me standing there, trembling.

After hearing what she had done and what would follow, I lost my appetite, but with Mommy standing over me, I forced myself to eat everything on the plate.

"I want you to take it easy for a few days, Noble. You've been through terrible things. Just concentrate on the reading I've given you and some of the science manual work. Don't worry about the chickens or any of our chores around the property," she said.

I did what she asked, but it was very difficult to remain so confined. I missed Cleo very much, too. Everything conspired to make me feel even lonelier. At night, when I listened to Mommy playing her piano or when I went up to my room to read, I couldn't stop the flood of images from passing through my head. Repeatedly, I saw Roberta taking off her bra. I relived that kiss. It all nauseated me, but at the same time, for reasons I couldn't understand, it titillated me and made me think more and more about my own sexuality.

Terrified I'd be caught, but unable to

prevent myself from doing it, I went into my bathroom and gazed down at my naked bosom. Of course, I was no way near as chesty as Roberta, but my breasts were becoming fuller and rounding out. It would soon become very difficult to flatten my chest enough to satisfy Mommy, I thought. The prospect of that day when she would look at me with such terrible disappointment was frightening. What would she do then? Would she make me eat more, become fatter, erase every possible curve? Could she erase the curves inside my head as easily?

I put my modified corset on again. I trimmed my hair myself. I pushed aside the memories of the makeup and what it would do to my face and what it had done to Betsy's and Harmony's and Roberta's eyes and lips. I fought back every urge to be Celeste and went about my work with new determination. I was back to my heavier chores, swinging an ax with vengeance, raking, shoveling, hammering until my shoulders screamed. Mommy looked pleased at my exhaustion every night.

"You're a good boy," she would say. "You'll be fine. We'll be fine. Our home is sacred again."

I hoped she was right. She did look quite

revived herself and stopped complaining about headaches and didn't doze off as much. I looked for her spirits, the spirits I seemed to see easily once, and I waited for Daddy's whispers from the shadows to tell me I was fine. I was redeemed, and as Mommy had said, all would be well.

But all I heard finally was Elliot's anger and threats.

He popped out of the forest as if he had been waiting for days and days behind some tree to approach me at the first opportunity. I had just finished feeding the chickens and repairing a gate when he came charging across the meadow. I thought he was going to leap at me, but he stopped a few yards away, his hands on his hips.

"You're a freak," he began. "You probably are a homo. I don't know why I tried to be your friend." He waved his fist at me. "You'll get yours someday."

"Look, I'm sorry my mother went to your father, but I didn't want to be with Roberta. She's disgusting."

"Disgusting? Why? Because she wanted to have sex with you? Is that disgusting? Is that what your mother teaches you? I feel sorry for you, even sorrier than I feel for myself, even though thanks to you, my father took my car away and grounded me for a month."

"I didn't mean for that to happen to you, Elliot."

"Yeah, right. Don't bother trying to make friends with anyone in this community. By the time I finish making up stories about you, no one will give you the time of day," he threatened. "You're a pathetic excuse for a man," he added, turned and marched back to the woods, his head down.

I felt tears burning in my eyes. I wanted to call to him, to find some way to apologize, but I was too choked up to utter a sound. I stood there watching him disappear.

Then I turned, my own head down, and started for the house.

When I looked up, I saw Mommy standing there on the porch, her arms folded under her breasts. She wasn't wearing a coat, just a blouse and skirt, but she didn't seem to care about the cold. As I drew closer, I saw she had a smile on her face. I was sure she had witnessed my confrontation with Elliot.

"Did you see that?" she asked.

"What?"

"He couldn't get near you. He couldn't

get close. He had to stand away from you and shake his fist and I'm sure make his stupid threats."

She looked off toward the forest.

"There is a wall between us and them, Noble, forever and ever, there is a wall."

She looked down at me.

"You are safe," she said. "You will always be safe."

She held out her arms. I stepped up on the porch, and she embraced me. Together we walked into the house, me pausing only for a instant to look back at where Elliot had entered the forest and disappeared.

He disappeared like a dream would when I woke up.

15

---•○●---

Awakened

During the weeks and then months that followed what had been my only real contact with young people my age, I often felt like I was shrinking. The world into which I had been born and in which I had lived with my family seemed to become smaller and smaller, perhaps because I did not venture far beyond the immediate grounds around our house and barn, and perhaps because I began to realize how much I was missing.

With more and more time on my hands, I turned to our wonderful library of leather-bound books and read far beyond what Mommy required of me. The pages of these books, the wonderful stories and characters I met, were the roadways, the pathways, that enabled me to leave the confines of our protected home and its boundaries patrolled by Mommy's spiritual army of ancestors.

These days I hardly ever left any other way. Mommy always seem to find good reason why I shouldn't accompany her whenever she drove off the farm to shop or complete an errand.

"I'll be away only a little while," she would say, or she would tell me she was just doing this or that and there wasn't time to do anything else; therefore, there was no reason for me to go along. She never put any value on my need to see other places, meet other people, or have a change of scenery.

"There will be plenty of time for that later on," she would tell me if I uttered anything that suggested it. "Besides, these people living here don't want to see you, meet you, know you, Noble. They'll just use whatever they see to build more nasty gossip to fill their empty little lives."

I could just imagine what they were saying already. Elliot surely fulfilled his threat and made up fantastic stories about me.

"Believe me," Mommy assured, "I know what's best for you. I've been told," she said with that finality that resonated whenever she said it.

In fact, *I've been told* became her reason and her justification for almost everything

I questioned, and once she said it, there was no other argument for me to make, for I had no doubt as to who had told her.

However, it was on the tip of my tongue to ask, "Why haven't I been told? When will I be party to all these discussions and revelations?"

I began to hope I never would be. Mommy was well into this other world and crossed back and forth at will, it seemed, but look at how isolated she was, I thought. She no longer had any men friends and never socialized with anyone. She refused to contact or return phone calls or letters from any living relative. Would this be my destiny?

Once, when I was very young, I desperately needed to make contact, to cross over, and when I believed I had, I thought I had won Mommy's deepest love forever and ever, but she still hovered over Noble, spreading her wings to protect and cuddle him. To be him was to be loved.

Many nights when I was by myself, I would stare out the window like she often did and wait for some sign. Sometimes I would gaze so long and hard, I eventually did think shadows took shape again. I did believe I saw faces, but they were all like bubbles floating by, bubbles that would burst as soon as they were seen. I also began to hear whispering again. On the shallow waves of the evening tide voices drifted. My brain became garbled with all these images and visions. I didn't know what to believe.

I told her about it, and she said it was normal. I was close. I was always close. Just be good. Just listen and do my work, and it would come. This loneliness would end, and I would be part of this wonderful community that had chosen us and our farm. I would inherit all of Mommy's powers and abilities. This was my real legacy, and how could I doubt it? After all, she had been told.

But this promise didn't stop me from feeling more and more boxed in.

When I read *Macbeth*, I was stunned by the witches' prediction that Macbeth would be destroyed when the woods came to his castle. Lately, feeling my world shrinking, I thought our woods was coming closer and closer. Perhaps it was just an illusion, but for me it was real. The entire outside world was pressing our boundaries, squeezing, pushing. Eventually, we would be swallowed up and gone. I thought about it often, but this was an idea I never expressed.

Although Mommy saw me reading more and more, saw me curled up under a light with a book well into the wee hours, she didn't say anything. Sometimes she smiled, and sometimes she looked thoughtful. She seemed unsure. Should she stop me? Should she encourage me? I was sure she thought that at least when I was reading, I wasn't questioning and complaining. Her world was quiet and comfortable, as it should be. We were safe.

The library we had was old. It had what I imagined were very valuable editions of famous novels and books. Great-Grandmother Jordan had begun to collect volumes, and Grandmother Jordan continued to do so. I suspected neither of them really had read what they had brought into the house. I was confident they wouldn't have approved of some of these stories. Nevertheless, they acquired them because of their vintage. They shopped at antiques fairs, used-book stores, and wherever they could find leather-bound copies. Some of them were gifts from Great-Grandfather Jordan and Grandfather Jordan. I saw the inscriptions, the scratchy signatures sprawled over a page: *On the occasion of your birthday,* *Merry Christmas,* even a *Happy Anniversary.*

Perhaps that was the real reason Mommy never stopped me from reading these books. There was a history attached to them, a family history, and anything that had to do with our ancestry was important. After all, my grandparents and great-grandparents had at least touched them once, and that touch made them into something sacred, another of the many parts of the spiritual world that circled us like planets in our solar system.

Some of these novels, however, were about great loves, and the descriptions of the beautiful women and the handsome men, the wonderful and gala events, the dresses, the celebrations, and the eloquence of their worlds fascinated me. It filled my nights with dreams in which I saw myself throwing off my jeans, flannel shirts, and boots and then plucking beautiful stylish dresses out of a magical closet.

The moment I put one on, my hair grew longer and was softer and more glamorous, the calluses left my hands, my eyebrows thinned and took shape, my lips were moist and bright with sexy lipstick. I was dainty, and I could spin about and laugh with a melodic sound that would fill the hearts of men who longed to hold my hand, to kiss my lips, to touch my breasts, my poor concealed and smothered breasts that sometimes ached and tingled beneath the tight wrap.

Perhaps because of my reading, memories of a little girl returned more and more vividly. Yes, I remembered my dolls, my teacups, my dollhouses and coloring books, and my beautiful ribbons. Yes, I remembered the scent of my clothes, my crinoline and silk, my beautiful pinks, my little fur jacket Daddy had bought me for one of my birthdays. All of it rested beneath the earth outside our house. I even dreamed of digging all of it up at night secretly.

But of course, I never would.

Nevertheless, these feelings that I kept in my heart as securely under lock and key as I could were heightened with every passing day. They clamored to be heard more and more as winter began its inevitable retreat and the fingers of warm spring and renewal crept in everywhere. The ice and the snow melted under the warmer, more frequent sunlight. Trees began to bud, and our meadow turned greener and greener. Side by side, Mommy and I worked the softened earth, turning it over in our garden. We planted, we cultivated, and then we began to freshen everything up around us, restoring color to the wood cladding, painting the porch floors with protective stains, washing down windows and shudders. There was always a lot to do after winter unshackled the earth and fled the warmer sun.

I was happy to have the work, to be able to occupy myself as much as I could. I wanted to be tired at the end of the day. It helped me fall asleep, which was something that lately had become more and more difficult to do quickly. Too many nights I lay awake for hours and hours hearing the music I read about in my books, seeing the handsome men flirting or dancing with the beautiful women, listening in on the whispered words of love between them, words I had memorized and whispered myself. Their silhouettes moved on my walls. I felt sure it was better than watching television Mommy forbid anyway.

Sometimes, when I thought about a love scene I had read, I let my hands move over my body. I thought about what Elliot had told me about his sister Betsy, and I recalled the sensuous way she touched herself and gazed at her body. The tingling I felt surging through me frightened and yet delighted me. If I longed for it too much, I pressed my face into my pillow as hard as I could. Mommy's footsteps would also set me into a mad retreat, holding my breath while I chased away the images and visions. But it was impossible to stop the dreams, dreams in which I felt lips on mine, hands on my breasts, and dreams in which I recited pages and pages of wonderful romance.

I tried to repent, to pray for forgiveness, to avoid Mommy's powerful eyes. The work did help, but it didn't completely stop it all from happening. Time's not on my side, I thought. Every passing day, passing hour, makes it harder and harder. How would it end? I wondered. Or more important, how would it begin? So much of my life was in limbo, I thought, so much had yet to start.

Of course, the promise that Mommy made to Daddy long ago, the promise that we would someday attend a public school, drifted away like smoke. To further ensure that, she made special arrangements for my scholastic testing this particular year. As if she anticipated how much more I wanted to see other students my age, she fixed it so that I was brought to the school hours after dismissal. There were very few students in the halls or on the school grounds. She whisked me into the building, hovering so close to me as we walked down to the classroom that she practically had me in blinders. I was in and then out with little delay. I wasn't there long. The test was easier than ever, which pleased Mommy.

On the way there and on the way home, with even greater intensity than before, I felt myself gobbling up everything I could see. My eyes were everywhere, looking at everything, every person, every color, style of clothing, even every movement people made, especially young women. Mommy warned me about gaping, of course, but I couldn't stop myself. I tried looking forward, but my eyes seemed to have a mind of their own, and like two steel marbles drawn to magnets, they shifted from one side to another.

By the time we got home, Mommy looked very annoyed with me. She rattled off some work for me to do and sent me to the barn to get tools. I worked, and I tried to forget, but it wasn't easy. The only place to go for any sort of peace of mind was back to the books and then, since the weather had turned so warm so quickly, finally back into the forest. Most of the trees were thick with leaves again, creating small shadowy areas. Walking within, I could look up through the translucent green ceilings and see a muffled sun. One day I just decided I would find a comfortable place and do my reading there, far from Mommy's critical or suspicious eyes.

"Don't leave our property," Mommy warned me, and I promised I never would without her permission or without her. Still, she looked unhappy about my going anywhere that was out of her sight.

Sometimes, to ease her mind, I would take my fishing gear along, even though I didn't do any fishing. Just south of the stream, I found an area shaded by pine trees. The perfumed air smelled wonderful, and my special place had a matted-down floor with rich, cool, dark earth. I could spread out, get some sunshine if I wanted, and relax. Squirrels and rabbits watched me curiously from a safe distance, twitching their noses to be sure the scents I brought with me didn't suggest anything threatening. Birds chirped and did their aerial acrobatics around me as if they had finally found an appreciative audience. Once, I saw a small doe. It was almost impossible to see it because it blended so well with the surrounding foliage, but I caught a slight movement of its ears, and then slowly I sat up and stared at it while it stared back at me.

"Hi," I said, and then it moved off quickly.

Our winter had been colder than usual, but our spring was already warmer and acting more like our summer. I wore my coveralls and my bland white short-sleeved shirt. I had brought *Romeo and Juliet* with me because I wanted to reread it. I had read it quickly two years ago, and I was sure that I didn't understand or appreciate it then. As I read about their defiance and determination to be lovers, my heart pounded with excitement. Being something forbidden, their love seemed more intense.

I put the play aside and lay back to look up at the sky through the branches of the pine trees. For a while I just watched the way the clouds glided with a wonderful silence across the light, icy blue heavens. I closed my eyes and thought about Romeo and Juliet's first kiss. And then, I imagined it happening to me.

I, too, suddenly found a great need to be defiant, to be in danger and to taste that excitement. My hands moved over my body, exploring, discovering. I slipped off the top of my coveralls and then lifted my shirt over my head. For a while I just lay there breathing hard, terrified of what I had already done, but now that I had, I couldn't stop myself from continuing. I undid the corset around my bosom until I was totally exposed to the air, my released breasts tingling with the sensation of being in the open, feeling the breeze over them. Slowly, I brought my fingertips to my nipples, and then I moaned and went on to slip completely out of my coveralls. I took off my underpants, and for a long, terrifying moment of exquisite excitement, I lay there naked and fully revealed.

Never had I done this outside my house. Waves of thrilling titilation flowed over me. I trembled so hard, I thought my bones were rattling. It felt like warm hands were moving up my thighs to my forbidden place. Suddenly there was such a rush of excitement — like an explosion — inside me. It was shockingly delicious and then so frightening, I hurried to put my clothing on again. As quickly as I could, I dressed and wrapped myself more tightly in the corset, pulling the strings until I could barely breathe. When that was done, I picked up my book and literally fled my wonderful spot.

Running helped me calm down. I ran as

hard as I could until I broke out of the forest and then stopped at the edge of our meadow to catch my breath. My face was so hot, I knew it was crimson. I didn't go back to the house. I circled through the woods, found another shady spot, and rested.

What had happened? What had I done? All I could think was that Mommy would know the moment she set eyes on me. Or, worse yet, she would be told.

When I felt sufficiently calmed down, I walked slowly back to the house. I'm sure I entered like a prisoner entering death row in some penitentiary. Mommy stepped out of the living room. She had her needlework in hand.

"Oh, Noble," she said when she saw me. "I just had the most terrifying thought."

I waited, my heart thumping.

"Here we are, approaching your birthday, and I have not planned out a single thing. I don't know what's come over me these days," she said and smiled. "But don't worry. This will be a special one. I promise."

She kissed me on the cheek and then went on to the kitchen.

I stood there watching her walk away.

She wasn't told anything.

She knew nothing.

I was all right. Everything was strangely all right.

Maybe it was because I had gotten away with it, or maybe it was because I couldn't get the feelings, the excitement, out of mind, but just the thought of returning to my special place filled me with exhilaration. I tried to stay away. I tortured myself, tormented myself, teased myself.

One day I started toward it and then turned around and hurried back. Another day I forced myself to sit at the edge of the pond and not go anywhere close to my special place. I put up as much resistance as I could, knowing in my heart that I would lose the battle, that I would soon surrender and return.

Finally, I did.

And I took *Romeo and Juliet* with me again. I couldn't reread it enough. I was at the point where I practically had the whole play memorized and certainly had memorized my favorite lines. When I reached my special place, I stood back hesitantly. It had become magical. If I go to the same spot and if I lie down again and start to read, surely the same things will happen, I thought. I closed my eyes and held my breath and tried to turn around and go home, but it was too powerful. There was a calling, and the voice calling to me was inside me. It could not be denied.

I sprawled out and tried to read, but my eyes kept drifting off the page. My heart was beginning to race. I felt my breathing quicken. Lying back, I looked up through the branches again. The sky was cloudless today, the blue looking softer. I closed my eyes. Once again warm fingers were beginning to travel all over me, caressing, exploring.

Slowly, I began to undress, and soon I was naked under the sun, lying there and feeling the warm breeze flutter over my body. I took deep breaths and touched myself everywhere, and everywhere I touched, there was almost an electric shock of pleasure. How powerful it all was, I thought, and how naive it was of me to think I could ever resist. I kept my eyes closed and envisioned the handsome men in my books, dreamed of what Romeo must have looked like, heard those beautiful words, words that were now being said to me.

And then I heard a branch crack.

It was more like a clap of thunder.

I opened my eyes slowly, and when I looked up, I saw Elliot standing there gazing down at me, his mouth twisted, his eyes wide. I felt every muscle in my body freeze. His lips moved, but for a few moments nothing came out, no words, no sounds. He looked like he was having trouble swallowing. I was still, deathly still. Finally, he spoke.

"You're a girl?" he asked to confirm what his eyes were saying.

With lightning speed, the realization about all that could happen followed that clap of thunder that still resonated in my ears. Exposed and revealed, I would be the biggest disaster in Mommy's life. All of our spiritual family would be blown away in the wind of outrage that would follow. And they would never return. Mommy would collapse in defeat and disappointment. Our lives would be ruined forever and ever. I could not leave the property and attend any school or be seen in the community. Where would we go? What would happen to us? What had I done?

"Please," was all I could utter.

His twisted, wry smile of astonishment softened.

"You're a girl," he said now with full realization. "Sure, that explains it all. I was convinced you were gay, and so were the girls."

His expression continued to change and

turn until his eyes were full of impish laughter and delight.

"And you're not bad, either," he said.

The chains of ice that had tightened over me melted away. I turned to reach for my clothing, and he surprised me by stepping on it all.

"Not so fast," he said. "I'm not through. Why do you pretend to be a boy? What is this? What's your mother doing?"

"It's none of your business," I said, my eyes now clouding with tears.

"Oh, yes, it is," he said with some anger. "You made a fool of me. You made a fool of everyone. You're wacky as hell, both of you." He paused as a new thought came to him. "Who disappeared in your family anyway? Were there two girls or what? What's going on here?"

"I said it was not your business," I told him. "Get your feet off my things."

Instead of doing that, he lowered himself to his knees and continued to widen his smile.

"So what's your real name, Noble? Nobella or something like that?"

"No," I said, my arms now over my breasts and my legs crossed.

"How did you keep those boobs so well hidden?" He looked at the clothing and held up the modified corset. "With this? Doesn't that hurt?"

"Leave me alone," I begged.

He dropped it and wiped his hands on his pants as if it was contaminated.

"Is all this some sort of magic thing your mother performed? Did she put a spell on you and turn you into a girl?"

I shook my head, the tears now climbing over my lids and falling forward to stream down my cheeks.

"Maybe I'm seeing things," he said. "A spell has been put on me, too, huh?" He laughed. "Only one way to find out," he added, and that surge of cold fear began at the base of my stomach and slid up and over my breasts like a thin layer of ice.

"Go away!" I cried.

He leaned forward to grab my shoulders and push me down. I struggled with him, but he was too strong and was able to pull my arms away from my breasts. He gazed down at them and then slowly brought his lips to my nipples. I tried kicking at him, but he was over my stomach, and I couldn't hit him hard enough. I couldn't prevent what was about to happen. He kissed and sucked, and then he lifted his head and smiled.

"Not bad for a boy," he said.

I continued to resist.

"Stop it," he commanded. "Or I'll tell the whole world what I discovered. The police will probably come to your house, I bet," he added.

The realization that they might just do that shut down my resistance. My arms softened, and he pulled them straight and down to my sides.

"So why were you so interested in looking at my sister? Are you gay?" he asked.

"No," I said.

"You were fascinated. You got a long look at her. Don't tell me you didn't."

"It wasn't for that reason," I said.

"Sure."

"Get off me, please," I begged.

He thought and looked at me again, and then he released my wrists, but instead of getting off, he brought his hands to my breasts and fondled them.

"Nice," he said. "You could be pretty if you let yourself be what you are," he added.

"Please," I begged. His fingers continued to touch and squeeze.

"Why were you lying here naked? You were getting yourself excited, is that it?" he asked before I could reply. "Why waste it?" he added.

The fear I had felt before returned behind a drumbeat that echoed through my bones. He was smiling wider, his eyes full of lust. I shook my head, but he leaned back, still sitting on my stomach, and began to undo his belt buckle.

"Stop!" I cried.

"Why? You've got to know what you've been missing, what you probably want anyway. Who better to show you than me, your only friend?"

I shook my head, and then, when he lifted off me, I turned, but he pushed me down and brought his mouth to my ear.

"You better not get me mad," he said. "I'll go right from here to the phone and tell the whole world what I have seen. You want that? Well?"

"No," I mumbled.

"Then stop fighting me," he said. "You won't be sorry. I promise."

I heard him continue to undress. I was sick with fear now, but in a strangely bizarre way, curious, too. It was almost like a baby putting her finger in a candle flame. Everything told her it was dangerous, especially the heat as she brought her finger closer and closer, but the light was mesmerizing and fascinating, and she could not stop herself until she touched it or it touched her and she screamed with shock and pain. Why was something so beautiful so harmful?

He turned me over so I was on my back again, and then he lifted my legs and put himself comfortably between them.

"Feel that?" he asked. "That's what you pretended you had," he said and laughed.

I shook my head.

"Don't do this," I pleaded.

"Do what? How could I do this to you? You're a guy, just like me," he said, and he pressed on.

It was painful. I cried out, but my cries just made him more aggressive, it seemed. He was in me, pushing forward. I felt my whole body shudder. I kept my eyes closed just the way someone terrified of what was in the dark might, but at one point, I couldn't contain my curiosity, and I opened my eyes and looked at him. He had his eyes closed, and he was obviously in some ecstatic state. His body trembled, and then I felt him quiver inside me, which despite my fear and resistance made me quake as well.

Then he seemed to collapse over me, his breathing so hard and heavy, I thought he might die. Slowly, he lifted himself away and sat back.

"A friend of mine used to say that was like breaking in a horse," he said and laughed. "I promise you," he said as I reached for my clothing, "it won't be half as bad next time, which means it will be twice as good."

"There won't be a next time," I said.

"Oh, yes, there will," he countered, and then he reached for my arm and pulled me back. "Yes, there will. Matter of fact, I want you here tomorrow, same time, same place."

I shook my head.

"If you're not here, everyone finds out what I know, understand? I'll be here. I won't wait a minute either. No show, everyone knows. That's the deal, get it?"

"You're a horrible person," I said.

"Me? Hey, I'm not the one telling the world I'm a boy, and I'm not the one with a mother who says that, too. Here she made herself out to be such a goody-goody to my father and got me in deep trouble. I still want to know, who really disappeared? Did anyone, or was that some sort of lie, too?"

I didn't answer. I put on my underthings and my jeans quickly. He sat back to watch.

"Let me see how you hide those boobs," he said. "Go on."

I tried doing it with my back to him, but he demanded I turn around so he could watch.

"That's got to hurt," he said with a grimace. "Why do you keep pretending to be a boy?"

I didn't speak. I continued to dress. He did, too. When I was finished, I started away, and he caught up to me, seizing my hand to spin me around.

"Remember," he said. "Same time, same place tomorrow, or else. I mean it," he threatened.

I lowered my head in defeat, and he laughed.

"It's not so bad. You're going to enjoy it more and more. I promise."

He released me, and I shot away from him.

"Hey," he called, "so what happened to that great dog? He find out what you are so you had to get rid of him or something?" he yelled and then laughed.

I charged through the woods and didn't realize until I was nearly to the meadow that I had left my leather-bound copy of *Romeo and Juliet* back there, but I wasn't about to turn around and get it. I was afraid he would mistake that for a desire to be with him if he was still anywhere near the now infamous special place. The book would be fine as long as it didn't rain, and it didn't look like it would tonight.

When I reached the meadow, I paused and then just sat myself down to cry. I sobbed and sobbed and then finally, my well of tears drained, stopped and just sat there staring at an anthill. I watched them working frantically. My thoughts went back to Noble and how fascinated he had been when he had discovered his first anthill.

Somehow, because of what had just happened, I thought I had betrayed him. I thought I had betrayed everyone and I would soon be punished for it. It was really my fault, after all. If I hadn't done what I had done, Elliot wouldn't have discovered me. I had pulled back a protective curtain and let someone outside of our precious world look in and see us as we were. What was I to do now?

I wiped away the tears that lingered on my cheeks, and then I rose and slowly walked toward the house. Before I went inside, however, I went to the old well, drew up some water, and washed my face. What I must do now, I thought, was tell Mommy everything. Surely she would be angry, but she would also know what we should do, or she would ask for spiritual guidance. What other choice did I have?

With my head bowed, I entered the house. I heard the melodic tinkle of one of Mommy's antique music boxes, and I walked slowly to the dining room doorway because it was coming from there. When I looked in, I felt the breath go out of my lungs. The room was decorated with crepe paper and with balloons, and sprawled in paper letters across the mirror were the words HAPPY BIRTHDAY, NOBLE.

Mommy appeared in the doorway to the kitchen. She wore an apron, and she looked very pretty with her hair brushed and pinned neatly. She wore lipstick, and she wore one of her nicest dresses, the light blue one with the sequin collar. The table was set.

"I told you I would do something special for you," she said.

I was stunned. I had forgotten it was my birthday. How could I?

"Remember that music box?" she said, nodding at the ivory box embossed with a seahorse in black. "My great-grandfather bought it in New York City for my great-grandmother Elsie. Recognize the tune? I play it from time to time on the piano."

"Yes," I said in a small voice. " 'Eine Kleine Nachtmusik' by Mozart," I said.

She blinked rapidly and then smiled.

"Yes. I would never guess you'd remember that. You were never good at remembering the music, Noble. How wonderful. I guess you are becoming a charming little gentleman. Go put on something nice for dinner and let's celebrate," she said. "I'm making your favorite meal, rack of lamb with mint jelly," she said and returned to the kitchen.

I stood there looking at the table and the birthday greeting. The music box played on. It tapped a new well of tears inside me. Before Mommy could see me crying, I turned and hurried upstairs.

I couldn't break her heart.

I just couldn't.

I showered and then dressed in a nice shirt and pair of pants. Even after all that, I was unable to stop the trembling. I saw it in my fingers when I went to button my shirt. Every once in a while I had to fight off an urge to cry, and swallow back what felt like a ball of hard candy in my throat. When I went downstairs, Mommy was waiting at the table. She looked at me expectantly and gazed about the room.

"Well?" she asked.

I knew what she wanted me to say. She wanted me to say I saw Daddy.

"He promised," she added, almost in a whisper.

I forced a smile, took a deep breath, and slowly panned the room, pausing when I reached her. Then I widened my smile. Mommy put her right hand on her left shoulder as if she was covering Daddy's.

"Happy birthday, dear Noble," Mommy said. "From both of us."

I stared. Was he there? Did I see him? Was he as young as I remembered? How desperately I needed him.

"Isn't it wonderful?" Mommy asked. "To be together again like this?"

I nodded.

"Now you sit down, Noble. I want you to enjoy every moment. I mean we both want you to enjoy every moment. I have your favorite cake, too, and afterward, there is a big surprise waiting for you in the living room," she said.

I turned to look back through the doorway.

"No, no, you have to wait. Patience. All good things come to those with patience," she said and rose.

I sat at the table and stared ahead.

"Are you there, Daddy?" I whispered. "Show me, please. Touch me, speak to me, please," I pleaded.

I closed my eyes and prayed.

And I did think I felt him beside me, touching my shoulder. I waited, and then I felt his lips on my cheek.

"Happy birthday," I heard and snapped my eyes open. I turned quickly, but he wasn't there. I hadn't seen him. Perhaps I had lost any chance to ever see him.

Mommy entered with our food and stopped to look at me.

"Everything all right?" she asked.

"Yes," I said quickly.

"As it should be," she said. "As it should be."

It was a wonderful dinner, and the cake was delicious. Despite the swirling ball of sadness that lingered in my stomach, I ate well. Mommy talked about so many things that she wanted us to do about the farm.

"I want a better, bigger garden, and I'm going to sell some of my herbs to Mr. Bogart. He has customers. I can make a handy amount of money for us. I want you to have new clothes, and I'm thinking of getting some new things for myself as well. Most of all, Noble, I'm getting us a new car. You're going to learn how to drive, too. Now, with this birthday, you're eligible for that, you know. I can't wait to begin to teach you how to drive," she said.

How wonderful it all sounded. If I got my license, I could go places. This world would no longer be shrinking for me. Surely she meant for that to happen. How could I say one word to discourage her or depress her? We must both be happy, I thought. We must.

After the dinner was over and we had eaten the cake, she declared it was time to go into the living room to see my surprise. Whatever it was, it was gift-wrapped and left on the floor. The shape of it confused me.

"Go on, Noble," Mommy said. "Open it."

I started to take it apart neatly.

"Just rip it open," she said and I did.

I stared down at a chain saw.

"You're old enough to handle that sort of thing now, and we needed a new one, but one small enough for you to handle well," Mommy said. "You'll be able to cut firewood for us, harvest our woods. Of course, you'll have to be very, very careful. There is an instruction book in there, too. I want you to follow the rules and procedures exactly. Well? I guess you're too overwhelmed to speak. I know how much you like things with engines, how you like to ride our mower and how much you loved your electric trains."

I continued to stare at it.

I wanted to think of it as Noble would. I wanted to be as excited as he would be, but I couldn't do it. All I could do for Mommy was smile and look at the booklet.

"My little man," she said and came over to kiss me on the forehead.

"I'm going to clean up. Read the booklet," she told me and left me.

I felt like I was turning inside out. I didn't want chain saws. I wanted jewelry and new clothes. I wanted a radio for my room. I wanted to know about the music they had talked about in Elliot's car. I wanted a television set. I wanted to have my own phone, but more important, I wanted friends to call. I wanted a birthday card that said, "I've registered you for public school. Happy birthday."

But I would have none of that. Not for a long time, maybe not forever now, I thought.

I sat staring at the window because I could see myself reflected.

Now who was I? I wondered.

Now that what has happened, happened, who could I be?

Maybe I'm nobody.

Maybe I'm one of Mommy's spirits, and

I don't exist. Maybe it was I who had fallen off the rock and who had died in the stream.

Mommy came back and sat at her piano. She called to me to sit beside her, and like a tired ghost, I rose and went to her. I really felt like I was floating.

Her fingers danced on the keys. The melody flowed. Mommy nodded at the windows.

"They've all gathered to listen," she said.

I looked but saw nothing. She was so sure of it.

Were they there, and were they happy that I had kept their secret?

Now I wondered, how long could I?

16

"Who Pushed Me?"

I was trembling almost as soon as I had woken the following morning. Never was the tick of the small clock on the nightstand by my bed as loud. I wished I could somehow reach up and stop the sun from moving across the sky. If I froze time, I would not have to face the decision that I soon could not avoid. Fortunately, Mommy was so excited about all the new things she was going to do, she didn't notice how distracted I was, nor how quiet I was being at breakfast. She ran on and on about what she was planning to do all day, and then she surprised me by offering to take me along.

"Especially to look at new cars. I know how much you're going to be interested in all that, Noble," she said.

Panic, like a Ping-Pong ball, began to bounce about in my stomach. If I went with her, I would not be able to meet

Elliot, and he would surely follow through on his threats. I had no idea yet what I would do when I did meet him. I raked up every scattered thought in my brain to put together ideas, ways to get away from him and yet stop him from hurting Mommy and me. I thought I might offer him money. I didn't know how much to offer, but I decided I would start with a thousand dollars, which to me was a fortune. I would find ways to get him some periodically until I reached that amount. Surely that would keep him satisfied and quiet for a long time, I thought. He needed money for his car, didn't he? It was worth a try.

"Oh," I told Mommy, "I was hoping to use my chain saw for the first time."

She stopped and smiled.

"Of course you were," she said. "How foolish of me to give you something so exciting for you and then suggest you put it off to go on shopping errands. I'm very happy that's more important to you, Noble. We can look for a car another day. I have to see Mr. Bogart and do some other things that would only bore you. You'd be on pins and needles waiting to get home. You just go about your business," she told me, and I breathed easier.

She didn't leave until after lunch, and

when I watched her drive off, I stood trembling. Never had I kept so many secrets from her. Every time she called my name or appeared, I expected her to reveal she knew, she had been told. I was holding my breath so much, I was sure I looked red in the face most of the time.

Her car disappeared around the turn at the driveway, and I was alone. The clocks ticked on. My confrontation with Elliot was only hours away. Think, think, think, I told myself. You have to bring this to a quick end. Distraught and feeling helpless, I decided to go to the little cemetery to pray for guidance, to pray for some sign, to pray for Daddy to come to me, to help me.

A partly cloudy sky made the granite tombstones darker. I stood where I knew my brother's body lay. Was his spirit in limbo, just waiting to see what I would do, how I would affect all our destinies? I hated to have all this responsibility. If Mommy only knew how both of us, all of us, tottered at the edge of some great dark hole into which we could fall and disappear, she would be in so much panic.

"Help me, Daddy," I pleaded. "Tell me what to do. Please, please."

I bowed my head, and I waited and hoped. Then I stepped forward as I had seen Mommy do so often, and I touched the embossed hands on Infant Jordan's stone. I kept my eyes closed, and I concentrated with all my powers. It did seem to me that the hands moved. I snapped open my eyes and looked at them. The breeze, although warm, grew stronger and stronger. It swirled around me, and then I thought I heard Daddy's voice in the wind that flew through the trees and over the house.

"Be patient," he said. "Be confident. All will be well. Never tell your mother any of this. Follow your heart. Promise. Promise me."

"Yes, Daddy," I whispered. "Yes, I promise."

The gust of wind that had come so suddenly just as suddenly stopped. The branches of the trees that had been waving were still again. In fact, it seemed as though the whole world was holding its breath and not just me. I sucked in mine, touched the tombstone once more, and left the little cemetery.

Of course, I had no intention or real desire to use the new chain saw, but I read the booklet and then followed the directions to start it so that Mommy would see I had tried it. It frightened me, and it was heavier than I thought. I closed my eyes, and when I put it on a fallen dead log, it bounced and nearly flew out of my hands.

By then, I noticed the time. I had to go to meet Elliot. I put the chain saw aside and started for what had once been my wonderful, special place. All this was my fault. There was no way to avoid admitting that. I had let something evil take me over, and now I was suffering the consequences.

As I trekked through the forest, I rehearsed what I would say, how I would make my offer. In the pocket of my jeans, I had two crisp fifty-dollar bills Daddy had given me a long time ago. They were brand-new bills. Along with it, I had another amulet. It was a red coral Mommy had given me last year. I would offer it to him as well. Surely, I thought, Elliot would be impressed.

When I stepped out of the clump of trees and gazed at my spot by the pine, I first thought he was not yet there. For a few moments, I considered the possibility that he had already decided to expose me and Mommy and he had no interest in seeing me again. He had taken what he wanted from me. He would be a big hero in the school, after all, and even after only knowing him a little, I understood how important that was to him. It was difficult for me because I had mixed emotions about it. I didn't want to see him again, but I didn't want him to betray me. What he had done to me had left me feeling violated, and yet, it had further opened an otherwise forbidden door through which I had glimpsed another world.

Suddenly I saw a movement at the base of the pine tree, and then I saw Elliot's red hair. He shifted and leaned forward enough to see me. He smiled, and I also saw a trail of smoke rise and drift into the breeze.

"Right on time," he said. "Lucky for you. I wasn't going to give you a minute. I don't want you to ever keep me waiting," he added.

I stepped forward and saw he was lying on a dark green blanket.

"What are you standing there for? Get over here," he commanded.

Slowly, I walked toward him. He puffed on his cigarette, which I could now see and smell was his marijuana. He ran his hand over the blanket.

"Why not be comfortable, huh?" he said.

I stood there looking down at him.

"Did you tell all your friends about me?" I immediately asked.

"If I had, would I be here?" he countered. "And if I had, believe me, you and your mother would know it by now. I don't welsh on a bargain," he said. "You promised me something, and I promised you something."

"I didn't promise anything."

"Yes," he said, smiling and puffing. "You did, whether you like it or not."

"Elliot, I can give you money," I blurted.

"Money? What kind of money?"

"I can give you a thousand dollars if you'll swear to leave me alone and not tell anyone about me. Look," I said pulling the two fifties out of my pocket to show him, "I have some of it here right now."

He puffed on his joint and stared. Then he smiled.

"I didn't know you could get your hands on money, too. That's great. Sure, I'll take your money, but that doesn't mean I don't want anything else," he added.

"What do you mean? If I promise to give you so much money, isn't that a bargain?"

He shook his head and looked more closely at my two crisp bills.

"It's not enough," he said.

"I can get more, but not right away. I'll give you as much as one thousand dollars,"

I added quickly. "I'll have to give it to you as I get it."

"Oh, you will anyway," he said. "Give me the two fifties!" he demanded and held out his hand. "C'mon, hand it over."

"But what will you promise?"

"Not to tell," he said. I hesitated. "Well, you want me to tell?"

I gave him the money. He folded the bills and stuck them into his pants pocket.

"Perfect," he said.

"I have something else for you if you'll promise to leave me be," I said, fingering the amulet in my pocket. I didn't like giving it away. It was something Mommy had bought for me, but I thought she would approve if she knew why I was doing it.

"What?"

"This," I said and showed him the red coral amulet. He grimaced.

"What's that?"

"It's a spiritual gift. It's red coral and it has powers. If you wear it all the time, it will make you courageous, improve your memory, calm your emotions, give you peace of mind, and prevent tension that can cause heart trouble," I recited just as Mommy had recited to me. "It's very, very valuable, Elliot."

He continued to grimace.

"You believe in all that?"

"I know it's true," I said.

He shrugged and reached for it.

"Maybe I'll give it to Harmony," he said. "I'll tell her it cost a lot. But I'd rather have money, understand."

"Yes. I'll try to get you more soon," I promised and started to turn away.

"Hey, where do you think you're going?"

"I've got to get home," I said.

"Not quite yet," he said. "Get yourself back here right now. Now!" he commanded.

"Can't you leave me alone?" I pleaded. What did Daddy mean when he whispered to me in the wind? How could I be patient under such circumstances? Did I imagine his voice again?

"No, I can't leave you alone, and you don't want me to," Elliot said, smiling. He leaned back on his rolled-up jacket he was using as a pillow and inhaled more of his marijuana. "All right," he said. "Take off your clothes again."

"What?"

"You heard me. Do it."

I started to shake my head.

"Do it and do it right there. Don't start acting modest or something and turn your back on me either. I know what you have hidden. Go ahead, start. I don't have all day."

I closed my eyes and bit down on my lower lip so hard, I could taste blood.

"If you're a good girl-boy, I'll let you puff on a joint later," he promised.

I shook my head.

"I don't want to puff on a joint."

"What you want and don't want is not important. Get started," he said. "Now, or I'm off to the local newspapers and radio station. They might even pay me for the story, you know," he said smiling. "Sure. I bet I could make a lot more than your promised thousand dollars, which I might never see." He looked serious. "Maybe I should just forget it and leave. Is that what you want?"

I felt like I was sinking in the earth, felt like it had opened and I was slowly descending. I wished it was so. I wished I could disappear forever.

"No," I said.

"Okay. Then ask me to stay. Say, Please stay, Elliot. Go on. Ask."

He put his hands down to push himself up, threatening to leave and do what he said, go to the newspapers and to the radio stations.

"Please stay, Elliot," I said quickly.

"All right. That's better. Start with that shirt. I want to see you take off that contraption and unwrap those boobs again. Go on. Start!"

I thought about just running off, but what would that accomplish? Apparently, he hadn't told anyone. He was right. If he had, we would have known by now. At least for a while, I rationalized, I was keeping us safe, and wasn't that really what Mommy wanted? For us to be safe?

My fingers fumbled with the buttons on my shirt. Elliot stared up at me, that lustful smile deepening, brightening his eyes, twisting his lips. He puffed and then squashed the joint in the damp earth as I took off the shirt and began to undo the corset. His smile changed to a look of real astonishment and fascination.

"I can't get over it," he said and laughed. "Here I thought you were just a tough country kid. Okay, now your jeans," he said. "Hurry up. You're taking too long."

To me it seemed as if I had stopped breathing again. I even felt like I was out of my body, standing off to the side of the pine tree watching the whole scene like some interested observer. I had to kneel down to undo my shoes and then step out of my jeans.

"I can't get over you wearing boy's underwear," he said. "It looks stupid. Get it off quickly," he commanded, waving his hand at me.

I did it, and then I tried to look away, but he snapped at me again.

"Face forward," he said. "Keep your arms down at your side. Just stand there," he directed and put his hands behind his head as he lay back and gazed up at me. "You know, even though you're chubby in places, you have a better body than Harmony. You're firmer around the rear, and you don't droop like she does. What a waste for you, dressing and acting like a boy."

"Won't you let me be?" I pleaded. "Now."

"You have to be kidding," he said. He started to undo his jeans. "Come here," he said and reached up for my hand. It was like bringing my fingers to a candle flame. I moved so slowly, and when he seized my hand and pulled me to him, I felt as if I had fallen into the fire.

"It's going to be better today," he whispered, his hands moving over my breasts, down the sides of my body, around my legs and over them, bringing me closer to him and then turning me onto my back. He pushed himself up and over me and gazed down at me.

"All this," he said, "and money, too. What a lucky guy am I."

He was in me again, turning and twisting me to fit himself comfortably between my legs. I kept my eyes closed and tried to put myself somewhere else, but my body would not cooperate. It seemed to rush to him and not away from him. He went longer before he shuddered inside me this time, and when he did, he moaned loudly in my ear. After it ended, he lay there over me, breathing hard.

"Told you," he whispered and finally turned over to lie next to me on the blanket. "Told you it would be better this time."

I turned away from him. What suddenly interested me was the silence. It seemed as if what we had done had silenced the birds. Nothing moved. Even the breeze had paused, and the world was still. I heard him sit up and fumble with something. Then I smelled the marijuana again. He poked me, and I turned back to him.

"Here," he said.

I shook my head.

"Take it and smoke it," he ordered and

kept it before my face. "Don't make me angry," he warned.

I took it and puffed on it as quickly as I could. He insisted I do it right and went through instructions once more. Then he lit one for himself. I went toward my clothing, but he stopped me.

"Relax," he said. "We've only just begun. Finish your joint. Enjoy the day. When will you get me more money?"

"I don't know. Maybe next week," I said.

"Okay. Let's plan on a payment once a week."

"I don't know how much I can get you if I have to do it every week."

"I don't want five dollars. Make sure it's at least fifty," he said. "Yeah, fifty will be fine. Fifty a week."

I had no idea how I would get that, but I said nothing.

"I want you to tell me more about yourself."

"What?"

"How do you live? Are you always a boy, even when you're inside your house and no one can see? Do you wear a dress in the house?"

"No," I said.

"Keep smoking. Don't waste the stuff. It was expensive, and it's good," he asserted.

I did what he asked. He stared at me and shook his head.

"I don't get this. I still don't understand, not that I'm complaining," he added, smiling. "Why can't you just be what you are, anyway?"

I didn't answer. The joint was making me dizzy again. I felt his fingers over my breasts and his lips on my neck.

"Huh? How come?"

"It's what my mother wants," I said. I was feeling like I was talking in my sleep.

"She's crazy. Your mother's really crazy. Maybe I should tell people. Maybe I should get you out of that house. Maybe you could even come live with us," he said laughing. "Just think of that."

I shook my head, and then I couldn't help sobbing. Real, thick hot tears began to streak down my cheeks.

"Take it easy," I heard him say. "I'm just kidding. You want to live with a loony woman, live with her. I won't tell. We have a good thing going. Don't worry about it. Relax," he said, and he was over me again.

This time I really felt as if I was floating. My body was supple beneath him. He turned and molded me to him easily. All resistance was drained out of me. I thought about my rag dolls, and I imagined I had turned into one. I went from crying to laughing, and he started laughing, too. When it was over, he was even more pleased and kept complimenting me.

"We're going to have good times," he said. "I'll make up for all you've missed. That's a promise. I don't want to keep calling you Noble, though. It makes me feel . . . queer. What should I call you? Huh? What?"

I looked at him.

"Celeste," I said, and the moment I said it, I felt I had done something worse than Judas had done. However, he didn't understand.

"Naw," he said. "I don't like that name. I'm going to call you Jane. You can call me Tarzan," he declared and howled and beat his chest.

I thought he was very funny. He got up and paraded around our blanket naked, pretending to be an ape. He lit himself another marijuana joint. Slowly, I began to return to earth. I felt myself falling back like a balloon that leaked air, and it was truly as if I was bouncing about the blanket. My stomach rumbled now, too. While he smoked and howled and laughed at his own silly remarks, I managed to get dressed.

He finally realized it and said, "Yeah,

I've got to get going, too."

He started to dress, but stopped every few moments to laugh and howl. I had never seen anyone drunk, but it seemed to me this was what it was like. Still puffing on his marijuana, he completed his dressing, and then he seized my hand.

"Come on," he urged. "Walk me back."

"No," I said shaking my head. "I've got to get home before my mother returns from her errands."

"You got time. I want to know more," he insisted. "Walk," he said and tugged me so hard, I stumbled forward and almost fell. That put him into another fit of laughter.

"What about your blanket?" I asked, turning back.

"Leave it. We'll use it tomorrow and tomorrow and tomorrow," he replied, which made him laugh again.

We stumbled through some brush and into the woods until we reached the edge of the creek, him pulling me along and holding onto my hand as if he was a blind person who needed me alongside. He did seem to have trouble navigating. He even banged his shoulder against a tree. I kept telling him I had to get home, but he just laughed and surged forward until we reached the water.

At this particular side of the creek, there were a series of large rocks that ran across to the other side. The water was still at a high level and rushing along the sides. The rocks gleamed like chunks of ice when the sun broke through some clouds.

"My shortcut," Elliot said, waving at the rocks. He stood there smiling stupidly at me. "I have an idea. Tomorrow, how about you come to me. I'm getting tired of this woods. My sister won't be home. She's onto a new boyfriend, and she goes to his house every afternoon. My father's on his daytime schedule this month, so we'll have the house to ourselves. I sorta like the idea of your being in my bed, and I bet you will love it, too," he added. "Just appear at the back door the same time."

He waved at the air between us as if that was that. Then he stared out at the creek a moment like someone who was indecisive. He was still holding tightly to my hand.

"I have to go home," I said softly.

"Huh? Oh. Yeah." He seemed to have difficulty focusing on me. "You didn't tell me much more about yourself and your mother. I want to hear it all tomorrow, understand? Understand?" He asked, raising his voice.

"Yes, yes, I understand," I said.

"Okay." He nodded and looked across the creek. "Okay."

He let go of me and started to cross, paused, and looked back.

"You're not going to pretend to be a boy forever, you know," he said.

It sounded like a prediction, and his face was so different, even his voice was changed when he spoke. I wondered if some spirit was speaking through him.

He returned to his navigating over the rocks. I stood for a moment watching him. He slipped once and got his right foot soaked.

"Damn," he shouted, and then he started laughing. I was still feeling unsteady myself, but rather than fall into a laughing jag, I wanted to cry. I sniffed back my tears and swallowed and swallowed.

Just as I started away from the creek, I heard him scream and turned to see him fall backward into the water. He started laughing again and waved.

"Who pushed me?" he cried and laughed again.

He splashed about and reached for the rock from which he had tumbled, but the raging creek actually turned him. The water was still quite cold, despite the start of spring. Most of it was coming from melting snow and ice from the mountains above, I thought.

"Hey," I heard him scream, as if he could talk to the water and bawl it out for interfering. "I think I feel a fish in my shoe," he cried and laughed again.

He was carried farther away from this rock bridge, and although his efforts to prevent it were futile, he didn't seem in any panic. I took a few steps back toward the water.

"Hey. Look. A shark's after me," he shouted, and then his head went down below the water.

He popped up and flailed about, turning as he did so. I saw he got some footing, but when he attempted to stand, he fell backward. He laughed again, even though this time he was carried more forcefully away. I ran to the shore of the creek, and from there, I watched him swinging his arms and struggling to take hold of rocks, branches, anything, until he went under again and then emerged just as he rounded the far turn. He waved at me and shouted, "Call the Coast Guard!" His laugh died away as he disappeared.

It was quiet, except for the gurgling sound of the water as it rushed by and over the rocks.

"Elliot!" I called. "Are you all right?"

I stared at the turn where he had disappeared from sight and waited. I called again. My voice was swallowed up by the sound of the creek. A large crow, however, shot off a high tree branch and flapped its wings madly. When it cried, it sounded like laughter to me.

He must have gotten out on the other side, I thought. He was probably lying there laughing at it all, especially laughing at me. I've got to get home, I realized. Mommy might already be back. I hurried away, avoiding brambles and branches the best I could. When I broke out of the forest and into our meadow, I could see that Mommy was not yet back. I sighed with relief and continued to the house.

As soon as I got there, I went upstairs to my room and undressed. I took a hot and then a cold shower, and it seemed to help me clear my mind. By the time I dressed again and went downstairs, Mommy had returned. She seemed very, very happy. Her face was beaming.

"Noble," she cried when she saw me. "I have wonderful news. Mr. Bogart has already found us customers who will buy everything that we can produce. We're going to expand our garden. Oh, I know

509

we don't need the money so desperately, but it will be fun to be doing something valuable, won't it? He was even talking about creating a brand. He suggested Sarah's Herbal Wonders. It would be something for you to inherit someday, too. Another legacy."

She paused.

"You look freshened up. What have you been doing?"

"I tried my saw. I have to get used to it," I said.

"Of course. I'm glad you're responsible enough to realize such a thing. I went to the supermarket and bought some very lean pork chops. I'll stuff them, and we'll have a little celebration," she decided and went off to the kitchen.

I went outside and sat on the porch, gazing off at the woods. What had I done? How much deeper had I fallen? I wondered. A part of me was treacherous. Even though Elliot was forcing me to do his will, I was unable to keep myself from confessing my excitement and pleasure over some of it. I wanted to harden myself against myself.

I imagined Mommy would say it was the Celeste in me again, but all this did was make me question and challenge my own identity. Who was I now? Who would I be? You can't be a boy forever, Elliot had said, but if I wasn't, Mommy would have to bury Noble again in a proper grave with a tombstone.

The image of her digging him up crossed my troubled mind. It was gross and actually made my stomach churn. I would have to help. I would have to take off Celeste's clothes and put Noble's on his decomposed body. I shuddered, stood up as though I was being haunted, and quickly walked off the porch and went to the barn to busy myself with cleaning the chain saw.

Later Mommy called me to dinner, and I had to force myself to have a big appetite. She had gone ahead and made an apple pie, too, and when she cut me a piece, she cut a large one as usual and plopped a chunk of rich vanilla ice cream over it. She was still keeping me overweight.

"I didn't actually stop at a car dealership, Noble, but I went by one and I saw this red sedan you would just love. It was one of those very fancy cars with the shiny wheels, you know. I sat back and saw you washing the car every weekend. Remember when you and your daddy would do that?"

"Yes."

"We're going to have wonderful times

again, Noble, wonderful times."

After dinner she went into the living room and played some of her favorite old-time songs, songs she said her mother had loved and even her grandmother enjoyed.

"They would stand around the piano and sing," she told me. "Our home was so warm, so full of love. Grandpa Jordan would pretend it was just a lot of noise to him, but when I stole a glance, I saw the happy smile on his face and the way he looked at my grandmother. She was a beautiful woman with an angelic smile.

"She still has that smile, of course. That's the wonder of the spiritual existence, Noble. You are frozen in your happiest, most beautiful and handsome moments. Some day you'll know what I mean. Someday," she said, her voice drifting off with the music.

Could we be that happy? I wondered. Would everything turn out all right after all? Would I be blessed and given the powers, all the powers, even though I had done what I had done?

Despite the events of the day, I went to sleep with an air of optimism about me. Mommy was so strong, I thought. She could change the face of time. She would keep me safe. I cuddled up beneath my covers and dreamed of the time when she would be playing the piano and I would see and hear all our family spirits who stood around and sang. Daddy would have his arm around my shoulders and he would kiss my cheek, and I would feel it, actually feel it again.

"See," he would say, "your mother is a special lady."

As soon as we finished our breakfast the next day, Mommy had me join her in the garden. We worked side by side for hours, turning the earth, planting her herbs. As we worked, she talked more about her early life and told me stories I had never before heard.

"You know, I wanted a little brother or sister for the longest time," she said. "I was lonely and it was always hard to have friends over to our home. My mother tried to have more children. She did everything Grandma Jordan told her to do, but nothing worked, and after a while, they concluded that because Mommy was only able to have me, I must be someone very, very special.

"My mother became my best friend," she told me and smiled at me. "Just like I'm your best friend and always will be, Noble. That's okay, isn't it?"

"Yes," I said. "But you went to public school. Didn't you ever have a close friend?"

"No," she said quickly and turned away from me. Then she hesitated and turned back. "There was someone once, a girl in the ninth grade, Sandra Cooke, but she became friends with very bad kids, and I knew I would get into trouble if I stayed friends with her. I told her mother on her, and she hated me forever afterward."

"What did she do?"

"She was, as they used to say, promiscuous. You don't know what that means because you don't read enough, Noble, but let's just say she was loose with her body, and she did things with boys she shouldn't have done."

Of course I knew what it meant, but I said nothing.

"She didn't seem to care who she was with. Your body can betray you sometimes," she continued. "People think pleasure is something good all the time, but it's not. Sometimes, it's just the evil spirits' way to open doors to your very soul. Once inside, they can rot you like an apple.

"But," she said, running her fingers through my short hair, "you must not worry about that. It will never happen to you."

She looked up at the sky.

"Let's work faster. It's supposed to rain hard today," she said, "and most likely tomorrow as well."

We did work until the rain began, and then we went inside and I sat by the window and read and watched the wind whip the sheets of drops over the trees and meadow. Daddy hated long rainstorms, but Mommy would tell him it cleansed the world and he should be grateful. Of course he retorted with, "It makes it harder for builders, and that doesn't help our bottom line."

"It's your soul's bottom line I would worry about," Mommy countered, and he would pull his ear and smile at me. "Can't argue with a mystic," he sometimes said. Mommy hated to be called that.

"There's nothing mystical about me. Nothing mysterious. What's mysterious to me is why so many people are blind to the beauty of the spiritual truths in our world," she said.

In the end Daddy surrendered and went off laughing about the futility of arguing with her. There was a different sort of music in our house then, a different sort of light, too. Would all that return as Mommy promised?

I watched the rain until I grew tired and went to sleep. The following day, as Mommy had predicted, it rained until late in the afternoon. It was almost dark before it stopped, in fact. I sat in the living room and completed some of my workbook assignments. Suddenly a sweep of light passed over the wall, and I looked up sharply. I heard a door slam and then another. Moments later the bell rang, and Mommy came out of the kitchen. She looked curiously at me and wiped her hands on her apron. I shook my head.

"Who could that be?" she muttered and went to the door. I stood in the living room doorway and watched.

A policeman and Mr. Fletcher stood there. The policeman was still wearing a raincoat, but Mr. Fletcher was in a sports jacket and slacks and looked like he had just come from a social event.

"Yes?" Mommy said. She looked at Mr. Fletcher.

"We're here to see if your son has seen my son recently," he said.

"What?" Mommy brought her hands to her hips.

"Mr. Fletcher's son Elliot has been missing for a few days, Mrs. Atwell," the policeman said. "His car and all his things are at the house, but he's not there, and no one has seen him. He hasn't been to school. We've questioned all his friends at school, and the only thing left to do is speak to your son."

"Why would Noble know anything about him?" she demanded.

The policeman looked at Mr. Fletcher.

"My daughter suggested he might."

"Why would she say that?"

"She said he had seen him recently," he told her, and Mommy slowly turned to me.

"Is that true, Noble?"

"No," I said quickly, maybe too quickly.

"I'm very worried, son," Mr. Fletcher said. "He's done some silly things, but he's never done anything like this. He's not here by any chance, is he?"

"Of course not," Mommy snapped. "Do you actually believe I would permit such a thing?"

"I was just —"

"We're checking every possible lead, Mrs. Atwell," the policeman said. "I'm sure you can appreciate what Mr. Fletcher is going through, having lost a child yourself."

Mommy's upper body snapped back so fast and so sharply, she looked like she might topple.

"Of course I appreciate it. I'm just telling you that we don't know anything about him." She looked at Mr. Fletcher. "I warned you he was into very bad behavior," she told him. "This doesn't surprise me. It doesn't surprise me at all."

He nodded and looked down.

"I know," he said softly, his voice couched in a tone of defeat.

"Well, we can't help you," she said. "I'm very sorry for your trouble."

"You sure you haven't seen Elliot?" the policeman asked me again.

I shook my head.

"No, not for a while," I said. My heart was pounding. Mommy didn't even look at me.

"Okay. Thank you. If you think of anything, please call the station," the policeman said, and they turned away.

Mommy closed the door immediately. For a moment she stood there looking at it. Then she spun on me, her eyes small, suspicious.

"Do you know where he has gone?"

I didn't, so I was able to shake my head.

She didn't look convinced, but she breathed easier and then, without another word, returned to the kitchen.

I stood there feeling numb all over.

I heard Mommy rattle pots and pans as she sifted through them, looking for something. When she made noise like that, I knew she was upset.

The sounds seemed to echo inside my chest.

At dinner Mommy went on and on about how much of a burden children were to their parents today.

"If you're blessed with a responsible, obedient, and loving child, you're a very lucky person, but the truth is, they reap what they sow. That was why I couldn't be as sympathetic to Mr. Fletcher as the policeman would have liked me to be. I know it's a hard face to wear, but if we don't wear it, things will only get worse.

"That," she said, "is why I feel so fortunate having a child like you."

She got up and walked over to me to kiss me on the forehead and then hold me tightly against her. I said nothing. I couldn't help but wonder if she felt me shaking. The trembling I had felt when the policeman and Mr. Fletcher came to our door was still going on inside me.

It followed me into sleep and turned every shadow in my room into a dark threat.

The search party came late the following

morning. It brought back horrid memories, both for Mommy and myself. We could hear the voices of the men shouting to each other in the forest. From our front porch, we saw the cars parking on the highway. A fire engine was brought up as well.

Only an hour or so after they had begun, we heard a gunshot to signal the others. That was followed by the sound of an ambulance screaming up to our road.

Mommy walked out and down the driveway, where she could speak with people.

Then she returned quickly.

"What's going on?" I asked her.

"They found him," she said.

"Where?" I asked, my voice not much more than a whisper.

"Washed about a mile downstream."

17

The Gift

Before they had found Elliot, they had found his blanket by the pine tree. We didn't know it all immediately, but they also found remnants of his marijuana cigarettes. However, it was what they had found in his pants pocket that brought the police back to our front door. They didn't come until early in the evening. I was upstairs in my room when I heard the doorbell ring. The sound made my heart race. With all the sirens, the sounds of far more traffic and people on our road and around our property, I couldn't help being anxious.

After we had heard that Elliot was found apparently drowned and washed ashore farther downstream, I had gone off to be alone as quickly as I could. I was sure Mommy would take one glance at my face and know I had lied to her and had kept things from her. I was more afraid of her disappointment in me than I was of her rage.

As I sat there thinking about the horror of it all, I told myself that even though I had seen Elliot get carried farther down the creek and around the turn, I had good reason to assume he would be all right. From the years when we didn't have much of a snowfall and spring rain, I knew the creek had so many rocks and hills under it, making it very shallow in many places. I had good reason to conclude he would eventually find his footing and pull himself safely to shore. He didn't really scream for help. I had no idea he wasn't a good swimmer, and in the beginning, when he dipped his foot in the water and even after he fell in, he was laughing about it and clowning around.

But what fascinated and even frightened me somewhat the whole day after I had heard the news was the possibility that this was what Daddy's spirit had meant when I thought I had heard him whispering in the wind to be patient. I recalled the way Elliot had toppled into the water. He did cry, "Who pushed me?" Had he really felt some force knocking him off the rock or was that shout and the surprise just part of his joking around with me?

Could it really be that our spiritual protectors had done this? If so, wasn't it all ultimately my fault? If I hadn't done what I had done that day and exposed myself to the world and to Elliot, none of this would have happened. Complicating it even further, I had not told Mommy. I had kept it all a secret, and I had let it continue. Now what would happen to us?

I heard Mommy calling for me from the entryway. Slowly rising from my bed, where I had been sitting and thinking, I walked to the door and then descended, feeling like a convicted felon approaching the gallows. Mommy stood there looking up at me with her arms folded under her breasts so tightly, they looked locked in place forever. The policeman and a man in a dark gray sports coat and tie stood just behind her, waiting for me. He had a chiseled face with a brow that hung like a cliff's edge over his eyes. His lower lip drooped just enough to show most of his lower teeth.

As I drew closer, I saw the fire in Mommy's eyes, each holding the tip of a candle flame. Her lips were pursed, pressing up the crests of her cheeks. Some loosened strains of hair fell over her temple and down to the right side of her mouth.

"Officer Harold and Detective Young want to ask you some questions, Noble. I want you to answer them honestly," Mommy said, pronouncing each word with crystal clear and sharp consonants and vowels, which I knew was how she spoke when she was battling to control the rage roaring inside her.

I nodded and turned to them. Detective Young stepped forward.

"Do you recognize this?" he asked and opened his fist to show me the red coral amulet.

I couldn't help looking up from it quickly at Mommy. She stared, her face a closed book to anyone else, but to me speaking volumes and volumes of angry disappointment. She knew it was the one she had given me, of course. Her eyes flickered, rage feeding the fire.

"Yes," I said in a voice so small, I wasn't sure myself that I had spoken.

"Elliot's father and his sister told us he didn't have this when they had last seen him, and in fact they had never seen it. They have no idea how he got it or even what it is, but his sister thought you might know."

"Why did she think that?" Mommy demanded, spinning on the detective.

Detective Young looked at her for a moment, obviously considering how to reply.

"Her brother told her things about your son and you that led her to believe it. I guess he described what your son is wearing right now," he said, referring to my amulet. He turned back to me. "What is it, and how did Elliot Fletcher come to have it in his possession at the time of his death?"

"It's an amulet," I said. "Red coral."

"An amulet?" Officer Harold muttered. "What is that, exactly?"

I looked at Mommy.

"An amulet is a talisman, a good-luck charm, if you will," Mommy explained for me. "Red coral is said to have certain beneficial properties for the wearer."

"This was yours, then?" Detective Young asked, still holding it out as if he was showing something to a jury in a courtroom.

"Yes," I replied.

"And you gave it to Elliot Fletcher?"

I nodded.

"When exactly?" he asked.

Again, I looked up at Mommy first.

"When?" she repeated for Detective Young.

"A few days ago," I said.

Mommy released a trapped breath like someone who had just been given terrible news.

"When I was here earlier, you told me and Elliot's father that you hadn't seen him for a while," Officer Harold said, practically leaping at me. "Now you're saying you gave him this thing a few days ago. Why did you lie to us?"

I felt panic running down the sides of my legs, freezing them in place. Why was this happening to me? If the spirits were protecting me, why did they let this happen? What was I suppose to say, to do?

I didn't look at Mommy. I shifted my eyes guiltily toward the floor and shrugged.

"Elliot made me promise not to tell," I said and recalled Mommy once telling me that lies pop out of people's minds like pimples sometimes.

I don't know what makes someone a good liar, if there is such a thing, but I suppose it has something to do with his or her ability to create, to perform, maybe even believe in the lie him or herself first, I thought.

"Why did he do that?" Detective Young followed.

"He was smoking something bad, and he said his father would take away his car if he found out," I said in a very convincing tone of voice. I felt confident that really wasn't a lie anyway.

"So? Why wouldn't you tell his father you had seen him?" Officer Harold asked, his face dark with exasperation and outrage. "You saw how concerned he was."

I bit down on my lower lip and kept my eyes fixed on the floor. I couldn't think of any excuse that would make me look good or even make sense.

"Was it because you smoked something bad as well?" Detective Young offered.

I looked up quickly. Mommy's eyes hadn't changed, hadn't moved. They were so fixed on me, I felt like she was boring a hole through my forehead.

"Noble?" she said. "Answer the question."

I nodded. The detective's theory was an unexpected gift, a way to rescue myself.

"Yes."

Both Officer Harold and Detective Young settled in the comfort of being right about me. I could see it clearly in the way they glanced at each other. They had probably discussed it before they had arrived at our door.

"But I didn't think anything terrible had happened to him," I added quickly.

"Tell us what occurred the last time you saw him," Detective Young said.

"We smoked that stuff in the woods, and then we parted and he started for home and I came home."

They stared at me, four eyes searching my face like spotlights sweeping over a prison wall, looking for cracks. I held my breath. Out of the corner of my eye, I could see a small movement in Mommy's lips. It was impossible to lie to her, no matter how good I was with other people.

"You didn't have any arguments or anything like that?" Detective Young asked.

"What are you suggesting? That Noble drowned him?" Mommy snapped at him.

"No."

"Then why ask such a question?"

"It's what we do. We try to get all the information we can in order to understand what happened, Mrs. Atwell. A terrible family tragedy has occurred here."

"I think I know something about terrible family tragedies," Mommy told him, speaking so sharply, he reacted as if he had been slapped.

"I'm sorry. We're just doing our job."

"Well, do it quickly and leave us be," she said.

He turned back to me.

"So you didn't know Elliot was in any sort of trouble when you left him that day?"

"No," I said and nodded at the amulet he was holding. "I thought he was protected."

Maybe that was the wrong thing to say; maybe it was the right thing to say. I didn't know, but it widened the eyes of both policemen.

"Huh?" Officer Harold said. "What do you mean, protected?"

"Red coral is a powerful gemstone. It can make the wearer courageous and have a very strong calming effect, reducing tensions. It has healing powers," Mommy explained. "Noble had good intentions in giving the boy the amulet, but the boy shouldn't have depended on it to protect him in every possible way.

"In fact," Mommy continued, "one problem with red coral is it might make the wearer too confident, too courageous. You know that saying about fools rushing in where angels fear to tread," she added in her typical educationalist tone of voice.

The two policemen stood speechless, staring at her. Finally, Officer Harold turned to me.

"You did a bad thing, not telling us you

had seen Elliot Fletcher recently. We would have concentrated on the woods a lot faster, and even if we couldn't do anything to help him, his father and his sister wouldn't have been left in limbo so long."

"Withholding information from the police is a criminal act, you know," Detective Young said.

I said nothing, and neither did Mommy. They looked uncomfortable.

"Here," Detective Young said, handing me the amulet. "Mr. Fletcher doesn't want it."

"We don't want it either," Mommy said, stepping in between me and the policeman. "Tell Mr. Fletcher he should bury it with his son. There are ways to protect us in the afterlife as well, and that can be even more important."

Officer Harold smirked. Then he turned away and shook his head.

"Okay," Detective Young said. He put the amulet back into his pocket. "If your son thinks of anything else that might help us understand what happened —"

"Why is it so difficult to understand?" Mommy practically shouted at them. "From what we've heard, the boy drowned in the creek. You said he was smoking something bad, and you just heard Noble confirm it. I'm sure it was marijuana, and that can affect your perception, can it not? I was a public school teacher once," she added. "We were always talking to the children about why using drugs was bad for you."

"Yes," Detective Young admitted. "The pot might have had something to do with what happened."

"It's a tragedy. It's terrible, but parents have to be on top of their children more vigorously these days," Mommy lectured. "I've said it before, and I'll say it again. I feel sorry for Mr. Fletcher. I know what he's suffering. No one knows better about that suffering than I do, but in the end, he has to live with his own failings. We all do," she concluded. "Now if you're finished here —"

She opened the door for them.

"Thank you," Detective Young muttered.

Officer Harold just glared back at me and followed him out of our house.

When Mommy closed the door, I felt like she had closed the lid on my coffin. Slowly, ever so slowly, she turned to me. I fumbled words in my mind, trying to find the right way to say I was sorry.

"Don't try to explain anything to me,"

she said. "I know exactly what happened."

Did she know? Exactly?

"Evil spirits have been at us ever since your father died. They have tried every way they could to pierce our protective shield. They made me sick once and gave me headaches. They even resorted to entering the body of a dog. It is no surprise to me that they concentrated on spoiling you, Noble, and tried to spoil you by using that young man. I should have been even more diligent when I learned of your initial contact with those people and you had told me of the bad things they were doing. It's not all your fault. I was too trusting, too dependent on those that watch over us.

"But thankfully, they continue to do so. I am not surprised about what had happened. Of course, I am disappointed in you, and there is work to do now to cleanse you, but I am grateful we are still safe, still being watched over and blessed."

She paused, squeezed her temples with her right thumb and forefinger, and took deep breaths. I held mine in anticipation. Finally, she looked up at me and nodded as if she had just been told exactly what to do.

"Go upstairs and get undressed," she said.

"Undressed?"

"Yes. I'll be right there," she said and walked toward the kitchen and the pantry.

For a moment I was too frightened to move. What was she going to do? I started up the stairs slowly and then walked quickly to my room, where I began to undress. I was in such a daze I didn't hear Mommy come charging up the stairs and into my room. Suddenly, she was there rushing past me into the bathroom. I heard her turn on the faucet for the tub.

"What's taking you so long?" she cried from the bathroom doorway. "Hurry up and get yourself naked and in here. There is no time to lose."

She turned into the bathroom. I continued to undress. When I was naked, I entered slowly. It had been a while since Mommy had gazed upon me and seen my body develop, but when she looked at me now, it was just a glance and it was as if she saw nothing different from the first day she had dressed me in my brother's clothing.

She stood by the tub and looked down at the water pouring into it. I saw the jar of black powder in her hands.

"What's that?" I asked.

"It's from my grandmother's secret closet," she said. "Her own recipe. Get in the water," she told me and stood back waiting.

I approached the tub and then slowly brought my leg over and my foot down. The moment I touched the water, I leaped back. It was scalding.

"It's too hot!" I cried.

"It has to be very hot. Get in," she said without emotion. She sounded as if she was under a spell herself.

"I can't. It's much too hot."

"Get in," she said again.

I shook my head and backed away.

"Get in, Noble. Get in."

"Make it cooler."

"Okay," she said suddenly, and she turned the cold faucet on and let it run. "Try it now," she said, and I cautiously dipped my foot in again. It was still very hot, but bearable.

"Soak," she said, and I sat slowly and endured the hot water.

She then sprinkled the black powder into the water, and it quickly turned the water into a dark blue.

"It smells terrible," I said.

"It's not supposed to be bath salts. Just soak," she said and left me.

"How long?" I called after her.

"Until I return," she said.

"What does it do?" I shouted, but she didn't hear me, or if she did, she didn't want to respond.

I had to turn my head because the smell was so gross. I felt like I was going to vomit. I leaned over the side of the tub and waited and waited. I thought she had forgotten me when she finally came into the bathroom. I looked up and saw she was carrying a large cauldron. Before I could protest, she rushed at the tub and poured out the contents, which was scalding hot water. I shouted and tried to get out, but she pushed down on my shoulders and held me in the water. I cried and cried and begged. Finally, she let me emerge. My skin was as red as it would be if I had lain out naked in the hot sun for a day. It was painful, too, especially where some of the boiling water had hit my body.

I grabbed a towel and began to wipe myself, but that hurt.

"Lie down," she told me. "I'll bring you some soothing salve."

I didn't trust her. When she returned this time, she had a jar of one of her herbal salves, but I cringed when she began to wipe it on my body, expecting some more pain. It didn't hurt. It brought relief.

"Hopefully we have driven what remains

of the evil out of your earthly body. Sleep now, Noble," she said. "And say your prayers. We have to pray you've been completely cleansed, that all that corrupted you has been exorcized."

She left, closing my door. I heard the familiar sound of the key in the lock.

I was going to be put on a fast again, I thought, and like someone condemned, I closed my eyes and listened for the tolling bells of doom.

She surprised me, however, by bringing me cups of tea, toast, and jam. She brought me no breakfast in the morning, but she did bring me some hot cereal for dinner and some fruit. She rubbed the salve over my body again and told me to rest. Later that evening, she burned her incense around me and held vigil. Every time I tried to speak or get up, she shook her head and said, "Not yet. It's not time yet."

I was permitted only to go to the bathroom. After two days, she opened my door and told me I should dress and go wait for her at the cemetery. Grateful I could finally emerge from my room, I hurriedly did what she asked. She didn't come to the cemetery for quite a while, and when she approached, I saw she was wearing her mourning clothes and was completely in black from her shoes to the veil she wore.

There, before the old tombstones, she held my hand and sang her hymns. Then she stopped and offered a prayer, begging the spirits not to take me from her. She had me plead with them as well, repeating the words she dictated. When it was over, we returned to the house. Mommy changed into her everyday clothes and then behaved as if nothing unusual had happened. She went about her house chores and gave me my schoolwork and the list of things she wanted me to accomplish around the house and the property. Not another word was said about Elliot Fletcher or the policemen who had visited us.

Every once in a while during the days that followed, I would catch her looking at me, or more accurately, around me, and nodding. She saw someone, some spirit, I was sure, and I held my breath and waited for some sort of verdict or conclusion, but she said nothing. I was happy she at least looked content.

Finally, one evening a week later, after we had eaten our dinner, she folded her hands on the table and leaned forward to speak to me. I could tell from the expression on her face and the tone of her voice that she was going to assume her teacher mode.

"There will be other times, other challenges like the one we just had," she began. "It is very important that you tell me immediately when anything like that occurs. Never, never again will you keep anything secret from me, Noble. We are all we have and all we will ever have."

She smiled.

"Once you were inside me, a part of me physically. Then you were born and you were outside me, but what tied us together was never untied. Do you understand? Do you understand now how very important it is to be trusting and truthful with me and how that keeps us bound together? Do you?"

"Yes," I said.

"Good. Because I have a wonderful surprise for you tonight," she said. "First, I'll clean up our dinner dishes and put things away. You go wait patiently in the living room," she said and I rose and left the dining room.

I sat in Mommy's great-grandfather Jordan's rocking chair. I really didn't think about it. I just did it, but when she came to me, I could see in her smile that she thought it was something significant.

"It doesn't surprise me to find you sitting there," she said. "We are often drawn to our ancestors through set pieces in our home. Remember that. Remember how important it is to cherish everything that binds us to them."

She held a candleholder and an unlit candle in her hand.

"I know that it was always upsetting to you that Celeste was able to cross over so quickly at so young an age while you were still waiting at the wall with no sign of any doorway. As we learned, that was because they had other plans for her, plans we didn't understand then. Now," she said, "they finally have plans for you."

I barely moved a muscle listening. What did that mean? What sort of plans for me? What was she going to do?

"Come with me," she said, smiling. "Come on." She lit the candle, turned, and walked to the doorway, waiting.

I tried very hard not to be afraid, but the memory of my scalding bath was still quite vivid. My skin cringed. She saw it in my face and laughed.

"There is nothing bad awaiting you, dear Noble, only good things now. Don't look so frightened. Come along."

I realized all the lights in the house were

turned off. In the darkness, with only the glow of the candle showing us the way, I followed her to the stairway. The shadows slid over the walls along with us. We walked up slowly, her cupping the small flame to be sure it stayed lit and bright, and then we continued to the turret room. She unlocked the door and entered first, turning to beckon me to follow.

When I walked in, I saw a mattress had been placed on the floor. Around it were all the pictures we had of the relatives, and in front of them were other candles, yet unlit. Next to the mattress was a black pitcher and a goblet, an heirloom we never used. Previously, it had been on a shelf in the armoire in the dining room.

"Do you know where you're going tonight?" she asked me.

I shook my head.

"Tonight, you will go through that door we spoke of, and as brief as it might seem to you, you will walk with them and you will finally hear them speak. It's a gift they have decided to bestow on you."

She looked about the dark room, holding the candle high to throw its glow over the walls, the windows, and the floor. She moved slowly in a circle so that the light washed across every part of the room, as if she was sterilizing it with the yellow glow. Then she stopped and turned back to me.

"I was younger than you when my mother gave me the gift, but it was just how it was, how it was meant to be. Afterward, just as it will be for you, I no longer needed anyone's help to cross over. Sometimes we need to do this, my mother told me. There's nothing shameful about that. Think of it the way you would think of a helping hand reaching out for you, guiding you, pulling you aboard a wonderful ship to take you on an dazzling journey. You are ready for this. I know you have wanted it for so long, and I know you were often jealous of Celeste, who did not need any help.

"But all that is over now. Tonight it ends."

She put the candleholder down gently and then picked up the pitcher and the goblet. I watched her pour something into it. Then she turned to me and offered me the goblet.

"First, you will drink this, and then I want you to lie down softly on the magic carpet, for that is truly what it will become," she said.

Hesitantly, I reached out and took the goblet. She urged me with her eyes and her smile. I couldn't help my hesitation, nor the way my hand trembled.

"Trust, remember? We must have trust between us. Drink, my darling. Drink it all in one long gulp. Don't sip it. Go on," she said.

A dark part of me wondered if this was going to be the end. Before morning's light, would she lay me down beside Noble? Would I become a spirit, too, and was that the way she would keep us together forever? Was that the way I would cross over?

Even if that was true, shouldn't I be happy? After all, I was soon to enter a perfect world, a world in which I no longer had to hide from myself, disguise myself, be someone I was not. Wouldn't that be the true gift, and didn't I finally deserve it?

Perhaps what had happened between Elliot and me had convinced her I was in danger of never crossing over. Perhaps she had been told, and that was why tonight I had been brought here and, like my Juliet in the play I so loved, given a potion to swallow that held the promise of endless happiness. There were so many forces greater than myself, than my little mind, my small fears, my tiny being. Who was I to challenge any of them?

I took the goblet and brought it to my lips.

If this was truly the end of one life and the beginning of another, to what was I to say good-bye? What would I miss? My chores, my spartan room, my fishing pole, and new chain saw? Was there anything I left behind that brought tears to my eyes?

Or was it truly the beginning, and on the contrary, weren't there so many things I would say hello to again? My dolls, my beautiful clothes, my jewels, my teacup set, all of it, just waiting for me.

Really, I thought, I have no good-byes to say, just hellos.

I tipped the goblet and let the cool, strange-tasting liquid flow over my tongue and down my throat, swallowing quickly until it was all gone.

Mommy nodded and took the goblet from me gently.

"Lie down," she said.

I did as she asked, and she slowly and carefully lit every candle in front of every picture. Then she stood up with her own candle and holder in hand and smiled down at me.

"What a lucky boy you are," she said. "I'll see you again," she promised and left the turret room, closing the door softly behind her. I heard the key turn in the lock, and then I heard her steps as she walked away.

The candles flickered around me, causing shadows to dance over the walls. Soon I felt my head spinning, and then it wasn't just my head. My whole body started to turn and turn. I closed my eyes and put my hands on the floor to steady myself. All sorts of colors and flashes of light streaked over my closed eyelids. I thought I shouted, but I wasn't sure. What I was sure of was that I could hear Mommy playing on the piano below.

Suddenly I stopped spinning, and then I saw something out of the corner of my eye. A puff of smoke rose. Did it come from the candle in front of the picture of Auntie Helen Roe or did it come from the picture itself? I shifted my gaze to my right because another puff of smoke rose in front of Grandpa Jordan's picture, and then another from Great-Aunt Louise, another from Cousin Simon, and yet another from Grandmother Gussie's picture.

All the puffs rose and merged in front of me, and then the shadows that danced on the walls turned into the spirits Mommy had promised. They circled me. I could hear them laughing. They moved faster and faster, their laughter louder, and then they stopped and returned to their pictures, the smoky forms almost sucked into the frames.

All was quiet. Mommy's piano music rose again, and there was Great-Grandpa Jordan sitting in his rocker, looking at me. He nodded.

"What a good child you are," he said. "I'm very proud of you. Very proud."

I heard giggling and saw three little girls kneeling beside me. When I reached out to touch them, they were gone like popped bubbles, but just as soon as they were gone, I heard someone clear his throat and turned to see Uncle Peter, Great-Grandma Jordan's brother, standing and looking down at me, that gold pocket watch of his that was in his photograph in his hand. He squinted and opened it.

"It's almost time," he said.

Then he was gone.

The shadows continued to dance on the walls.

"Daddy!" I called. "Daddy."

The music seemed to get louder.

I felt fingers in my right hand and looked up to see him, my daddy, standing there, as young as he was when I was five.

"You've been a good girl," he said. "We

all love you, and we'll never let anything bad happen to you again. That's a promise."

"Where's Noble?" I asked him, and he nodded toward my left.

There was Noble, smirking.

"You have no right trying to be me," he said. "You can't fish for nothing, and what about that new chain saw? You barely can hold it. What a waste. You don't have an ant farm going either.

"And when was the last time you played in my fort? You let it rot in the woods."

"What did I ask you, Noble?" Daddy said. "What did I ask you to do?"

"Be nice," Noble answered.

"Are you being nice?"

"No." He shook his head at me. "You don't want to come here," he said. "You've got to be nice all day and night."

I heard Daddy's laugh, and then all of them laughed, my uncles, my grandparents, and cousins. The laughter got louder than the piano music.

"I want my electric trains!" Noble screamed.

He popped and was gone.

Daddy remained there, holding my hand.

"Don't leave me, Daddy," I begged. "Please."

"I never will," he said. He sat beside me.

Together we looked at the wall and watched the pictures run by like a movie, all the pictures of me and Noble and our happy days, our walks, our swimming, our fishing together. There were the pictures of our trips, too, our rides, the times we went to the fun parks, our birthdays, on and on they ran, flashing faster and faster until they began to run into each other.

"Daddy," I said nervously and fearfully.

"I'm here," he whispered.

The pictures were soon indistinguishable balls of light that grew so bright, I couldn't look directly at them. I had to close my eyes.

"Daddy . . ."

I heard my voice echo.

I was falling and falling into some dark place.

"Daddy . . ."

"I'm here," his voice echoed back, and then . . . all was black.

I woke to the sound of the key in the lock and heard the door opening. Sunlight was streaming through the window so brightly, I knew it was late in the morning, if not early afternoon.

All of the candles were burned down in front of the pictures.

Mommy stepped in and looked at me.

"Good morning," she said. "You can tell me everything after you wash and change for breakfast, okay?"

I started to sit up and groaned. I felt so stiff, and there was a tiny beating of blood in my temples.

"You'll be fine," Mommy said, helping me to my feet. "Once you have something substantial in your stomach, you'll be fine. And guess what? It's a beautiful day. You should see how our herbs are growing, too."

I followed her out, the brightness still hard to take. I had to shade my eyes.

"You've got an old-fashioned hangover," Mommy said, laughing. "But don't worry. I have all the remedies, and the remedies that really work, too. You'll be yourself in no time."

We stopped in front of my room.

"Take a nice shower. I'll be waiting for you downstairs." She shook her head and smiled at me. "You look just the way I did afterward. The main thing to remember now, Noble, is you've crossed over, really crossed over, and you'll be seeing and hearing them all the time. It's the gift, the gift that binds you to me forever."

She kissed me on the forehead. Then she

left me and descended the stairs.

I went into my room and began to undress to take that shower. Before I did, I went to my window and looked down. Something had drawn me to it.

There below, walking slowly and talking, were my three cousins who had died years and years before I was born: Mildred, Louise, and Darla, all sisters. They were exactly as they were in the pictures on the hallway wall below, wearing the same calico dresses, their hair the same style. They paused as if they had heard something, and then the three of them looked up at me.

And they smiled.

I watched them walk on until they were entering the woods and disappearing in the shadows.

I wasn't trying hard to see them just to please Mommy, I thought, and this was certainly not a dream.

After all, weren't they all there for me as well?

And wouldn't they be forever and ever?

18

———•○•———

Celeste

Shall I say that never a day passed now without my seeing or feeling a spiritual presence? It wouldn't be a lie. Finally, I was truly like Mommy with her powerful spiritual vision. We shared the world as would two sisters who had inherited heaven and earth, happy for each other.

In the evening after all our daily chores were done and we had eaten a wonderful dinner, she would play the piano and I would sit nearby and read or sometimes just sit and listen with my eyes closed. On wonderful nights like that we were often not alone. Many members of our spiritual family were there sitting on the settees and chairs or just standing about and smiling. Children, my many cousins, were sitting on the floor, being quiet and behaving. All of them stole glances at me and smiled and waited anxiously for me to smile back.

Although I still didn't tell Mommy, I saw Noble more and more, too. He followed me about the farm, criticizing my work, telling me he could do it better. At first he made me nervous, and then, mainly because of Daddy, I humored him and didn't take his comments to heart. I could almost say he haunted me, however, because as he grew more comfortable being in my presence, his complaints became more personal and more frequent. He was like a bee buzzing at my ear. No amount of swatting at him would drive him away.

One night I woke and saw him squatting beside my bed. He looked up at me, and I saw he had been crying.

"Why are you crying?" I asked him. "I thought there is never any sadness where you are."

"Maybe just for me," he muttered.

"I'm trying my best, Noble. I'm doing everything you would do as well as you would do it. I've even begun to rebuild your fort, haven't I?"

"I'm not crying because of all that," he said as if I were stupid.

"Then what? What's making you so sad?"

He looked like he wasn't going to tell or he was afraid to tell. His eyes shifted about the room to be sure we were alone. I saw no one else either.

"I don't like wearing your dress," he said, "and your amulet. I want my own. I like my worm."

I simply stared at him. I didn't know what to say or what to do. I could never mention such a thing to Mommy, of course.

"You're not wearing a dress now," I pointed out.

He smirked.

"You don't know anything. I have to be like this when you see me, but every other time I'm in that dress, and I don't like it. Our cousins are laughing at me behind my back," he told me.

"Daddy never says anything about that."

"He's just trying to keep Mommy happy."

"I can't do anything about it, Noble," I said.

"Yes, you can," he insisted. "You can be you. As soon as you are, it will stop."

His request took my breath away.

"I can't do that," I said in a loud whisper.

Now the conversation was making me dizzy. Luminous white smoke circled around me. Was I really awake, or was all

552

this part of a dream?

"Yes, you can," he insisted.

"I can't. Mommy would . . . would be very upset, and besides, she was told what had to be done and what I must do," I pointed out. "She can't go against it, and neither can I."

"You will," he said, his eyes small and angry like they could be when we were younger and I had done something that irked him. "You will," he threatened.

He popped like a bubble.

Soon after that, I began to vomit in the morning. I was so nauseous, I had trouble getting dressed and going downstairs. I was sure it was somehow Noble's doing, his way to get even with me, and I was confident that he couldn't keep it up. Daddy would stop him. I was still afraid to tell Mommy anything about him. I was sure she would be so unhappy if she knew some of the things Noble had told me, especially what he wanted.

And then one day when the morning sickness diminished, I realized that my monthly bleeding had stopped. There were other times when it had stopped for a few months and then started again, but this was different. It was accompanied by a new sensitivity about my nipples and a change in color. Also, I found myself drifting off more, napping, being tired. I was going to the bathroom more often, too. I kept anticipating Mommy asking me about it, but she didn't appear to notice, and I thought it might all just pass soon.

One morning while I was examining myself, noting how much bigger my breasts had become and the small swelling in my stomach, I looked in the corner and saw Noble smiling.

"You won't be able to be me much longer," he said with an impish grin.

"Get out!" I screamed. "Get out!"

He laughed, but he disappeared. Mommy came up the stairway, calling to me.

"What is it, Noble?"

I began to wrap myself as quickly as I could.

"Is something wrong?" she asked from the doorway.

"No," I said. "I'm just being teased. Like I used to be," I added.

"Teased? Teased by whom, Noble? Who would tease you?" she asked, standing in the doorway with a confused smile on her face.

I turned away from her quickly.

"I didn't mean teased, exactly. I meant

annoyed. I'm annoyed with myself."

"Why?"

"I'm just not getting as much done as I want, and we're already well into fall."

"Oh. Well, you will. Be patient. I'm not unhappy with your work," she said.

She kissed me on the forehead and cheek and then left.

I stood there looking after her and wondering what would I do.

Days and then weeks went by with me keeping my secret locked in my heart. Sometimes, my heart felt more like a closed fist battling to keep itself closed. It burned in my chest, too. I would stop working and find myself out of breath, gasping for cool air. There were even times when I would have to keep swallowing to prevent words from charging up my throat, into my tongue, and out of my tight lips.

"How can I stop this?" I cried. I would just pause in whatever I was doing and, feeling certain Mommy couldn't hear me, scream my pleas and wait for some response, but a strange new thing happened.

Daddy wasn't appearing.

Neither were any other members of my spiritual family. Only Noble was visible and heard, and usually it was to gloat and to irritate me. He would always follow with his complaint.

"I don't like wearing your dress, and I want my amulet back."

Some nights, I practically leaped out of sleep and sat up, a cold sweat over my body, my heart pounding. He was weaving himself into all my dreams, crawling slowly like a worm through my brain. His face was everywhere. Once, I saw a bobcat saunter out of the woods and cross the meadow. When it paused and turned toward me, it had Noble's face and it was smiling.

There was no escape. Even the wind began to repeat his complaint.

"I don't like wearing your dress, and I want my amulet back."

The tree branches and their leaves were like multiple hands of symphony conductors moving to the rhythm of that sentence. I would have to stand there with my palms pressed tightly over my ears and wait for the breeze to calm and the chanting to end.

Once Mommy caught me doing this and asked me why I was doing it.

I told her I had a buzzing in my ear, and she gave me something to stop an infection from developing. Now, evenings when she played her piano, I pretended to be busy doing something else other than reading. The last half dozen or so times when I was relaxing with her, I didn't see anyone but Noble, and all he would do was squat below me and stare up at me with that mean-spirited smile on his lips. It was on the tip of my tongue to shout at him, but I caught myself in time and just rose and went to get myself some water.

He tracked after me everywhere, cloaking himself in shadows sometimes and then just sliding out along the wall before he disappeared.

Another month passed without anything changing. My appetite went from hardly anything to my sneaking meals between meals. The more weight I gained, however, the happier Mommy was. The woman in me was sinking under the added pounds. Even the postman who saw me occasionally shook his head with disgust.

One result of Noble's haunting of me was to make me want to succeed more at doing the things he thought were his things to do. I mastered the use of the chain saw, and I cut many logs. I split them and piled them to dry. I had calluses upon calluses, but I didn't moan and groan. Mommy had good herbal remedies to soothe the pain, and I began to soak in an herbal bath every night. It helped me sleep.

Fortunately, she never came in on me, and she didn't see how my waist and my breasts had expanded. She didn't notice the stretch marks or how my ankles were swelling. It was getting more and more difficult to tighten the corset around myself, but it gave me the idea to use one of my grandmother's girdles to keep my swelling stomach from showing. As another precaution, I stopped going places with her. For months now, no one off our farm but the postman and an occasional delivery man saw me. I didn't return to the school either. That was all ended.

"You're at the age where you don't have to attend any school anyway," Mommy told me when I made a vague reference to our failure to appear for my periodic testing. "Who wants those busybodies interfering in our lives? Not me," she answered.

Not me either, I thought, especially not now.

I used to wonder how Mommy could be so contented, living alone as we were. Didn't she miss the company of men, of other women her age? Didn't she want to get out in the world and see what was new in fashion?

Now I thought I understood her better. I didn't wake up longing to leave the farm as much anymore. I wasn't interested in meeting young people my age. After all, look at what that had led to when I had. I didn't even think as hard about the public school.

But I knew my time was running out. Despite all I had done and continued to do, Mommy would soon realize what I realized but refused to acknowledge. Only Noble gloated about it, and he would never stop saying, "I don't want to wear your dress. I want my amulet back."

"I can't do it," I shouted back at him. "Why don't you stop?"

He just stared.

Everywhere, he stared and he waited and the weeks went by and I grew bigger.

One night I woke up absolutely terrified. I had dreamed of Mommy looking at me in the morning and bursting into tears and rage and great sorrow, so great, it broke her heart and she died. I would be alone, and because of what I had let happen, no spiritual ancestor would comfort me or care to be in my presence ever again. Where do people go when they can't go to the warm, happy spiritual places? What dark hole awaited me?

"I don't want to wear that dress any-more," Noble chanted from the darkest corners in my room. "And I want my am-ulet back." He was on my right, then my left, then behind me, then in front of me. I slapped my hands over my ears, but he was whispering in between my fingers like someone whispering through the cracks in a door.

I threw off my blanket and, dressed only in my stretched pajama bottom and top, I fled the room.

Like a ribbon tied to the back of a car, he trailed along.

I charged out of the house, down the porch steps, and across the yard, not caring about how the small pebbles and gravel tore at the soles of my feet. I went to the barn. I was crying now, the tears streaming down my cheeks.

The sky was thickly overcast. I felt the first drops of rain, but it didn't deter me. I found the spoon shovel, and I rushed across the yard and up to the small ceme-tery. I was even surprised myself at how well and how easily I moved through the inky darkness. When I reached the tomb-stones, I saw Noble standing there, waiting.

"If I take the dress off of you and give

you back your amulet, will this stop? Will I stop growing in my stomach?" I asked him.

"Yes," he said.

I dug the shovel into the grassy earth where I knew he lay buried in my dress. The ground was soft enough, but the work was hard. I dug and I dug with such intensity and determination, I was blind to anything else. I didn't see the light go on in the house. I didn't hear the front door open and close. I didn't see the beam of the flashlight streak over the ground until it found me. I didn't hear Mommy coming quickly. I dug, and then I felt her grab my arm.

It surprised me so, I spun around.

She stood there looking at me, her face aghast, her mouth twisted, her eyes wide. She spoke in a hoarse whisper.

"What are you doing?"

"He doesn't want to wear the dress, and he wants his amulet back," I said, looking to where Noble had been standing, but he was gone, lost in the darkness.

She shook her head and then lifted the beam of the light so it washed over me. In a moment she saw it all, my bigger bosom, my swollen stomach. I held my breath. My heart seemed to stop. I went completely numb. She reached out and ripped the shovel from my hands.

"What have you done?" she screamed, and then she dropped the flashlight and lifted the shovel with both her hands, raising it to bring it down on me.

I fell to my knees and waited for the blow, but it didn't come.

I looked up and, in the glow of the flashlight at her feet, I saw her frozen, her head slightly tilted, her mouth in a grimace. She was listening, and then she started to nod.

When she looked back at me, her grimace was a smile. She put the shovel down gently, and she reached for me.

"Come," she said. "Come back inside the house. It's all right. It's all right."

I rose slowly and hesitantly took her hand. She saw how frightened I was, and she put her arm around me.

"Everything will be all right," she whispered.

The rain started to fall harder, but neither she nor I took note of it. Without another word, she led me back, her arm around me the whole way so she could hold me close. We entered the house, and she led me upstairs to my room. She sat me on the bed, and then she went to the bathroom and got a basin of warm water. She washed my feet, cleaning out any and all scratches and scrapes. Then she helped me off with my damp pajamas and wiped me down.

When that was done, she directed me to lie back. She put her hand on my stomach and stood there with her eyes closed.

"What a wondrous thing has happened," she said.

"What wondrous thing, Mommy?" I asked. How could she see it as anything else but a disaster?

She looked down at me in the strangest way. I felt she was looking through me, not at me. It was truly as if she didn't see me at all.

"Mommy?"

"You'll be fine," she said. "Everything will be fine. They have told me. It will be a miracle."

"What sort of miracle, Mommy?"

"No more questions. Rest and do as you're told," she replied.

After she left, I saw Noble gloating in the corner. Why was he gloating?

"What is it? What's the miracle?" I asked him.

He just laughed.

My mind reeled with so much confusion, I felt nauseous. I closed my eyes and tried to meditate, but I heard him come to the side of the bed and bring his lips to my ear.

"I told you," he said. "You can be you."

He was gone when I opened my eyes and turned. There was only darkness. I was never more willing to sink into a pool of deep sleep.

The next morning so much began to change. Mommy forbade me from doing any of the hard labor. I couldn't use the chain saw anymore, and I couldn't split wood or pile it. Even my gardening work was reduced. No more digging and bending. No more weeding. She modified my diet and gave me herbal pills she said were important for me, but she had that look on her face again. Her eyes were glassy, far-off, giving me the feeling she wasn't speaking to me. She was speaking to the baby growing inside me.

There were nights when she woke and came to my bedside because she said she had heard the baby crying. I was so confused the first time she did it, I asked her, What baby?

She just shook her head and told me she would make something warm for me to drink, which was really the way to get the baby to drink. Some nights she would sit there and sing and hum an old folk song designed to calm the baby. She said it would help the baby sleep.

All this made me feel no more important than a wheelbarrow. I soon understood that in Mommy's eyes, I would be bringing the baby to the table or putting it to bed. I would move it out of the hot sun when I moved or cover it to keep it warm and secure when I covered myself. There was no longer a me. I was slowly disappearing, and the baby was emerging.

And Noble gloated.

He was always there in some shadow, in some corner, or just walking slightly behind me, especially after Mommy had spoken to the baby inside me.

"When the baby is born," he said, "you're going to disappear completely.

"And I won't have to wear a dress, and I'll get my amulet back."

Even though I had less and less to do, I didn't feel life was easier for me. Almost overnight, perhaps because I no longer could or had to hide was happening inside me, I grew bigger and bigger. I waddled when I walked, struggled to rise out of a chair, climbed the stairs slower, and groaned about the pain in my lower back. I saw how it all made Noble laugh. Sometimes, his laugh echoed and was joined in a chorus of chilling laughter out of the dark.

I felt the chill everywhere. It was colder in the house.

This winter was even more severe than the previous. It was so cold, tears would freeze as soon as they escaped my eyelids. To me, it often looked like the world might crack like a piece of ice.

Mommy thought it was dangerous for me, or more to the point, for the baby, to spend too much time outdoors. We had weeks and weeks of below-freezing temperatures and weeks and weeks of temperatures below zero at night. I rarely went out of the house and spent hours and hours alone in my room, reading, sleeping, or just staring out the window.

The cold took its toll on everything. Mommy had trouble with our car. One day after she had left to get some groceries, she didn't return until a little after eight o'clock in the evening because some hose or something had broken, and she had been stranded for hours waiting for help and a tow truck and then for the mechanic to repair the damage.

We had problems with our oil burner. The pipes nearly froze, and the snow was so heavy with one storm after another, Mommy had to give in and hire someone to plow our driveway, two, sometimes three times a week. I recalled how Daddy used to do that with his truck and how Noble and I would ride with him, or we would be permitted to drive the little tractor and plow with it, and then how he and I had done it together after Daddy's death.

Toward the end of these severe winter months, we had ice storms and branches cracked on trees continually. The moonlight would dance on the icy bark, creating a dazzling show in the evening, but Mommy called it the "smile of cold Death, gleefully enjoying its triumph over fragile and vulnerable living creatures surprised by Nature's treachery."

Mornings now, I would make little effort to get up. Mommy brought the "baby's breakfast" to me, and I remained in bed until almost midday. I began to hate going downstairs because it meant I would have to walk up. Mommy warned me about being too lazy.

"It's going to make everything harder for the baby," she said. She didn't mention how it would be harder for me. Everything was the baby, the baby.

She didn't seem to notice or care that all this time while I was confined to the house, my hair grew longer and longer until it was down to the base of my neck. When I knew it was safe because she was busy downstairs, I would go into her room and look at myself in her vanity mirror. I imagined my hair even longer and envisioned how I might cut and style it. Every day, however, I anticipated her realizing and taking the scissors to me.

I tried to keep the baby's kicking a secret. The truth was, it frightened me. One afternoon, however, I had fallen asleep on the sofa in the living room, and the baby's kick woke me with such a jerk, I cried out. She put down her knitting (she was making the baby a hat and gloves) and walked over to me to place her hand on my stomach. She waited, and then her face lit up with more brightness than I had seen in her face for years.

"It's almost time," she said. "It's almost time."

I rarely if ever thought about the impending birthing. It was more as if I believed I would be the way I was forever and ever. The fetus within would never leave me. I tried to learn as much as I could from the books we had in the house, but it was still quite a mystery for me.

The first time I felt a labor pain, I screamed so hard and so shrilly, I frightened myself. Mommy came running. I was in the kitchen, seated at the table, sipping some tea. The cup fell from my fingers and shattered. I thought she would yell about that, but she didn't seem to care or notice as soon as she realized what had occurred.

She made me walk even when the pain began again. She led me up the stairs and to my room, where she had me lie down. The labor pains stopped after a few more minutes, however, and life returned to what it was. I hesitate to say *normal*. It was so different from what had been my life, even after Noble's tragic death.

The next time the labor pains came, they were accompanied by something even more frightening to me: a stream of water running down my leg. I was standing in the hallway, and I couldn't move an inch forward or an inch backward. Mommy had been outside. She entered the house and saw what was happening immediately.

At first she started me for the stairway, but the pain was so intense now, I couldn't lift my feet to climb the steps, so she turned me into the living room instead. She had me lie down on the sofa, and then she smiled and said, "This is amazing. I just remembered that my great-grandmother Elsie gave birth to my grandfather on this very sofa. There wasn't even time for the doctor to come, and no time to get her to any hospital. Do you sense her?" she asked me with that same far-off look in her eyes. It was eerie. It was as if she was looking at a face behind my face, and all I had was a mask.

All I sensed was excruciating pain anyway. I grimaced and cried out.

"It will be all right," she said, and she went for towels and hot water and one of her herbal concoctions. I heard her mumble about it being something her grandmother had created. I swallowed two tablespoons of it, but I didn't think it did much of anything. The pain only grew worse.

I don't know how long I was screaming. I know my throat became scratchy and my voice hoarse. I drifted in and out of consciousness. At one point when I awoke, I saw the living room was filled with members of our spiritual family. They were all sitting or standing calmly, talking softly and watching me. Behind one of my uncles, more in the doorway, was Noble, looking frightened, I thought.

On and on my labor went. Mommy wiped my face with a warm wet cloth, but did little else. And then, right after nightfall, with darkness closing around our house as if some giant had dropped a black sheet over it and the windows, I saw the relatives drawing closer.

"Push," Mommy screamed. "Push, push, push."

I did, and again she screamed, and again I did it. The room turned red. I thought I was looking through some crimson veil at everything and everyone. Even Mommy's face was a bright scarlet. I heard a cheer and a cry of joy, and then there was the sound of a baby's cry.

Mommy worked quickly to cut and tie the umbilical cord. Noble, who had edged closer and closer, stood with his eyes so big, they looked like they would explode. Mommy held the baby up for all to see. I saw that it had a full head of red hair, Elliot's red hair.

"It's a girl!" she declared.

And then she turned and carried the baby away in her arms, wrapped in a blanket. I heard her going up the stairs. The entire roomful of spiritual relatives followed. Even Noble left, and I was alone.

I fell asleep, or really passed out, and when I awoke, I could see the first light of morning. Every part of me ached. I ached in places I didn't know I could. Mommy

571

came in with a tray and put it on the small table she had brought beside the sofa.

"You have to eat," she said. "I need you to be healthy and strong."

"Where's the baby? How is the baby?" I asked quickly.

She didn't answer. She left me and went up the stairs. I drank the juice and ate the oatmeal and the toast. Just as I finished, Mommy returned. She was carrying something very strange.

"What is that, Mommy?" I asked immediately as she pulled a chair up beside me.

"Unbutton your shirt," she said instead of answering. "Quickly."

I did as she asked, and she leaned forward and pulled it apart so my breasts were fully exposed. Then she brought the strange thing to my right breast and fitted it over my nipple.

"Just lie back and relax," she said.

She began to pump the bag, and I watched as my milk filled the bottles she attached. At one point I cried out that it was painful, and she went easier and slower. When she was finished, she stood up and turned to leave me again.

"Where is the baby?" I asked.

"Just rest," she told me.

She didn't return for hours. I rose and

moved about the room and then, when I heard her coming down the stairs, I went to the foot of them and looked up.

"Go back to the sofa!" she ordered. "I told you to rest."

"But I wanted to see the baby," I said.

"Not now," she told me, and she physically turned me away from the stairway.

She made me stay in the living room to have my lunch and even my dinner. I wanted to go up to my room, but she told me I couldn't climb the stairs yet. Periodically, over the following few days, she brought back the pump and filled the bottles with my milk.

One night I rose and went quietly up the stairway. I wanted to change my clothing, to bathe and freshen up. I saw that her bedroom door was closed. I listened, and then I went into my room, took a shower, and changed into a fresh pair of pajamas. I saw no reason why I couldn't sleep in my own bed now, and I did just that.

In the morning she came rushing into my room, her face full of rage.

"I told you to stay downstairs," she cried at me. I wasn't even fully awake.

I ground the sleep out of my eyes and propped myself up on my elbows. She was hovering over me and looking so furious and so strange, I was frightened.

"I needed to get clean and I wanted to sleep in my own bed, Mommy," I said.

"I don't want you up here. Get dressed and go back downstairs," she told me.

I heard the baby crying.

"Can I see the baby first?"

"No," she said. "Go downstairs!" she screamed. Then she left the room.

After I dressed in a fresh shirt, under-wear, and pants, I went out and paused in the hallway. Her bedroom door was shut tight again. I waited a moment, and then I went downstairs and fixed myself some eggs and toast. I was very hungry. She appeared and made me take some of her pills again.

"Why can't I see the baby, Mommy?" I asked her, but she didn't reply.

Later that afternoon, she did a very strange thing. She wheeled the old television set into the living room and hooked it up. I watched in amazement. Suddenly, my watching television didn't matter. She was no longer worried about what harm it could do to my studies or anything.

"Amuse yourself," she said. She made it sound like an order. Then she left me again. For days afterward, she continued to bar me from going upstairs. She brought clothing down to the living room for me. She insisted that I eat my meals there. And periodically, she brought in the pump.

She spent little or no time with me, barely speaking to me when she was around. I was desperate to see the baby, of course, and not seeing her filled me with a painful emptiness, but I realized there was something more.

Ever since the baby's birth, I had not seen Noble, nor any other family spirit. Even the soft sound of whispering was gone. When I turned off the television set, except for the sounds of Mommy moving around above me or the baby's crying when I could hear it muffled by the walls, there was cemetery quiet. Every corner of the house, every shadow, was empty. With Mommy ignoring me except when she wanted to pump my milk or when she brought me something to eat, I was never more alone, and my desperation to see the baby grew stronger and stronger until I could think of nothing else.

Hours at a time, I'd wait to hear the sound of the baby's voice, and when I heard Mommy's footsteps on the stairway, I rose eagerly, praying that she was finally carrying the baby down for me to see, but she never did.

On the one day Mommy left the house to get things she needed, I went upstairs and hurried to her bedroom door. I heard the baby. She wasn't crying, but I could hear her making baby sounds. I tried the doorknob, but found the door was locked. It was frustrating and brought tears to my eyes. I tried to talk to the baby through the keyhole and even tried to get a glimpse of her, but I saw nothing that way.

When I heard Mommy drive up, I hurried downstairs again. I offered to carry in the groceries for her, but she told me to just return to the living room. She didn't want my help.

"But I'm going crazy in there, Mommy. I need to have things to do. Why can't I see the baby? Why can't I help you?"

She didn't respond. She worked on putting away her groceries, and then she went upstairs. I returned to the living room, where I sulked and stared blankly at the television set. Even though it was a novelty for me, I was unable to keep myself from thinking about the baby and what Mommy was doing with her upstairs. I saw that it was taking a toll on her as well. She looked more tired, more haggard, every passing day.

And all this time, not a vision, not a

voice, nothing. I began to wonder again if I had ever seen or heard anything spiritual. It had all been a hallucination, something Mommy had caused with her secret potions, maybe. Noble spoke to me only in my mind, after all. It was just my conscience or my fears. I was not special. I had inherited no powers. Perhaps Mommy finally realized that, and that was why she was being so indifferent to me now.

Finally, a good two and a half weeks after the baby had been born, Mommy came downstairs, prepared my supper, served it to me, and then went to have her own. I ate and listened hard because sometimes I could hear the baby's cries better now.

Sure enough, she began to cry and then cry harder. I anticipated seeing Mommy come quickly down the hallway and go up the stairs. It did no good to follow her because she would turn on the steps and chase me back. This evening, however, she did not come down the hallway and hurry up the stairs at the sound of the baby's crying.

I rose and cautiously entered the dining room. I saw her sitting at the table, only she had her head down on her arms and she was fast asleep. Taking the greatest care I could, I tiptoed up to her, and then as gently as I was able to, I put my hand into her apron pocket and brought out the key to her bedroom. She didn't budge. I saw her breathing remained regular, subdued. She was in a deep sleep. Perhaps she had passed out just as she had once done when she had gone to see our attorney. I couldn't help but take advantage of this great opportunity.

I moved as quickly and as quietly as I could down the hallway and then up the stairs. At the top of the stairway, I paused to be sure she had not waken. All was quiet below, but the baby was crying harder behind the locked door of Mommy's bedroom. I inserted the key and entered.

Mommy had set up a crib right beside her bed. Her bed was unmade, and her room was messier than I had ever seen it. It was actually in disarray: clothing scattered about, diapers piled on the vanity table, some dishes with food from days before lying on tables, and even some dishes on the floor.

I went quickly to the crib and looked down at the baby. For a moment I thought something was wrong with her, and then I realized what it was.

Her hair was dyed my color. She was no

longer a redhead. I got over the shock of it quickly and lifted her into my arms. It was obvious she was hungry. I glanced around to see if Mommy had left any bottles, and then I thought, how stupid.

I opened my shirt and brought her lips to my nipple, and she began to feed, her eyes on me with what I thought was great excitement and contentment. It brought a smile to my face. I sat in the chair beside the crib and watched her suckle.

Shortly after, I felt a dark shadow fall over us, and I looked up to see Mommy standing in the doorway. She looked angry enough to lunge at me, but she didn't move.

She just watched and waited for the feeding to end.

Then she walked calmly across the room and gently took the baby out of my arms, cupping her in her own. Her face blossomed with happiness.

I was trembling inside, but she didn't notice. She never even looked at me. She rocked the baby in her arms until the baby's eyes closed, and then she placed her back in the crib and covered her little body with the tiny pink blanket.

I stood up and watched over her shoulder.

Finally, she turned and looked at me.

"You have to go back to your room," she

said, "and wait until you're needed."

"But Mommy . . . the baby's hair. Why did you dye it a different color?"

She shook her head as if she had heard pure gibberish and smiled at me.

"I didn't dye her hair, silly."

"But . . . it was redder. It was —"

"Of course it wasn't," she said sharply and turned me to walk me out of the bedroom.

She practically pushed me into the hallway and started to close the door.

"Mommy, why are you keeping me away from her?" I bawled, my eyes awash in tears.

She held the door halfway closed and gazed out at me for a long moment.

"It's just not time for you to be with her yet."

"But there's so much more to do. Don't we . . . shouldn't we . . . I mean, she has no name."

Mommy smiled.

"Of course she has a name, Noble," she said.

She started to close the door again. I put my hand out, and she looked at me.

"What's her name?" I asked.

"Her name's Celeste," she said.

And she closed the door.

Epilogue

<hr>

Welcome Home

Not long after Mommy stopped using the pump and the baby was put on Mommy's special formula — the formula she had used for both Noble and me — I was able to tighten the corset around myself well enough to hide my curves and bosom again. I did not lose weight quickly, and only a few pounds at that after all. My face was still chubby. I wasn't happy about it, but I could see Mommy was pleased. She even told me to go up to her room and cut my hair.

I sat for almost an hour staring at myself in her vanity mirror, dreaming of my hair flowing freely down the back of my neck like some of the women I had read about and had seen on television. Finally, she called up to me because she wanted something done, so I had to bring the scissors to my long strands, chopping away until my hair was close again and the fantasy gone.

She wanted me to help her with baby Celeste, and I was afraid if I didn't do exactly what she asked me to do, she wouldn't let me near the baby.

In time she permitted me to hold Celeste or feed her and change her by myself.

"It's no shame for a big brother to help out," she said.

It didn't matter what she said as long as I could do it. Those hours were my happiest. I was pleased just to be in the same room and watch the baby sleep.

As soon as the red would start to get more prominent in the baby's hair, Mommy would wash in her dye, and it would be returned to my color. Usually she did it at night after I had gone to sleep. No one else would have known anyway. Even though no one other than the postman or a utility man came to our farm, Mommy was very careful about when she would take baby Celeste outside. No one in the world but us knew she had been born.

"When the time comes, we'll reveal her," Mommy said and added, "when they tell me."

Everything we did in our lives now emanated from those famous three words: *they told me*. New ideas, changes, anything and everything, came to us from the whispers that rained down from clouds only Mommy could see. I hadn't seen or heard anything from the spiritual world for so long, it all lodged in the back of my mind like some dream I had years and years ago, and I began to suspect more and more that it was all just hallucinations.

Together in our secret world, Mommy and I watched baby Celeste grow stronger and more alert. When she began to crawl and be at things constantly, Mommy gave me more and more to do with her until I was spending most of my day minding her. There were some close calls when the man who read our electric meter monthly almost saw her and then when we had a seed delivery and the driver surely heard her crying.

But no one came to inquire about her. I used to think about the Fletchers, who still lived next to us, and how surprised Mr. Fletcher would be if he ever learned he was a grandfather. Would he be angry or happy about it?

Baby Celeste was certainly a beautiful baby. How could anyone not be happy about her? She had the same blue-green eyes, which Mommy expected her to have and which helped support what she had been told, of course. I could see baby Celeste wasn't just alert, too. She was bright and very curious about everything she saw or heard. When she stood up and then tottered, but then stood up again and again until she could do it well enough to take a step at eleven months, Mommy was convinced she was a blessed child.

This is not someone we can keep secret forever, I thought, but Mommy wasn't a bit worried about anything. She had such trust in her voices.

Where were they? I wondered again and again. Why had they gone from me? Were they ever with me? Or was it all just as I feared: something I wanted so much, I made it happen?

I did my work. I sat with baby Celeste in my lap in the evening, and we listened to Mommy play her piano. I read more when I could, and I waited.

What was I waiting for?

The following spring I began to take walks in the woods again, but for the longest time, I avoided what had been my special place. Finally, I got up enough nerve to go there, and when I looked at it now, it seemed innocuous, so common to the rest of the forest. There were many places where the pine trees shaded the ground and where the ground was matted in a carpet of fallen needles and smelled as redolent and fresh as this one, I thought.

And I thought, The truth is, all our special places come from inside us. Something within makes them special for us, and when that changes, they change. Beauty surprised was the most impressive because of what exploded in our hearts when we confronted it, whether it was an unexpected waterfall, a doe, a beautiful bird. Once we had seen it and seen it again, it was still beautiful, but it was different, as different as a magnificent animal stuffed was from the animal or a painting of a beautiful place was from the place itself. Something of it was captured forever, but it would never be what it was in the beginning, that first time.

I wanted to tell Mommy that all this awareness had come to be without my being told, but then I thought, Maybe that's where the spirits really are, inside us. Maybe she was right, and maybe when we realize it, surrender to it, believe in it, they appear.

Had I ever really believed, or was I like Noble, skeptical? Sometimes desire can be greater than the thing itself. You make it into something beyond what it is, and then you suffer when you face reality. Was it less painful to never fantasize, never believe, and never be disappointed? Or was that an empty life, a life with shadows that never took any form, clouds that never had any interesting shapes, winds that were only winds and carried no voices?

What would be baby Celeste's world, her choices, her visions?

One late afternoon, that time when daylight is caught for a final moment under the impending curtain of night, that special time we call twilight, Mommy permitted me to take baby Celeste outside for a little walk. This time Mommy didn't come with us as she always did.

For a moment that made me hesitant. What had she been told? Why was she not accompanying us outside?

We left the house. Baby Celeste clung to my hand and looked at everything with dazzling eyes. I had no special direction in which to walk the baby, but for some reason, we turned right and slowly made our way to the little cemetery. The moment she saw it, she was intrigued. When I let go of her hand, she entered and went straight for the tombstones. She paused, looked at them, and then she reached out slowly and she put her tiny hands on the embossed hands of Infant Jordan.

I watched, mesmerized.

She turned to me, keeping her hands pressed to the stone, and she smiled. Had she felt them move?

I held my breath and watched.

And then I felt something, some warm touch on the back of my neck, and turned toward the oncoming shadows marching out of the woods toward us, slowly bringing the stars out of the sky with every step they took.

Leading them was Daddy.

And Noble.

And all our spiritual ancestors.

They were coming to make us a family again.

They were coming to welcome me home.